D0553445

PINPOINT

By the same author

Ringmain
The Double Tenth

PINPOINT

George Brown

C
CENTURY
LONDON SYDNEY AUCKLAND JOHANNESBURG

First published 1993

1 3 5 7 9 10 8 6 4 2

First published in the United Kingdom in 1993 by
Century Limited
Random House, 20 Vauxhall Bridge Road, London SW1V 2SA

Random House Australia (Pty) Limited
20 Alfred Street, Milsons Point, Sydney,
New South Wales 2061. Australia

Random House New Zealand Limited
18 Poland Road, Glenfield
Auckland 10, New Zealand

Random House South Africa (Pty) Limited
PO Box 337, Bergvlei, South Africa

Random House UK Limited Reg. No. 954009

A CIP catalogue record for this book
is available from the British Library

ISBN 07126 4997 2

Phototypeset by Intype, London
Printed in England by Clays Ltd, St Ives plc

For Dennis and Valerie Wombell – With love

. . . I count myself in nothing else so happy as in a soul remembering my good friends.

Richard II.

ACKNOWLEDGEMENTS

Lt/Col Fred L_ _ _ _
whose advice has been invaluable – both in this work, and, in an earlier life, when we stood in the shadow together.

My thanks also to Gaby Violle – the real one.
And my son, Jerome, for helping me retrieve the past in Paris.

pin+point ('pin,p) /nt vb (tr) 1. to locate or identify exactly; . . .
Ponctuelle (fr) 2.ph: pin/point . . .
'Operation Ponctuelle'; OAS execution

ANTI-OAS SHOCK FORCE.
CARTE-BLANCHE FOR BARBOUZES TO LIQUIDATE THE OAS

The new anti-OAS formations will not belong to any classical hierarchy. They will be autonomous organisms, not subject to normal authority . . . They will act largely outside the army and the police.
Above all, this new force will be secret. An absolute secrecy will cover the activities and above all the identity of the members of the anti-OAS formations

France-Soir; November 1961

France, autumn 1961, a country riven in pieces. De Gaulle is preparing to pull out of Algeria; the Army, which has fought long and hard to keep the colony French, has grown disenchanted, rebellious and even murderous. As the Organisation de l'Armée Secrète, or OAS abducts and assassinates Gaullist Ministers, open rebellion is just around the corner. In September, de Gaulle narrowly escapes death when an explosive charge on the Pont-sur-Seine fails to detonate as his car passes over it. There will be other attempts on his life.

Meanwhile, in a car park beneath the Boulevard St-Germain, two men wait to play their part in France's internal war . . .

PART ONE

The Killing Fields of Paris

1

Paris 1961

FROM THE SHADOW of dead ground at the back of the car bay, where the inadequate strip of neon built into the underground car-park ceiling failed to meet its neighbour, two darker shadows, shapeless, indistinct, waited, unmoving.

'Philippe, this is a waste of time – he's not the one we want, he's insignificant, small stuff. We should be going for Big Nose, not the bloody street cleaners!'

The whisper barely reached but it was enough to earn a quiet, warning 'Shhh!' A hand shot out, grabbing the shorter of the two shapes, cautioning silence. It wasn't enough. The whisperer was uncomfortable, he was dying for a cigarette. He was dying for anything to alleviate the tension of waiting.

'And we don't even know that he'll come,' the whisperer continued, slightly louder, as if having broken the hour-long silence it didn't matter any more.

But the other man's voice stayed on the lower key and hissed into the crouching shadow's ear: 'For Christ's sake shut up! If you don't keep quiet, I'll stick my boot in your mouth!' The speaker rolled up the sleeve of his thick sweater and strained his eyes at the faintly luminous dial of his watch. The hands appeared not to have moved since his last check. *When was that? An hour ago?* He stared hard, in disbelief, then brought the watch slowly up to his eye. *Jesus! Only five minutes ago!* The slight movement brought a tiny reflection of light from one of the silver buttons on the cuff of the police uniform he was wearing; it startled him for a moment and he stared into the shadow beside him for a similar give-away. But there was nothing, the gleam was insignificant, nobody standing a metre away would have seen anything to break the shadow. He gave a fractional nod of satisfaction and this brought another slight but duller gleam from the shiny visor of the uniform kepi jammed on his head. Half-past ten. He allowed his wrist to drop slowly to his side.

He controlled the doubt in his own mind with a hoarse whisper: 'Lucienne won't let us down.' It was for himself; he needed the reassurance. His crouching companion had already given up. 'Listen,' he hissed, 'don't let go. Anything could have held them up. She'll keep her word . . .' *She had better!* he added under his breath. But she was three-quarters of an hour late. Something had to be wrong, and his instinct told him that if it started wrong it would end wrong. He had great faith in his instincts, but he stood his ground. 'We'll give it another ten.'

'It's a waste of time!'

'Shhh!'

A revved engine in neutral gear echoed from the concrete dungeon walls and a car's headlights bounced erratically from ground to ceiling as it negotiated the ramp, out of sight of the two waiting men, before turning the corner. The two men pressed themselves hard into the wall behind them and froze rigid as the car's wheels squealed impatiently, then shot off to the far end of the garage and disappeared down the slope to one of the lower floors. The standing man relaxed and touched the arm of his companion, who rose slowly to stand beside him. The machine-pistol he held across his body touched the wall with a dull metallic thud, causing the taller of the two men to hiss urgently, 'Shut up, Paul! I'm not going to warn you again. Be careful with that bloody thing and don't make a bloody sound!'

The warning had barely left his lips when the lights of another vehicle bounced off the wall, briefly illuminating the empty bays and lighting up the sign warning that the landing was reserved for special-permit holders, Government and VIPs. The lights steadied for a second, then gave a double flash on high beam and dipped again.

'That's ours!' The taller of the two men nudged his partner. 'Don't forget, the eyes of those in the second car'll be on me. I'll let them see the uniform. It'll calm them down. You look after the Minister. Shoot him in the leg if he argues, but that's as far as you go. I want him alive, not on a bloody slab! And Paul—'

'For Christ's sake!'

'Make sure there's room for Lucienne to make a bolt for it.'

'Jesus! We've been all through this, there's no need to keep on repeating things – I'm not a bloody idiot.'

'That's debatable . . .' He raised his voice from the whispered hiss and spoke normally: 'The second car'll be full of pros, so don't distract me. Just do as you've been told, and nothing else, OK?'

The second man made no reply.

'I said, OK?'

'OK, OK!' It came reluctantly. But he wasn't perturbed. He was quite a few years younger, less experienced in the gun game, and he had a younger man's excitability, but the excitement was well controlled and the adrenalin was pumping healthily. 'Just stop worrying about me. Do what you have to do. I can look after myself.'

The tall man, Philippe, took the machine-pistol from him and quickly checked that the magazine was firmly home before easing the bolt out of its safety recess. It was a serious killing tool: a Schmeisser P40, 60 × 9mm in a double magazine, the stock removed for ease of movement. He handled it like an old friend. The barrel fitted comfortably in the crook of his arm whilst, with one hand lightly grasping the pistol grip, he remained in the shadow and watched his companion step out into the path of the Peugeot. Its lights dipped as it bounced over the ramp and crawled towards him.

Ten metres behind a second car bumped gently in its wake and fractionally scraped its sump on the ramp.

'Philippe!' Paul's warning barely carried. His uniform clearly visible, he was now standing in the full glare of the Peugeot's lights. He hissed again out of the corner of his mouth, without moving his lips, 'Philippe! Four – probably five in the second car!' In the car nearest to him, silhouetted against the other's lights, he could see only two heads.

The Peugeot stopped. The second car continued moving at a snail's pace until it was four metres away, then it, too, stopped and waited. Without moving from the passageway, Paul held up his hand and pointed his finger at it. There was no response from the driver or the front-seat passenger, who stared back with indifference. The three men on the back seat appeared to be asleep.

The policeman shrugged his shoulders and approached the driver's side of the Peugeot and peered into its interior. A girl's white face peered back at him. He lowered his head and studied the man in the passenger seat.

Heavy-featured, his lips thick and wet, the passenger ignored the policeman and stared straight ahead. There was no acknowledgement, no greeting; he wasn't interested. The policeman took his eyes off him and glanced down at the woman's lap. Her short skirt was rumpled around her hips and the passenger's hand was firmly between her slim thighs.

'Gautier,' the passenger grunted after a moment. It was a condescension; a command to get your eyes off and get on with your job. He didn't remove his hand. He didn't look at the policeman. 'You know who I am?'

The policeman touched the peak of his kepi. 'Yes, Minister, I know who you are – and what you are.' The Minister was too preoccupied with the working of his fingers to notice the lack of servility in the policeman's response. Paul stared at the side of his sweating face for a moment, then touched the girl's shoulder and pointed to an empty bay further along on the left-hand side of the garage. 'Please park there where I can keep watch on you. Are these people behind with you, monsieur?'

'Yes, of course they bloody are – idiot! Get on with it!' The Minister's preoccupation didn't extend to the common gendarme. Whatever he wanted to do, he was in a hurry to do it.

The policeman looked briefly at the back of the Minister's hand, attracted for a moment to its sinews, raised like cords as his fingers worked and probed between the girl's legs. He glanced openly at the girl. The probing and feeling was having no effect on her; she was upset, nervous, and it wasn't the Minister's hand making her so. The policeman turned his eyes briefly back to the Minister. He wasn't concerned about her feelings. There was only one person who concerned him. And his wrist was beginning to ache. 'I said get on with it – and get your bloody eyes off!'

The girl glanced shyly into the policeman's face. She didn't smile. She eased the Peugeot forward into the space the policeman had indicated and switched off the engine. The second car moved up.

The windows were down. The driver didn't give the policeman time to speak. 'The Minister's bodyguard.' He flicked his half-smoked cigarette out of the window. 'His little friend wants to eat couscous. We all know what he wants to eat!' His snigger was echoed from the loaded back seat. The policeman didn't join in the mirth. He bent from the waist and peered into the car at the grinning faces. 'Would you mind putting on the interior light, please?' he asked politely.

The driver stopped grinning and reached above him to switch on the roof light. It was a normal request; he didn't argue. The policeman glanced unconcernedly at the automatic in a shoulder-harness revealed by his arm movement and turned his head to study more closely the three men bunched on the back seat.

The driver said, 'Come on, get a bloody move on!' and raised his arm again to switch off the light.

'Leave it on.' Philippe's voice was calm and authoritative. It had an instant effect. Nobody had noticed him move out of the shadow and into the artificially lit tunnel. He moved back slightly and stood by the offside wheel where they could all see him. All heads turned, but nothing else moved. The driver's hand remained just above his head.

When he'd got their full attention, Philippe showed them the Schmeisser. But they'd already seen it. He moved it gently to the left and then to the right so that they each had a good look down the short barrel. They stared like so many rabbits caught in a car's headlights and, paralysed, sat stiff, rigid, careful not to move their hands from where they'd rested them while talking to Paul.

'Go and get the Minister and take him to our car,' ordered Philippe. He didn't look at Paul; he didn't take his eyes off the men in the car. 'Be quick!'

Paul didn't acknowledge. He turned quickly on his heels, the heavy police 9mm MAB automatic out of the holster on his belt and in his hand as he sidled up to the passenger side of the parked Peugeot. The Minister glared round in anger when the police uniform filled his side-window again. His hand remained between the girl's legs, but was locked, unmoving – and then he saw the pistol as Paul brought it up from his side and rested its barrel on the open window-ledge. It took a second to register, then his stomach dropped on to his bladder, threatening to burst it in terror as he stared first at the automatic, pointing directly at his head, and then at the no longer familiar or reassuring sight of the dependable French gendarme. But the paralysis lasted only seconds. He came to life and started to move his hand away from the girl, then stopped dead as Paul raised the MAB and touched its muzzle to the side of his temple.

'What do you want?' There was no more arrogance there; no more the Minister. He was a man very afraid. But Paul gave him no time to consider the situation. He squeezed the trigger and part of the Minister's head splattered over the girl in the driving seat. She screamed and dragged his hand from between her thighs and tried to open the door on her side. There was another ear-shattering explosion as Paul fired again into the shuddering body beside her. She went out of control. It wasn't supposed to be like this. She opened her eyes to the sudden silence and then her scream rose higher when she became aware of the horror of the mess that had hit her and, beside her, thumping up and down on the ridge of the dashboard, the rest of the Minister's exploded head. She stopped struggling with the door handle and closed her eyes and stuffed her knuckles into her wide-open mouth, but still her screams built up, a white searing crescendo of noise.

'What the . . . !' bellowed Philippe, and for a fraction of a second turned his head towards the Minister's car. It was only for a second. One of the men on the back seat thought it was long enough and his hand shot under his arm. But it wasn't. Philippe recovered as quickly as his attention had lapsed. He stroked the trigger. Three rounds thumped into the man's chest as his hand reappeared with a cocked automatic. Two of the others thought they too had a chance. The Schmeisser thudded again, this time a longer burst, and all three men on the back seat tumbled together like three old bundles of washing, their bodies jerking like puppets as Philippe emptied the first of the magazines into the back of the car.

He reversed the magazine without taking his eyes off the twitching bodies. None was alive. Neither was the front-seat passenger, who, in his panic to get out of the car, had managed to get the door open, only to catch on his way out two bullets from the edge of the burst, both in the neck, one just below his ear. There he stayed, half in and half out of the car, one arm hooked over the window-ledge, his shoulders shuddering with the shock as his life dribbled out of the two holes. Just one more: the driver. Philippe dare not take his eyes off him.

'*Paul!*' he bellowed again, his voice rasping with the inhalation of blow-back cordite fumes and his ears ringing with the explosions.

'*What the fucking hell's going on? For Christ's sake! What the bloody hell are you doing?*'

There was no answer.

Paul leaned into the car and touched the girl's head with the muzzle of the automatic. 'Shut up!' he rasped urgently.

The screams died in her throat. She opened her eyes and stared with horror into his face. But the tableau lasted for only a second and then she half turned and jerked her shoulders against the door as, once again, she struggled to get it open. But her shaking hands kept slipping. 'Help me . . .' she hiccuped, and then choked: 'Please! Please! Get me away from here! Where's Philippe? Quick, help me get out . . .'

She turned sharply in her seat and stared appealingly into Paul's cold eyes. The MAB hadn't moved. Rock steady, it was still only two inches from the side of her face.

'Sorry Lucienne,' he murmured. 'They'll tear you to pieces.'

She didn't have time to register his words. Without flinching, he squeezed the trigger once. The explosion sounded even louder this time as the bullet tore a passage just below her ear lobe and ploughed downwards. It was a careless shot. He cursed silently to himself as her head crashed on to the steering-wheel. But she wasn't dead. He leaned across the Minister's dead body, resting one hand on his shoulder, and placed the muzzle against her temple. She was making a barking, coughing noise like a dog with a piece of bone stuck in its throat and her shoulders were jerking up and down, making a clean shot difficult. He pushed himself further through the open window and reached out with his other hand and grasped her hair to steady her head. Then he fired. Everything stopped. He picked up her handbag, wriggled his way out of the window and backed away.

Without taking his eyes off the driver, Philippe moved back until he was almost level with the Minister's car. He gave a quick glance over his shoulder.

'What's happened? Where's the Minister? Where's Lucienne? What the bloody hell . . . !'

'I'll tell you in a—' Paul elbowed past Philippe. 'Watch it! There's one still there!' He pointed his automatic at the windscreen of the car and looked in. 'Jesus!' Then he stared at Philippe. 'You've killed the whole bloody lot! God, what a fucking game! I'm enjoying this!'

Philippe turned to stare at the bodies in the Minister's car. For a second he was speechless. Then he exploded in a cold rage.

But Paul was not listening. The younger man's blood was thudding behind his eyes; he was unstoppable.

'Forget it, Philippe – it's bloody war! Come on, get out of it. I'll tell you all about it later. Finish that bugger off and let's go.'

The tall man stared grimly at his companion for several

seconds. 'But why Lucienne?' He swung the Schmeisser round, ominously, so that it was pointed at Paul.

Paul wasn't perturbed. He shook his head. 'I said I'll tell you about it. Quick, you go. I'll cover you in case anybody here moves.'

Philippe hesitated for a second, but time was running out. He growled something incomprehensible, then turned and walked briskly into the depths of the car park. He didn't look round.

Paul poked his hand with the MAB into the window and tapped the crouching driver's hands. The driver came to life. He seemed to know what was expected of him. He wrapped his hands round the steering-wheel where they could be seen and began to plead incoherently for his life. He had only seconds in which to do it. Their eyes met. 'Please . . .' His hands and wrists jerked uncontrollably. He was swarthy, with tight, pock-marked cheeks, sallow skin, jet-black crinkly hair – Corsican – but the normal hard cruelty of his face was softened by the fear-driven quivering of his facial muscles. Paul squeezed the trigger twice and the dark face disappeared under the force of the two 9mms.

Philippe halted in his tracks and began to turn back. A bellow from Paul stopped him. 'Duck, Philippe!' He went down on one knee and saw the younger man, with a grin splitting his face, toss a small object through the window of the car and then, at a crouch, double towards him. A second later the grenade exploded with a whoof, and a whoosh of hot air funnelled towards him as the bodyguards' car disappeared in a ball of white, then red and black oily flames.

Paul shot past him. 'Come on, Philippe! Let's get the bloody hell out of here!' He had to shout to make himself heard over the roar of the flames, but he didn't wait for his partner and pounded into the gloom at the far end of the car park.

The taller man followed at a slower pace, a gentle trot, turning every so often to study the carnage they'd left behind them. When he joined the younger man he handed him the Schmeisser and, grim-faced, took the automatic from him and tucked it into the back of his trouser-band. The anger showed through his drawn expression. There were a lot of questions to be answered.

A simple kidnapping, a well-organized, bloodless exercise had turned into a bloodbath, and the reason for that bloodbath stood grinning at the roaring flames and the crack of exploding pistol ammunition from under the cremating Corsicans' armpits. Paul was enjoying himself. And he wasn't finished with the killing. The adrenalin was still coursing.

'What about them, Philippe? Do we kill them?' The bloodlust showed in his red-rimmed eyes as he pointed the muzzle of the Schmeisser at another recess in an empty bay where, kneeling side by side, their hands tied behind their backs and their faces pressed against the cold concrete wall, two uniformed gendarmes shivered with fear. One had given up. The other, less experienced, strained to turn his head to see what was going on. He stopped straining when he heard the sentence of death.

'No. There's been enough killing, you vicious bastard!' Philippe turned his back to the two policemen and his partner. 'Come on. Leave them as they are.'

'They'll recognize us.'

'I said leave them!' His anger burst. 'Just do as I bloody say for once, will you! Without fucking argument!'

The young man's face showed nothing. He shrugged his shoulders, but continued staring at the heads of the two bound gendarmes. The adventurous policeman had stopped trying to see what was going on. He'd heard enough. He didn't want to see anybody's face; he didn't want to recognize anybody.

'Come on!'

Paul shrugged again and moved away.

There was no look of relief on the policemen's faces, now highlighted by the gushing, roaring flames of the torched car. They weren't going to be shot – but they could just as well be burned to death. They could feel the heat already, here in the bowels of the car park, and even deep in one of the bays, with the flickering of the roaring flames reflecting off the concrete walls around them, it felt like the approach of hell. They began to scream, and the new fear showed in their bulging eyes as they stared at each other. It was like a silent horror film with their screams reduced to gurgles of terror behind the thick wrapping of plaster that covered their mouths and lower part of their faces. Their plight didn't worry Paul as he left them behind.

Still in their bogus uniforms, Philippe de Guy-Montbron and Paul Vernet descended at a trot to the lower floor, and then, more casually, to the sub-basement. Above them the Boulevard St-Germain, after a period of shocked paralysis, was beginning to react to the sound of muted gunfire and the dull thump of underground explosions, and the sirens were converging from all directions. But the two men didn't panic. They stopped by a nondescript, old-model brown Renault and with controlled haste stripped off their uniforms and tossed them on to the back seat of the car. The Schmeisser went in last of all. They opened the boot and dressed themselves in their everyday clothes. Philippe removed the magazine from the butt of the MAB, threw it on to the clothes in the car and replaced it with a full one. He cocked the weapon, applied the safety, tucked it into his belt and pulled his sweater down over it.

'Wait for me over there,' he snapped, and jerked his chin at the upward slope and a door marked 'Emergency Exit'. He was finding it difficult to talk to his companion. He kept his words to a minimum, turning his back and then leaning into the boot of the Renault. He shifted an old sack and inspected beneath it the packet flattened over the petrol tank. He ran his hands over it and checked that it was firmly in place, then compared the time on the small clock attached to the packet with the dial on his wrist. Nothing registered on his face. He looked tired. It was the aftermath of battle. He brought the two loose wires together and twirled them into a join, studied the packet for another second, then dropped the boot and joined Paul Vernet at the exit.

They surfaced at street level on the opposite side of the car-park entrance. Avoiding the confusion of police, ambulance, fire and emergency services they walked, without hurrying, away from the chaos. They passed no one. The few cars they saw were all hurrying to the party to add to the confusion and nobody had time to give the two men a second glance. Without exchanging a word they walked up the Rue de Rennes as far as the intersection with the Boulevard Raspail.

'We make a bloody good team, Philippe!' Paul broke the silence. He was impervious to the older man's silent anger. 'We'll show the bastards, won't we?'

Philippe stared at him. This wasn't the time – or the place. He didn't reply. Finally he nodded in the direction of Montparnasse. 'Walk to Montparnasse and take the Métro. Go straight home and have a bath. Wash your hair. Keep your head down and don't go out for two days. I'll be in touch – usual manner – be there.' He watched as the younger man turned away towards the Métro. 'Paul,' he called, softly.

'What?'

'Why did you kill Gautier?'

Paul smiled. 'I didn't like his fat face. And the bastard called me an idiot!'

'You killed him because he called you an idiot? Jesus Christ!'

'It wasn't only that – he was going to be awkward. He'd never have gone with us, and it was my life on the line as well. I reckoned it was the easiest way out.' The younger man's face took on a look of truculence. 'I still think kidnapping the old bastard was a silly idea. This was much easier – it'll make a much bigger splash.'

Philippe kept his temper. 'Even though all my planning and instructions were that he remain alive? Didn't you think, for one idiotic minute, that there was a reason for that? If I'd wanted him killed, don't you think I'd have said? Christ! Was that too much for you to understand?'

Paul shrugged his shoulders and again turned to go, but Philippe gripped his arm. Paul didn't try to pull away. 'Philippe, what's done's done. I reckon we're better off this way.'

Philippe let go of his arm. It was a waste of time. 'Why'd you kill Lucienne?'

'Because you'd have been too soft to do it yourself. It's all very well telling her to run and forget, but what would have happened when the *barbouzes* shoved her up against the wall and started knocking the daylights out of her? D'you think she'd have stood there shaking her head and saying she knew nothing about it? D'you think she'd have whistled with joy as they were breaking her arms and asking who's the bastard who killed the Minister? She bloody wouldn't have, Philippe. She'd have screamed at the top of her voice it was Philippe de Guy-Montbron and Paul Vernet who did it, and this is how you can find them . . . !'

'What happened afterwards was none of your business,' said Montbron with as much control as he could muster. He might as well have saved his breath.

'My life is my business.'

'Then it's time you packed your bloody bag and buggered off back into the mountains.'

'No can do, Philippe. You need me. There's no one else.'

He was right. Philippe studied him for a moment and tried hard not to shake his head in exasperation. There wasn't much else he could say, or do. He said, tamely, 'There was supposed to be no killing tonight. Next time . . .'

But Paul was on firm ground; he was still riding the blood trip; the adrenalin was still coursing. He grinned into the older man's face. 'They were only fuckin' Corsicans!'

Philippe de Guy-Montbron shook his head sadly. His unhappy features were a permanent legacy of an unpleasant profession. 'You're a mindless young bastard,' he said through his teeth.

'Yeh, I know – but I'm still your brother.'

Whatever else he was going to say was cut off by the sound of a muffled subterranean thump. There was a faint rumble, a vague movement under their feet. The old Renault had disintegrated, exploded under a two-kilo wad of PE. Nothing drastic – just enough to blow the thing, and everything in it, to tiny pieces, and give the forensic people an interesting hour or two before they shook their heads and went home.

The two men looked at each other. No more words. Montbron stood in a shop doorway and watched the younger man until he disappeared up the Rue de Rennes towards the Boulevard Montparnasse. He waited a few minutes longer, then crossed the road, skirted the Jardin du Luxembourg, cut through a side-street and then joined the Boulevard St-Michel. He glanced casually around him. He knew nobody had picked him up, but he wasn't relaxed. Nobody was relaxed. It was like wartime, and as in wartime, the best-laid plans go wrong. As this one had. He found his car where he'd left it and sat at an adjacent café and drank a small glass of beer while he studied his surroundings.

The car had no watcher, but it had a ticket for overstaying its welcome. He'd have been very suspicious if it hadn't.

When he finished his beer he changed to coffee and cognac and waited another three-quarters of an hour. There was plenty of life about. The Boulevard St-Michel was at its most vibrant and the tall, slightly balding man in his early thirties sitting outside the café with his back to the wall, sipping cognac and coffee, caused no interest. Montbron suited the Left Bank. Clean-shaven, with a firm chin and grey eyes that, with a trace of mockery gazed at the thronging mass without interest. He looked the part. A dark roll-neck sweater and rust-coloured suede jacket kept his appearance within the bounds of mature student/youngish lecturer. The fact that he was sitting alone might have raised an eyebrow, but it would have been nothing more than that and it didn't seem to concern him. He glanced down at his watch. The minute hand was creeping towards ten-past twelve. Unhurriedly he tipped the remains of his cognac down his throat, swirled the coffee-cup absently and drained it as he picked up the little tab, stood and squeezed his way past his neighbours through the café to the bar. He paid his bill and bought half a dozen telephone *jetons*, then, after a brief glance through the café door at the spot he'd just vacated, he strolled to the end of the café and locked himself in the phone booth. He looked at his watch again. One minute to quarter past. He began to dial. It was a Metz number on the Army network.

The phone rang three times before it was picked up.

Montbron listened for a second, then said, 'Diderot.'

'I've just heard the news,' said the voice at the other end. It didn't sound too pleased. 'What went wrong?'

Montbron told him.

'A simple kidnap turns into a bloodbath – that's going to take some explaining at the end of the day. Who's this mad bastard you've picked up as a partner?' The voice didn't wait for an answer. 'You're supposed to be on your own. If you need backup, I'll supply it, but that wasn't in the drawing. What happens now, Philippe?'

'You want me to abort the programme?'

There was a longish pause. Montbron coughed lightly to show he was still there, then pressed another *jeton* into the slot. It wasn't necessary; the phone came to life again. 'No. Pick the cards up again and carry on – but I repeat, get rid of that bloody maniac. They'll have your head in the bloody bucket if it happens again. Is that clear?'

'Yes, sir. I'm sorry about Gautier.'

'It's not as bad as it seems.'

'Even so—'

'Forget it.'

Montbron waited for a few seconds longer with the receiver jammed against his ear. But the line was dead. No goodbye. Nothing. He put the phone down and went outside, ordered himself another cognac, no coffee, then sat down and watched his car for another ten minutes before getting into it and driving away.

2

THE MURDER OF the Minister of Special Affairs, one of the country's senior Government administrators, and his bodyguards, reverberated well beyond the walls of the underground car park in the 6th arrondissement and even beyond the thicker, albeit more ornate, walls of the office of the Central Control for the Analysis of OAS Activities – the CCAOA – housed in a security complex overlooking the Auteuil racecourse.

All the major branches of the national security service were represented by the CCAOA's committee, and on this occasion, the day after the outrage, the chairs around the long table were occupied by the senior members of each organization. It was presided over by the President's Director of Intelligence, Maurice, whose presence underlined the sense of urgency – the near panic – which the assassination had provoked. The surprising aspect of the event was the lethargy of the OAS (Organisation de l'Armée Secrète) publicity machine. Not normally reticent in claiming a success, they hadn't said a word on the operation. More than surprising – it was worrying!

But that was the least of the CCAOA's problems.

The anti-OAS machine was losing itself in a dense fog of suspicion, mistrust and overelaboration. It was in danger not of shooting itself in the foot but of blowing the leg off altogether. There were too many cooks, too many bubbling pots and no direction. They were all running around shrouded in secrecy, not only from the enemy but from themselves, their only common purpose to kill the OAS. If they killed each other in the process, too bad. And that's exactly what was happening. This meeting wasn't going to raise the fog. The DST and SDECE would ensure that.

The DST (Direction de la Surveillance du Territoire), the secret organization entrusted with the responsibility for the internal security of Metropolitan France, considered the prosecution of the war against the OAS in France its sole prerogative and acted accordingly. As the battle developed it had augmented its main thrust with irregular units, splinter groups and teams of infiltrators whose missions and identities were closely guarded secrets, even from each other. That confusion reigned at times was putting it mildly and when, finally, in 1961, an élite group of undercover agents was put into the field, the confusion was complete. This group of official no-mercy killers was made up almost entirely of Corsicans bent on wreaking vengeance for an OAS massacre of a large number of their compatriots in Algiers. They rapidly became known, and feared, as *les barbouzes* – the false beards.

SDECE disagreed with the DST contention that the war was purely domestic property. SDECE (Service de Documentation Extérieure et de Contre-Espionnage), the Secret Service and lineal descendant of the famed Deuxième Bureau, was concerned with carrying out espionage abroad and preventing foreigners from doing the same in France. General Grossin, head of SDECE, considered the OAS an overseas organization and went into action on that premise. But SDECE, to an even greater degree than the DST, was riddled with pro-OAS sympathizers, and, in several instances, with active supporters. After the SDECE head of station in Rabat was discovered to be a senior leader in the OAS, information and consultation between the two main organizations dried up completely. In many instances, SDECE operatives were forced to act without the prior clearance of their own HQ at Tourelles for fear of being betrayed to the OAS by many of their questionable colleagues. Department Maurice, nominally within the SDECE order of battle, remained, as always, a law unto itself and answered to no one. Its highly specialized agents worked individually and were, again as always, totally anonymous, even to each other.

As if the mixture wasn't sufficiently balanced for disaster, the Army had entered the fray without the agreement or permission of the main intelligence groups. Agents of the BSLE (Bureau de la Statistique de la Légion Étrangère), the Secret Service of the Foreign Legion; of the CCI, the Inter-Army Coordination Centre, and its special Section A; and of the Action Branch of SDECE, with its offshoot the 11th Shock Troops, had all introduced agents into the battle on their own behalf and were guarding their identities with unusual tenacity. The OAS silence regarding the assassination of the Minister of Special Affairs was indeed the least of their problems.

The committee sat well into the afternoon before the Chairman finally bent the representatives to his will and forced a broad agreement that their activities, however diverse, should not be disrupted, and nor should they, the directors, be sent into a panic of martial-law type operations. Indeed, he argued, no outward manifestation of the frustration felt by the heads of the various organizations should be allowed. No retaliatory show of force. No additional media oxygen for the criminals.

'You mean we tiptoe through the crisis as if this massacre at the Boulevard St-Germain hadn't happened?' suggested a man from the middle of the table. His voice dripped with sarcasm. 'We treat the murder of one of our most senior Government officials as an everyday happening in France? Is that what we've come to?'

'I mean', said the Chairman, patiently, 'that we do not show these thugs they have hurt us, that they have dealt us a shattering blow. We do not give them the satisfaction of seeing us running around like frightened schoolgirls. We show them, and the world, that this outrage means nothing to our resolve. We carry on with a shrug, and promise the vultures of the world's press that these bandits will be caught, tried and treated according to the law. They will be punished like the ordinary criminals they are. The man who fired the bullet into the Minister will be caught, however long it takes. His name will never be erased from the criminal records until he has paid the final penalty. On that I give my word.'

'Fine sentiments, my friend,' said his critic. The rest of the table appeared to have given him the right to speak their thoughts; but whether they had or not, he was not going to sit quietly while the President's man poured balm over their unresponsive heads. He locked eyes with the Chairman. 'I'm sure the world at large will be enormously cheered by that pronouncement and will derive great comfort from the vision of a little old man coming forward, maybe at the turn of the century, to have his head removed for the murder in 1961 of the French Minister of Special Affairs!'

'You exaggerate, as usual.'

'Perhaps. But I'm concerned with today, not sometime in the future. It doesn't matter what you offer us or what you offer the President and his supporters. It's what you offer the people of Paris that'll decide this issue – the people of Paris, the bastards who'll have us all in bloody tumbrels if they think we're losing this particular war. They're fickle at the best of times and I wouldn't bet a dud centime piece on one of the buggers shedding a single tear if they saw the nose and kepi of the President poking out of a wicker basket in the Place de la Concorde! So, tell us, Mr Chairman, for the sake of our bloody noses and kepis, what can we offer the people *today*?'

Nobody smiled. The Chairman fumbled with his matches and lit another cigarette. His throat was dry through smoking too much and his head thumped behind his eyes from bashing it against the brick wall of the rifle-and-bayonet mentality of his colleagues who wanted to see blood being soaked up by the sand of the gun pit at Vincennes. All he wanted, at the moment, was a large glass of whisky, but he knew if he started now he wouldn't stop until he'd finished the bottle. He decided to reserve the temptation for the peace and tranquility of his apartment.

'It is my belief,' he said tiredly, without looking at or replying to his tormentor, 'and I know most of you have reached the same conclusion, that this atrocity does not bear the usual hallmarks of the OAS/Métropole Central Committee and that its handwriting indicates a new executive brain and a new way of thinking. The actions of these perpetrators are more akin to the dentist's drill than the usual gangster tactics of OAS Central Command.'

'You think a freelance expert has been invited to take part?'

'Not at all. You don't kill Government Ministers and carloads of security agents for money, you do it out of conviction, for your principles. The man who organized this is one of them all right, but he's different. He's barely poked his nose above the parapet and he's pulled the biggest coup so far. He's not exposed himself or given us anything to look at him with.'

'What about the two gendarmes in the car park?'

'They were too busy worrying about their lives to take notice of the killers.'

'But they were spoken to?'

'They didn't see them.'

'That's not what I mean. Were the killers Frenchmen?'

'What d'you mean?'

'You know, were they Metropolitan?' There was an embarrassed pause while the speaker considered the origins of his colleagues. He was content. 'Were they Corsican? Algerian?'

'Breton?' added a new voice.

'I don't think we need to stick our heads into that bucket,' said the Chairman, archly. 'They were Frenchmen – and only two of them. That should be enough to satisfy this committee. The assassination team would have been made up of a leader and a subordinate, and as I remarked earlier, it's only his nose the leader of this pair has shown us. I reckon that's all he's shown anyone else, even his own command. That's why they're quiet. They, like us, are mystified. They haven't been brought into the picture yet.'

A new voice broke in. 'It is my opinion that this new creature is being directed from Madrid by one man.'

' "Soleil"?' suggested another.

'Don't play their bloody game,' snapped the Chairman. 'He's got a name.'

'OK. Salan?'

The Chairman nodded. 'Or by Vanuxem. But the question we ask ourselves is, who've they chosen for the next show of cleverness?'

But they didn't have to ask themselves. They knew who usually came next – Charles de Gaulle. But the name was unpronounced.

Like reciting the words of the benediction when making the sign of the cross, it was unnecessary. The Chairman shook his head slowly. 'This assassin has shown his resourcefulness. He mustn't be allowed to move up the ladder, which is why he has to be identified and dealt with without delay.'

'We have OAS people in custody,' murmured the Director of the DST. The statement hung in the air. It wasn't necessary to elaborate. Harsh times meant harsh methods. As long as none of the men at the table had to pull on the rubber gloves.

The Chairman answered bluntly. 'I don't think we're going to get to this one via the bollocks of run-of-the-mill OAS troopers. He'll have a very safe bed somewhere, probably in Paris.' He stopped, thought a little more about it, pulled a face, and breathing deeply said, 'Definitely in Paris. A rabbit in a bloody rabbit warren! And he'll have his target indicated through a treble cut-out system. He won't report to his command. They'll get his sitrep through the front page of *La Libération* – or the comic papers!'

'He's got to contact somebody, and we've got most of OAS's Metropolitan capos covered in one way or another. How's he going to manage for money? He'll have to break out and contact somebody, even if it's only for that.'

The Chairman grimaced and crushed his half-smoked Gitane into the glass ashtray in front of him, then reached for a bottle of Vichy water to wash away the taste. His colleagues watched him pour the water into his glass as if they'd never seen it done before. He knew they were watching but he didn't hurry. When he'd drunk and replaced the glass on the table, he sat back in his chair and said, 'Not necessarily. He'll have an unattached banker, a wealthy sympathizer, a rich friend, or there'll be a special drop – a box dug into concrete some time ago for just such an operation as this. One thing these treacherous bastards are not short of is money.'

'Or rich sympathizers,' murmured someone at the other end of the table.

The Chairman ignored the interruption. 'Personally, I don't

think he'll take a chance on a pick-up when he can help himself from the Crédit Lyonnais!'

'I didn't realize we had so many bank robbers in our Officer Corps,' said one of the earlier interrupters. 'Is that a standard course at St Cyr nowadays?'

Nobody laughed, least of all the Chairman. 'He'll need an arms and explosive cote, and that'll have to be here, somewhere in Paris, or its environs—'

'That's a very small element in our favour. But I reckon we've covered everything we can here, except' – the Director of DST sitting at the far end of the table decided to lift the boiling pot off the stove – 'what we're going to do about him.' He stared at the Chairman from under dark grey bushy eyebrows. He was not known for mincing words. 'The only impression you've given me so far, Maurice, is that you could be the man's publicity agent! So, having got us all madly in love with this new star of the thuggery circus and kept us away for the best part of the afternoon from the job of putting the bastard in a cage, perhaps you would be good enough to point us to the road you've decided to trot us all down.'

'Nicely stated, Édouard!' The Chairman wasn't put off by the blast of sarcasm, in fact he bared his teeth in the semblance of a smile. 'What I'm going to suggest is that we meet fire with fire. We put into the field our own one-man army to counteract the OAS new thinker. One man to catch and destroy one man.'

'If you don't mind my saying so,' riposted Édouard, 'you've left me behind there. At the last rough count we had some fifteen thousand specialists whose sole occupation was looking hard at anyone with a suntan. And that fifteen thousand doesn't include the special-action units that have been cobbled together for purely counter-OAS measures.'

'But there's no central direction. Everybody's doing his own thing.'

'And we're going to continue doing so because we're not getting in each other's way—'

'Not much we're not!' interjected a voice, which was silenced into a growl by the heavy, bushy eyebrows frowning in his direction.

'And the overall success rate in putting these people away precludes any change of tactics. I can't for the life of me see what one man can do that this lot haven't.'

The Chairman lit another cigarette. It was against his better judgement and as he coughed on the first mouthful he said, gruffly, 'And how many members of the OAS have you got among those fifteen thousand, and these famous action groups you're talking about?'

'Pardon?'

'This is not black and white, Édouard. It's not France on one side and some other fuckers on the other. This is a bloody civil war. It's Frenchmen against Frenchmen, and if they're not in the ring fighting each other, they've taken sides. So, I'll ask again: how many of our people are OAS sympathizers and collaborators?'

They got the message.

In the heavy silence that ensued the Chairman went back to his theme: 'Our one man will be known only to us in this room. He will have *carte blanche* to go anywhere he wants, do what he wants, and order the removal of anyone getting in his way. His sole mission is to find the man responsible for Gautier's assassination, destroy his apparatus and either bring him home to be shot, or cut his head off himself. He can do whatever he chooses.'

The silence, broken only by the Chairman's hoarse cough, continued for almost a minute. Then a voice, hitherto unheard, said, 'That's an awful lot of power and authority to invest in an unknown. Are we agreeing to give someone, legally, the power to kill one of us if he so desires?'

'If you're a member of the Organisation de l'Armée Secrète embarked on overthrowing this Government and murdering its ministers, that's exactly what might happen.' The Chairman's expression was set in concrete; he meant what he said.

'What a preposterous suggestion!'

'If you choose to take it that way. Does anybody have any interesting questions?'

They all had.

'How's he going to be controlled?'

'By me.'

'What authority?'

'A Presidential "K" authority.' He paused for a moment. 'The service number of which I will make known, exceptionally, to each of you. It will be issued as a special Department Maurice authority. But if you want to know when he's stepping on your toes, there'll be a code-name for anyone at gutter level who gets in his way.'

DST wasn't happy. 'What if he oversteps his mandate and runs into one of the orthodox agencies? What do I tell my people – Force H in particular?'

'You call H and the *barbouzes* orthodox?'

'That's neither here nor there.'

'You tell them nothing. The same applies to everyone else. This man goes on to the streets totally anonymous. Anonymity – that's the strength of the operation. He stands on his own two feet and if your people get in his way, they'll go.'

They were running out of arguments.

'Have you got anybody in mind?'

The Chairman nodded his head but didn't speak. They knew what he meant.

'When will this individual start his campaign?'

The Chairman studied the speaker for several seconds. 'He started this morning.'

ACCESS MAURICE ONLY
Confidential – NOT TO BE REMOVED FROM FILE

GÉRARD XAVIER DEODAT, BARON NEURIE

Born:	15/3/1923; Oloron, Béarn
1938	Naval Academy, Brest
1940	Commandeered small fishing boat and with 3 other cadets sailed to British port.
1942	After two years' service at sea volunteered for French Marine Commando and saw action with Canadian Forces at Dieppe. Made aide to Admiral Foixeau and made several clandestine pre-invasion trips to French coastal towns.
1944	With French Special Forces landed France on 4th June and cleared and held beachheads at Juno and Gold. As bodyguard to Admiral Lafoix took part in every action involving French SF in Belgium, France and Germany. Wounded at Cabourg and again at Bassenville but on both occasions discharged himself from hospital to rejoin unit.
1945	From Lieut. Commander – wartime, acting – to sous Lieut. substantive and posted to A/Carrier *Jeanne d'Arc* for service in Far East.
1946	Transferred back to Marine Commando and saw action in all theatres Indo-China. As Commander Special Force (F) dropped behind enemy lines and operated until force wiped out. Severely wounded, captured, and tortured. After five months escaped and made way back to Saigon.
1947	Hospital Marseille. Discharged Navy with rank of Lieutenant and placed on reserve. Recruited into SDECE, posted Far East station.
1949	Active against Communist terrorists in Malaya as part of Anglo/French MI team, intelligence gathering and analysis and military action against armed units in Malayan jungle. Wounded.

1952–56	Singapore and Kuala Lumpur as Deputy Head of SDECE presence. Nominally Commercial Attaché, French Embassy. 1955 married Monique de Cantenac. Divorced 1958, no issue. (Cross-ref. de Cantenac, Robert; file D/C/513.)
1956	Recruited by Dept. Maurice. Principal duties: internal security. Special duties: elimination of enemies of State.

Section 2

Additional qualifications:

Languages: English; German; Russian; Spanish; Arabic; Italian.

Grade: A/12

Operational Status: Unrestricted.

3

TALL, A FRACTION over six feet two, with a hawk-like nose and a receding hairline, but an otherwise full mop of light brown hair, Gérard Neurie was sufficiently unhandsome to appear anonymous in a normal-size crowd.

He folded his newspaper, drank the last of his coffee, then stood up and threaded his way through the pavement tables and chairs and into the cool interior of the restaurant.

The telephone was being used.

He moved to the counter and ordered a small beer. Propping himself on a bar stool, he stared thoughtfully at his reflection in the ornate gilded mirror that ran the entire length of the bar. It was a short communion. His expression didn't betray his findings or conclusions as he moved his eyes away and glanced down at the thin black diary he held in his hand. He opened it at the address section and reminded himself of a number. He had plenty of time to finish his beer before the unhappy-looking occupant of the phone booth finally gave up whatever was making him unhappy and vacated the box.

Neurie waited a few seconds, drained his glass and then bent his shoulders into the small cabinet. There was a slight suggestion of sweat left by the previous occupant but he closed his nose to it and allowed the two sections of the door to click together. He felt, as he usually did in café phone booths, a slight claustrophobia, as if he were locked in an upright coffin; it was a legacy of Viet Minh hospitality in Indo-China, where he *had been* locked in an upright coffin for days at a time. It was the claustrophobic's ultimate nightmare, but he shrugged this one aside, stuck the *jeton* in its slot and dialled. It was a local number, just around the corner.

'DST,' answered a clear female voice. 'What department please?'

'E2.' Neurie didn't waste words.

Another female voice. 'Can I help you?'

Neurie stared over the top of the booth's half-frosted window. He could see beyond the bar and restaurant to the outside world and the animation of a lunch-time Champs-Élysées. Life out there looked very clear-cut and definite. He didn't give her time to repeat the question. 'Superintendent Violle.'

'Who's calling?'

'Jean Joffre.'

Violle wasn't surprised. He knew who Jean Joffre was.

Neurie said, without preamble, 'Gaby, d'you fancy lunch?'

'Where?'

'My place.'

'Half-past one?'

'See you there.' Neurie's 'place' was a small café in a side-street off the Rue de Miromesnil, a short walk from the DST HQ in the Rue des Saussaies – no outside tables, only nine inside, and no view. Discreet.

Neurie walked there slowly, then stood at the tiny bar and drank a glass of house red while he waited for the occupants of the only table for two in a corner to leave. A food-only café, no coffee, it dissuaded those with nowhere else to go from sitting for another hour gazing into each other's eyes. The owner of the café was replacing the soiled paper tablecloth as Violle arrived.

'Gautier?' asked Violle as he sat down. Nowhere near as tall as Neurie, he was a solidly-built Breton with a stiff, bristly crew cut of prematurely grey hair. Three years older than Neurie, his expression had no give in it, but remained permanently sombre. He was a professional; he'd seen a lot of unpleasantness. It showed.

Neurie poured him a glass of wine from the bottle on the table and gave a slight nod. There was no need for preliminaries. He and Violle had landed at Juno beach together, had dropped from the same Dakota on the other side of the Rhine, and later Violle had pulled the strings of the fellowship of the Croix de la

Libération to have himself posted to Indo-China as a sergeant in Neurie's Special Force. He'd been wounded and evacuated before Neurie's last action, and after a tour in Algeria, and another wound, he had been recruited into military intelligence and, in a sideways skip, to the civilian internal intelligence organization, the DST. 'Jean Joffre' was the identification code used by him and Neurie. Known only to them, it was the name of an agreeable young buffoon who, like many of his generation, had died uncomplainingly in the Normandy sand.

Neurie refilled his own glass and said, 'Gautier – and other things. I want a pair of eyes, some delicate finger-work, and a good reliable legman.'

'And you want me to lend you these three men?' Violle frowned in concentration, but it was affectation; he knew what Neurie wanted. 'When?'

Neurie ignored his friend's frown. 'Right away – say, as from tomorrow. But let it come from the top. I'll get Maurice to make a request for an Arabicist with special qualifications for temporary attachment to the Élysée. He'll suggest you.' Neurie smiled at Violle's raised eyebrows. 'Maurice's suggestions are other people's death wish! Bring with you the names of a couple of street-corner boys, just in case. We'll have them smuggled in to save you having to make the coffee yourself! But Gaby, make sure they're yours. They've got to be trusted and loyal – if that's possible!'

'It's the times we live in,' said Violle as he studied the menu. 'This bloody OAS thing has thrown up some very funny attitudes in our trade. I'm even beginning to look sideways at the lady who brings my coffee every morning, and I've known her for ten years.'

'Which brings me to the reason I'm spending my hard-earned wages on putting another inch round your waist,' interrupted Neurie as he took the menu from Violle's hand. 'Who killed Gautier?'

Violle shook his head. 'Who held the gun? No idea, but the thinking is definitely the boys from the desert. We haven't really had time for a detailed analysis. At the moment none of the former "ultra" people who built up a specialization in this type of butchery in Algeria before they changed their name to OAS fit the outline of the operation.' Violle allowed his mouth to droop, although whether due to his choice from the menu or his thoughts on the killing wasn't apparent. 'This particular show has different hallmarks. I think he's your sort of man.'

'How d'you make that out?'

'The guy who carried this out had no sentiment, no feelings. He's a hard bastard – a surgeon.'

'And that makes him my sort of man?'

Violle shrugged. 'Think about it. Everybody had to die, and when they'd been done they were burned, just in case. It shows a certain clinical regard for detail. We haven't had a hard bastard go to the lengths of cremation before.'

Neurie took a mouthful of wine and broke the crust off a baguette. 'Go on.'

Violle did the same, and speaking through a mouthful of bread said, 'Initial indications show two weapons were used. The Minister and his passenger – a girl – were both shot at close range with a 9mm or 7.62. The guys who were cooked in the second car took a load of 9mm – there was a full magazine's worth of empties lying around. Somebody who reckoned he knew all about it suggested a Schmeisser.'

'Tell me about the girl.'

Violle shook his head sadly. 'Pretty little thing – nice body, good legs . . .'

'Come on, Gaby.' Neurie went to work on another piece of bread. 'They all look like that – depending on when you last stuck your knee between a pair of tightly clenched thighs! Who was she? How did she get into the driving seat of a car with one of the country's leaders? Whose car was it? And why was she killed—' He broke off when the café owner put plates in front of them and refilled the bread basket. Neurie didn't continue, but left Violle to think about the question he'd asked while he poked his knife into a communal bowl of fat-encrusted *rillettes*.

'Nothing's known about her – yet.' Violle stared flatly at Neurie's plate. He made no attack on the *rillettes*. 'Renseignements Généraux have got it all on the table and are sifting through the debris. DST only gets the conclusions. All those tiny little details are considered too complicated for us – unless, of course . . .' He dragged his eyes away from Neurie's plate and stopped talking to concentrate on cutting out a large wedge of rough *pâté de campagne* from another bowl. When he got it settled on his plate he continued, in between mouthfuls, 'they intrude into the realms of national security.' He looked up. 'And that includes OAS activities.'

'You can poke around where you like and as much as you like from now on,' said Neurie, 'and with Élysée authority. Start cracking as soon as you get Hausmann's letter of assignment. I want to know everything about that girl and whatever you can shuffle together about the man who put this game into play. No time to spare. The man's got to be identified, traced, talked to and—' Neurie popped a small piece of bread with a mountain of *rillettes* balanced precariously on top of it into his mouth. It stopped him talking, but it didn't matter; there was no need to go on.

Gaby Violle wiped his lips with a napkin, then pursed them and raised his eyebrows as his eyes locked on to Neurie's. 'D'you want to be a bit more specific about that "and"?'

Neurie shrugged. He seemed more concerned over what he was about to eat than Violle's question. It received only the bare suggestion of a shake of the head and a short 'no', nothing more.

Violle lowered his hand and wrapped it around his glass. After a long sip he allowed the suggestion of a smile to touch his otherwise sombre features. 'You have an extraordinary way of earning your living nowadays, *mon capitaine*!'

Neurie didn't smile back. 'It takes all sorts to make good *boudin*, Gaby, as young Joffre used to say!'

The two men met again that evening, this time in Neurie's sixth-floor flat in the Rue Jacob, just behind the Boulevard St-Germain.

Neurie had picked up the whisky-and-water habit from the English and poured himself a large one. Violle was much more set in his ways. 'Ricard with ice, no water,' he said as he came back into the room from the balcony.

Violle was the perfect intelligence operative, average in almost everything – average height, five ten; eyes, average for his part of the country. Brown – and a tenacity of purpose that made him a very difficult man to shift once he got his teeth into something. His face, at the age of forty-one, had set into a loose baggy shape, its lines relieved by a grey-tinged David Niven moustache. He'd practised for a long time in front of the mirror to acquire the smile that matched the moustache. The result was a habit of pressing his top lip up against his teeth whilst fractionally dropping the lower one. It had a very pleasing effect. At least he thought it had. He didn't use it enough, although he was never short of women friends.

'Three of the five gorillas killed with Gautier were Corsican,' he said now. 'Action Association people specially drawn in to the bodyguard group as a wedge against OAS plants. The other two were regional – one a long-serving permanent chauffeur, the other a contract shooter from SDECE's Algier's Bureau 24. They shared something like thirty rounds between them. Forensic reckons one of the Corsicans must have still been alive when the car went up in flames. They put his death down to "causes over and above gunshot wounds".'

Neurie placed the small glass of Ricard in front of Violle and watched as he dropped, with a healthy clunk, four cubes of ice into it. He tasted his own drink again, and with the glass still resting lightly against his lips said, 'Which shows the men knew what they were doing with the finishing touch – or at least one of them did. You said there were only two weapons used?'

'That's what they say. I reckon a two-man job. No fuss, no tripping over each other's feet, but—'

Neurie drank another mouthful from his glass then lowered it and raised one eyebrow quizzically at Violle as he stopped in mid-sentence.

'One of them forgot what he was supposed to be and took his eye off the ball. He used his bare thumb to load the machine-gun magazine. There are parts of a print on every empty case.

Only segments, mind you, but they reckon they can join them into an almost complete thumb.'

Gérard Neurie wasn't impressed. 'If anything comes of that, it'll be the name of the boy who fetches the sandwiches. It still won't tell us where he lives or what he looks like, or who the genius is who tweaks his bit of string. At this stage of the game, Gaby, they'll have imposed a cut-out, probably double. Your jigsaw prints, if they tell us anything at all, will end up on the fingers of a dead-end street. These bloody things usually do. It's not a question of him taking his eye off the ball, it's just that they couldn't give a bugger because neither of them has ever had his thumbs on a criminal ID pad.'

Violle stared at the rapidly clouding liquid in his glass. He didn't taste it, but swirled it lightly and watched the ice cubes slowly melt. 'I'm not arguing that one,' he said. 'I'm agreeing. The OAS has attracted some funny buggers to trot with it behind the colours: fanatics who've crawled out of drains for the duration and who're likely to shove the hot end of a machine-pistol into their mouths and pull the trigger if it looks like they're going to be taken in for a chat with the friendly *barbouzes*. And talking of the *barbouzes* – this little effort's not going to soften their expressions. Another shoot-up like that one with more Corsican dead and the buggers'll be totally uncontrollable. They're almost that now. They're running their own little no-rules war, and they've even been given their own space somewhere on the edge of the 16th. They should have given them the Gestapo's old place on the Avenue Foch!' Violle didn't smile. Corsicans running amok legally weren't a funny subject. 'But, that apart . . .' He brought the glass up to eye level and studied its contents against the light. 'I'm interested in this girl. I think she might have been part of the crew.'

Neurie stared pointedly but said nothing. He let Violle have his head.

'She doesn't start anywhere. This was only the third time she'd been with Gautier.' He paused again. 'D'you know anything about his private life?'

'Tell me about it.'

'He was not nice to know. Had all the vices – the lot! Little boys, little girls – not women, girls, as young as they come. He was a pig! He'd got filthy habits, disgusting manners and used his position like a senator of ancient Rome. D'you want any more?'

Neurie shrugged and raised his glass to see how far he'd got with it. He drank another mouthful and prepared to refill it. Violle continued.

'The bastard collected these little girls and boys around him and then set about ageing them with his particular brand of fetishism. The girl who was killed with him had been round the course but still had some distance to go.'

'She won't finish it now.'

Violle ignored Neurie's remark. 'She'd got quite a few marks on her body but he hadn't really got down to nailing her to the kitchen table.'

'Is that what his staff say?'

'He's got a servant who helps – helped. Used to hold them down for him. He's an Arab, from the backstreets of Algiers, from Belcourt. Ambidextrous fetishists are the norm there. This guy says his master met the girl at a dinner or a soirée – a drinks do of some description.'

'He was sure about that?'

'No, it was what he reckoned. I've got two lads on the payroll who're going through Gautier's social calendar, official and unofficial, to find out where he might have picked her up. Personally, I reckon she was planted just for this operation.'

'And killed to muddy the tracks?'

'Right. Any private little dinner party he attended over the past couple of weeks is going to have to be awfully pro our great Leader if the hosts or organizers don't want to find themselves sitting on a hard stool over at Ivry. I'm glad he didn't come to dinner at my place!'

'Are these men of yours secure?'

Violle finally sipped from his glass. He gave a little smack of the lips to show that he was satisfied and smiled crookedly. 'As houses! They're too young to have developed such antisocial habits as revolutionary tendencies. *Le grand Charles* would be perfectly safe sharing an outdoor shithouse with these people. They've been hand-picked. I've also drawn a couple of good youngsters on attachment from SDECE Tourelles. Boys with good safe hands. And anyway, they're already on the job, so stop worrying!' Violle looked up and studied Neurie's sceptical expression. 'It'll look like a routine investigation – closing the file on the Minister's last week or so, eliminating any question of forces other than the OAS being involved in, or responsible for, the man's death. Don't worry!' he repeated.

'I'm not. Have another Ricard?'

4

A WARM AUTUMN DAY – mid-morning – and the golden shafts of the sun's rays cut through the ageing foliage of the trees standing sentinel on either side of the broad expanse of the Avenue Beauchamp. But Gérard Neurie, sitting in the passenger seat of Violle's dark green Citroën, wasn't interested in the sun's rays or ageing foliage. He was staring straight ahead, studying the road, assessing the importance of the large, prosperous-looking houses that took up more than their fair share of space, and watching men hard at work.

The Citroën was comfortably parked, well concealed at the bottom end of the avenue where it joined the Boulevard Malesherbes. About three hundred yards at the other end of the avenue a yellow and blue public works department repair van was parked half on the kerb and half on the road. A man in brown overalls leaned against a metal extension ladder, one hobnailed reinforced boot resting solidly on a brown leather tool-box and the other on the ground. He gazed into space, an unlighted cigarette hanging disconsolately from his lips.

'You're going to get your toes jumped up and down on, Gaby,' murmured Neurie, 'if you get caught messing around with the sort of people who live in these places.'

Violle wasn't interested. He sat relaxed in the Citroën's spongy seat and continued studying the notes balanced on the steering-wheel in front of him. He didn't look up. 'This is one of the three non-official dinner parties Gautier attended in the ten days before he was killed. His man reckons it was during these ten days that the girl appeared for the first time.'

'And you're now convinced she had a fairly senior role to play?'

'It was your suggestion, Gérard. And, yes, I do. The kill was calculated, but the arrangements were loose. They were worked around her, she persuaded Gautier into the killing zone – his regular chauffeur said so, remember? He was the lucky one; he wasn't in on the fun and games. What a bloody card to draw – to be told to put his feet up for the evening because the girl liked driving! Jesus! I'd never stop smiling at myself in the mirror if it happened to me . . .'

'The girl, Gaby?'

Violle twitched his nose. He'd liked to have expounded more on lady luck, but he went back easily to the story. 'Sure, the girl. I reckon there's a good chance she knew her killer, the man with the precision weapon. She just sat there and allowed him to put a gun a few centimetres from her forehead and pull the trigger. She didn't even put her hand up to try and stop it.' He stuck his finger on the sheet in front of him to remind himself. 'Nine millimetre, probably a MAB according to the markings on the empty cases. Distance, about six centimetres. The same weapon used on Gautier and the driver. They were both treated to a couple of bullets each. The girl was privileged – she got two as well, but the second was from a distance of less than five centimetres.'

'Maybe he didn't like to see her jiggling up and down after the first with that unhappy look in her eyes.'

'More like he was making absolutely sure of her because she knew him. He'd put her up to it. Incidentally, it was definitely a Schmeisser that sorted out the body-watchers on the back seat. Ex-Boche Army, no history, probably lifted by the Resistance during the war and cached.'

'What else have you got on the girl?'

'Eighteen. Lucienne Maillot, born in Le Mans. Her parents, middle-class people, moved to Paris when she was twelve. She left home about a year ago and rented a small studio flat in Porte d'Italie. We're digging, mainly the last eighteen months, but I don't expect too much. The boy with the gun seems too much of a pro to have been seen with her. He probably picked her up in a Boul' Mich' discothèque a couple of weeks ago and gave her a romantic story about the new Resistance.'

'Is that how you'd have done it, Gaby?'

Violle smiled wryly. 'They're very impressionable at that age, particularly if the boy's Army, or ex-Army, and has a sad look, sand between his toes and an Algerian suntan.'

'*Putain*?'

Violle's smile remained in place but his mind had gone ahead of it. He hunched his shoulders, then allowed the smile to droop as he indicated with his chin the large house in its own grounds where the men were working. 'Somehow I don't think a whore would be on that house's social list. The big-head who lives there is a prominent *juge d'instruction* with fairly powerful political connections. Apart from posh dinners, he doesn't spend a lot of time there, although his wife does – and you can read into that anything you like. But he's a solid de Gaullist and wouldn't let anyone like us piss on the doorstep. He's no prude and doesn't need to mix with the not-so-nice girls when he has an unlimited choice of enthusiastic and dedicated amateurs.'

'So she could have been one of those?'

Violle had lost interest in Lucienne Maillot. He stuck a cigarette in the corner of his mouth and handed another to Neurie. 'We'll see if anything comes up. In the meantime this and the other two places where Gautier had dinner are starting-points. We'll watch and listen for a bit and see if any likely new face appears on the streets talking about what a clever fellow he is.' He removed the cigarette from his lips and indicated with it a point beyond the windscreen. 'The chap up that pole is installing a camera link. We gave the district a power cut and a telephone breakdown, so a fitter up a pole won't excite curiosity.' He snorted and put the cigarette back between his lips. 'Personally, I don't think the snotty buggers who live around here would notice a man up a pole. They probably think a man in a boiler suit's some sort of visitor from one of the other planets.'

'Gaby, I didn't know you harboured all these social prejudices against your betters. Are you sure you're on the right side in this war?'

Violle snorted again. He didn't swallow the bait. 'Well, just in case my social prejudices are all to cock, he's going to do the rest of this avenue, and there's another plumbing crew attending to the other two places.'

'Phones?'

'We've got a tap on all three.'

'Who did you ask?'

'No one. I referred GIC to your governor. They didn't quibble with me, just asked me how many, when and what, and there you go! Trouble is, though, that camera up there'll only give us daylight callers. It will relay to a cupboard we've acquired in the post office over there—' He jerked his finger over his shoulder. 'Very convenient – on the corner of Malesherbes and Monceau. They'll make a still of all comings and goings so that we can study them at leisure. When it gets too dark for the camera we'll have a physical watch lined up.'

While he was speaking the man at the top of the ladder threw his bag of tricks to the ground and began to climb down. He made heavy going of his descent. On the ground he took a cigarette from his mate and lit it as he gazed conscientiously up at his handiwork. He looked every inch the municipal repairman. After a few moments he crooked his finger at his mate and ambled along the pavement towards the next post. He stopped an arm's length away, tapped it with his open hand and leaned back to study its top whilst he smoked his cigarette. His mate busied himself with the ladder and equipment. The two agents from the highly specialized Groupement Interministeriel des Communications had the municipal-worker hierarchy down to a tee.

Violle turned his head and blew a stream of smoke through the open window. 'And if anybody asks, we're looking for B&C – bribery and corruption – money for favours in high places.'

'What about that Schmeisser? You mentioned thumbprints on cartridge cases – anything come of them?'

Violle allowed his mouth to droop again. 'Nothing. They don't belong to anybody. Whoever pumped those rounds into the magazine hasn't got a record and didn't do National Service.

Until he spits at a *flic* or hangs around a girls' school with his fly buttons undone and gets run in, we haven't got a name.'

'Could he have failed the medical for military service?'

'Could be a number of reasons why he didn't get in. Why d'you ask?'

Neurie didn't explain immediately. 'There'd be a record of failures and exemptions?'

'Sure – but too many. The Occupation buggered up the records. It'll take years before that source of fingering becomes reliable again. Sorry, Gérard, but we'll have to wait until Sammy the Schmeisser makes another mistake. He wound down his window and flicked the half-smoked cigarette on to the road. 'Anything you want to do while we're here?'

'Nope.'

'Then I suggest we get together tomorrow to look at pictures and listen to confessions.' He glanced sideways at a blank-faced Neurie. 'And I bet you an undercooked *boudin* to a *Lapérouse caneton collette* that the OAS is not mentioned once – and I'll throw in the wine for free!'

5

WHILE VIOLLE'S MEN went discreetly about their business, Philippe de Guy-Montbron stood to the side of a window at the back of the house being prepared for surveillance and gazed out at the green expanse of the Parc Monceau.

Montbron and his friends believed in the principle that the safest place for a bee to feed was in a hive. And there was nothing more like a beehive than a rambling three-storey house, one and a half kilometres from the throbbing heart of Paris. If he'd stood on his tiptoes, he could probably have read the stirring inscriptions on the Arc de Triomphe. Here he felt secure. He wasn't complacent; safety was simply something that neither entered his head nor worried him.

After a few more moments staring at the mist rising from the ornamental waters on the edge of the park, Montbron glanced down and studied the face of his watch. When the two hands joined together at five to eleven he flicked the switch on the small two-way handset he was holding and put it to his ear. It crackled for two or three seconds, then emitted a single word.

'Diderot?'

'Voltaire,' responded Montbron.

There followed immediately: '*Trente et un, trente-deux, quarante et un, trente-deux. Midi cinq exactement. Nom: Xavier.*' The crackling resumed; there was nothing more to be said. Montbron switched off the set and replaced it in the sink cupboard where it shared a dark niche with a bundle of cleaning materials. He glanced at his watch again. He'd been given an hour to find a safe telephone and ring a Monsieur Xavier at 31 32 41 32. He pursed his lips for a second. The number meant nothing. It could be anywhere in Paris – a phone perched on the end of a café bar, or, more likely, a public phone box. He screwed up the small piece of cardboard on which he'd written the number, lit a cigarette, and with the match burnt the number out of existence.

One hour.

Montbron took care with his appearance: a clean white shirt, a plain navy-blue knitted tie, a good but unpretentious dark grey suit. He polished his shoes with a rolled-up pair of socks. When he'd finished he slipped the socks back into the drawer and arranged them, with several other pairs, over a loaded and cocked Browning resting at the back of the drawer. He studied himself carefully in the mirror and nodded his approval, then, turning abruptly, he moved towards the camp-bed that occupied the wall on the blind side of the door and ran his hand under the crumpled pillow. He felt more comfortable with this than with the heavier Browning – a snug 7.65 Sauer & Sohn automatic, one previous owner, a Gestapo officer with ideas above his destiny and his dead hands stiff around the Sauer's butt. Small, unobtrusive and very, very useful when the unexpected breathed down the back of the neck and a snub-nosed police-issue MAB ground into the soft flesh below the left shoulder-blade. But the thought didn't trouble Montbron as he slipped its short barrel into the small leather toggle on his belt and tucked a fully loaded spare magazine into his waistband. Eight lead-nosed bullets in the magazine, one in the breech. No need to check it. He studied the effect for a few moments in the mirror then turned and spread the counterpane over the rumpled bed.

He left by his own special back door, which, hidden by disuse, led out into a garden shed. He slipped through the partially concealed wooden door and then through a gap in the surrounding wall. A stealthy exit from the untidy bush copse led him into the park promenade and out into the Boulevard Malesherbes.

He waited until three minutes past twelve and rang the number he'd been given from a café near the Gare St-Lazare.

The public phone in the wooden cabin by the tobacconist at the entrance to the Invalides terminus clicked under the fingers of the man holding down the receiver rest before bursting into sound. He took his hand back and stopped talking to himself. The exchange was familiar.

'Diderot,' said Montbron.

'Xavier,' responded the man in the booth, then took time to gaze out of the glass-framed door of the booth. It looked the normal terminus rush and bustle. Nobody paid any attention to the man at the phone. He neither recognized nor sensed interest in himself, but it was no consolation and did nothing for the damp fear-sweat building into a pool at the back of his neck where his collar cut into the fleshy folds. He stopped looking outwards and turned his head back to the cabin wall.

'You still there?' he murmured.

'*Oui.*'

He read out from memory a phone number and instructed Montbron to call it in fifteen minutes. When he put down the receiver he cut the link. The perfect cut-out: no names, no place, and not the slightest idea who or where – or what – he'd been talking to.

Montbron didn't move from his café. He drank a small chilled beer, smoked a cigarette and thirteen minutes later picked up the phone again.

It was the same procedure. Different instruction.

'Half-past one,' said the voice. 'Fouquet's, inside bar.' That was all. Montbron's phone went dead. The call had taken five seconds, including the ring.

There was plenty of time. He stopped for a coffee in the Place St-Augustin and watched the crowds. It was getting near lunch-time, people were becoming animated and losing the drawn looks of a starving populace. There was nobody watching him.

He left the café and walked down the Rue La Boétie, turning left when he reached the Champs Élysées, then made his way to the back row of tables under the awning outside the café opposite Fouquet's. He ordered a Pernod and relaxed as he watched the comings and goings across the road. Philippe de Guy-Montbron could afford to relax. The system was working. While all the resources of the security services and the vast network of

Renseignements Généraux peered down the alleyways in the traditionally red-tinged, revolutionary working-class districts of north-eastern Paris, and made nuisances of themselves around the cheap Left Bank student lodging areas, Montbron went to ground in comparative luxury in the exclusive parts of fashionable Wagram. But it couldn't last. They hadn't yet realized that this was no ordinary rebellion. These weren't peasants screaming for the blood of the better-off and mounting set-piece barricades as in previous arguments. This was a right-wing revolt, the Army officers, not the corporals; it was the rich and comfortable who weren't pleased with their leader, not the raggy-arsed rabble normally at the forefront of the paving-slab assault on law and order. As long as the blinkers remained firmly in place in the Préfecture on the Île de la Cîté, and the Intelligence Service HQs on the Boulevard Mortier and the Rue des Saussaies concentrated on looking inwards for officers with Algerian sand between their toes, people like Philippe de Guy-Montbron would be free to come and go.

But it definitely couldn't last.

Fouquet's was snob country, gin and tonic, Johnny Walker Black Label, cashew nuts, and swizzle-sticks with the champagne. Montbron went for gin and tonic and sat inside on one of the bench seats near the bar, his back to the wall. He saw his man long before he sidled into the leather-covered chair opposite him.

It couldn't be anybody else. A navy-blue pinstriped suit with waistcoat, crisp white shirt and shiny black shoes of quality. He looked at home, the sort who would consider aperitifs at Fouquet's and a lunch of *jambon à l'épinard* under the awning overlooking the George V a perfectly normal happening. He didn't shake hands, but ordered, like Montbron, a large gin and tonic: ice? Naturally. Slice of lemon? Of course!

'Beautiful weather we're having,' he said heartily. It was a cultured voice, which went with his appearance. Then he sipped from his glass. Montbron didn't respond. This was Xavier. He'd met him in another life. Xavier was Colonel Vaucoulet, now Director of Operations OAS/Métropole, a normally shadowy figure who'd learnt to duck and weave with the French Section during the Occupation and had fought a good war against the Viet Minh, more recently attracting attention for his outstanding work against the *fidayine*, the guerilla fighters of the Algerian Front de Libération Nationale, before the conflict in Algeria became a normal breakfast topic in Paris. His anti-de Gaulle stance and utterings had made him Salan's natural choice to command the OAS military structure in Metropolitan France, and it struck Montbron as extraordinary that a man with his reputation should be allowed by the numerous security groups to wander the streets of Paris at will. It struck him as even more bizarre that the man himself was not affected by his freedom. He looked comfortable, at ease and complacent. Perhaps long years in the undercover game had gone to his greying head? Montbron sipped his gin and tonic and waited for the rocket.

'A special team has been formed to find the killers of Gautier,' said Xavier in a voice that had Montbron straining to hear. 'You've stirred up the nest, which is something we didn't need at the moment. You've set us problems that we could well do without.' He paused and regarded Montbron from under his thick, bushy eyebrows. 'Well without,' he repeated. 'I've a bloody good mind to have you put in a sack and dumped on the DST's front doorstep . . .' He paused again and swallowed a mouthful of gin. It must have cleared the bad taste in his mouth for he looked Montbron in the eye and said, reluctantly, 'But I must, nevertheless, concede that it was a bloody good job well executed.'

Praise, like medals, had been suspended by the OAS for the duration. Montbron didn't blush. Neither did he respond. He merely sat with his back against the wall and sipped from his glass of gin and tonic and gazed, unobtrusively, over Xavier's shoulder at the entrance to the restaurant.

Xavier was content to leave the surveillance to him. If his neck itched he didn't show it. He continued in the same low voice: 'But I'll qualify that by saying it would have been a job better done if you'd wrapped Gautier up in a blanket and taken him into the country – alive. Better publicity, good clean Army action, and we'd have had a bargaining chip for Roger Deguel-dre, Machotte, Laconte and some of the others sweating their balls off in the Santé while de Gaulle "fixes" his impartial tri-bunals for their deaths. We could have bargained his life for their release, but still . . .' He shrugged his shoulders. 'Too late to worry about it now.' It was Gautier's epitaph; probably a more generous one than any of his friends would have suggested.

Montbron kept his thoughts to himself. There was no point now in telling the OAS's master chef that great minds had been thinking alike; that his intention had been kidnap, not murder or slaughter. But he wouldn't understand. He was a soldier, an old one, and orders meant blind obedience, not a basis for improvisation. He'd have more than Paul Vernet's balls hanging from the telephone wire if he knew the true extent of the cock-up. Montbron would have to hope that Vernet knew how to keep his mouth shut better than he did how to follow orders.

Xavier was still talking. '. . . Now that I've got you under my command I would like you to hit them again, but my way, my orders. I choose the target, you choose the method. You have a team, loyal people . . . ?'

Montbron nodded.

'How many?'

'One.'

Xavier stared at him while he considered this. He didn't disap-prove; he marvelled. One leader, one follower – the perfect team, though risky when it went wrong. This man was an asset. He narrowed his eyes and continued: 'Now we've got them in the mood for the smell of blood over here, I want more of the same; to hit them while they're still hopping up and down; the "brutal tap". You understand?'

Montbron understood. 'The brutal tap', '*opérations ponctuel-les*': the OAS had brought an interesting new vocabulary into the conflict.

Xavier spoke softly, but there was an edge of fanaticism in his voice that brought a slight quaver to it, and it barely carried to the other side of the table. To illustrate what he meant he edged his almost untouched drink jerkily with his finger towards the edge of the glass-topped table and whispered again, 'A brutal tap, and then another' – the glass of gin and tonic jerked forward another inch – 'and then another.' The glass reached the edge and almost tottered and he took his finger away. 'And when the realization comes that we are everywhere, that we cannot be stopped, then they will remove him themselves . . .'

Montbron touched his bottom lip with the cold edge of his glass. His expression didn't change. 'Had you anything to do with the attempt to kill de Gaulle last month?'

'Which one was that?'

'That idiotic firework display at Pont-sur-Seine?'

'No. It was done by a group such as yours – unofficial, uninvited and interfering. They subject themselves to problems, as indeed you did until I recognized who and what you are. You are acceptable. They are not.'

Montbron leaned forward to dispute the point, but was cut off by the tightening of Xavier's lips. 'No argument. I stress the point, we are not out to kill de Gaulle. He has to be remembered for his treachery and his stupidity, not for the martyrdom of political assassination. With all his faults and arrogance, de Gaulle is still the peasants' hero and they'll turn on us like hungry rats if he dies before his time. At the moment they're not interested in what's going on in our part of the gutter, and the soldiers are with us because he's made them taste defeat again when a victory in Algeria was assured.'

'You're preaching to the converted,' said Montbron dryly. 'If I'm invited into your tent, just make sure those idiots who want to put a rope round his neck or turn him into a candle don't foul my tracks. If there are factions in your organization who ought to be in a lunatic asylum, then either you winkle them out and get rid of them or we might as well drop our weapons into the Seine and join Salan in Madrid. I'd like to put a suggestion to the Métropole Committee—'

'Diderot, you're not in a position to put suggestions to anyone. I've invited you to join us; I haven't invited you to sit on the Board of Directors!' The corners of Xavier's lips curled.

Montbron wouldn't have noticed if he hadn't been sitting so close; Xavier's lips hadn't twitched in humour for several years. 'But, to amuse me,' he said after a pause to allow the flash of humour to die a death, 'what would you suggest to the most secret committee in France?'

Montbron wasn't abashed by the older man's sarcasm. His expression remained bland, almost disinterested.

'That if there's any more killing to be done, any more punishment, any more *opérations punctuelles*, they be done under a single command—'

'Yours?'

Montbron ignored the interruption. 'One man in direct contact with the OAS/Métropole Central Committee who will carry out any sentence imposed by them. It's the only way. Any other method – groups, units, people with grudges, people without authority settling old scores – and we get back to the chaos that existed in the Resistance and the mayhem that followed the Liberation. Carry on the way you are going and we'll end up killing each other. It's unavoidable.'

'Are you volunteering?'

Montbron considered it for several moments. He drank, replaced his glass on the table, then nodded his head. 'I don't think I need prove myself.'

'Your suggestion is worth considering.'

'Thank you. Then let's talk about today.'

'Very well. A target for you.' Xavier's voice dropped until Montbron was almost lip-reading. He sat forward casually. 'I'll give you the name. You'll assess the feasibility, outline the method, suggest the team, the time, and the place. You'll submit the framework to me, and if I approve you can put the design yourself to the Committee.'

Montbron allowed smoke to trickle through his pursed lips, raised his head, and waited.

The pause was significant.

'Bouchard,' whispered Xavier.

'Jacques Bouchard?'

Xavier nodded.

Montbron continued staring at him through the spiral of smoke that drifted in front of his eyes. But he didn't notice it. 'Bouchard's impossible,' he said at length.

'We reckoned Gautier was.'

'Gautier had a weakness. He was a pervert, which made him vulnerable. I merely exploited that vulnerability. He was happy to walk barefoot among the thistles – people of his ilk are like that. He got himself pricked! Bouchard is a different animal. As Minister of the Interior he has a screen as impenetrable as de Gaulle's. But that's not all. He's popular. He could be President—'

'Exactly—'

'Let me finish.'

Montbron squinted his eyes against the cigarette smoke but didn't move his hand. He glanced again, still casually, over Xavier's shoulder and studied the drinkers at the bar and the other occupants of the restaurant. Nothing suspicious. Nobody bending their heads in their direction. Everything was perfectly normal.

'Bouchard comes from the people. He had a good Resistance war.'

'I know all that—'

Montbron didn't let him in. 'De Gaulle himself handed him lieutenant-colonel patches and almost offered to sew them on for him. Bouchard's progress came through intelligence and he's never put a foot wrong. He's been a P2 agent since his first trip to London in '43, when even the British liked him – and still do! He's hands-on-shoulders and kisses-on-both-cheeks with de Gaulle, and the same with most of the Government. He's an impossible target, Xavier. Kidnap or kill, an attempt on him would be the worst possible move.'

'I'm not seeking your advice, Diderot. We didn't invite you – you asked to join the club. You came in through the back door; you can go out the same way before you damage the system. You can either undertake this contract with the full weight of the OAS staff and organization in support, or you can go back to the Army before your name goes up on the notice-board, and we'll disown any knowledge of your temporary work on our behalf. But don't forget, a word either way and there's a place for both of us against the wall at Fort d'Ivry.'

Montbron shook his head contritely. 'You misread my intentions, Xavier. I'm not falling out, I'm outlining the comparison between Gautier and Bouchard. I'm asking you to consider the impracticality before we even consider the operation.'

'It's already been considered. It's to be planned. You've been elected, if you so choose. I repeat, *you* asked to join *us*. We're not short of men who know how to kill. By Christ, we've had enough experience of that over the past twenty years, so you don't have to consider yourself unique in the killing department! Nor are we short of men who can think while they're doing it.' Xavier's eyes locked on to Montbron's, and he relented. 'But go on with your impracticalities.'

'Bouchard has no gaps in his armour,' stated Montbron. 'He's married, unlike Gautier, has a beautiful wife, and gets all he wants there. He's got three children, no mistress, and no hang-ups. Not only does he lead a perfect life, but – and this "but" is important – he knows how people get knocked off. He did enough head-banging himself, as quite a few Boche headstones will testify. Ergo . . .' Montbron lowered his cigarette. He'd finished trying to talk himself out of a job. 'He knows how to look after himself.'

Xavier continued studying him for a few moments with a stony expression. His hoarse voice still didn't rise above a whisper.

'If that wasn't the case I could call in any one of a thousand twenty-year-old pioneers to pull the lever on this man. That is why I am sitting here swirling the bubbles from my gin and tonic and repeating the recommendations of the Central Committee, firstly, to bring you to book for interfering, and secondly, to offer you congratulations and an invitation to present yourself to that Committee. Bouchard's elimination, one way or the other, will be that little push that sends de Gaulle into the wilderness. When his yes-men see Bouchard's head in the gutter, they'll move him – they'll have to in order to survive. De Gaulle will bury himself in Colombey-les-Deux-Églises to write his story on how he and France won the war against the Boche; meanwhile we take the throne and determine the direction of the Fifth Republic for the foreseeable future and put a stop to this bloody nonsense about independence for Algeria.'

Xavier shifted his bottom on the chair. He'd been in one position too long; he was ready to move on. 'And that is your future too. Ring me, as arranged, in two days – that'll be Sunday the fourth – so that I can listen to your proposals and, if I like them, arrange for you to be presented to the future leaders of our country. Don't fail us, Diderot.' He stood up. He made no offer to shake hands but disappeared through one of the internal doors. Montbron didn't see him leave the restaurant.

6

MONTBRON REMAINED WHERE he was, sipping his drink, smoking another cigarette. There was much to think about. He'd dug himself a nice deep hole and found a lot of interesting things crawling about in the mud at the bottom of it. But he'd got what he wanted: he had been accepted by the grown-ups. He was in there with the bemedalled revolutionaries. It could have been South America. He didn't laugh, not even to himself.

He'd give himself another ten minutes and then it would be time to make a move. Xavier would be in the crowd by now, back in the Paris undergrowth, and would have taken the followers – his and theirs – with him. He ran his eye again over the people in the bar. Nothing spectacular. Very normal. He lingered a little longer over the man and woman standing at the bar with drinks in their hands. Nothing suspicious, he'd seen them come in. He gave her another glance. It was purely personal – she was far too attractive to be with the undersized, slightly unkempt individual who appeared to pay her little attention. Montbron turned his eyes away when the two picked up their glasses and moved into a newly vacated seat by the window. She sat facing inwards and, after a brief, uninterested glance at Montbron, turned her attention fully to her companion.

They were still sitting there when Montbron left the restaurant. He didn't see the woman move down the bar to the entrance, and although he stayed for several moments on the corner of the Avenue George-V and the Champs Élysées, he didn't see her standing in the doorway of Fouquet's. She spent some time fiddling with the flap of her handbag and then, as if in exasperation, she turned and descended to the basement toilet. She was joined there by her companion and after a brief conversation the two of them left hand in hand and caught a cruising taxi as it crawled out of the George-V. They looked like a couple who'd sorted out their differences and were now in a hurry to consummate their new happiness as quickly as possible.

But not in her flat. Nor in his. The taxi dropped them on the corner of the Boulevard de Montmorency and the Rue Raffet and they walked back a few metres and went through the iron gates that barred the entrance to the impressive new office block set back off the boulevard. They both waggled identification wallets at the small guardroom in the entrance and then again as they passed through the plate-glass security doors of the building. They went to the sixth floor, where the woman handed her bag to a man in a scruffy, stained white coat who was waiting at the lift door.

'Bring whatever you find to Monsieur Filli's office. We'll be there for about another hour,' she told him, then turned and caught up with her partner as he entered the main door at the far end of the corridor.

The room was a command centre, with one wall covered in maps, diagrams and small photographs, mainly poor quality snapshots mounted in little unsymmetrical blocks. Most of the pictures were of men in uniform. There was the odd woman, as well as quite a few men in what appeared to be unaccustomed civilian clothes. They looked out of place.

'Any luck with Xavier, Michèle?'

There was only one man in the room. He sat at a large desk – more like a pine kitchen table – in his shirtsleeves, his tie fully done up but with the top button of his crumpled shirt undone. He was about forty-five years old, with jet-black, short, stubbly hair and he looked as though he'd forgotten to shave that morning, and the morning before that. It didn't worry him; it was a normal half-day's growth. He was Georges Filli from Bastia in Corsica. He was head of Action Association, a group of hard men from the Military Intelligence Section specially recruited to combat the ever-growing menace of the OAS. They were mostly Corsican or Frenchmen from Marseilles. Their enemies called them the *barbouzes*; their friends? They had none, and it didn't worry them what they were called; they were happy in their work, helping to suppress the Army revolt and, as an aside, settling old scores on mainland France.

As a fringe group of the DST's Combined Council for Action Against the OAS; the *barbouzes* made their own rules. They shared no information, and with the Government's unofficial approval and their own special self-granted powers, they carried out on-the-spot executions. Feared by both sides in the conflict, their information-gathering techniques would have made the Gestapo wince with embarrassment. For administration and logistical purposes they were loosely affiliated to the Department for Internal Security – the DST – and Filli, as head of the Association, held senior rank within that department. Most of Filli's group were former NCOs who'd seen front-line service in Indo-China and less glamorous activities in undercover operations against the Algerian FLN in the *bled* and the backstreets of Constantine and Orleansville. Most bore scars from one of France's recent lost colonial wars.

It was significant that Filli addressed the woman first.

Michèle Bourdier was the widow of a young lieutenant of the élite Commando de Chasse who had been one of the first victims of the OAS; an officer who had refused the invitation to revolt. The invitation had come from his commanding officer, one Lieutenant Colonel Vaucoulet, now known among the whispering-out-of-the-side-of-the-mouth brigade as 'Xavier'. Xavier was their plum. They'd broken his cover, thanks to Michèle Bourdier, and the dividends this had returned were incalculable.

'A new face,' she informed Filli. 'He looks hard and intelligent. I gave the handbag camera a chance inside but I don't hold out much hope. Fouquet's is quite gloomy at the best of times. I had another couple of goes at him outside, but he was covering his departure. I didn't dare try full face when he turned, but I think I've got a couple of profiles. I can fill in the details when I see the prints.'

'You didn't follow him?'

She shook her head. Filli didn't pursue the question. It was understood that with a ripe lead like Xavier it was best not to put any member of the organization on their guard. If they rushed around collecting everybody who spoke to Xavier their lease of contact would end after they'd picked up the first two. As it was they had a dossier, and in most cases a photograph, of some forty OAS members and subsidiaries who'd shaken hands with the good Colonel since Filli's group had been formed and Xavier identified by Michèle. They were all marked men; their days were numbered.

Philippe de Guy-Montbron was about to join them.

The man who'd relieved Michèle of her handbag entered the room after a discreet knock. It had taken about half an hour and in his hands he carried an enamel tray. In the bottom were half a dozen sopping-wet 15cm × 10cm black and white prints. They were nearly all the same: full length, the face in half-profile.

He handed the tray to Michèle first. 'That little lens won't cope with anything less than good sunlight. You're wasting your time trying indoor shots.' He pointed to a wodge of contact prints stuck to the side of the tray. 'Underexposed. Bugger-all, not even the wall. These aren't much better, but if I take them any bigger the outline'll disappear into grain the size of grapes.'

Filli stood up, lit a cigarette from a packet on the table, and without taking it from his lips leaned over Michèle's shoulder to study the wet pictures. His face remained expressionless.

'Does that look like the face of a man who could kill five agents in the back of a car?' he said to no one in particular.

'Not to mention the Minister of Special Affairs,' murmured Michèle.

'Bugger the Minister of Special Affairs!' spat Filli, and took the cigarette from his mouth. 'Those men were my people. They're the ones who concern me, not poncing Ministers of Special Affairs – or any other bloody Ministers!' Without looking up from Montbron's picture he said, 'How about you, Rosso? Did this guy mean anything to you?'

The scruffy man who'd been Michèle's companion in Fouquet's looked up from studying his black and broken fingernails. He was a man totally devoid of humour; his mournful jet-black eyes had never softened under a smile; he didn't know the meaning of the word. Neither was he a conversationalist. 'He means nothing.' His eyes scoured the wall with its many photographs before coming back to Filli. 'But he's of the Légion.' He uncrossed his legs and stood up, then walked across the room to stand beside Filli and stare into the tray. 'There'll be a better picture than that in Records.'

'How d'you know?'

'How do I know what?'

'Stop pissing around, Rosso!' hissed Filli. 'You know what I mean! How d'you know he's Légion?'

Michèle turned her head to stare into the swarthy Corsican's blank, humourless face. She too was curious, and didn't try to conceal it.

Rosso let it run as long as he dare, then said quietly, 'He was wearing a Légion ring . . .' he waggled the little finger of his right hand '. . . like that one.'

'Jesus Christ!' Filli wasn't sure whether he was amazed or delighted by the stupidity of conspirators who wanted to change the world and yet wandered in and out of the dark and narrow alleyways of treachery with their antecedents tattooed across their stupid faces – or, in this case, with the regimental banner stuck on the end of their little finger like a flashing white light! '*Quel con*!'

Rosso didn't go overboard. 'D'you want me to go to Records?' He jerked his chin at the wet pictures. 'I won't even need that.'

'Christ, no!' said Filli. 'We're not giving those bastards a new face on a plate. Let them find their own bloody targets. Michèle . . .' He stuck the cigarette back between his lips and dropped his hand on her shoulder. 'Do it under the blankets. Get one of those pictures dried off and show it to some of your friends. Don't go near Tourelles, not for the time being.' He squeezed her shoulder. 'But don't take any chances. The bastards we're dealing with don't want to look up your skirt. If this is one of the crew that did the St-Germain job, the least he'll do is cut your throat, so be discreet and be choosy who you ask. And just in case, Rosso'll be hovering in your background . . .' He looked across the room. 'Won't you, Rosso?'

7

GABY VIOLLE PRODUCED a pack of fuzzy and very grainy pictures of the comings and goings in the Avenue Beauchamp and slid them across the table to Gérard Neurie. 'Before you look at those,' he said, 'listen to this. That house is owned by a Madame Marie-Claire Massotte, married to Claude Massotte . . .' He paused.

'So?'

'He's that *juge d'instruction* I mentioned.'

Neurie looked up from the spread of pictures on the table. 'Does that make them respectable and one hundred per cent Fifth Republicans?'

'Him, yes.' Violle ignored the tone of Neurie's question. 'But not her. She belongs to the Bonapartists, that group of semi-weirdos who believe that the greatest thing since, and including, Jesus Christ was Napoleon Bonaparte and that his lot should still be sitting on some sort of golden throne and ruling the country as in the days of yore. According to them, he's a cross between a god and a king, and at the very least the product of a Virgin birth!'

'Which means?'

'That de Gaulle is not it and Algeria is *Française*. The mixture makes them rabidly anti-Gaullist.'

'And that makes them agents and supporters of the OAS?'

'The two usually go together. On top of that, her father made his money in Algeria at the turn of the century – quite a packet – and when he died six years ago the whole bloody lot was shared between her and her sister . . .'

While Violle was talking, Neurie picked up a wad of photographs and glanced at the top one. He looked as though he had lost interest in Mme Massotte. But he hadn't. His head came up with a frown. 'Sister?'

Violle tried not to look smug. 'A Mademoiselle Jeanette Fabre. She owns a bloody great mansion out at Buc, between Versailles and St Cyr. Very appropriate! She also has another extravagant spread in the Camargue. It's a farmhouse, but it probably looks like the Louvre!'

'Mademoiselle? She's not married, a rich girl like that?'

'She was once, but I gather the guy was too expensive for her. My people tell me he was eating all her money, so she filled his pockets with hundred-franc notes and shipped him off to the colonies, or words to that effect. She's supposed to have a man in tow at the moment, but we haven't pushed in that direction yet. I should think that after the first guy this one would have to be well off, which would make it a purely bedroom friendship. She reverted to her maiden name.'

'And what are her politics?'

'I'd say extreme Right. There's nothing secretive about Mademoiselle Fabre. She shoots her mouth off on a variety of doubtful causes. Prudence doesn't come into it.'

'Even if it means her head in a basket?'

Violle shrugged. 'She's a great believer in the right of free speech . . . The only thing she shares with her sister is a jaundiced attitude towards our Leader's carryings-on with his new Republic, and particularly the way he scuffed the sands of prosperity from under the feet of the *pieds noirs*. She's been inflicted with a mouth that won't stay still and has been a bit more outspoken about her dislike of de Gaulle than Madame Massotte.'

'How does that make her pro-OAS?'

'As I said earlier, the mixture's there.'

'Had the Minister of Special Affairs been stretching his feet under her dining table?'

'Not within the last couple of months.' Violle had finished his report. He pointed to the pictures. 'Have a look at them. See if there's anybody you know.'

Neurie flicked the pictures over one by one. He didn't dwell on any particular shot. They were of appalling quality and lacked any sort of definition; one or two were almost totally blurred, like old Box Brownie snaps, which they could well have been. But there was one that didn't need intensifying. It was the last one in the pack, probably deliberately so. Not quite studio quality, but clear enough. Neurie studied it for a moment, then looked up at Violle. 'You remember?'

Violle shrugged his shoulders and lit a cigarette. He flicked the packet across to Neurie. 'Interesting, though. She features on the other sister's guest list as well.'

Neurie was studying a full-length photograph of a woman coming out of the Massotte house. Even its poor quality could not disguise an extremely beautiful woman. Beside her, with one hand familiarly on her shoulder, strode a well-built man in his thirties dressed in a blazer, its shining buttons picking up the sun's rays and glinting star-like into the camera lens. He looked English. Neurie removed a cigarette from the packet, lit it, then stood the packet on its end and propped the photograph against it.

'Monique Bonnet,' he said, without taking his eyes off it. 'Née Monique de Cantenac, formerly Baronne Monique Neurie . . .' He blew a mouthful of smoke that gently enveloped the picture before dispersing. Violle sat back in his chair and said nothing. 'Divorced 1958, no children. Married Pierre Bonnet 1958, divorced 1959. Nineteen sixty-one photographed leaving a house suspected of harbouring a mass killer . . . What extraordinary people we bump into in our line of business, Gaby.'

'D'you still see her?'

Neurie tossed the photograph on to the table. If he had any post-marital regrets it didn't show in his face; in fact he managed a bleak sort of smile for the easygoing Violle. 'Children who are brought up together shouldn't marry; it never works out. It's suggestively incestuous – something to do with growing up like brother and sister. You know too much about each other, there's no mystery.'

'That last bit sounds like every marriage I ever heard of. She was unkind to you?'

'That's putting it mildly! But there's nothing vicious about

Monique. She's beautiful – everything about her's lovely. She's also fun to be with and has lots of nice ideas – knows how to use a bedroom . . .'

Violle studied Neurie curiously. 'And she's still there, under your skin.' When Neurie made no response he shrugged his shoulders and said, 'Any idea who the guy is?'

Neurie didn't look up. He shook his head absently. 'Could be anyone.'

'He looks English.'

'Why not? She's a beautiful woman, she attracts men. The English are not immune to attractive women.'

'She seems to like that one.'

'Forget it. Let's think how we can make use of Madame Monique Bonnet.'

'I'm not with you.'

'Wouldn't it save us buggering around outside the front door of *Monsieur le juge d'instruction* and give us peace of mind, as well as the opportunity to redeploy our meagre resources to a more fruitful occupation, if we knew whether there was a well-organized cosy-hole in his house?'

Violle frowned. 'Sure. But if we go sniffing any closer than we already are we could invite a very severe bollocking, and a stampede. If there's nothing doing, the good judge'll have seven kinds of shit fall around our ears for violating his property and defaming his good character, not to mention upsetting his wife, children, pussy-cat and mistress. And if there *is* a hidey-hole, we're going to blow it without even knowing whether it's our man in it or some tenth-grade squaddy who's hiding out because he was seen spitting on our Leader's picture. First I'd like to know a bit more about the guy with the Schmeisser and his master. I want to know which way to duck when we come face to face with him.'

'If we come face to face, Gaby. That's what I'm getting at – let's work out a way of using Monique to tell us who's living in that house apart from *Monsieur le juge* and his good lady. And whatever way we look at it, it's still a long shot. We don't even know that these people are active. All we've got so far is that

Gautier might have picked up the girl who led him into an ambush in one of three houses . . . Incidentally, we've got ourselves nicely warmed up over the Massotte household, but what about the other houses on your slate?'

'I think we'll push them into the background until we've used up all the mileage on this one. About your ex-wife . . . ?'

'I'm going to have a talk with her. She might have seen or heard something . . . I'll let you know. Erm, you mentioned something about the good judge and a mistress?'

'Right.' Violle scrabbled in his jacket pocket and brought out a crumpled sheet of paper. 'Jacqueline Mericourt. Has an apartment in Montparnasse. Massotte didn't pay for it, it's her own. He sees her regularly – at least three times a week.'

'He must be quite an acrobat . . . How often does Madame Massotte get herself seen to?'

'By him? Not at all I should imagine – different bedrooms, separate lives. She has a boyfriend but doesn't bring him home.'

'What's the matter with him – does he pick his nose in public?'

'He's only nineteen. Madame Massotte's daughter who lives in the house is twenty-two. I think she's worried he might have the energy for her as well, so she keeps him wrapped up in a nice little studio flat on the Boulevard Murat.'

Neurie shook his head and grinned, then uncurled himself and stood up. 'I don't think I can swallow much more of this, Gaby. Carry on with the surveillance, keep your ear to the ground for anything else that might be worming around, and hope like bloody hell that our bloodthirsty friends mount another little caper fairly soon. I'll let you know, after I've had a chat with her, whether Monique wants to come and play in our game.' He took the picture of his ex-wife and her boyfriend and stuck it in his top pocket.

'That's the only one we've got with that man on it,' warned Violle.

'What d'you want it for?'

Violle shrugged. 'Make sure I get it back.'

8

MARIE-CLAIRE MASSOTTE'S staff were carefully chosen. There was no old *nounou* brought forward from the judge's childhood to make sure Madame toed the line. This lot were Marie-Claire's own selection, and if there was to be any toeing of lines it wasn't going to be her toes that did it. For two women, a girl in her late teens and a man acting as a sort of understaffed major-domo, discretion guaranteed the security of a well-paid and unarduous job. They knew where their wages came from and to whom their loyalty was pledged. Lieutenant Colonel Diderot was Madame's friend. In what capacity they could only speculate among themselves, but that was as far as it went – among themselves.

With the pictures of these four people in a line on the desk in front of him Violle decided to move the game two squares forward in advance of Neurie's ideas about recruiting his ex-wife into the sniffer game.

He pressed the button on his intercom.

'Where's Morel hiding himself at the moment?' he grunted.

'He's off duty,' responded the tinny instrument. 'Doesn't go back to the Avenue Beauchamp until six this evening.'

'Get him. I want to see him.'

'But—'

Too late. Violle had taken his finger off the intercom button.

Marc Morel was twenty-three. He had all the advantages – good health, rich father, good education, and incredible looks. He wasn't of a modest disposition, he knew all about his looks and admired them regularly, particularly first thing in the morning. It helped start the day. But it wasn't helping it at the moment.

His mood was bad and he tried not to show his feelings at being called back to Violle's office after an all-night stint leaning against a tree staring at the back of the Massotte house. He composed his schoolboy features into an expression of unfriendly attentiveness as he stood, unshaven and slightly red-eyed, in front of Violle's desk.

'You look bloody awful.' Violle's greeting wasn't out of character. 'Come round here and look at these.'

'D'you mind if I smoke?'

'If you must.'

Morel moved round to Violle's side of the flimsy trestle-desk and stared down at the three pictures as he lit his cigarette. He waited for the rest of it.

'Which of those women would you choose to spend the night with?' Violle didn't look up until the whoosh of smoke had passed over his shoulder. 'If you had the opportunity.'

Morel didn't need to think about it. 'None of them.'

'I'll rephrase it. You've got to spend the night with one of them. Which one d'you choose?'

'I'm not altogether sure that male prostitute was one of the duties specified in my contract, sir.' Morel managed a thin smile, but it didn't mollify Violle. He'd had a bad night as well.

'Your duties are what I specify, young man. You'll do as you're bloody well told or I'll put you down for a tour of picking up dog shit around the Eiffel Tower. Pick one of these bloody women!'

Morel pulled himself together and pointed his finger at the younger of the three women. 'I think that one, sir.'

Violle smiled happily. 'I'd have bet money on that. OK, go and get yourself some sleep and then clean yourself up and take the girl to bed. With a face like that she'll probably come out of a night of your funny ways with a credit balance.' Morel didn't laugh. She wasn't pretty – the photo didn't flatter her – and by the look of the size of her hips it was going to have to be a lights-out job. Violle picked up the photograph and held it in front of him, making a pretence of studying the girl's image. He was still studying it when an affected cough followed by a gush of cigarette smoke over his shoulder reminded him that Morel was still around. He swivelled his chair and looked the young man in the face. 'Try not to fall in love,' he said without a smile. 'You're getting all the perks. The important thing is to find out who else was picking their teeth at the big table at the Massottes' when the Minister of Special Affairs last came to dinner. I'm interested in unattached females, in particular one named Lucienne Maillot. You've seen a picture of her?'

'Only dead.'

'Well, describe her to your new girlfriend. She might have used another name. Also, find out whether there's anybody staying in the house as a sort of permanent guest. They might have one of those idiot rooms, doors locked, curtains drawn, full of cobwebs, where they store the old, the mad, the relative who's gone too far over the hill and has to be kept out of sight for fear of upsetting the neighbours. You've probably got somebody like that in your ancestral home, all that rich blue blood and interbreeding . . .'

'I don't think—'

'I'm joking, boy. But you know what I mean. Find out if the odd tray of food goes upstairs and if the lavatory seat is sometimes left up in Madame's bathroom. But don't push too hard, son, and be bloody careful. We don't want her rushing home to Madame saying she's been fucked by some good-looking boy from SDECE and she's told him all her guilty secrets . . . Prise these things out of her in between squeaks – and Morel . . .'

'Sir?'

'Don't take too long over it. I shall expect to hear something this time tomorrow, or at the latest the day after tomorrow.'

'Christ!'

'Exactly.'

9

MICHÈLE BOURDIER CAUGHT only a brief glimpse of the Corsican, Rosso, on the far side of the road as she sat under the thin mid-morning sun at a pavement table outside the café Corbusier in one of the broad avenues off the Place des Invalides. Her companion waited until she'd folded the small sheet of paper he'd given her and dropped it into her bag before reaching sideways across the table and resting his hand on hers. She didn't take it away.

'And now,' he said firmly, 'I'm going to insist on your telling me what your interest is in this man.'

Michèle smiled coquettishly. Playing the coquette wasn't her nature but like all beautiful women she knew when to do it, and how. 'Don't press me, Henri, please. It's nothing sinister . . .' Lying wasn't a problem for her. 'A friend of mine who's – well, you know what I mean . . . ?' She raised her eyebrows and let the tip of her tongue show provocatively through moist, slightly parted lips. 'I'll tell you all about it tonight, if you're still interested . . . ?'

'I don't think I shall be under those circumstances, my lovely Michèle.' He was a good-looking man in his early fifties. He had the bearing of an Army man – a young general or a colonel with his time running out. But Henri Gillet was neither. He was in limbo while his loyalty to de Gaulle was held over the flames to see what colour it turned. A former member of the CCI – the Inter-Army Coordination Centre, which grouped together the Armys myriad intelligence-gathering organizations – he was perfect for a senior sideways shuffle into SDECE. But in their eyes he wasn't yet pure enough. He'd shared the same changing room in Algiers with some of the Army's, and CCI's, more adventurous

OAS adherents. But he still had friends, some of them sitting cross-legged on the razor-like fence waiting to see who won, and he looked like being a winner either way. And besides, it couldn't be too bad a thing to help the curiosity of the attractive widow of a former junior colleague, and widows repaying debts had been known at times to be awfully generous. 'Just as long as your friend realizes the sort of fish she's trying to tickle out of the water.'

Michèle replaced her tiny coffee-cup in its saucer and glanced sideways at Gillet. 'Is there more I should tell her about this man – other than what you've written here?' She moved to open her bag but his hand stopped her.

'Digging into Army records in these unsettled times, *ma chérie*, can lead you into the company of some very strange people. Producing fuzzy pictures taken under questionable circumstances and asking for information could, given the wrong conditions, result in your meeting these strange people in your underwear, possibly with your feet in a bowl of cold water and two little electrical clips attached to two pretty little nipples . . .' Her expression didn't change. He was telling her nothing she didn't know. But he softened the rebuke with a little smile. 'Lucky for you you came to me with your friend's problem.'

Michèle widened her eyes into an innocent, little-girl expression. He felt a surge of sympathy for her crawl into his groin and allowed a little smile to quiver the ends of his carefully trimmed moustache. He forgot about the problems of digging into Army records.

'Good God, Henri! Don't tell me this man's involved with the OAS?'

He sipped his Rémy Martin and controlled the urge to look over his shoulder. But he couldn't control the instinctive lowering of his voice. 'I doubt that very much – more likely the other side, but I really don't kow. The man is a career officer, fought the Germans as a seventeen-year-old with de Lattre, then St Cyr and the Foreign Legion – all the right things. According to his record he's never put a foot wrong and is expected to go all the way. At thirty-three he's probably the youngest lieutenant colonel in the Army, so he is already more than half-way there. I'm very curious about the origins of this picture you have – perhaps . . . ?'

She didn't allow him to develop his curiosity and eased him off course. But Henri Gillet wasn't silly; he filed the question of the picture at the back of his mind and handed the lead back to her.

'But you said, Henri, something about him being a tricky customer – what did you mean?'

'I said, Michèle, that you and your friend ought to be careful sticking your noses into the private business of people like this. He's not an ordinary soldier, he's one of the few officers to have won both the Médaille Militaire and the Légion d'Honneur since the end of the "real" war. He fought with great distinction in both Indo-China and Algeria, and in between, as a sort of appetizer, he managed to squeeze a three-year operational tour on attachment with the British SAS in Malaya. They are a very tough and very special bunch of people. You have to be an exceptional Englishman to serve in that unit, so imagine what sort of Frenchman you'd have to be to be accepted . . .'

'I think I'm going to have an orgasm!'

'I beg your pardon!'

'You make him sound like a cross between Joan of Arc and Maréchal Ney. I'm getting quite excited.'

Gillet crossed his legs, thought briefly about Michèle Bourdier having an orgasm, then composed himself. Sipping his Rémy Martin again, he decided to close the file on Lieutenant Colonel Philippe de Guy-Montbron. 'Don't get too excited, he's with his regiment in Germany. He won't be allowed to come and flaunt his medals on the Champs-Élysées until the Army's purged itself of these grandiose ideas about changing governments. It could take years.'

Michèle shrugged and stroked his hand. She didn't dislike Gillet and was quite happy to share his silk bedsheets occasionally in the interest of good relations. And this was the sort of dividend it payed. But what she wanted now was the quiet of the Boulevard de Montmorency and a long-distance telephone connection. She suddenly glanced down at the tiny diamond watch on her wrist. 'Oh, *mon Dieu*, Henri. Look at the time! I have a hair appointment. Damn, I'm going to be late!' She was up and on her feet before he had time to react. She leant over and kissed him quickly on the side of the mouth. 'I'll see you tonight . . . I'll ring you. Bye bye!'

10

MARC MOREL SPENT a fruitless morning watching the camera monitor on the Massotte household. Two new shifts came and went but still he watched. He had a ham sandwich brought to him for lunch, with a rum baba and an almost cold cup of black coffee for pudding. He wasn't enjoying his special assignment and his throat felt like the inside of an old tennis shoe by the time he screwed up a second empty packet of Gauloises and tossed it over his shoulder to join the other one in the corner of the small hut. Maybe she wasn't coming out today. Maybe she wasn't even in the house. Maybe she was having a week's holiday. He scowled to himself and reached for the fourth time for the log-book. She came out every day, so stuff that one! Midnight staff check: three female, one male. *Stick that up your arse, Morel*! He changed the grimace for a near-smile and coughed his way into another cigarette. And then the monitor flickered and there she was – all five foot three and twelve stone of her, tripping out of the front gate in her going-out-for-a-plate-of-cakes-and-chocolate-gateau clothes. It was half-past three.

Marc Morel could smile his way into bed with a dedicated twenty-three-year-old novitiate. Poor fat Lilli Blancard and her three wobbly, bewhiskered chins would have spread herself on the busy pavement at the first tentative smile. She was surprised at the expert pick-up but got over it very quickly and decided that this very good-looking man must see something that she looked for every morning in the full-length mirror but had, so far, failed to recognize. But Gaby Violle had misjudged her; so had Marc Morel. She didn't want a quick bang, she wanted it done properly, after a little courting – not too much, but a little

– and in a nice bed in a nice room. Morel wasn't disappointed. Sitting face to face in a café just made things that little bit more difficult.

After the third chocolate éclair had disappeared, he went to work.

She remembered Mlle Maillot: 'Fancy you knowing her!' The Minister of Special Affairs had been to dinner that evening. He had been quite taken with her. 'And I'm not surprised, she had on that lovely rich-yellow mini-dress, and, of course, she was wearing nothing underneath, everyone could see that. He couldn't take his eyes off her – or his hands . . . Wasn't it awful the way the poor man was murdered? They say it was the OAS, you know.'

'She was sitting next to him at the table?'

'Almost in his lap.'

'Who set the places?'

'You mean who decided who the Minister should have to play with on his right? He was a randy old bugger, you know.'

Morel shrugged. He'd already worked it all out. The girl was a set-up, no question about it; they all knew that. 'How many people at dinner that evening?'

'Fourteen. Isn't it funny? There he was eating, drinking, tickling Mademoiselle's fanny and having a marvellous time and a couple of days later – dead! You never know, do you?'

'You don't. Were they all couples?'

'Why are you asking me all these questions?'

Morel pulled himself up. Ugly didn't necessarily mean stupid. He shrugged his shoulders and smiled disarmingly; it was going to have to be a two-day job – unless: 'Want some more coffee?'

She didn't pursue it. 'No thanks,' and glanced down at her wrist-watch. Her good intentions about beds and soft lights were under attack. It didn't take her long to shove them to one side as the afternoon passed over the yard-arm. In this life, she had no difficulty convincing herself, you take what you can, when you can get it – and where. She fancied Marc Morel very much. 'I have to be back by seven for dinner. How about a walk in the park?' She glanced at him coyly from the corner of her eyes. He got the message. *Jesus! The things I do for France*!

He tried again as he lit a cigarette and watched her drag the barely adequate briefs back over her cellulite-loaded thighs. She turned round to face him, shyly rearranging her dress. Her eyes were sparkling. She was in love. 'This girl you were telling me about,' he said casually. 'The one in the yellow dress . . .'

'What about her?'

He feigned indifference. 'Oh, nothing really. I was just curious. I wondered whether she was on her own or came with a husband or something.'

'I think you're a journalist.'

Morel smiled enigmatically; why not? But he didn't respond. She was no longer suspicious. 'I don't think she was married. She came with Madame's friend.'

'Friend?'

She hunched her shoulders, pursed her lips suggestively and repeated the word 'friend'. 'He's got his hand there. I'm not sure about anything else. But he's awfully good-looking, as most soldiers are . . .'

Morel didn't rush her. 'I was a corporal myself.'

'And I bet you looked a very pretty one too in your uniform. But this one's not a corporal, he's a colonel.'

'Oh?'

'Colonel Diderot—' She suddenly stopped, guiltily, as if realizing that she'd said too much. She'd been warned: 'Don't talk about people who come to the house, or you'll be looking for another job. Madame insists on discretion and won't stand for tittle-tattle.' But Marc wasn't going to say anything – was he? She hauled herself on to her tiptoes and kissed his mouth. 'Or was it something else? I've probably got it all wrong, but it's only gossip, isn't it? D'you want to walk me home?'

'How about tomorrow?'

She slid her hand between their bodies and rested it on his groin. In public? Marc Morel for the first time in his life was embarrassed. He looked around furtively. There was nobody watching. She said, 'I've got a half-day the day after tomorrow. Can we go somewhere?'

'My flat?'

She squeezed her agreement.

He winced.

'I'll meet you at the café. One o'clock?'

She squeezed again. 'Don't be late.'

But Lilli couldn't keep it to herself.

Later that evening, Cook took a delicate sip from dinner's left-over Pichon-Longueville and said to the butler, 'Lilli's got herself a pretty boyfriend. He picked her up in the Café Faubourg. She's meeting him again tomorrow.'

The butler paused with his glass half-way to his lips. 'Quasim odo would be pretty in her eyes if he was kneeling between her legs with his cock in his hand. He must be blind – or a bloody masochist!'

'She said he was very curious about people who came to dinner, particularly when Gautier was last here . . . Asked lots of questions.'

'Forget it.'

'It could be perfectly innocent, Philippe.' Marie-Claire sat on the end of the camp-bed and watched Montbron load butter and jam on to a piece of toasted baguette and dip it into his large bowl of coffee. She considered all possibilities and argued for, and against, an innocent meeting of a good-looking young man and the ugly duckling among her hand-picked staff. Montbron continued eating his sopping toast and drinking the coffee without interrupting her. When he finished, he wiped his mouth with a tablecloth-sized napkin, lit a cigarette and laid the tray on the floor. He got out of the bed and sat on its edge.

'Don't say anything to her. You've told André to check this person out? Let's wait and see what he says.' He remained sitting on the edge of the bed, his elbows resting on his knees as he smoked his cigarette and stared contemplatively at the pattern of the carpet. He didn't look up when he spoke again. 'Have you noticed anything unusual, anything different happening outside the house in the last forty-eight hours or so?'

Marie-Claire shook her head automatically, without thinking, and said, 'No, nothing at all.'

He looked up. 'Nothing? Are you sure? Think about it.'

She stared into his face. 'Give me one of your cigarettes.'

He lit one from the embers of his own and stretched out to place it between her fingers. He didn't hurry her but went back to his original place on the edge of the bed. He didn't have to wait long.

'No,' she repeated, 'I can't think of anything out of the ordinary. Shall I ask André and Cook?'

He didn't help her. 'OK. Tell me something usual that's happened.'

'What do you mean?'

'Did the postman come?'

'Of course.'

'The usual postman?'

'Philippe, for God's sake, I don't deal with postmen! I shall have to ask André.'

Montbron didn't lose his patience; he knew where he was going. 'How about the telephones? Anybody been to check them?'

She exhaled a mouthful of smoke with a noisy whoosh and stood up abruptly. Walking to the window, she looked out across the lawn at the back of the house. 'The telephone people,' she said, half to herself, without looking round. 'Yesterday they were doing some repairs to the line across the road. You don't think . . . ?'

But Montbron wasn't listening. He pulled on trousers, a dark sweater, and slipped his feet into a pair of rubber-soled shoes. 'D'you have the key to Claude's gun cupboard?'

Marie-Claire's eyebrows pinched together. 'Philippe, you're not going to—'

'Don't be stupid! I want a power scope. Somebody's repaired your phone. Were you told it was going to be out of order while they did that?'

She shrugged. 'André would have told me . . .'

'But he didn't.' He crushed out his half-smoked cigarette. 'If somebody's sounding out your staff, they have a watching team – and if they've got a watching team, they'll have left their mark somewhere. I'm going to have a look.'

Marie-Claire's consternation came to the surface for the first time. Her agitation showed. 'My God, Philippe! Are you sure? What are we going to do? What am I going to do? How did they find out?'

'Marie-Claire, for Christ's sake stop worrying. It's probably nothing. Your fat little servant could be exaggerating – she could even be lying. Carry on as normal. Say nothing, don't use the phone other than for normal things until I've had a look around, and for God's sake don't panic.' He allowed the suggestion of a smile to soften his features. It didn't reach his eyes. 'Not until you hear me screaming and running up the wall. Then you can join me!'

Montbron's words had the right effect. She looked almost embarrassed at the crack in her composure but covered it by leading him out of the door, along the corridor and down the backstairs that led from Claude Massotte's bedroom to his study on the first floor. She opened the solid wooden door, revealing a large walk-in cupboard, and switched on the light. Claude Massotte's passion for weapons was evident. He wasn't just a collector, he was a user, and the row of sporting rifles and shotguns, every one a piece of the finest quality, showed that the wealth of his wife was not confined to her own obsessions. But Montbron wasn't interested in fine weapons and didn't linger on the collection in their racks. He turned to the shelves. One was filled with neat boxes of cartridges and rifle ammunition. He wasn't interested in this either. On the top shelf, shimmering in the gentle glow of a humidifyig lamp, were three hard leather boxes. He reached up and brought down the first one that came to hand. There was nothing on the boxes to indicate their contents, but there was no mistaking their shape.

He unstrapped the belt binding, flipped the catch and lifted the lid. He didn't dwell on it. A glance was sufficient: a German

S&B power scope, long distance, with a light-intensification capability. He closed the lid. It wasn't what he was looking for. He put it back in its place and brought down the second. It was smaller and lighter, and when he opened it it was exactly what he wanted, a simple distance magnification with a zoom action and a sharp definition adjuster. Massotte wouldn't have bothered using this since he'd acquired the sophisticated Schmit und Bender, but like a true collector, he just couldn't bear to part with it. Montbron closed the lid and tucked the box under his arm.

'Shut the door, put the key back in its place,' he told Marie-Claire, 'and carry on as normal. I'll be in your office overlooking the front.'

Everything had suddenly become urgent. Even his normal sang-froid had a slight edge to it, though Marie-Claire was too agitated herself to notice. 'I'll come with you,' she said. He didn't argue as she followed him out of the study and into her office overlooking the Avenue Beauchamp.

'Don't go near the windows,' he warned. He went down on his knees and crawled across the room, settling himself with his back against the wall to the side of one of the room's two large, lace-curtained windows. Marie-Claire lowered herself gingerly into an armchair at her desk and lit another cigarette as she watched Montbron remove the optical gun sight from its case and, with a barely perceptible movement, edge the curtain fractionally to one side, leaving a tiny gap for the sight. Moving only his head, he placed his eye to the lens and inched the bevelled ring in smooth, tiny movements until he'd focused on the base of a tree on the far side of the road. It was crisp and clear. He zoomed. The bark of the tree hit him, almost physically, in the eye. With a tiny gleam of approval he returned to normal magnification and began to inspect the area.

As he'd anticipated, there was nothing in the avenue, or its surroundings, to confirm his earlier misgivings. But he was saving the best bit for last. He did another turn up and down, as far as his angle of vision permitted, then inspected the solid concrete base of the street lamp. He followed it up slowly and when he reached the top, where the metal overhang protected the neon strip from the weather, his finger found the zoom lever and turned it as far as it would go. There it was. Exactly what he'd been expecting: the wide lens, coated against reflection, with the bulk of the camera neatly concealed in the overhang. He could almost reach out and touch it. He traced the thick black cable and lost it when it plunged into the standard's housing. He followed the trunk of the lamp to ground level, and, without being able to see round the other side, could readily visualize the locked compartment at the base containing the powerful image transmitter probably joined to the telephone system. Without getting up to look, he knew where the signals would be going; he'd already reconnoitred the post office. The whole bloody crew would be comfortably installed in a nice, cosy cabin. The idle bastards didn't even have to suffer! He returned to the camera and studied its angle. It was fixed. That was the first bit of good news. He slowly removed the gun sight from the window, went down on his belly and crawled to the other side.

'What is it, Philippe?' Marie-Claire crushed out her cigarette and immediately lit another.

'They've got a camera on the house,' he announced unemotionally.

'Oh, *mon Dieu*!' Marie-Claire's eyes popped out of her head. 'What are we going to do? Who are they? Oh my God, Philippe! How did they find out . . . ?' She threatened to go on and on but he silenced her quickly with a wave of the hand and moved carefully, on his knees, until he was squatting beside her.

'I've no idea,' he said thoughtfully. 'DST. It could be routine. They watch all sorts of people. Claude might have upset them.' He knew that was highly improbable; he knew exactly who they were watching, and why. He'd made the classic mistake – he'd underestimated the opposition. But it wasn't too late. They couldn't be sure of anything, otherwise they'd have kicked the door in. That was why Lilli was being given centre stage – they were doing a house census before risking upsetting the judiciary. He slipped the extra earpiece out of its slot in the telephone and said, 'Is this phone on the main circuit?'

Marie-Claire was still struggling for composure; it took several seconds for her to work out the question and its meaning. 'It's my personal phone,' she replied. Her voice was husky where her mouth had dried out with fear. The continual puffing of cigarette smoke wasn't doing much good except by keeping one hand occupied. It didn't stop it shaking.

'Does it have a different number from the rest of the phones in the house, or is it an extension?' Montbron persisted, trying to keep the impatience out of his voice.

'It's a different number.'

'Good. Ring your hairdresser and book an appointment. Make it natural. Write down the number, and the time you want your hair done.'

'But—'

'Do as I say,' he said sharply. 'Now calm down. Good. That's it. Now, when you pick up the phone, don't dial until I point . . . Don't ask questions. OK?' He forestalled the quizzical look in her eyes and stuck the extension to his ear. 'Pick it up,' he whispered, then listened. 'OK,' he mouthed, and pointed at her face. As each digit was dialled he frowned in concentration; in the background of the whirring made by the dial returning to its stop, was the tiny echo of the digit being transferred to the recording tape. When she finished dialling he waited for the hollow cut-in as the voice transfer was manually checked, and then the barely discernible click as the magnetic tape took up her conversation. He waited until she replaced the receiver, then slipped the earpiece back in its slot and stood up. He lifted one of her cigarettes from the packet on the table and lit it. 'Don't use the phone for anything other than your usual calls,' he said.

'I won't use it at all.'

'Do as I say. Don't change your habits, or that *will* drop us in the shit. And for Christ's sake, try to sound a bit more normal than you did just now. One more thing. When you go out, don't stand at the front entrance like a star going on stage. Forget the camera, forget the watchers.' He stared coldly into her face for a few seconds. 'You've got a friend you trust?'

She stared back. 'Of course.'

'Go and have drinks with her this morning, then make a phone call from her house. Call this number – don't write it down.' He gave her a north-east Paris number. 'Introduce yourself as "Éliane" and say "Diderot has changed his habits, he'll be in touch." '

'What does it mean?'

'It doesn't matter, just say it.'

'Nothing else?'

'Nothing else. They'll understand. No conversation. Put the phone down and forget everything you said.'

'Philippe, what are you going to do? Where will you go? When? How can you go if the house is being watched?'

'Better you don't know where I am going.' He pretended not to notice her sigh of relief. 'I'll be gone before you get back. Don't worry, there'll be no trouble for you. Nobody's going to come barging in, not without concrete proof that you're harbouring criminals. And you're not doing that, are you? There's nobody here; there never has been anybody here. In any case, they wouldn't risk having Claude jumping up and down on their feet.'

'You didn't say how you are going to leave.'

'Their little camera is on a set angle. It doesn't swivel – they have no control. It's pointed at the entrance and covers a few metres on either side. There's a blind spot, and there'll also be a blank spot when the light fails but it's still too light for a physical watch. That's when I'll go. I shall be able to walk out like the man at Monte Carlo!'

'Which one?'

'Was there more than one?'

'There was the one who broke the bank and lived happily ever after – and the other poor sod who crawled into the bushes and stuck a gun in his mouth because he'd lost all his money! Philippe, how can you be so flippant at a time like this?'

'It worries me too sometimes, Marie-Claire.'

11

FILLI WENT THROUGH all the motions even though he knew what the outcome would be.

'The Rhine Army', he told Michèle, 'says that your man, Lieutenant Colonel de Guy-Montbron, went on accrued leave four weeks ago. That's two months' leave entitlement. The bastard's done his groundwork very well. He's untraceable, according to the Army, until his leave is complete and then, would you believe it, he goes direct to a six months' course – NATO staff college, it says here – with the British Army somewhere in the south of England.'

'Clever little man,' said Michèle, which brought Filli's head, and scowl, up from the hunched position he'd allowed it to drop into whilst reading the summary of Michèle's findings. But he found nothing in her face to doubt her serious intent.

'Not as clever as he could have been,' he snapped. 'The bastard's shown himself. He should have used the phone, or met bloody Xavier in the park in the dark. That's the trouble with these smart cocks, they think St Cyr gives them brains and the God-given right to think that everybody else is a bloody idiot! Well, he's met someone who's not. I'm going to nail this supercilious bastard.'

'How d'you know he's supercilious, Georges?'

'You trying to be clever?'

'No – objective. If you're building up a character study, let's get the thing right. Let's not begin by giving him disadvantages he doesn't possess.'

'I hope you're not taking the piss, Michèle.'

Michèle didn't answer. She shrugged her shoulders and stared at the sheaf of papers in Filli's hand. 'What else does it tell us?'

'Nothing, but let me tell you what my instinct is . . .'

'Is your instinct going to help put him against the wall?'

Filli didn't react. He went on as if she hadn't replied. 'My instinct tells me that this smart bastard killed the Minister of Special Affairs and five of his personal security screen. My instinct tells me that this smart bastard planned the whole party. My instinct also tells me that he's been specially recruited – probably by one man – and brought to Paris for the sole purpose of running a high-powered assassination group. I think that group comprises just him and one other, and I also think that he's not going to stop at Gautier – and that's how the bastard's stuck his head in the hole. He's been given his next target, and the silly buggers chose, of all bloody places, Fouquet's in the Champs-Élysées in the middle of the day to stitch up their conspiracy. It's going to cost him his commission! I'm going to have him splattered against the wall at Vincennes and the dogs can come and lick him off the fuckin' brickwork!'

'I don't suppose, Georges, it ever occurs to you to moderate your language – just a little bit – in deference to ladies being present?'

'You asked to join – you take whatever comes. And if you don't like the fuckin' language you can fuck off and join a ladies fuckin' sewing circle.'

'Thanks.'

Then Filli smiled. It was a most unusual occurrence. It took Michèle by surprise. 'And to prove to you that your being a beautiful woman has no effect on my attitude, I'm going to take you out and buy you a nice glass of champagne and tell you what I want you to do next.'

'Do you normally take Rosso out for champagne?'

Filli smiled again. Things must be going well – or she was about to step out on to the tightrope. 'Never. I don't like his perfume, and his knees aren't as pretty as yours! Come on.'

'I'm not going to ask who gave you this duff info on Montbron,' Fillie said to Michèle as he tipped and emptied his second glass of champagne, 'but next time you're lying there hanging on to his ears, see if you can find out whether the Firm has anybody specializing in the Gautier business and whether they've made the Montbron connection – or any other connection. Is he capable of that sort of talk?'

Michèle treated her glass with more respect and sipped her champagne delicately. She wasn't offended by Filli's crudeness; she expected it. He was, after all, Corsican, and a country boy at that. She played the game that suited him. 'He's not capable of any sort of talk when, as you delicately and romantically put it, I'm hanging on to his ears, but without going to that extreme, I shouldn't think SDECE would be the least bit interested in Gautier's trip. More likely a DST caper, and I reckon they'll be flat out.'

'Find out.'

'Not from him. He plays footsie with the big boys over at Tourelles; I doubt whether he has an entrée into the DST's Rue des Saussaies HQ or the Renseignements Généraux people. They're all fairly cagey with one another.'

'Cagey?' spat Filli. 'Cagey be buggered – it's a fuckin' balls-up. Nobody knows what the bloody hell's going on on the other side of the street. It's like a bloody girls' school . . .' He stopped swearing for a moment and looked over his shoulder at the waiter. When he caught his eye he held his empty glass up with one hand and two fingers with the other. He didn't ask Michèle if she wanted more. She got it whether she wanted it or not. When he swung back in his chair he regarded her suspiciously. 'You brought the DST into the conversation deliberately,' he said accusingly.

She tried not to smirk. It wasn't often one could lead the little Corsican into a minefield. 'Something I heard. Do you know Violle at the DST?'

'Know of him,' replied Filli, guardedly. 'What about it?'

'It's only a whisper, Georges, nothing more than that. I wouldn't want my name down as a source, but it was hinted that he'd locked up his drawer in the Rue des Saussaies and was last seen squeezing through the back door of the Palais.'

Filli thought about it, but not for long. 'The Élysée Palace? What do you read into that?'

'Same as you—' She stopped talking at his warning glance and waited until the waiter had refilled their glasses and moved back to his counter. 'That he's been called by someone to set up a special shop with special powers. It's too close to Gautier's murder to be anything but a direct response to that.'

Filli sipped from his new glass. 'It stinks of Department Maurice.'

'I didn't want to say.'

'Did Violle take anybody with him from the Rue des Saussaies?'

She shook her head. 'The whisper didn't say.'

Filli took time off to concentrate on the taste of his champagne, but it took second place to the new thoughts that Michèle's rumour had germinated. He lit a cigarette to help them grow but didn't offer one to Michèle. He could have been sitting at the table all on his own, but it didn't upset her, she was quite happy to sit and watch his mind at work. It seemed to go on for quite a long time and just when she was getting used to being on her own, he stood up and called for the bill. 'See you tomorrow,' he said as he paid it, then looked down and gave her a long, hard look. There was no trace of the earlier humour in his eyes; this was the ordinary, everyday Filli. 'And by the way, if you get into trouble don't look around for Rosso, he won't be behind you for a day or two.'

She inclined her head. 'I'll try and live without him. D'you want me to guess what he'll be doing?'

He smiled again – he'd have to watch it, it was becoming a habit. 'Your little whisper's just changed his life. He's going to sit on the President's front doorstep and wait for one of Monsieur Violle's friends to pop in for a cup of tea, then take him home to see if he can't turn a few favours our way.'

'You wouldn't think we're all on the same side.'

'Only marginally, sweetheart. We're like strangers in a dodgy cable car: we don't talk, we don't want to know each other, but very shortly, when the string breaks, we're all going to end up wrapped around each other in a bloody great heap in the same pile of shit!'

'It'll be snow.'

'Whatever!'

12

ROSSO WATCHED PIETRI out of the corner of his eye. He was like a coiled spring; he should have been leading a bayonet charge, not sitting in a dark Peugeot under the trees on the corner of the Avenue de Marigny. The gendarme on duty on the far side of the road checked them every so often without interest. He knew what they were. He didn't envy them. And he wouldn't have changed jobs.

Félix Pietri, like Rosso, came from the same corner of France. One of the few regular Corsican DST operatives, Filli had had him transferred from the Rue des Saussaies as soon as he'd been given the green light to move against the core of the Army renegades. But Pietri was no watcher; he was an action man with a savage, violent streak that belonged more in the hills behind Ajaccio than the broad boulevards of Paris.

From their shaded viewpoint they had a clear view of the traffic entering the one-way system along the Faubourg-St-Honoré. But Rosso was only interested in taxis.

For perhaps the two hundredth time that day a taxi glided past them and pulled up just past the entrance. Neither man moved. There was no excitement; it had been happening all too frequently since early morning.

But this was different.

Pietri's eyes narrowed. He leaned forward, peering through the mud-spattered windscreen, and hissed noisily.

Rosso, without moving, studied the young man who got out of the taxi, paid it off and then strolled with assurance through the side-gate. He wasn't stopped by the guard. 'You know him?' asked Rosso out of the corner of his mouth.

Pietri's teeth gleamed. 'Morel – Marc Morel. Glamourboys.'

'DST?'

'No, SDECE. Ex-E2, DST.'

'Any known connection with Violle?'

Pietri's lip curled into a sneer. 'That's a joke!'

Rosso said nothing.

'Violle is head of E2. Morel was recruited by him to run down to the canteen for his croissants every morning – he used to sit on his knee and dip them into the coffee for him. Then he went to SDECE at Tourelles. Like I said, the glamourboys. Is that enough connection for you?'

Rosso opened his door and put his foot out on to the pavement. It was warmer out there than in the car. 'I'll do the footwork,' he said, 'in case he goes on the Métro. Keep me in sight. He might head for the taxi rank in the Rue Royale. I don't want to have to fuck around explaining to some bloody Breton driver the rudiments of cops and robbers, so if he takes wheels, follow him, mark it and then phone the Shop. I'll do the same.' He got out of the car and crossed the road, then strolled down on the opposite side to the Élysée entrance and waited on the corner of the Rue d'Aguesseau near the English Church.

Pietri lit another cigarette, flicked the match out of the open window and allowed his head to rest on the back of the seat. But he didn't close his eyes. Pietri at work was like a snake eyeing a live breakfast.

Violle studied Marc Morel as he spoke and thought he looked much too young. He ought to be at university studying medicine or sociology, sitting in cafés on the Boul' Mich' spouting revolutionary claptrap with the scruffy intelligentsia instead of creeping around in the mud of military politics. Which just went to show the difference a few years made . . . Violle's eyes closed for a second. At this child's age he had been shivering with fear, his face pressed into the sand at Courseulles-sur-Mer while German machine-guns tried to cut him into little ribbons. The silence made him open his eyes. Morel had stopped talking and was regarding him curiously. But he hadn't lost the thread.

'Diderot is a new one,' he said and reached for a file on the shelf behind him.'

'She said *Colonel* Diderot,' Morel reminded him.

'They're all colonels,' said Violle as he turned the pages. 'They picked that up during the war. You ever hear of a lieutenant or a captain running a Resistance cadre? Of course you bloody didn't; they were all majors or colonels! At the end of the war even the local butcher became a colonel. De Gaulle once met all the Resistance leaders in a town in Normandy and they all turned out with brand-new colonel's chevrons sewn on to their scruffy jackets – all except one, who, in the great man's honour, wore his old pre-war uniform with a lieutenant's badges. De Gaulle tapped them with his finger and said, "What's the matter with you, my friend – can't you sew?" ' Violle studied Morel's polite smile for a second or two then dropped his eyes back to the open file. 'We've got them all here – Colonel "Jean", Colonel "Troyes", Colonel "Xavier", Colonel this, Colonel that, and Colonel the bloody other. But alas,' he looked up with a sad smile, 'no Colonel Diderot, which means we can't barge into the judge's bedroom and hoick the bugger out just in case he's as innocent as you and me, because then, my young Marc, the shit would really hit the fan. So it looks as though you're going to have to bed the lovely, shy virgin again and get a few more details about the good Colonel. You're meeting her this afternoon, you say?'

Morel nodded, but his lack of enthusiasm didn't deter Violle. 'Then I suggest you get out there and start stuffing raw eggs down your throat. Make her happy, make her voluble. I want a good description: age, shape, colour of eyes, the lot. And, Marc—'

Morel looked up suspiciously.

'Persuade her to lift one of the glasses from his tray – before it's washed, of course.'

'I think that might be pushing things a little too far, sir. She might be bloody ugly, but she's not stupid enough to think that I'm collecting souvenirs. She might even blow the whistle.'

Violle shrugged. 'Play it by ear, then. I leave it up to you.' He picked up another file, took from it one of the photographs of Lilli and studied it. Then he shook his head. 'I wish I was your age again. You young people get all the good jobs! Ring me here when you get some strength back into your legs.'

He didn't hear what Morel said as he went through the door.

13

LILLI HAD ALREADY reached her third climax and was lying supinely while she waited for Morel to reach his. He was making very heavy going of it and she watched him curiously, trying to see through his tightly closed eyelids, until after a moment she decided to try and steal a little more and closed her eyes again.

Neither of them heard the two Corsicans come to the side of the bed.

Rosso had made short work of the lock on the door to Morel's apartment. Pietri had closed it quietly behind him. They stood for a moment watching the two heaving bodies, then, exchanging quick glances, they moved silently across the room. Rosso, without taking his eyes off Morel's juddering body, pointed to the girl, while with his other hand he removed a stubby-barrelled revolver from the back of his waistband and from a distance of two feet aimed it at the side of Morel's head.

'OK,' he said.

Morel took a second to realize what was happening. But there was no time left. 'Don't move an inch,' said Rosso and Morel stopped dead as his erection died inside her. Lilli wasn't quite sure. She opened her eyes, studied the two swarthy men, then opened her mouth. But the scream didn't materialize; it was absorbed, wetly, by the pillow that was rammed across her face, and faded into a muffled gurgle. Her body heaved, throwing Morel off, but Rosso's revolver followed his head. Morel kept his hands open and his body still, and remained where he'd been thrown.

Pietri was having trouble. Lilli was a big girl, of peasant stock, and she could have thrown a full-sized sow on her back if she'd had the advantage, though lying on her back, stark naked, the struggle was almost even. Pietri took Morel's place and sat astride her, pressing the top part of his body on to the pillow, but it was like sitting on an unbroken pony as she tossed him up and down like a cork. With difficulty he managed to get one hand round his back and pulled from his belt a heavy Colt automatic.

'Don't kill her!' snapped Rosso from the corner of his mouth. His eyes never left Morel's face and the pistol pointed unwaveringly at his head.

'F-f-fuckin' w-woman!' spat Pietri jerkily, and with a quick movement he whipped off the pillow and with a hammer-like swing hit Lilli across the side of the head with the solid barrel of the automatic. It only slowed her down and a new scream began to form. He hit her again and the scream gurgled into nothing. It was enough. Without looking at the suddenly bloodied face, he rammed the pillow back into place until there was no more movement.

'For Christ's sake, I said don't kill her,' hissed Rosso. 'That's enough. Come and help with lover boy here. You!' He waggled the stubby revolver at Morel. 'Get over there.' He jerked his chin at the low *bergère* standing near the wall on the cosy side of the apartment. It was a nice armchair; Morel had good taste. He'd found it in a junk shop and had it renovated. He was very proud of his *bergère*. He stooped to gather around him the duvet that had been thrown to the floor by Lilli and allowed himself a few seconds' luxury of wondering what the hell was going on and who the bloody hell these two evil-looking buggers were. He had time to feel sorry for Lilli and the battering she'd been given, but it wasn't long enough to reduce him to tears.

'Leave it. We've seen cocks before!' Rosso moved to one side and waggled the pistol again. 'Go and sit in that chair. Félix—' He was far enough away from Morel to allow a quick flick of his eyes in Pietri's direction. 'Get something to tie this bastard into that chair. Look in the cupboard – and close that bloody window and shutter on your way past.'

'My pants?' asked Morel.

'Shut up and sit down!'

Pietri backed away from the wardrobe with a bundle of silk ties in one hand and Morel's compact issue 7.65 MAB automatic in its skeleton belt-holster in the other. Watching the ugly Corsican ruin the silk ties by knotting them together was bad enough; the loss of the pistol set up a shiver of fear. And he hadn't yet worked out what it was all about. He was about to find out.

Pietri pulled Morel's hands tightly round the back of the *bergère*, gouging his shoulder-blades hard into the backrest. From behind the chair he grabbed both ankles. With his feet pressed against the back of the chair, he twisted Morel's legs until the cartilages almost snapped and forced them round the low-slung armrests. Morel's legs almost broke at the knees. He screamed. But Rosso was waiting. They'd done this before. While Pietri was squatting like a rower with Morel's ankles in his hand, he'd been busy folding several pairs of Morel's socks into a fair-sized ball. When Morel's mouth opened for the scream he shoved the socks in as far as they'd go. Morel had to abandon the scream or suffocate. Instead he fainted.

He came to reluctantly. A wet towel was being slapped across his face and the surplus water, dripping down his chest and over his stomach, had collected around his crotch so that he was sitting in a small puddle. He didn't consider the ruin of his nice *bergère*. The pain in his knees was excruciating. Not as bad as at first – the knees were getting used to the unusual position and had gone numb – but there was still enough feeling left to bring tears to his eyes and another scream to his throat. When the tears cleared he noted they'd thrown a sheet over Lilli's body. But she wasn't dead – he could see movement. They must have tied her as well. Poor little bitch!

A hand reached over his head and ripped the plug out of his mouth. 'What is Violle up to?' said one of the voices.

Oh, Christ! So that's who they are – they're bloody OAS stormtroopers! How the hell did they manage this? How did they find out about Violle's business? They've got a bloody spy in the Élysée office. That's it then – end of game!

'Who's Violle?' He ought to have known better.

They both came round to the front to look at his face. The one called Félix looked happy, as if he'd given the right answer. They both stood staring, saying nothing, and then the one with the happy expression lifted his jacket and pulled from behind him the big Colt automatic again. 'Go behind and hold his head,' he told the other one, and then: 'OK, hold him still.'

Morel had a sudden, urgent desire to urinate.

Pietri turned away and then, pivoting on his toes, brought the automatic round and hit him with the barrel with all his vicious strength. It was aimed very deliberately – just below the nose. Morel's top lip split like paper, and suddenly his mouth was full of loose teeth and blood. The shock kept him conscious and suddenly the realization that there was nothing to keep his tongue in his mouth made him spit and bellow with horror. His front teeth shot out like little white bullets and the blood showered over his chest and thighs like a burst tap. Rosso pulled back his head brutally and rammed the rolled up socks into the gaping red hole of Morel's face. The silence was like cotton wool, the only sound in the room the bubbling, snotty mess around Morel's nose as he sobbed and fought for air, and the solid but cushioned thump, thump, thump of his shoulders beating agonizingly against the backrest of the chair.

The two Corsicans watched dispassionately.

After a moment Rosso glanced down at his wrist and nodded to Pietri. Pietri reached forward with the Colt, then, at arm's length, placed it under Morel's chin and lifted his bloody face. 'We're going to ask you again,' he said. The boy's ruined good looks had no effect on him; he could have been talking to a sheep's head on a butcher's counter. 'You're getting a second chance, but no third. Can you hear me?' It didn't matter to Pietri whether Morel heard him or not. He repeated the question. 'Violle – what's he up to?' He removed the pistol from under Morel's chin and reached forward with his other hand and dragged the blood-sodden socks from his mouth.

Morel came out of shock. The thundering in his ears, the blood, the pain, the agony in his arms and legs, and all he could say, at the top of his voice, was, 'You fuckin' bastards!' But it didn't sound like that. It sounded like a wounded animal in its death throes; no single syllable was intelligible. But the meaning was clear. Rosso and Pietri acted instinctively; it was if they'd rehearsed the move earlier. Pietri even had time to shake his head and say, 'I said you don't get three . . .' as Rosso grabbed Morel's hair and steadied the wildly shaking head. Then Pietri swung his arm and the automatic slapped wetly against Morel's lower lip and displaced the rest of his front teeth. Morel's good looks finally vanished in a welter of blood. He looked like a wizened old peasant farmer, toothless, with his bottom lip split all the way down to his chin. This time, mercifully, he fainted.

The two Corsicans exchanged glances over his bowed head. Pietri shrugged his shoulders. 'He'll tell us next time. If not, I'll keep hitting his face until he does.'

They untied his hands but left his legs cruelly wrapped round the bottom of the small chair. The sounds that came out of Morel's disfigured mouth were still totally indecipherable, so they put paper in front of him and thrust a Biro between his fingers. In answer to their question he told them what, as far as he knew, Violle's mandate was, and what, again as far as he knew, had so far been achieved. The two Corsicans weren't impressed, but they were convinced he was telling the truth. He could have saved himself a lot of trouble, a lot of pain and an awful lot of dental work if he'd told them in the first place. Morel had heard the two men discussing his plight and he wasn't assured.

'Is this Diderot Guy-Montbron?' asked Pietri and pointed at the paper on Morel's knee.

Who he scrawled.

'Guy-Montbron, friend of Xavier's.'

Morel shook his head. He knew of Xavier; he'd never heard of Guy-Montbron.

'You shouldn't have mentioned that, Félix.' Rosso scowled at his partner. But Pietri wasn't contrite.

'Fuck him! We only have to tear the paper up.' But it wasn't that easy. And they both knew it. 'Let's talk to the girl. She can tell us whether Diderot is still in the house. This silly bastard's just a waste of time. He hasn't got a fuckin' clue.'

They showed Lilli the photograph of Philippe de Guy-Montbron. She didn't hesitate. She told them everything: Gautier's last dinner at the Massottes', Montbron's girlfriend Lucienne, Montbron's age, the colour of his eyes, how many pairs of trousers he had – everything she could have told Morel in the café yesterday and saved them both a lot of trouble. They didn't slap her around any more, they didn't hurt her – they didn't have to – and when they'd finished they left her as she was, naked, tied in a bundle with the duvet thrown over her. The bed looked as if it had a mountain of old clothes on it, but she was alive, and she didn't make a sound from the dark security of her covers.

'Go and get in the car.' Pietri had assumed temporary command. 'And I'll tidy up here. I'll join you in a minute.'

'Don't make a mess.'

Through the throbbing pain, Morel watched the short-legged Corsican pull on skin-tight leather gloves and wander around the small apartment rubbing anything he and his partner might have touched. There wasn't a great deal and it didn't take very long. He didn't remove the gloves when he finished up standing in front of Morel, studying the mess he'd made of his face. Morel stared back through eyes beginning to close with the puffiness of his cheeks. There was a vague sense of familiarity about the face in front of him, but he wisely kept it to himself. He'd sort this one out later; he was sure he'd seen him before.

But there wasn't going to be a later.

Pietri moved round to the back of Morel's chair. Morel didn't try to follow him but kept his head to the front and his eyes on the carpet. He'd had enough of looking at Corsicans. Pietri picked up Morel's MAB from the round table where he'd dropped it after the initial search, and removed it from its leather holster. He checked the magazine and cocked a round into the breech. At the sound of the metallic click, Morel began to turn his head, but he'd hardly moved when the bullet slammed into the side of his head. He was already on the floor dragging the armchair on top of him when the second bullet splattered part of his forehead on to the carpet.

Pietri didn't stop to check his handiwork. There was no need; it wasn't the first time he'd shot a man in the back of the head. He threw Morel's automatic under the bed and without a glance at the shuddering body in the middle of the room went out on to the landing. Closing the door, he unhurriedly descended the stairs and stepped out into the street.

14

'I TAKE FULL RESPONSIBILITY for this,' said Violle. He and Neurie were sitting on the edge of the bed in Morel's apartment. It was in chaos. The police had done their stuff and almost wrecked the place in the process. Morel had been photographed in all the gory details, then untidily stuffed into a cheap, plywood coffin and carted off to the mortuary and Forensic. Lilli had been spared police interrogation – for the time being – and had been rushed off to hospital, where she'd been placed under police guard. She'd have a lot to say to the Sûreté, but later. Violle didn't intend waiting that long, however; she was going to start talking to him that evening, with or without police cooperation.

'You've no need to,' replied Neurie coldly. 'These young buggers know what the job's all about when they come into your office and ask to be taken on to your staff. This is one of the drawbacks of a glamorous occupation.'

'You're a hard bastard, Neurie.'

'And I'm a live bastard. What did you get from the concierge?'

'Two men, dark-skinned, one with a little moustache.'

'Arabs?'

Violle shook his head. 'He said *basané* – swarthy – not *noir*. He's been around long enough to recognize a Muslim when he sees one, and besides, when did you hear of an Arab working for the OAS?' Neurie pulled a face but let him get on with it. 'Anyway, the girl'll sort that out for us, if they didn't pull her bloody tongue out whilst they were on the job. Morel was looking for an OAS connection here, a name to go with the Diderot he picked up yesterday.' He gazed around the room with a cold stare but saw nothing. 'This has all the hallmarks of an OAS off-the-cuff job. Nasty . . .'

Neurie's eyes also did a tour of the room, but unlike Violle he was totally insensitive to the atmosphere of death, pain and torture still hanging about the small apartment. He could have been sitting in a deck-chair on the side of a pool in Cap-Ferrat. 'You could have saved your breath, Gaby. Why didn't you suggest these two "*basanés*" were a couple of Corsican rat-catchers sniffing after the same Diderot as you and Morel?'

Violle stared back flatly. Anger, which had replaced the sorrow he felt over Morel, was bubbling dangerously near the surface. The smell of the young man's death was very fresh; it would take a long time to eradicate it from the fabric of the room. It affected Violle's attitude. 'I wanted to hear you say it. I was hoping it might have been a love war, but I've seen a picture of the girl and no one could have loved her that much, so that's what I reckon it is, the Action Association bringing their nasty little manners to Paris and not giving a bugger for anyone just so long as they score points. Well it's not good enough, Gérard. I think I'm more in sympathy with the OAS than these merciless fuckers. I'm going to stop looking for the Diderots and the Xaviers and start making spaces against the wall for bloody Corsicans!'

Neurie's smile broadened into a grin. He'd grown from boy to man in a very short time in the company of Gaby Violle. He fully understood the workings of his mind. He even agreed with his sentiments. 'It's nice to know who our enemies are,' he said, and passed him a cigarette.

Violle almost bit the cigarette in half and when it was lit he whooshed out smoke like an old-fashioned locomotive and shot Neurie a sideways glance. 'What do you mean by that?'

'We both know who we're talking about – Action Association. We can play them at their own game. They've just laid down a new set of rules, so if they get in the way, you can barge them aside the way they've just barged your boy away. D'you know Georges Filli?'

Violle's lips tightened over his cigarette. 'Algiers?'

Neurie nodded.

Violle took the cigarette from his mouth. 'A very nasty piece of work. Discovered his forte before, during and after the Battle of Algiers in 1957. Godard, when he was Massu's Chief of Staff, used him as a special interrogator and when he showed everyone how good he was he moved on, again in a "special" capacity, to organize a group within one of the colonial parachute regiments, which, under his guidance, copied FLN methods and then improved on them. One of their little habits with Muslim shadow-men was to hunt, then kill and collect the cocks to show how well they were doing – a sort of head count. But it got too easy; they liked to hear the screams; so they collected the cocks and sent the poor buggers back into the world without them. Not very nice people . . . But Filli obviously didn't dirty his fingernails over that, because he vanished for some time and resurfaced as a major in SDECE's 11th Shock Troops – and that wasn't all that long ago.'

Neurie didn't look surprised. The Algerian conflict had thrown up some very strange attitudes, and even stranger people, in the French Army. 'Filli was just one of many,' he said casually. 'They'll be crawling out of the dunghill for quite a few years yet. But I didn't know this one was heading for respectability. He seemed quite choosy about what units he'd offer his services to. You sure he didn't start life as a gas-chamber operator with the SS?'

'He's working here in Paris. He's got a little abattoir on the Boulevard de Montmorency staffed by some of his ex-Algeria Special Group dustbin men – all Corsicans. He's under the anti-OAS committee umbrella. Free rein. There's no record of his people and no record of their activities. He hands damaged OAS people over to DST's Special Reception.'

'I'm going to put a watch on him.'

'Don't. Concentrate on what you're doing. Gautier's assassination comes first. We want Diderot and his team before de Gaulle's becomes the second. Leave Filli to me. Don't worry. We'll have a fair pound of flesh for this little effort. Come on, let's get out of here – the smell's beginning to get to me.'

Violle needed only fifteen minutes with Lilli and the only thing to come out of it was the name de Guy-Montbron.

After he'd finished with her he went through the same procedure as Filli had done earlier. The Army at Metz sat up and began to take notice when the second lot of enquiries concerning one Lieutenant Colonel de Guy-Montbron came in from civilian intelligence circles in Paris. Suspicion, and curiosity – but Violle managed to calm them down and after a long session with Army Records and Postings ended up only slightly wiser about Montbron's movements than Filli.

They gave him a contact address in Paris: mail only, probably collect, they thought, it was the best they could do. It turned out to be a café/restaurant on a corner looking onto the Place de la Bastille. It wasn't much of a lead, Violle told Neurie, but a little better than nothing, and he promptly had an official-looking letter sent to the address. With it went an agent who took up permanent residence in a second-floor studio overlooking the shop, with a direct line to the person responsible for checking letters in and out of the collect address. 'No contact,' Violle impressed upon the agent. 'You check, you follow, and you report where he goes to ground. If you balls this up and try in any way to be cleverer than you're capable of being, you'll end up as the dustcart driver's tea boy – and I mean it!'

But Violle had miscalculated. He'd assumed that Filli's people, if Filli's people it was who'd killed Morel, had picked him up through watching the housemaid. In his reckoning there had been no other way. Pietri and Rosso had forgotten about Morel by the following day – but they hadn't forgotten where they'd started. Their car was back in its Avenue de Marigny slot the following afternoon, and the day after that. It was early morning on the third day that Pietri spotted another of Violle's E2 operatives leaving the familiar side-door of the Élysée Palace.

This one took them to the café at the Place de la Bastille, where they separated and from different points watched him settle into his own watching routine from his window on the opposite side of the road. They didn't know what they were watching for; it was sufficient that the man had come from

Violle and was interested in the café/restaurant. Morel had told them that Violle's interest was purely in the men who'd killed Gautier; that was all Filli needed. The men who'd killed the Minister of Special Affairs were the men who'd killed the Corsicans. Rosso and Pietri had a serious chat with the café owner and settled down for a long one-on, one-off watch. They were in no hurry.

'The girl's been taken home by Madame,' Violle told Neurie over the phone. 'Stormed into the hospital in high dudgeon and demanded to know what the hell was going on.'

'Understandable.'

' "*D'you know who I am? D'you know who my husband is*!" Stupid bitch!'

'Just as well her husband's not a ticket collector on the Métro! Is that what you rang me for?'

Violle snorted. 'These bloody people get on my nerves. No, I didn't ring for that. I sent a uniformed lad round to have another talk to the girl and she told him, when the bloody aristo left them alone for two minutes, that the mysterious house guest was no longer in residence. And, no, she didn't know where he'd gone.'

Neurie didn't reflect on it. 'Close everything down. Remove the cameras and bugs and get everybody out of the area. Don't bother the girl any more. I want Madame Massotte calmed down and any trace of interest in her house or movements removed. Today, Gaby – and then forget her.'

'You going to tell me?' Violle couldn't hide the sarcasm in his voice, but it had no effect on Neurie.

'Meet me in the Chandelier tonight. We'll have a couple of drinks in the dark and then go and have a meal at Louisette's. And, Gaby . . .'

'Yup?'

'Watch yourself.'

'I always do. Is there something worrying you?'

'I'm not happy about this Morel business. I think they got on to him, not the girl, which means your move might have been logged and your new place blown. See if anybody's been standing on the street corners of the Faubourg-St-Honoré. Ask about a bit, but when you jog about outside have the odd look around.'

'Christ! I hope you're wrong. But I think I'll change dressing-rooms anyway! See you tonight – sevenish.'

Neurie rocked back precariously in his chair, put his feet up on the desk and studied the picture of his ex-wife and her escort. He stared hard at the grainy image of the man, then, with a tight-lipped smile, picked up the phone again and dialled a London number. After a brief conversation about the weather that fooled no one, he said, 'How can I get hold of Harry Metcalfe?'

'No idea, Gérard.' The London voice was suave and casual, but there was a lot of thought behind the answer. It waited for a few seconds and without prompting from Neurie continued, 'He doesn't work for us any more. Totted up his pension points and decided he'd earned enough to allow him to do what he's always wanted – lead a life of doing bugger-all. What's your interest?'

Neurie ignored the question. 'Is he still in the Business?'

'Are we ever not, Gérard? But you know Metcalfe. He's got a mind of his own, although it has been suggested that he might lift a finger for the right incentive – money or women.' He tried again. 'Why?'

'I fancied a little chat about old times. We go back a long way, we're old friends.'

The voice thought this one over for another few seconds, then broke a rule and made a decision. 'Oh well, if that's all it is I don't suppose it can do any harm. I'm not sure he'd thank me for telling you this, but he's not at home, he's gone abroad.'

'Was he covered?'

'Of course. You should know our funny little ways by now. We don't allow the people we've honoured with the privilege of signing the Official Secrets Act to wander willy-nilly amongst our competitors without our knowing it. It's not good for trade.'

'Which of your competitors is he wandering amongst,

Michael?' Neurie continued to stare at the picture of Harry Metcalfe. At least it looked like Harry Metcalfe and coincidence didn't stretch to *doppelgängers*, not in this business. And it helped to get confirmation from the horse, if you could.

'Sorry, old boy, I can't help you, but if I had heard a whisper or two, would there be anything here for us?'

'Like what?'

'Oh, come on, Gérard! What are you up to and how can a former British intelligence officer be of use to you? It might be contrary to our interests.'

'There's nothing except a little return favour in the future for you, Michael. I'm not asking for the colour of the Queen's knickers. I'm asking for the whereabouts of Harry Metcalfe on a purely private matter – nothing to do with Her Majesty's problems. It's nothing to set the bells clanging, nothing more than a little French domestic matter that he could advise me on.'

'Then you'll owe me a drink?'

'Where is he, Michael?'

'Paris.'

It wasn't very difficult. Neurie found Harry Metcalfe in the Montalembert, a hotel on its way down the ratings in the Rue du Bac just off the Boulevard St-Germain.

He strolled into Metcalfe's room behind an elderly chambermaid bearing a large breakfast tray. Metcalfe didn't look all that surprised to find Neurie in his room. But then Metcalfe wasn't the sort of man who was easily surprised and wouldn't have shown it even if he had been.

The chambermaid hurried out before they asked for extra cups and more croissants. Neurie closed the door behind her and turned to study the man on the bed in his pyjamas, his back propped against the headboard, with, until now, only thoughts of breakfast on his mind.

Metcalfe gazed back at him with an untroubled expression. He sat at ease, six feet two, solidly built, with no fat to show for his new life of leisure. It was a friendly face, until something happened to change it, and it didn't take much. Fair, his short hair was no more unruly from a night's sleep than it would be after a comb had been dragged through it, though his chin, tight and slightly aggressive, betrayed what was going on behind the otherwise even expression.

'What are you doing in Paris, Metcalfe?' Neurie walked across to the large window and without disturbing the lace curtains gazed down on to a quiet Rue du Bac where the street washer was splashing away yesterday's and last night's dust. He watched for a few moments, then turned. 'Didn't you hear what I said?'

Metcalfe smiled. It wasn't a genuine smile; there was a slight air of uncertainty about all this. He tried to lighten it. 'Is that your new job, Gérard? Checking for foreigners in the Paris doss-houses?'

There was no reaction from Neurie.

After a few moments regarding the Frenchman, Metcalfe shrugged. 'I'm having a holiday – a bit of this, a bit of that . . .' He raised an eyebrow. 'What's your problem, Gérard?'

'When did you last see Monique?'

'Monique who?'

'Monique Bonnet, the woman who was happily married to your best friend and whom you were fucking behind his back in Singapore. That Monique.'

'Oh, Jesus! You haven't come for another bloody fight have you? I thought it was all over and done with. That was five years ago. And as I told you then, you were asking for trouble, taking a beautiful woman out to Singapore and then ignoring her and spending all your time climbing in and out of bed with other people's wives. What was she supposed to do – sit at home knitting? But, bugger you, Neurie, we did all this in '56. I'm not going to spend the rest of my life singing the same bloody song for you whenever you feel the urge for a bit of self-flagellation. I'm on holiday, so if that's all you wanted to talk about, perhaps you wouldn't mind buggering off and letting me have my breakfast . . . ?'

Neurie took a cigarette from the packet in his shirt pocket, lit it and blew a stream of smoke upwards. It had no effect on the already heavily brown-mottled ceiling. He watched it disperse. 'When did you last see her?'

'Five years ago in Singapore.' Lying came naturally to Metcalfe; it went with the profession. No blushing, no beating around the bush, a clean statement right between the eyes; at least it was honest lying. He and the ex-Mme Neurie had been very close friends, very close indeed for the three years since her almost brutal divorce from the stone-faced man standing by the window, and a hasty, rather silly union with Bonnet to show Neurie that she didn't care. Metcalfe was in love, though he didn't know what to do with it. But one thing was for sure: it was none of Gérard Neurie's business. Metcalfe should have known – it was the Trap.

Neurie slid the picture of Metcalfe and Monique out of his pocket, looked at it for a moment, then walked across to the bedside and placed it on Metcalfe's lap.

'So when did you meet her twin sister?'

Metcalfe stared up into Neurie's set features. It had always been a thing about Gérard Neurie: he never showed anger. He could kill and he could love, he'd even gaze benignly at a howling child – provided the mother was young and pretty – but his expression was the same for all three. Metcalfe regretted the passing of their friendship. It had been a good one; they'd been through a lot together. But he hadn't regretted Monique. He still didn't. He left the picture where it was, lowered his eyes and glanced at it briefly, but it was long enough for him to realize that this was trouble. He found it hard to believe that Neurie was having him followed because of Monique. It was no longer necessary, divorce was divorce, you didn't have to keep on piling up evidence years after the absolute. So who was taking pictures? And why?

Neurie looked as though he'd lost interest. He picked up a croissant from the basket on the tray, tested its freshness with his forefinger and thumb, then dipped one of the pointed ends into a bowl of apricot jam and bit it off. He continued chewing while Metcalfe, with a casualness he didn't feel, picked up the photograph for a closer look.

'Who are these two people?' he asked.

Neurie took his time. He swallowed, dipped the croissant into the jam again, but didn't carry it to his mouth. 'You were photographed coming out of an OAS safe house – a safe house suspected of harbouring a senior OAS assassin. You've committed a crime. It comes under the category of a foreign national knowingly consorting with enemies of the State actively engaged in armed conflict to overthrow the Government.'

'Bollocks!'

'Your situation is somewhat worse. You are a member of a foreign intelligence organization—'

'Ex—'

'And under emergency regulations you can be detained, without trial, for as long as I choose. At a rough guess, bearing in mind that I owe you a bad turn, you could be put away in the Santé for a minimum of three years, or at least as long as this emergency lasts and somebody asks who this Englishman is rotting in one of our prisons. You could end up like the Count of Monte Cristo . . .'

'What do you want, Neurie?'

Neurie ate his croissant. 'What I want, Metcalfe, is the answer to a few questions, your total cooperation should I need it, and for you to leave Monique alone and bugger off back to England when I've finished with you.'

Metcalfe got the message. In typical Murphy fashion he'd come to Paris to rekindle the heady past with Monique and he'd walked straight into the Paris branch of the Algiers war. And, of course, it had to be Monique's ex-bloody husband running that particular corner of it! How bloody lucky could you get. But he wasn't going down without attempting a kick at Neurie's crotch. 'Jesus, Neurie, I don't understand your hang-up over Monique. There's something bloody sick about it. You're divorced. *You* divorced *her* – remember? She's your ex-wife twice removed, she married another guy purely on the rebound, though that lasted only months. That was your fault, too. Monique's nothing to do with you any more, Neurie. She's your ex-wife, not your bloody teenage daughter.'

'You finished?'

'Fuck off!'

Neurie wiped his lips with a serviette from the tray, took his time over lighting another cigarette, then sat down.

'How long have you known the Massottes?'

'Who are they?'

'The people you had lunch with last Friday.'

'Then that's how long I've known them – since last Friday. That's the only time I've been there. She, Marie-Claire, is a friend of Monique's – or rather Monique's a friend of Marie-Claire's sister. She took me along for the smoked salmon. I hadn't seen her before, and probably won't see her again. She in trouble?'

'You're all in trouble if I like to make it so. Who else was at this luncheon?'

Metcalfe held up the photograph and flicked it with his fingers. 'What happened – your camera break down after it took this one?'

'Answer the question.'

'Why don't you ask Monique, she'd know better than I would.'

'I'm asking you – and I'm not going to ask again. Tell me about the men. I'm not interested in the women.'

Metcalfe lit a cigarette, stuck it between his lips and made himself more comfortable on the bed. Crossing his ankles, he clasped his hands behind his neck and closed his eyes. He looked as though he was about to start making up for lost sleep. But Neurie wasn't deceived. He had patience – it was part of his trade – and he knew his man. He waited. It wasn't long in coming.

'There were one or two insignificant odds and ends, fringe politicos with a lot to say but nothing of interest, and a couple of soldiers.'

'Ranks?'

'An elderly major who's missed the boat and a young lieutenant colonel who hasn't.'

Neurie wasn't amused. 'Names?'

'No idea. One had a double-barrelled name, though.'

'That name wouldn't have been de Guy-Montbron?'

Metcalfe opened his eyes and blinked through the spiral of smoke rising from his cigarette. There was nothing in Neurie's face; no expression, just a bland, disinterested look.

'You know him too?'

'Was Guy-Montbron the name of the man you met at the Massottes?' persisted Neurie.

Metcalfe shrugged. 'No, nothing like it.'

'Then how do you know this name?'

'We *are* talking about *Philippe* de Guy-Montbron?'

'We *could* talk about him,' said Neurie casually. 'Have you met him recently?'

Here it comes again. We know what Monique did to him, but what's Philippe Montbron been doing to ruffle the bugger's feathers? Play it as it comes. Look honest, look him in the eye. 'No.' The lie was automatic. No reason; an instinctive response. 'I haven't seen him since you and I were doing that thing together in Singapore. He was SAS. But you probably know that?'

Neurie didn't bite. 'How did you meet him?' His eyes were frozen.

It wasn't lost on Metcalfe. He frowned for a few seconds and brought his memory out of its hiding-place. 'On the night mail train from Kuala Lumpur going up to Butterworth. Some time in . . . I think . . . 1953, or thereabouts. Remember how the bloody thing was always getting itself shot up?'

'I'm not interested. Tell me about Montbron and your meeting him on the way to Butterworth.' Neurie poured himself a cup of Metcalfe's breakfast, no milk or sugar, just black. He didn't drink it, but left it on the tray and waited for Metcalfe to continue.

'The only person, except myself, who hadn't hung out of the window blasting nine millimetres into the night air or thrown himself on to the deck and stuck his hands over his ears, was this tall suntanned guy in a light khaki uniform with a red beret wrapped up in a webbing belt and a holstered Colt on the bar. He looked foreign, but one of us, if you know what I mean. He just carried on sipping his brandy and soda and gazing at the bottles on the shelves behind the counter. He looked like the sort of chap who was quite used to having bullets whistling round his ears. I liked the look of him. After a minute we started chatting and by the time the train pulled in and out of Ipoh we were well away. He told me he'd come down from Indo-China on an SAS attachment, but the KL people had sent him for a few days' leave to Penang while they found room for him. As we were quite good friends by the time we got to Penang we stuck together and spent a couple of days whoring and drinking around the place. After a bit he went back and I stayed for another week. I saw him once or twice afterwards in Nanto's in Batu Road and we had a few drinks together. On another occasion we bumped into each other in Prince's in Singapore, but I was doing an earwig on a Russian merchantman captain. Philippe G-M got the message and didn't make contact . . . Just a minute – you were with me.'

Neurie didn't relax his expression. 'I remember the Russian. I don't remember the Frenchman.'

'Your memory's very selective, Gérard,' said Metcalfe reflectively. 'I suppose you've even forgotten that time in Singapore when you led me into that bloody whorehouse off Bugis Street where the MCP were holding their annual meeting . . . Very nice girls in this place, you said, you bastard. You didn't say anything about having to fight for my bloody life against the Central Committee of the Malayan Communist Party, or having to drag out by the scruff of his neck a deputy head of SDECE Far East named Gérard Neurie who had a bullet in his chest, and not getting any thanks for it . . .'

But Neurie wasn't in the mood for reminiscences, at least not those sort. 'There's only one abiding memory I brought back with me from Singapore, Metcalfe, and that's your nasty, sneaky little ways with my wife. Now let's get back to Montbron.'

Metcalfe shrugged again and stubbed out his cigarette. 'That was the last time I saw him, or heard his name mentioned until just now . . .' *Apart from the fact that I spent a week with him last year in the Cercottes house of tricks in Corsica and that we played soldiers with the SAS's toys at Hereford earlier this year.*

And, as old friends should, we get pissed occasionally both here and in London, though that is not the point. The point being, what's Montbron done, or doing, to get the cameramen out of bed? 'What's your interest in him?'

'Nothing to concern you. If you see him, or make contact, ring me direct.' Neurie scrawled a number on a piece of hotel notepaper and stuck it between the two remaining croissants. 'That number. No message, personal contact. OK?'

'I'm not likely to. With your interest in him, he sounds to me the sort of bloke well worth avoiding. What's he been doing – upsetting the Establishment?'

Neurie ignored the question. 'Keep your nose out of things, Metcalfe. Don't stay around too long.' He stood up and walked to the door. 'Eat your croissants and go back to sleep. And then think very seriously about returning to London. You're not welcome here.' There was no goodbye, no thanks for the old times and favours rendered, just a long, searching look and the door closing quietly behind him.

Metcalfe didn't move for several minutes after Neurie had gone. His appetite had left him; he didn't fancy either croissants or sleep. He lit another cigarette and settled back into the pillow, staring at the pretty nicotine patterns on the ceiling. It seemed that the time had come to look up friends from the old days, particularly as they seemed to be in Paris, moving in the same circles and exciting the interest of a very serious spy hunter. *Sounds very OASish, and sounds to me as if you're on the wrong side, Philippe. Could be interesting! I think it's time you and I had another little chat, for old times' sake, and to make sure you know there's a very heavy breather sniffing into your game. I owe you that favour at least . . .*

15

NEURIE LEFT THE Montalembert, crossed the road and went into the Café du Consulate on the corner of the Rue du Bac. He ordered a cup of coffee and an early-morning cognac and whilst the coffee was filtering into its squat little cup he locked himself in the telephone booth. He dialled the private Department Maurice number at the Élysée. 'Can you locate Violle for me, please – urgently. Tell him to ring me at . . .' He glanced down at the telephone base: no number, incoming calls not encouraged. He shook his head. 'Forget the phone. Tell him to grab a cab and meet me at the Café du Consulate. It's the Rue du Bac, near the Montalembert Hotel . . .'

'He's no ordinary *Anglais*, this one,' explained Neurie when Gaby Violle joined him in the café. 'He's a smart operator. Last known employment, MI6; now running free, and dangerous. He and I worked together on quite a few projects in Malaya and Singapore and he knows how to move. He looks like an overgrown choirboy but he's a ruthless bastard, and a brave one. Not to be under-estimated. He once dragged me out of a very nasty situation in Singapore when he could quite easily have turned away and nobody would have been any the wiser. I had a bloody great hole in my chest from a Chinaman's .45 but Metcalfe hung around and nearly got his arse blown off for his trouble.'

'Metcalfe?' Violle's memory wasn't at fault. His forehead creased into a frown. 'Wasn't that the name of the guy who . . . Monique . . . ?'

Neurie nodded. 'That's the one. We were very close friends –

but not as close friends as he and Monique became. He was the cause of the split, and the divorce.'

'Perhaps you were lucky.'

'I loved her, Gaby.'

'And still do by the sound of it.'

Neurie shrugged aside Violle's observation. He didn't need telling what he already knew. He called for two more cognacs and ordered another coffee with his. 'I've just been to see this fellow Metcalfe. I thought I recognized him from that grubby little picture the boys produced from the Avenue Beauchamp so I made a few enquiries and found the bugger in one of the rooms in that hotel over there.'

Neurie pulled a curtain to one side and glanced across the road. 'While I was there I tossed a couple of balls in the air and he caught one.' He brought out the small passport photograph of Montbron and laid it face up between them on the table. 'I mentioned this guy's name to him and he picked it up and ran. He knows – or knew – him and I think he might be interested in picking up on the old friendship. I don't think it's anything more than that, mind you, but you never can tell. The English have never been averse to stirring puddings in other people's quarrels, particularly ours, and this is just the sort of guy they'd send. But that's another little road I shall get a lot of pleasure from trotting down. I think by his reaction that Metcalfe might start looking round for his old chum. I dropped one or two names that might tickle his fancy, so I'm interested in his first moves. I think this one's big enough for your personal touch, Gaby. But watch only. Don't take him on, not even if he makes contact with Montbron. If he *does* make contact, drop him and concentrate on Montbron. I'll sort Metcalfe out later in my own way . . .'

'I don't like the sound of that, Gérard.'

'Neither will Metcalfe. Don't lose sight of the fact that it's Montbron and his operational circus we want, and that gets priority. Once you're in touch with him I can join you and we'll roll them up together, but don't forget, we want Montbron running for a spell, so look after him, don't let anyone kick his head in until we've had him in the confessional. Then we'll do it! OK?'

'OK. But what if some other team wants to cripple him?'

'Keep him upright – Montbron, that is. Metcalfe can play his own game. If he interferes and gets thrown into the gutter, leave him there. Montbron's the bloke to cosset. You can go all the way to keep him healthy. I'll move in with you the minute you find out where he's working from.' Neurie sipped his black coffee and stared out of the window towards the Montalembert. 'Of course, this could all be a total blank. We could be sitting on bugger all and Metcalfe may decide that reunions with old Malayan chums have a very low priority whilst he's happily jogging Monique up and down on his knee. And with that in mind, if you don't pick him up here, you can always find him at her place on the Boulevard Raspail . . .'

Violle finished his third mid-morning cognac. 'OK, Gérard, I've got all that. Metcalfe and Montbron. Simple. But—' He placed his empty glass on the table and flicked it with his finger. It skidded across the tabletop and came to rest against the ash-tray. Both men stared at the manoeuvre. 'You can tell me it's none of my business if you like, but have you considered trying again with Monique?'

'You're quite right, Gaby. It's none of your business.' Neurie offered Violle one of his rare smiles. He'd already considered it, several times, and it seemed like quite a good idea. But not yet. Metcalfe had to be shifted first – one way or the other. 'Let's stick to Metcalfe and Montbron. Keep the names simple on the phone. Montbron remains "Diderot". Metcalfe?' He stubbed his cigarette out in the ashtray. 'Call him "Pigeon".'

'Sounds appropriate.'

16

GÉRARD NEURIE HADN'T been exaggerating when he described Monique Bonnet as an attractive woman. If anything, he'd understated it: Monique Bonnet was an exceptionally beautiful woman. She stood out in a city where beautiful women are the norm and when she walked into a restaurant it wasn't only the men who gave up eating and talking to check that the rest of her did justice to the lovely face. It did. Her legs were exquisite, her body perfect. Harry Metcalfe was growing up: love had replaced lust; he wanted her for ever.

He hadn't bothered looking over his shoulder when he left the Montalembert about two hours after Neurie. He hadn't spotted Violle. He wouldn't have spotted him even if he had been worried and looking. Although Neurie had tapped his curiosity glands, given him plenty to think about, a middle-aged watcher wasn't one of them. But it didn't take long for Monique to bring him back to earth when he met her for lunch. Away from the crowd, travelling in her car, they moved downstream to an interesting restaurant just outside Paris. It was the peasantry's turn for a thrill. She drove well, a bit aggressively for Metcalfe's taste, sitting on the wrong side of the car without a steering-wheel, but there was no messing about with men in fast cars who wanted to show her how they flexed their muscles. Metcalfe sat quietly and smoked Gitanes while she got on with it.

Bougival was her idea. Out of Paris by Neuilly and across the bridge and there on the bank of the Seine, inside with the inevitable check tablecloth, or outside on the river's edge, was one of those small restaurants where the food was exceptional and its whereabouts as yet fairly private property. But too good to last.

'Marie-Claire's invited us for dinner tonight.' Monique sipped her Corton-Charlemagne appreciatively as she continued gazing at the hurried progress of the Seine as it sparkled its way to Rouen and the Channel. She spoke English with the hesitant, slightly husky accent of a woman who knows what she wants to say but needs a fraction of a second's thought before translating the French word; she was sufficiently unfluent to make frequent and interesting grammatical errors. It added to Metcalfe's ever-increasing fascination with her. 'Half-past eight. She thought you were nice – even after all the things I said about you! She's worried . . .'

Metcalfe pursed his lips but his expression remained bland. *Oh God! So bloody Neurie's sniffing in the right area. Marie-Claire Massotte's running an OAS cell and Neurie reckons her punching power's one Philippe de Guy-Montbron with a permanent place at the dining table. She bloody well ought to be worried!* 'What's she worried about?'

'Me. That's why she wants to have another look at you. She thinks something serious is happening to me. There's a new vivacity about me, she says!'

Metcalfe drank deeply from his glass. It was a wasted luxury. This was like the old days, you made a guess, an assumption, and you were invariably wrong; it showed how the mind was fitting into the cloudy atmosphere of near civil war. And it had taken Gérard Neurie only half an hour and two croissants to get him gnawing at the bone. He lowered the glass and searched for the new vivacity. Marie-Claire was right. Women were always right. The timing of the invitation was frightening, but it was a bloody convenient coincidence. Had Neurie been to see Monique for breakfast as well and put her up to it? *Jesus! Where're we going?*

'When did all this happen?'

'What, my new vivacity?'

'No, but I think she's right. I think you've found the right man at last! I meant when did the invitation drop through your letter-box?'

'Pardon?'

'The invitation . . . ?'

Monique pouted her disappointment; she would rather have talked about vivacity. 'Ah, that. It was this morning. We spoke for several hours on the phone. She's curious about the man she thinks is going to whisk me off to England. To Marie-Claire, England is Outer Mongolia – though a little bit less of a cultural desert than the last place . . .'

'The last place?'

'Singapore – Gérard.'

Metcalfe kept the grimace from his face. 'Did you put the idea about being whisked off to England into her head?'

Monique smiled disingenuously. She had beautiful teeth too. 'No, she thought it up all by herself.' The smile seemed to lose some of its warmth as her thoughts moved on, but she recovered quickly and wrapped the smile seductively round the rim of the tall, condensation-covered glass. 'Harry, why didn't you tell me you'd seen Gérard this morning?'

Harry Metcalfe's *turbot au champagne* turned into a mouthful of bran and for the second time that day he lost his appetite. He put down his knife and fork and picked up his glass. To Gaby Violle, watching from his car on the other side of the river, they looked like a couple of chess players gazing into each other's eyes over the rims of their long-stemmed wine glasses, each trying to see what the other had in mind for his next move. Metcalfe sipped delicately and gave himself a few seconds' grace. 'Seen'? Christ, it sounded like a visit to the bloody doctor, or a brief sighting of a friend from the far side of the park! What the bloody hell was going on?

'Do *you* see him very often?'

'No.' She sounded tentative – a trace of regret? To Metcalfe it felt like a knife in the groin. 'I was surprised.'

Not as much as I am, darling! 'What did he want, apart from telling you we'd met?'

'Nothing really. He said he was passing by. He mentioned that you'd told him we'd been to lunch at the Massottes and then he asked if I'd like to have dinner with him this evening.

Funny, I don't think Gérard has asked me out to dinner since the divorce. I was quite touched.'

'So am I.'

'Harry, you're jealous!'

'Of course I'm bloody jealous!'

'How quaint!'

'So, how did you leave it?'

'What, dinner? I told him you and I were going to the Massottes. He didn't seem terribly interested.'

'Did you expect him to burst into tears? So when are you having dinner with him?'

'That's funny as well. He didn't suggest another time.'

'Gaby, take the day off.'

'What d'you mean. The day's bloody finished!'

'Go home and put your feet up. Watching's a young man's game. You shouldn't volunteer for things like this . . .'

'Fuck off, Gérard! Is that what you've got me to the phone for?'

'More or less. Look, I know where Metcalfe's going tonight. I'll look after him – tomorrow as well. You be ready to pick him up the day after at the Montalembert. Use the café. If there's any panic, I'll ring you there.'

'You're all heart, Gérard. See you around.'

'*Ciao*!'

After hearing that Neurie was edging back into Monique's frame Metcalfe didn't have to act the part of a dog with its mate on heat. When he and Monique arrived at the Massottes', Marie-Claire's needle-sharp intuition wasn't put to the test; everything showed on Metcalfe's face. If it was left up to him, Monique was about to move out of Paris to grace the uninteresting and damp society of the boring people on the island the other side of the Channel. It might just as well have been ten thousand miles away, like the last time her mate had had that look in his eye. Monique's friends were looking distinctly worried.

Metcalfe weathered the early storm and after three or four

sturdy whiskies sat down at the large dining table and studied the form.

Unlike during his previous visit, the conversation round the dining table was entirely political. And it was heavy politics – anti-de Gaulle but not quite pro-OAS – until halfway through the meal, when the vacant place at the table was filled. Metcalfe had half hoped the missing guest was Philippe de Guy-Montbron – Neurie had almost promised that he was somewhere around this little corner of Paris – but he wasn't really disappointed when, in a flurry of kissing and explanation, an attractive and animated woman about five feet one with cropped pure blonde hair and a figure that made her into a miniature beauty, sat in the empty chair. She was Jeanette Fabre, Marie-Claire's sister, a total opposite in every way: bright, cheerful, optimistic and, observed Metcalfe to himself, a girl who looked as though she knew what fun was all about. She studied Metcalfe with an experienced air. Monique was an old friend. She didn't have to say anything; Jeanette Fabre could work it out for herself. In any case, these Englishmen were so transparent.

Metcalfe enjoyed her attention. What he didn't like was her accent. She must have been sixteen or seventeen when the Americans came to town in 1944 and it sounded as though she'd exchanged her virginity for American-accented English. It spoilt the effect and removed some of the sexiness from the delightful French vowels. But Metcalfe tried not to let it interfere with his admiration. She was direct and to the point, and the rest of the table sat and listened with rapt attention to her views on the Fifth Republic, the leader of that republic, and the modest triumphs of robbery and murder committed in the name of the OAS. She seemed to be well informed, but was either very indiscreet or knew her companions to the point of intimacy. The Englishman wasn't considered a political threat. He was a friend of Monique's – he had to be clean.

After dinner and cognac with coffee came whisky or champagne. Metcalfe was suffering withdrawal symptoms and from a distance watched Monique enchanting two middle-aged colonels in civilian clothes who played their political – and military – affiliation cards with the dexterity of professional gamblers. Unlike Marie-Claire and Jeanette, they viewed the Englishman with caution, though they would have had the same reservations in the most normal times. French Army officers are born with a jaundiced view of the English; *perfide Albion* is engraved on their mothers' nipples. But Jeanette had no such hang-ups. She attached herself to Metcalfe, poured his champagne, lit his cigarettes and invited him to lunch at her place in Buc. She'd already asked the blushing bride, she told him.

He tried once to draw Marie-Claire on the subject of Montbron but she wasn't interested. He mentioned his experiences against terrorists in Malaya and the interesting sort of people one met in the jungle – and on trains – but she didn't nibble. She wasn't interested in Malaya, she was only interested in France, and if Frenchmen found themselves touching elbows with English people in English colonies, that was their business. He discreetly mentioned Montbron's name and it brought no reaction. Marie-Claire was well in control of herself – she could afford to be now – and she didn't even glance at Jeanette out of the corner of her eye. Metcalfe didn't press the point.

But Jeanette was most interested.

17

JEANETTE FABRE SAT on the edge of an overstuffed armchair in a converted attic room in her mini-château in Buc, on the south-west extreme of Paris, and spoke in an undertone to Philippe de Guy-Montbron. He lay on the bed, relaxed, dressed in a dark shirt, drab trousers and a scarf around his neck. His hands were clasped behind his head and a cigarette drooped from his lips, which, every so often as he listened, he pursed, raising the cigarette to the horizontal and giving a sharp puff down its side, expelling the lengthening section of ash.

The room had always been waiting. They'd expected he'd eventually have to move from the Avenue Beauchamp – in these days nothing was 100 per cent secure – but he hadn't planned for such a rapid evacuation. On that day almost a week ago, he'd waited until dusk and, with knowledge of a definite physical watch on the rear of the house, had avoided using the back exit, making his way instead into the surveillance camera's blind zone just at the time he judged the operators would be substituting the mechanical watch for the physical watch and moving into their new positions. He'd judged it to a nicety and by the time routine had been re-established around the front of the Massotte house he was into the Métro and commencing his evasion programme.

It didn't take long for him to determine that he hadn't been followed, but he didn't relax his vigilance. He continued the system of change, counter-change, backtrack, back-mark, stop, retrace and retrace again until he reached his destination and surfaced at Mabillon. He cut through the backstreets to a small café in St-Sulpice and had a casual meal with a *pichet* of *vin ordinaire* and after two more cigarettes, moved on again.

He was still alone.

He doubled back to the Boulevard St-Germain, joined the meandering masses and crossed over at the traffic lights and entered a crowded Café Deux Magots. He bought a *jeton*, descended the stairs, and locked himself in the telephone booth.

The phone rang for some time before the receiver was lifted off its hook. It sounded reluctant and nothing was said for several seconds. Montbron broke the silence.

'D'you recognize my voice?'

'*Oui.*' Paul Vernet's relief was unmistakable; it came down the line and into Montbron's ear in a searing whoosh. 'Where've you been? I've been worried sick. No news, nothing since—'

'Don't say it,' warned Montbron. 'Listen. I'm moving to a new lodge – nothing to panic about. Stick to your change times, don't move about unnecessarily. You know the meet we agreed?'

'Yes. But—'

'Don't interrupt, just listen. OK, you know when; you know where. Be on time. One more thing . . .'

'What?'

'On the way, call in at the post office and see if there's anything for me. If there is, bring it with you. Once you leave your place, don't go back. Go on to the Square and I'll meet you in the café where we met last time. I'll be there first. You sure you know where I mean?'

'I'm sure. See you then.'

Montbron dropped the phone into its cradle and slipped out of the Deux Magots and back into the crowded Boulevard St-Germain. He blended. There was nothing to distinguish one of the leading new assassins of the illegal Organisation de l'Armée Secrète from any other pedestrian going about his pleasure on a warm autumn evening. Montbron was in no hurry. He cut through the Rue St-Dominique to the Invalides and spent several minutes watching his car in the large gravel-based parking area as he went through the motions of looking for it. He saw nothing to disturb his peace of mind and was able to concentrate on his roundabout route through Paris, crossing the *périphérique* to Malakoff before turning west at Vélizy-Villacoublay and across country to the village of Buc. He was installed in his new safe house before midnight and by the time he laid his head on the pillow he'd already sorted out his next move to satisfy Xavier's assassination schedule.

But Jeanette Fabre was not as calm and relaxed as Montbron was. She'd offered a safe house, support. It was the romantic aftermath of the Resistance, she was doing her bit, and Philippe de Guy-Montbron was an attractive man. But patriotic duty was shouting 'Down with de Gaulle!' and '*Algérie Française!*', encouraging the boys with the bombs; it didn't extend to the possibility of squatting in the corner of a damp cell at Fort d'Ivry because some idiotic bugger had no sense of security. Jeanette's instincts had forced her nerves almost to the surface; they were bubbling just short of hysterical.

'This partner of yours,' she said hoarsely, the day after Marie-Claire's dinner party, 'is he totally trustworthy? I'm not nagging, Philippe, but if you make one mistake, this individual could place you directly in the hands of de Gaulle's rat-catchers. One slip on his part, one miscalculation, one careless moment, and you are finished. They'll either hang you or take you quietly out to Père Lachaise and bury you – probably alive. They'll now know who Diderot is. It wouldn't have taken them long to drag a description out of that ugly creature of Marie-Claire's. You must make sure of this man, Philippe.' She stopped, but she wasn't finished. Montbron waited. She was getting it off her chest. 'I can't understand why you've lumbered yourself with what sounds like a total nutcase. What do you need him for? For God's sake get rid of him, Philippe. I don't like the sound of him.'

Montbron smiled gently. 'This was never a one-man bike ride, Jeanette. It's not a game I can play on my own, and it was never the intention that I do a solo run. I needed backup, someone I could trust, someone safe and anonymous. He was all that, but he is only backup. He's no threat to you, I promise. Stop worrying. He might go over the top, but he won't let me down.'

It wasn't enough for Jeanette. 'How anonymous? How safe?'

'I'm the only one who knows him. That's his strength – he's

unknown, he has no name and . . .' He paused to light another cigarette. Jeanette reached out and removed it from his lips, but it didn't assuage her agitation, which showed by the quick, jerky puffs she took on the cigarette. Montbron continued. 'If there's any single person in this country who would die rather than betray me, it's him. He owes me his life. I trust him with mine.'

Jeanette still looked sceptical. 'Just so long as he doesn't lead the *barbouzes* to my front door.' She stared Montbron in the face. 'Tell me more about this very special person. How does he owe you these things?'

Montbron shrugged and smoked quietly for a few seconds. Jeanette thought he'd ignored her question, but he hadn't; he was thinking about it. Why did he trust Paul Vernet? What a bloody silly question. He'd already answered it: he had to trust someone. Paul Vernet, mad as a bloody hatter, probably psychopathic, met all the requirements for loyalty and obligation. But with all that he was going to have to go. Jeanette was right about that. Another disaster like the St-Germain car park and Lemercier himself would come down off his perch and hang him personally! Jeanette studied Montbron curiously as, staring at, but not seeing her, he pulled a face. *I'm going to have to get Vernet into the open. It'll have to be done at the next meeting. Lemercier'll help. We'll tuck him away in the country . . .* Montbron kept it vague in his mind, but he knew there was no other way. Loyal or not, Vernet was mad. It was going to have to be a hospital, and a bloody secure one at that, one with barbed wire and broken bottles on a fifteen-foot-high wall. Montbron felt more relaxed, and it showed on his otherwise taut features, now that he'd brought into perspective the fears Vernet's actions in the underground car park had raised. He lit a cigarette for himself, drew heavily on it and, without removing it from his lips, clasped his hands behind his neck.

'His mother was my father's mistress before the war. She had a baby in '34 or '35 but he never acknowledged it or gave it a name because she was Jewish and he thought it might dilute the aristocratic blood that he presumed ran through the veins of what he imagined to be the pure-bred Guy-Montbrons. But he did what people of his ilk considered the honourable thing: he made her an allowance and provided for the baby. She remained his mistress. When the Germans arrived they listed her as an unmarried Jew with one male child and put a large yellow star against her name – yellow for extermination in due course. My father turned his back on her.'

'Your father, if you don't mind my saying so, Philippe, sounds an unmitigated bastard.'

Montbron didn't take umbrage. He agreed. 'But he came right in the end. Later, in about '42, the SS Special Groups came round sniffing for fuel for the Auschwitz chambers. My father had advance warning and took the boy, who was then about seven or eight, and hid him, but when the Germans began inspecting the town-hall records and found this lady's, they threatened to hang her there and then in the boule park unless she told them where her son was. She didn't, but some kindly soul in the audience did and they promptly arrived at the Guy-Montbron stately home looking for little lost Jew boys. This is where the gambler in my father came to the fore. He produced me and, although I was thirteen, he told them I was her son – and his. He had a likely Hun to play against – one of his sort, a German aristocrat, if you can imagine anything less likely!'

Jeanette pulled a face. 'There's no such creature.'

Montbron shrugged. 'Something must have existed, because my father's argument worked. Half the kid's seven pints of blood had to be blue, he insisted, and that was enough to even out the Jewish share. Then he ruffled my hair and stuck his fingers under my chin so that I could look the Boche in the eye. And anyway, he said, look at him: fair hair, grey eyes and a complete cock! I thought he was going to drag my trousers down and show the German my little winkle, but by now the two of them were already clinking goblets and looking for an empty fireplace to bung them when they'd finished with the old man's ninety-year-old cognac. How could anybody possibly imagine a fine-looking lad like this being even the tiniest bit soiled? Good God! He could even be a German! The glasses splattered into the empty hearth, the two aristocrats thumped each other on the back and it was: "Very well, then, Monsieur le Vicomte, we'll forget about the boy – and I hope your other son soon recovers from the *variole* . . ." '

'You made that up!' said an open-mouthed Jeanette.

Montbron crossed himself in reply.

'*Mon Dieu*!' Jeanette shook her head. 'So your father adopted the boy and gave him his name?'

'That might have been his intention, but he didn't get that far. He changed the boy's name to that of his favourite spa – a place in the Pyrenees; there's no need for you to know which – and then the silly old bugger recruited the local banditry, which now went under its new title of the Maquis, and tried to organize a rescue of the Jews, including his girlfriend, who were now on their way to the ovens. And he almost succeeded.'

'Almost?'

'They got the old man's woman and about a dozen of the others away. The SS massacred the remainder and then went into the hills after those who'd escaped. They surrounded them – my father, the Maquis brigade, the rescued Jews, the lot – and slaughtered the whole bloody bunch. No quarter. No one spared. News travelled fast. The boy and I were whipped away by the local Resistance just before the rampaging Huns arrived and were tucked away, out of sight, in the mountains. By then the gentle Boches, led by the kindly arisocrat, had lost their temper. They blew up the Guy-Montbron house and village and tried to set fire to the old men, women and children in the church. They hadn't really got it down to the fine art they achieved later and some of these people got away, but nobody was ever able to point the finger at the Germans responsible. With luck they all ended up at Stalingrad!'

'Fascinating!'

'It's not finished.'

'I'm not sure I can take much more!'

Montbron nearly smiled. 'I'd always been a father figure rather than his elder half-brother, so the poor little bugger had another major disruption to come. We were looked after by the people of the Maquis until the end of the war, when one of the

Maquisards, a hotel owner, took the boy in and brought him up. I'd had enough. I slipped out and joined up with the Army in Normandy. I didn't see him again until well after the war. He was the only family I had left – and the same went for him. Blood is thicker, you know . . .'

'So they say.' Jeanette was no sentimentalist; neither did she believe in biblical aphorisms. She tried, unsuccessfully, to keep the scepticism out of her voice and turned the remark into a yawn.

But it didn't matter. Montbron was finished with the life story of his half-brother. 'So, in answer to your doubts, we're talking of more than blood. His whole existence is due to the Guy-Montbron family, and they've suffered on his behalf. He is conscious of his debt. He doesn't need to be told. So don't, Jeanette, question the loyalty, or the integrity, of this man.'

But Jeanette wasn't all that moved by Montbron's story; she was made of different stuff. She was cynical, a pragmatist who'd tasted the frailties of those whose loyalties had been above question. 'So you don't think he minds being a bastard and wandering through life named after his father's favourite steam bath and watering-hole? It wouldn't inspire an awful lot of loyalty in me.'

Montbron had the grace to laugh. But Jeanette didn't join in. She didn't need the gift of foresight to realize what would happen to her and her family if Montbron's protégé and half-brother turned out to be anything less than perfect. And then she remembered what she should have told him in the first place.

'There was somebody asking about you at Marie-Claire's last night.'

Montbron wasn't surprised. 'Who?'

'An Englishman.'

'An Englishman?' This was different. 'What was his name?'

She pulled a face. 'Arry.'

'Harry what?'

'I don't know – well, I did know, but I've forgotten. He came with Monique Bonnet. You know Monique Bonnet?'

'No.'

Jeanette stared at Montbron's face. It was serious. She should have mentioned it earlier. She tried to make up for it. 'Monique's no threat. She's nothing to worry about. I've known her for years. She's warm-blooded, kind and thoughtful. No politics. I like her.'

But Montbron wasn't interested in Monique Bonnet. He stood up thoughtfully, then walked across the room and gazed out of the small skylight set into the sloping roof of the attic. He stared down at the enclosed grounds, the fringe of trees and bushy shrubs that surrounded the perimeter. His lips tightened. It wasn't the most secure of holes, in fact it left itself vulnerable to some very nasty surprises. Someone could hide three-quarters of a platoon in that fringe and keep them supplied from the road for weeks without being detected. But it was a question of choice. There wasn't any. Or was there?

Without turning round he said, 'Tell me about the Englishman.'

'I think she's playing games with him. I'm sure she can't be serious . . .'

'Not that. What's he doing over here?'

'I don't know, and he didn't say. He said he'd been in Singapore and places like that, which was when he mentioned your name and wondered if anybody had heard of you, but he didn't say what he's doing now. I really wasn't paying all that much attention. I didn't think it was going to be important . . .' She tailed off and stared at the back of Montbron's head. He didn't appear to be listening.

But he was. And with suspicion. Coincidence? Or providence? He ran his eyes along the top of the wall, which in places could just be seen through the trees, and over the top of shrubs that hadn't quite reached maturity. In the far distance he could see the glistening tops of a complex system of greenhouses, now bordering on the dilapidated thanks to an unsupervised gardening staff. Jeanette, unlike the previous owner – her father – had no interest in gardens or garden produce. Even at this distance Montbron could see a large number of broken panes. But it wasn't broken panes of glass that were causing the frown of concentration, it was coincidence, and Montbron, like any other man in the killing business, had no space in his armoury for coincidence.

'Can you remember what he looked like?'

Jeanette wrinkled her eyes; she might forget names, but not what a man looked like. 'He was good-looking . . .'

'That doesn't help.'

'Tall – taller than you. I came up to about here on him . . .' She ran her hand sideways across her breasts. 'Good physique, fair hair, and a little hole in his chin.'

Montbron turned away from the window. Coincidence! Very suspicious. But it could be the other thing – providence. 'Is this Englishman staying with your friend Monique?'

'I've no idea. By the silly expression he puts on whenever she's near him I should imagine he is – and that he's found something quite unique there.'

'That sounds like Harry.'

'You know him?' Jeanette's eyes opened wide. 'Is it safe? What's he doing, Philippe? Does he mean something?'

Montbron shrugged the questions aside. 'Forget it, Jeanette. How close a friend are you with this Bonnet?'

'Fairly good. Why?'

'Ask her to bring her friend to lunch tomorrow. I'd like to have a close look at him – alone.'

Her face dropped. 'Oh dear!'

'What's the matter?'

'I've already done it – but there are seven other people as well. What do I do?'

'Don't do anything suspicious. You cancel a large luncheon party at ten minutes' notice these days and you'll find the gardens and the front of the house surrounded by tanks and men with little moustaches! Let it go ahead. I'll find a way of gazing into his eyes . . .'

'Don't wander around, Philippe, whilst it's going on. There'll be temporary servants getting in the way and I can't vouch for them, only for Aldolpho. Be careful of the others . . . Are you going to tell me what this 'Arry is all about?'

Montbron smiled lightly. He looked like a man who'd had a

glimpse of a break in black thunderclouds overhead. But the smile didn't last; it was as brief as the break in the clouds. 'Just make sure that your friend Monique brings her Englishman tomorrow.'

18

PAUL VERNET WAS bored. He was bored with being cooped up in one room, his only view the neighbour opposite's sloping tiled roof from a small, weather-dirtied window at the back of a tenement block. Nobody else was going to ring, unless – he almost burst out laughing – it was the man who worked the guillotine wanting to know his neck size! So why not a short stroll? He'd earned it. He'd check on Philippe's mail, a glass of *rouge* here and there, a stroll down to the station to look at the trains, and then back to a solitary lunch and a good afternoon's sleep. He'd got it all worked out.

He checked the magazine of the squat German HK4 automatic, replaced it and worked a round into the breech. He flicked the catch on to safe, slid the automatic into his waistband and closed his coat over it. He glanced once around the scruffy one-room flat and, without regret, closed the door behind him. One more day in this dump and then a move. He was looking forward to a new view. Four days was the maximum he spent in any one place. It didn't worry him.

He approached the Café Sorbonne in the Place de la Bastille without undue caution. There was no need for it and in any case, as he'd told Montbron, he was clean, and had been since he'd arrived in Paris. There was no possibility of his being on anybody's list; he was a face in the crowd and behaved that way. He sat at one of the café's outside tables and drank an indifferent, tourist-style cup of coffee and smoked a cigarette as he glanced through the sporting pages of *France-Soir*. He was in no hurry. When he'd finished the coffee he strolled into the café, paid the tab and moved along the counter to where the proprietor was filling a row of *pichets* from another row of unlabelled litre-bottles of red wine. The man didn't look up or stop what he was doing when Vernet appeared in front of him.

'Monsieur?'

Vernet lowered his voice. 'Is there anything in the box for Colonel Guy-Montbron?'

The café owner finished the *pichet* he was attending to and stared hard at Vernet. 'And you are?'

'His batman.'

'I'll go and see.' He pushed a clean glass across the counter towards Vernet and filled it with purply-red wine from the bottle in his hand. '*Santé*!'

'*Santé*!' responded Vernet and picked up the glass. Turning, he leaned his back against the counter and gazed absently around the empty café. There was nothing troubling him. He hadn't a care in the world.

The man behind the bar studied his back for a brief moment before vanishing through a curtain and then through a door that slammed shut with the movement of the air. He went straight to the phone and with shaking fingers dialled a number. Violle's man answered immediately. The café owner didn't announce himself, but in a whispered voice that rasped through the dryness of his mouth said, 'A man claiming to be his batman has called for the letter. Medium height, dark hair, pale blue shirt done up at the collar, no tie, brown jacket . . .' He paused, then: 'I don't know his trousers – I couldn't see . . . Hello? Ah, look, I don't want any trouble in the café . . . Approach him outside.'

As he gently lowered the receiver on to its rest, the café owner glanced furtively over his shoulder, then opened the drawer of the table where he was standing and took out the letter Violle had posted to the café. He wiped the sweat from his forehead and face and returned to the bar. Vernet was standing as he'd left him, his glass still half full. He dearly wanted to join him with a large glass of the rough *rouge* but he didn't trust his shaking hands to carry out the manoeuvre. Instead, he placed the envelope on the counter and controlled his nerves by wiping his hands with the damp cloth tucked into his apron-string. He didn't offer Vernet another glass and saved his sigh of relief until Vernet was out of the front door.

Violle's man was in the street and waiting when Vernet, after a brief glance in the opposite direction, turned away from the café and headed south down the Rue de Lyon. Rosso followed them on foot and, after a fraction's hesitation, Pietri turned the car into the one-way system and leap-frogged his way behind them. When he saw Rosso cross the Avenue Ledru-Rollin, he went ahead quickly and found a parking place just before the entrance to the Gare de Lyon. He hurried back on the opposite side of the road, then, after a decent interval, crossed it and walked alongside Rosso.

'The Élysée man's following that guy in the brown jacket,' Rosso muttered out of the side of his mouth. 'What have you done with the car?'

'Up there.' Pietri jerked his chin in the direction of the station. 'We gonna take this one out and let the other guy run – or what?'

'No,' snapped Rosso, too quickly, then changed his mind. 'OK, yes, but no blood. Obstruct this bastard, but don't hurt him. I'll go and intercept the muggins up front and we'll ask him what his game is. When you've thrown your guy, dash for the car and bring it to the Rue de Chalon car park. I'll have grabbed mine by then. I'll work him into the car park and we can bundle him up and take him home for a quiet chat. OK?'

'OK.'

Pietri sounded disappointed. It brought a sharp, sideways glance from Rosso and another warning: 'If you hurt him, Pietri, you go too, right through SDECE's front door – and you can explain the other one as well. Got it?'

'Piss off! Say when . . .'

At the end of the Rue de Lyon, Vernet went down the steps and into the subway of the Gare de Lyon Métro. As his head vanished from sight Rosso said, 'Now!', then quickened his pace to overtake Violle's man and pick up Vernet's scent. He was just in time to see Vernet take the subway tunnel for the main-line station.

Pietri moved up next to Violle's agent and they began the descent side by side. It looked like an accident. Even Violle's man agreed afterwards that it could have been. But Pietri knew exactly what he wanted. A slight trip, a stagger, an instinctive grab at the nearest thing – the arm of the man next to him – a gentle push, and the unsuspecting agent was tumbling out of control. Bouncing awkwardly, he landed on the sharp edge of one of the steps and the top of his arm, with all his weight coming down on it, snapped like a rotten stick. But it didn't stop him from falling further. A bellow of pain, and then silence as with shock he thudded from one step to another until he came to rest in a bundle at the halfway landing. There was a short, confused break in the movement of the crowd as the people about him stopped, uncertain, staring with curiosity as he lay groaning until the good Samaritans pulled themselves together and went to his aid. By this time Pietri was halfway back to his car.

Vernet strolled unhurriedly across the concourse of the station and stopped beside a coffee-dispensing machine. He studied the menu casually as he dug into his right-hand trouser pocket for change. That was as far as he got. A hand with fingers of steel clamped on to the muscle of his arm and a voice hissed in his ear, 'Stand still. Don't move. Look down.'

Vernet froze. His stomach contracted and pressed on to his bladder. He did as he was told. He allowed his eyes to drop. The stubby barrel of Rosso's revolver was touching his belt just above his hip-bone; the gun was cocked and rock steady. 'W-wha . . . ?'

'Don't say anything. Stay like that. Keep your hand in your pocket.' Without moving his position, Rosso slipped his hand under Vernet's coat, followed his waistband round and lifted out the compact HK4. He didn't inspect it but dropped it in the pocket of his jacket, straightened up and pressed the muzzle of his revolver deep into Vernet's side. 'D'you know the way to the car park in the Rue de Chalon?'

Vernet turned his head fractionally and stared into the cold dark eyes of a short, thin-moustached man with oily skin.

'*Oui.*'

'D'you want to walk to it or be dragged there with a shattered hip-bone?'

Vernet continued looking into Rosso's face. The urge to pee was becoming unbearable; he could almost feel the warm liquid trickling down his thigh. The walk would do him good. 'W-whatever y-you s-say . . .'

'OK, start walking. If you try to run or do anything silly, I'll cripple you. It's all the same to me.'

Vernet stopped looking into the expressionless eyes. He could see the man meant what he said. There was nothing theatrical here. This was professional. The whole incident had taken only a few minutes and not a person in the station had noticed anything out of the ordinary.

Pietri held the rear door open whilst Rosso said to Vernet, 'Get in and lie on the floor. Then don't move and don't say anything.'

'I'll bet the bastard feels like a good piss.' Pietri had made a study of fear; he knew exactly how Vernet felt. It gave him a slightly erotic feeling and he offered to sit in the back and guard the man on the floor. Rosso was different. He was a professional, with no feelings either way. As far as he was concerned, Vernet was dead – or would be after he'd screamed his life story into the condensation-covered concrete walls of the small, airless room at Montmorency. 'Drive the car, Félix. And don't do anything stupid.'

'Montmorency?'

'Back door.'

Paul Vernet couldn't hold it any longer. When he felt Rosso's shoe on the back of his neck, pressing his face into the dusty carpet at the bottom of the car, he closed his eyes and allowed his bladder to empty.

19

VERNET STOOD IN the corner of the bare, whitewashed room and stared at the blank wall opposite. Pressing his shoulders into the two walls seemed to give him some small measure of comfort, a minuscule feeling of security. But it was totally misplaced. The room had nothing in it, not even a broken wooden stool or a window. He would have liked a window, but the room was lit by a grid-protected bulb set into the ceiling. It produced enough light for him to realize that the whitewash was recent: it still felt slightly damp under his hands as they pressed against the walls, and here and there brown streaks and blotches showed through where the colour had been applied too thinly. He didn't study the brown marks too closely.

He had no idea of the time. He had no idea how long he'd been there. There was no way of telling. He'd been shown politely into the room after his coat had been taken from him, his trouser pockets emptied and his shoes removed. There were no gaps around the door, no keyhole, no skylight, and no little peep-hole for his jailers to check on his welfare. He was puzzled. It was like none of the films he'd ever seen about prison.

It was six hours later that they came for him.

He was squatting, still in the corner of the room, when the door opened and the two men came in. They weren't the same two men who'd picked him up at the station, but they were very similar; they could have been cloned off the same branch.

One stood by the open door and one came in. He didn't say anything but waited until Vernet looked up, then waggled his finger for him to stand. There was no expression on his face as he studied Vernet; then, after a second or two, he crooked the same finger and jerked his head towards the door. Vernet hastened to obey and joined the other waiting man, who at a gesture led him along a windowless corridor. It was more like a tunnel, with every so often a dark, solid door set into the left-hand side of the wall. They were all shut. No sound came from beyond them. He heard his own door close with a heavy thud behind him and then the footsteps of the other man echoing hollowly as he caught up and, without touching him, urged him along so that he was almost running. So far nobody had said a word.

The next room they took him to was totally different. It was more frightening. Bright and airy – too bright. It was like a very modern kitchen with a lot of pure white tiling and stainless steel and in the middle of the room, incongruously, stood a simple stripped-pine kitchen table.

There were three men in the room standing near the table, talking in undertones. Two of them he recognized from the station, the other was another clone, shortish, sallow-skinned, with jet-black short and slightly crinkled hair and a thin gigolo-style moustache. He appeared to be in charge. He stopped talking with the other two and glanced up casually when Vernet came into the room, but otherwise ignored him. The two men who'd brought him from his cell turned away without a word and Vernet was left standing by the door, which was closed softly behind him. His bladder began playing him up again.

Rosso detached himself from Filli and Pietri and took his jacket off. He hung it on the back of a chair and rolled up his sleeves. His arms looked like the back legs of a Dobermann pinscher, black hair straggling out from under his rolled-up shirtsleeves all the way down to his wrists. He turned and studied Vernet as if meeting him for the first time.

'Drop your trousers and go and sit on the table,' he said.

Vernet stared. 'Pardon?'

Without replying Rosso turned his back on him and said to the other two, 'I think this is going to be a waste of fucking time. I don't think he knows a bloody thing.'

'We can try,' said Filli. 'He had this envelope, he had a gun; there must be something he'd like to talk about.'

Vernet wondered if the man talking had seen him – he seemed

to be talking about somebody else he'd met who had an envelope and gun.

Rosso turned and looked at him. 'Didn't you hear what I said?'

'I didn't understand.'

'I said take your trousers off and go and sit on the table.'

Vernet shook his head in puzzlement and slowly dropped his trousers.

'Et les caleçon.'

He removed his underpants and with only his shirt-tail offering a modicum of dignity he stood staring at Rosso.

Rosso jerked his head. 'Table.'

Vernet looked at the kitchen table, glanced down at his bare feet and legs – and something snapped.

'NO!' he bellowed at the top of his voice, then turned around, threw himself at the door and scrabbled for the handle. There wasn't one. The three Corsicans watched: Pietri with a crooked smile; Filli shaking his head sadly. Vernet began to scream when he found the door was solid and immovable and that he was going nowhere. He didn't hear Filli say to Pietri, 'Stop that bloody racket, Félix,' neither did he see Pietri go to what looked like a broom cupboard on the far side of the room, open its double door and remove from one of the hooks a thin, leather-covered pouch about twenty centimetres long. It was shiny, malleable, and in places lighter patches of skin showed through where the leather had worn with use. At its thinnest end was a strap; this fitted over Pietri's wrist like the band of a favourite wristwatch. He tapped it in his other hand with a dull thwack and squeezed it into a sausage shape as he strode across the room to the hysterical Vernet. Vernet saw nothing, heard nothing. One second he was scrabbling at the door, shouting at the top of his voice, the next a blinding white flash behind his eyes – then nothing.

When he woke up he was lying face down on the pine table, his head dangling over the end. He tried to touch the back of his head where the pain was coming from, but nothing happened. He tried to drag himself to his knees, but again nothing happened. And then his eyes shot open as if on springs and he stared at the shiny floor. He tried again to pull his hand up and then looked to his right: his hand was tied to the table leg. The left hand? Same. He kicked out. Nothing. His legs were spread wide apart, as far as they'd go, stretched across the table as if it were an over-wide wooden saddle. His feet were tied together underneath. Apart from his shirt, rucked up under his armpits, and his socks, he was naked.

His brain worked on it for about ten seconds, then he began to scream again. Something was stuffed in his mouth and the scream, halfway up his throat, turned into a paroxysm of choking that blocked his breathing and almost sent him back into a very welcome darkness. But his luck was out. The stuffing was removed while he got over his coughing fit and when his eyes cleared of tears he saw that a chair had been placed near his face and he could now see a pair of knees, crossed and relaxed. A waft of cigarette smoke hit the top of his head and dispersed around him. He began to cry.

Filli allowed him a few seconds to sort out his emotions, then tapped him gently on the top of the head with something sharp. The tears stopped and he raised his head as far as it would go and looked into the flat, cold eyes of Georges Filli. He dropped his head again.

'Where is Lieutenant Colonel Philippe de Guy-Montbron?' asked Filli.

Vernet didn't hesitate. 'He's—'

The sharp instrument pricked him again. 'Don't answer yet, my friend. Think first, think carefully, and make sure that every reply is correct, truthful and without embellishment. We don't want to have to waste time breaking your fingers and things because you haven't thought the question over, do we?' He didn't give Vernet a chance to reply. 'D'you know what this is?' Filli showed him the thing he'd been using to tap his head.

Vernet focused his eyes on it and stared uncomprehendingly. It was an eighteen-inch strip of new barbed wire – clean, ordinary, galvanized barbed wire. But not quite ordinary. The barbs had been removed from the bottom six inches and leather wound round to form a handle; the rest of the barbs had been bent back towards the handle so that it looked like a strip of four-pointed arrowheads.

Filli waggled it tentatively, then said to someone out of sight: 'Raise his head up, Félix.'

Vernet felt a hand grasp his hair and his head was pulled up, straining his neck. He choked again.

'I said, d'you know what this is?' Filli hooked Vernet's nostril gently with one of the barbs and eased his head so that he was looking directly into his eyes. It was unpleasant more than painful.

'It's a piece of barbed wire.'

'That's not a bad guess,' said Filli. 'Tell him what it is, Rosso.'

'It's a lie-detector.'

Filli hooked Vernet's nostril again. This time it drew blood and a little whimper from Vernet.

'Watch,' ordered Filli. He shaped his forefinger and thumb into a tight circle and held it under Vernet's eyes. 'That's your arse.' He placed the tip of the wire in the centre of the circle and gently eased it in as far as the point of the first arrow-shaped barb. He paused, studying the device as if seeing it in operation for the first time, then shook his head in wonderment and slowly pushed in the first barb, then the second set of barbs, and then turned his hand over. 'Goes in quite easily, doesn't it?' he said, sharing the observation with Vernet. There was no threat, no venom; he was quiet, matter-of-fact, like a tutor explaining a practical exercise to a perspiring student. 'But . . .' He paused and raised his eyes from the demonstration to make sure Vernet was still paying attention and that his concentration hadn't lapsed. 'The problem is trying to get the bloody thing out again.' He turned his hand over so that Vernet could see the barbs on the inside of the ring resting in the palm of his hand, and tugged gently on the wire. The points gouged into the curled finger. He held it like that, studying the effect for several seconds, then, without raising his eyes, said conversationally, 'Imagine if I shoved that as far as it would go up your little bottom.'

Vernet's buttocks instinctively tried to close protectively, but nothing happened. Instead, his stomach contracted and its contents roared up his throat and splashed on the floor around Filli's shoes. The last thing he heard was Filli's roar of disgust and Pietri's guffaw of laughter. Then, mercifully, he fainted.

20

NEURIE WATCHED METCALFE and Monique into the Massottes' house, allowed them to settle down and then went for something considerably less sumptuous in a bistro down a side-street off the Boulevard Malesherbes. He returned in time to see them leave at about half-past one. He'd really had no doubts about where they would go after and what they would do. His motives in letting Gaby Violle off the treadmill weren't altogether altruistic. Gérard recognized the symptoms even if he didn't acknowledge that he had them. Three years after divorcing her he was still in love with Monique. Worse, he was jealous of Harry Metcalfe. But it didn't show. It never would.

He saw them home to Monique's flat and waited for her light to go out before driving slowly and thoughtfully through the deserted streets to his own bed. After two strong whiskies he picked up the phone. He didn't bother looking at the time; the number he rang had a permanent watch.

The voice at the other end wasn't even sleepy.

'Tell Lisanne', he told it, 'to prepare a fair imitation of a Ministry of the Interior immediate exclusion order and have it sent round by special messenger at ten o'clock tomorrow morning—'

'You mean *this* morning?'

Neurie looked at his watch. It was quarter to three. 'OK, this morning. Send it to this address.' He gave Monique's Boulevard Raspail address. 'The name on the order is Mr Harry Metcalfe, staying at the Montalembert Hotel, St-Germain-des-Près. Lisanne can think up a reason why Mr Harry Metcalfe should be excluded – anything will do. OK?'

'OK. Good night.'

Neurie didn't respond. He replaced the phone, poured himself another whisky, topped the glass up with water from the tap and went to bed. After he drank his whisky he set his alarm for eight. Five hours' sleep was, nowadays, par for the course.

Monique was sleeping comfortably when Harry Metcalfe got out of bed and pulled on a pair of white boxer shorts. She didn't stir, but lay on her back, her head to one side, sunk into the pillow, her mouth half open as if ready to continue where she'd left off a couple of hours ago. The thin cotton sheet was pushed down so that it rucked in an untidy bundle over her knees. Oblivious to her nakedness, she was dead to the world, worn out. Metcalfe stood and stared for a moment, hesitating, but only for a second. He whipped off the shorts and lowered himself gently on to the warm, silken body. Her thighs opened automatically with his weight and from her deep sleep she responded eagerly, matching her movements gently with his and when he'd finished, without opening her eyes, she went back to sleep. She'd said nothing and made no sound. Everything was instinctive with Monique.

Metcalfe had a brisk shower and then, still damp, padded into the sun-drenched kitchen. He made a large pot of coffee, poured half into a bowl, topped it up with half a pint of hot milk, unwrapped four sugar cubes and dropped them into the bowl, one by one, and waited for them to dissolve. He lit a cigarette, drank half the coffee and stared tiredly at the wall. It was a hard life!

He was still in this position when his exclusion order arrived.

It was ten o'clock.

Neurie arrived at ten minutes past.

He was no friendlier than the last time they'd met, but he did pour his own coffee, still black, no sugar, before sitting down on the other side of the table. He looked relaxed and comfortable, as if he belonged there.

Metcalfe opened the batting. He picked up the stiff, folded document, opened it as if to remind himself of what it was, and then handed it politely to Neurie. 'Is this your doing?'

Neurie didn't take it; instead he reached across the table and helped himself to one of Metcalfe's cigarettes. 'Monique still asleep?' he asked as he lit the cigarette and sat back in his chair, lifting his head to allow a thick stream of smoke to find its way up to the ceiling. It was like chess. You made a move, or asked a question, then put your own interpretation on the lack of an answer. Neurie moved again. 'Have you come across your old friend Montbron yet?'

There it was, all wrapped up in the exclusion order: "I don't like you buggering around with my ex-wife, and you haven't come up with any goodies on the man I'm looking for, so now you're just an aggravating, useless prick and you can fuck off back across the Channel, or unroll your sleeping-bag in a cell in the Santé until we kick you out officially . . ."

Metcalfe sat still. He dropped the order on the table and left it there, waiting for Neurie's next move. There had to be one – there always was.

'There was no sign of him at the Massottes' party, was there?'

Metcalfe said nothing. Neurie didn't want answers; he was just letting him know that wherever Metcalfe went Neurie was right behind. He continued. 'But he has been staying. He left rather suddenly, but he's still got to be somewhere in Paris. You sure he hasn't been in touch? You sure, Metcalfe, that your old friend Philippe de Guy-Montbron didn't send for you to come across and help carry his gun bag?'

Metcalfe smiled sadly and shook his head. It was the best he could do under the circumstances. He felt uncomfortable and vulnerable sitting in the kitchen on a hard chair in nothing but a pair of white boxer shorts, and just behind the door, spread out like an altar sacrifice, naked, and, hopefully, still fast asleep, this stony-faced bastard's ex-wife, whom he still thought himself responsible for. He recovered his cigarettes from Neurie's side of the table and lit one; his previous one, unfinished, still smouldered on the saucer in front of him. 'No to all three, Gérard. I know you've got quite a few problems over here, but Jesus, you must have better leads to the naughty boys than a simple Englishman over here to take the waters . . . You know, the silly thing about this Montbron business is that I don't think I'd recognize him even if you hung him up in a net in front of me. I haven't seen him since 1950-something. Surely you must know someone who's seen him since then? What's he done – or doing? As if I couldn't guess.'

'Go on then.'

'I can't be bothered. Why don't you get out of my bloody hair, Gérard, and go and tread on some other poor sod's toes? I thought you were an assassinator, and here you are nothing more electric than a bloody gendarme looking for someone who hasn't paid a parking fine . . .'

Neurie almost smiled but managed to control it. 'Still the same old clever, cocky Harry Metcalfe!' He put his fingers into the top pocket of his coat, brought out the passport photo of Philippe de Guy-Montbron and laid it on top of Metcalfe's expulsion order.

Metcalfe picked it up and studied it. He pulled a face. 'Jesus! Is this him?' He hadn't changed a bit since Metcalfe had last seen him. 'God, the poor old bugger, he's changed out of all recognition! I was right – I wouldn't recognize him if he was sitting on my knee.'

Neurie wasn't upset. He picked up the photograph and slipped it back in his pocket. 'I'll ask you again. You haven't seen him in the last two or three weeks?'

Metcalfe shook his head.

'OK. I've got a little job for you.'

Metcalfe shook his head again. 'No thanks, I don't want any little jobs—'

Neurie stopped him. He picked up the folded paper, opened it and glanced at the wording. 'It says here "immediate". In French official terms that means you start moving towards England on receipt of the notice. If you've got any gear here, go and get it. I'll give you a lift to the Montalembert where you can collect the rest of your stuff and catch a taxi to Le Bourget. You can be back in London for lunch. Or . . .'

Metcalfe stared at him. The bastard was bluffing. Or was he? He knew Gérard Neurie. Once the move was started, he wouldn't back down. What was the weather like in London? He wanted to glance at Monique's bedroom door. Christ! There was nothing like her in Bayswater!

'Or what?'

'I could have the order rescinded.'

'What sort of job d'you want doing?'

Neurie looked almost unhappy as he reached across to collect his winnings. He shook his head. 'Earwigging. You must like us over here an awful lot, Harry. Either that or you can't stand that bloody awful place you call home.'

The 'Harry' sounded encouraging, but it was probably a slip of the tongue. Metcalfe didn't join in the refound camaraderie. 'Let's talk about the job, Neurie.'

'You're going to lunch today with Jeanette Fabre over at Buc—'

'How d'you know that?'

'Don't be bloody silly, just listen. Whilst you're there, I want you to use those crafty habits of yours and have a look around. If you see anything that doesn't look right, don't disturb it, just ease your way out and ring me – same number as before.'

'Who am I looking for?'

'You trying to be funny? You're still looking for your friend Montbron. He was staying with the Massottes. He did a bunk. The Massotte sister is the same way inclined; she could very well move over in her bed and make room for a guy like Montbron. He'd appeal to their sense of stupidity, same as you would . . .'

'Is that it? You going to tell me what you want him for?'

Neurie stubbed his cigarette out in the saucer and stood up. 'No. And yes, that's it, and it gets you scrubbed off the expulsion list. But the advice I gave you yesterday is still on the books.' He nodded towards the bedroom door. 'Stop playing around with Monique. You're bad news for her. You'll get her hurt again. Go up to Pigalle and buy yourself a *putain* – something that can handle your sort of trouble. Keep away from Monique, Harry. Take that as a warning rather than advice.' He picked up the expulsion order, slipped it back into its envelope and put it in his pocket. He didn't allow Metcalfe to ponder on why it was addressed to Monique's apartment and not the Hotel

Montalembert. 'One way or the other, I'll expect a call from you about five o'clock this afternoon.' He didn't wait for Metcalfe's reply; he didn't say goodbye. He took a moment to drink the remainder of his cup of cold black coffee and left with just a casual sideways glance at the bedroom door.

Gaby Violle took the remains of his third croissant with him when the café proprietor signalled him to the phone booth.

'Gérard?' It couldn't be anybody else.

'Monique and Metcalfe are going to lunch at a place called Buc,' said Neurie. 'D'you know how to get there?'

'Yes, road to Versailles, isn't it?'

'You've got it. I've just lit a fire under the Englishman's sense of security, so if there's anything in, or under, Mademoiselle Fabre's bed he might shift it for us. Don't count on it, though – he's a crafty bugger. But stick with him all the way, Gaby, I've got a feeling about this. Are you all right?'

'Don't ask.'

'OK.'

21

JEANETTE FABRE CALLED luncheon at her house at Buc a simple meal.

Metcalfe spooned a quarter of a pound of finest beluga on to his plate and moved his shoulder to allow the tall, skinny Spanish manservant to lift the chilled five-kilo barrel and carry it to the person on his left. The same manoeuvre was going on across the other side of the long table. He took time out to sample the vodka. He'd been daring. Having been offered the choice of a dozen, he'd chosen the pale pink Petrovska, its little grains of raw cayenne now settling gently on the bottom of his glass. It felt like a red-hot poker working its way down his throat. A large mouthful of the cold caviare helped quench the flames and Monique's thigh pressing against his helped take his mind off it.

It was a very neutral gathering. Preprandial drinks had thrown up no disgruntled colonels, only a couple of old colonials from the eastern reaches of the French commercial empire, and the talk was politics pure and simple. They all took a turn at trying out their English with Metcalfe, even though his French was bordering on the fluent. But it was a waste of conversation. Nothing drifted into the realms of revolution, and treason and the OAS didn't exist, at least not round this table – maybe they'd been warned to be on their best behaviour. In any case, no Philippe de Guy-Montbron. Metcalfe gave up. He stopped looking under the table and got down to some serious eating.

For a moment, whilst Monique was distracted by a question from her right, and Jeanette was arranging for the next course to be presented, Metcalfe, with another mouthful of fiery Petrovska, was, for a minute or so, unattended.

As he put down his glass and fought to keep the tears from

his eyes, he glanced at the end of the room, beyond the table, to the dining-room entrance. The door was being held open to allow the skinny Spaniard to glide through with the two savaged barrels of caviare. Before the door was closed Metcalfe saw, briefly, a pair of hands grasp one of the barrels and place it on a tray held out by another pair of hands. He just had time to see on the tray the makings of a picnic lunch; a small carafe of colourless liquid and a tall brown bottle of what looked suspiciously like Gewürztraminer. Before the door closed the Spaniard paused, bowed his head and, catching Metcalfe's eye, inclined it slightly to the right. It could have meant anything. Or nothing. Metcalfe watched surreptitiously as the Spaniard went one way and the Gewürztraminer the other. Then he lowered his eyes and went for the final drop of fire-water in front of him as Jeanette again turned her charm in his direction.

The second course came and went. Then the third and the fourth and by the time they'd filled the room with inter-course cigarette smoke and caused havoc to a complete round of Brie, Metcalfe had almost forgotten the picnic tray and the Spaniard's manner. Perhaps he'd imagined it. Perhaps the Spaniard liked the look of him and had been inviting him to a private picnic. Perhaps . . . It was after a couple of large cognacs from an unlabelled bottle and a momentary lapse of his hostess's attention that his curiosity was rekindled.

'Is there a loo through that door?' he whispered to Monique, and directed his eyes to where he'd seen the caviare, the wine and the tray disappear. People were standing up and beginning to make their way through to the drawing-room, still talking, still smoking, still drinking.

'Yours is in the hall,' responded Monique. 'Let's go through. We pass it on the way.'

'Is there one through there?' he persisted.

'Sure to be. Why there?'

He didn't answer her. 'Make excuses for me,' he muttered and, wandering round the room looking slightly lost, managed to slide out of the door unnoticed. To the right the passageway led, by the sound of clanking tins and dishes, to the kitchen, but halfway along on the left was a fairly wide staircase, not the main route upstairs, but a substantial set of servants' stairs. He looked round briefly as if searching for a lavatory, just in case anyone was watching, then ran briskly up to the first landing. The stairs continued. *In for a penny!* He steadied his breathing and, in deference to the last huge cognac, which by its unnatural thumping was just beginning to circulate around his heart, went up the next flight at an old man's step-by-step pace. Discounting the very narrow flight of uncarpeted service stairs that led, presumably, to the attic and the water tanks, this was the top floor. There were four doors on this landing and another corridor leading off that made its way back to the main part of the upstairs, where it joined the broad central stairway.

He wrinkled his nose. There was a faint smell of cigarette smoke – fresh cigarette smoke – but he shrugged it aside. With the number of people smoking down below some of it would had to have found its way up here; all the other exits would have been overloaded! He waited for a moment in one of the doorways and heard a lavatory flush in the distance. Then a door opened and, peering along the corridor, he saw one of the female guests make her way down the stairs. He made a note of where the lavatory was, just in case, and opened the door behind him. It was a bedroom. Nobody was using it. The one next to it was the same. He was luckier with the third. It was just below the service stairs and he knew what it was even before he opened the door. It had a bidet in a rich shade of lilac, the same as the bath. The loo was conventional white, with a wooden seat. The seat was up.

He slid round the door and shut it behind him, then realized that the one thing he wanted at the moment was to pee. But it would have to wait. This bathroom, unlike the bedrooms on the same landing, was in regular use. The towel was damp and the soap in its tiny dish was soft and wet; it had been used sometime that morning. One of the servants? Maybe. He walked over to the lavatory and gave a sigh of relief as his bladder settled back to normal. It was just as he was straightening himself up that he heard the faint squeak of the floorboard behind him.

There was nothing else he could do. He put on a surprised expression and turned, his knee relaxed and his weight transferred to his left leg. He kept his hand to his side, out of sight, with the fingers bent inwards and the palm open, ready to ram the intruder's nose up into his brain if he didn't like his face.

'You took your time, Harry.'

Metcalfe didn't relax. 'Hello, Philippe.'

Montbron closed the bathroom door behind him with his foot and leaned back against it. He folded his arms, tucking the Sauer automatic he held loosely in his hand behind his left elbow. Metcalfe noted he hadn't applied the safety, but his expression, and his eyes, showed a wary pleasure. 'You got the signal, then?'

'I wasn't sure. I'm a bit dopey at this time of the day, Philippe – I thought your waiter fancied me!'

'You're not his type. Are you working?'

'Depends what you mean.'

'Have you taken sides?'

Metcalfe grimaced, then shrugged. 'I think I'm supposed to be against you. A guy named Neurie has got my balls in his *pétanque* carrier. D'you know him?'

'Tell me about it in a minute, Harry. Go out into the corridor and up the stairs on the right. There's a little door that opens inwards. I'll be behind you. Just a minute—' Montbron stepped to one side and inclined his head. Metcalfe knew what he wanted. He relaxed his fingers and allowed his limp hands to droop as he lifted his arms out to the side. He barely felt Montbron's hands run round his waist and down his legs to his ankles. There was no ill feeling; he had said he might have taken sides. He did as Montbron instructed and went into the attic room and sat down in the chair Jeanette had used the previous evening. He lit a cigarette and tossed the packet on to the bed for Montbron to help himself. The Sauer had disappeared, but Metcalfe knew that Montbron had tucked it no more than a flick of the hand away.

After Montbron had lit a cigarette, he said, 'D'you want to tell me about Neurie?' He waited a second, studying Metcalfe, then smiled. 'Unless, of course, you've signed on with him . . .'

Metcalfe shook his head. He put on his serious expression, although Montbron knew him well enough to have doubts about it, and told him what Gérard Neurie was, past and present, and where the ball had come to rest. He finished with, 'Like I said, Philippe, he's got me by the short and curlies. No fault of mine, it was coincidence. They were watching the Massottes' house and I walked through their screen. I didn't know what it was about. When Neurie popped in for breakfast with his little pictures, I thought he'd got a watch on Monique and was doing the jealous ex-husband bit. No such luck. He was looking for you and I didn't realize it and dropped both you and me in the shit. He thought I'd come over to hold hands with my old friend Philippe de Guy-Montbron and the more I told him the truth the more he decided it was what I'd come for. So, that's the story. He's put me in the stocks to drag you out. What've you done – apart from joining the revolution – to cause all these flashing lights?'

But Metcalfe hadn't proved himself yet. It was a funny old game. Old friendships weren't investments to be cashed in easily when the going got complicated; they had to be checked and tested to see what their current value was and whether somebody else had bought them behind the curtain.

Montbron had a glance at the small print. 'How much are you committed to Neurie?'

'Only this place. If you're not here, I'm free to run. He won't stop me. But I think he's got a serious team that wants your head. If I give a nil return he might drop me from the game; on the other hand he might think that as I'm honest I could be pushed down another hole. It all depends, I suppose.'

'How long did you say you'd known him?'

'Most of my working life. We were close until the bedroom door opened.'

Montbron smiled sadly. 'Angry husbands, Harry. They never stop being angry, and they never forget. Sometimes they forgive the woman, but never the other man. I think you can forget any favours you owed each other – you've got an enemy for life.' He thought for a moment and drew heavily on his cigarette. All the signs were there for Metcalfe and he picked them up one by one; he was shuffling into the market-place, he was buying. The smile vanished into a frown and he leaned forward with his elbows on his knees. 'But if it's in your interest to play seriously with your ex-friend, you could give me a little start by delaying your story until tomorrow. By then you wouldn't be wrong in reporting that there's nothing of interest here, and you'll be fulfilling your brief. I'll be gone by this evening. What do you say?'

Metcalfe didn't even think about it. 'I've just said, I owe him nothing. You going to be all right on the streets?'

'I'll be clear after this evening.' Montbron studied Metcalfe through eyes narrowed against the smoke from his cigarette. Metcalfe waited. Here it came. 'And talking about friendship, and non-specific favours . . .'

Metcalfe glanced down at the watch on his wrist. 'Keep it neat, Philippe. Just say what you want.'

'I've got a bit of a problem at street level. I've got a partner who's running wild—' In measured tones Montbron laid out his misgivings over Vernet's stability and his unpredictable actions. It didn't take long, no more than a couple of minutes, and it sounded to Montbron, as he voiced his fears to someone who knew what a dodgy partner was all about, as bad as it could get. 'I think Vernet's reached the end of his term. He's too hot-blooded for the modern game and I want to get him out of Paris and buried in the country. That's the fringe of my troubles, Harry, that's what I want your help with . . .'

'What's the main thrust, Philippe? You haven't gone native just to give your little half-brother a taste of life in the trenches. What's the rest of it?'

'Harry, for the time being let's work on the theory that what you don't know they can't screw out of you . . . But it's lethal stuff. I wouldn't ask your help if there was another source.'

'Thanks,' said Metcalfe sarcastically. 'I presume the reward for joining your little caper is a trip under the guillotine!'

Montbron shrugged. He knew Metcalfe – and he knew Metcalfe had bought it.

He was right. 'I'm in. For old times' sake,' said Metcalfe. 'But going back to your team-mate – what if he doesn't agree that there's nothing more for him in this business? What if he's enjoying the sport and tells you to piss off, he doesn't want to chew grass and watch the cows banging each other? That he's enjoying the war so much he'll go freelance if you don't want him?'

Montbron thought for a moment, then his mouth drooped. 'I'll pull him into a meeting and show him the facts of life. This is why I want cover – just in case.'

'Just in case of what?'

'Just in case of what you said – he doesn't want to go. I want someone backing me up with a car if he needs a tap on the head to get him on the way.'

'And that's all you want?'

'Sure.'

'When are you getting together?'

'This evening. It's out in the open, there'll be people about, but it shouldn't pose too much of a problem. There's always the possibility that I can talk him into the car and persuade him to take holy orders! Wishful thinking, but you never know. If that happens, you can fall out and continue waltzing your lady-friend . . .'

'Where shall we meet?'

'I thought we'd go on from here. Incidentally, does the former Madame Neurie know that your balls are in the custody of her ex-husband? Does she know what you're up to?'

Metcalfe shook his head. 'She knows nothing about this business. She thinks Neurie's shoving me about because of her. She thinks I'm jealous. She finds it quaint! I'm buggered if I do. Anyway, quaint or no, how are we going to play this? Shall I drop her back in Paris, then meet you somewhere, or have you something much more complicated drawn up?'

Montbron almost smiled. It took the wariness from his eyes. 'As much as I like you, Harry, I don't think I want to lose sight of you until I've cleared the rendezvous I planned with Vernet.

You might make a little slip and I could find your Monsieur Neurie sitting next to me at the café where we're meeting!'

'It's nice to be trusted!' But Metcalfe understood; he knew he'd been told too much. He'd joined the troupe and his hands were going to stay entwined with Montbron's until Montbron decreed otherwise – whether he liked it or not.

Montbron stubbed out his cigarette and stood up. 'Jeanette'll get Monique back to Paris. Don't worry about that part of it. She'll think up a reason. As soon as these people clear the house and Jeanette and Monique are on their way, you and I can make a move. Oh, and I think you'd better have this—' He put his hand under the blanket and brought out the Sig/Sauer, then held it out, butt first, to Metcalfe.

'Bit small . . .' Metcalfe didn't reach out for it.

'A P-230 .38. It's the guy holding it, Harry, that makes it big or small. You wouldn't want to enter a marathon with a couple of those lodged in your chest. Here, spare magazine.'

Metcalfe caught it, removed the magazine, checked it, and dropped the gun in his pocket. This made it serious – very serious. 'Where are you meeting him?'

Montbron looked at Metcalfe but said nothing. Instead, he picked up the bottle of Gewürztraminer and a glass and held them out to Metcalfe. 'Why don't you finish this up while I find Jeanette and let her into the new rules of our game?'

22

GEORGES FILLI CLEANED his fingernail with the point of one of the barbs and studied first the harvest on the point and then the now spotless nail before moving on, apparently satisfied, to the next finger. The operation seemed to be absorbing his entire attention. But that was illusory. He was listening very carefully to what Paul Vernet was telling him.

They hadn't touched Vernet, not physically, not yet, but they'd done terrible damage to his fear ducts.

'Let's get this clear, Monsieur Vernet,' said Filli, looking up briefly from his manicure. There was no threat in his voice; there was no need for it any more. 'You were forced into backing up this Guy-Montbron under threat of reprisal against your family? That's correct, isn't it?'

Vernet had given up trying to squirm himself into a more comfortable position. The unnatural spread of his legs and the terrible vulnerability of his unprotected anus had long since faded into a numb pain where his thigh joints had locked and deadened; the rest of it he tried not to think about. Lying? They'd warned him about that, but they meant lying to protect Montbron. He had no interest in protecting Montbron – he could bloody well protect himself. *And I hope the fucker gets washed down the drain . . .*

Vernet's brain was alight now. The more he thought about Montbron the more his fear-driven anger bubbled. What did he owe him? Fuck-all! Less than fuck-all. The bastard's family had done nothing for him except bring him trouble, and look where they'd brought him now! They couldn't even give him the name he was entitled to because he didn't fit their bloody image. Well, he'd see about that! Philippe de Guy-Montbron, war hero, smug, condescending, patronizing bastard! If Vernet had been born with the same advantages he too would be strutting around giving the orders, getting the praise. So who had made the headlines at the Boulevard St-Germain? Not Montbron, but Paul Vernet, the man who had taken charge and made the whole bloody country gasp. *Well* fuck Philippe de Guy-Montbron. If they wanted help nailing him to the shithouse wall, they only had to ask! When it got to this stage, the only person needing protection was the poor bugger tied to the kitchen table with his bare arse cocked in the air and a length of barbed wire waiting to prove a point. So no lies – only juggled history.

'That's right, it's—'

'That's enough, don't go into detail – we're not interested in what happens at home. So—' Filli abandoned work on the new fingernail and laid the barbed wire lightly on top of Vernet's bowed head. Vernet closed his eyes tightly; even without pressure the points of the barbs pierced the skin. 'You gave cover while he murdered the guards and then killed the Minister and the woman?'

'Yes.'

'And you didn't kill anybody – it was all done by him?'

'That's right.'

'I have a copy of the police forensic report . . .' Without looking up, Filli raised his hand and clicked his fingers. Vernet heard a rustling of paper as the report was put into Filli's hand by Rosso. 'Which says that fingerprints were found on empty nine-millimetre cases that had been fired by a Schmeisser. Would those fingerprints be Monsieur Guy-Montbron's?'

Trap! The length of barbed wire moved from the top of his head to his nose. Once again he felt it hook into his nostril and he followed the pull so that he was no longer looking at the tiled kitchen floor and Filli's knees and feet but gazing directly into his black eyes. Tell the truth.

'I think—'

'Yes?'

'I think they'll be mine. I loaded the magazines.'

Filli didn't say whether he was happy with the answer or not;

he didn't have to. 'But he killed the Minister with a different weapon.'

'An MAB automatic.'

'And you did nothing except stand and cover him?' Filli exchanged glances with Rosso. It didn't really matter what part this one had played, he was nothing more than a camp-follower. Another threat or two, another little tickle between the buttocks, and he'd be their man. He had no piss left in him at all. 'Never mind. D'you want to help us?'

'What's in it for me?'

'You mean what's in it for you if you don't!' Pietri wasn't happy.

'Shut up, Félix. I'm going to be serious with you, Paul. Félix doesn't like you. If you fuck me about, I'll walk out and leave you with him. I don't think you'd like that. So listen. If I let you help, Paul, I want to be sure that you're not likely to turn over in bed. I don't want you volunteering to help us and then as soon as you get out of the door go snuggling back into this Guy-Montbron's arms. What do you say?'

Vernet didn't hesitate. He'd worked it all out. 'No chance of that. I owe him fuck-all! He'd drop me like a bloody brick if it was the other way round. Besides, he's already going to do that when I don't turn up.'

'Loosen him,' said Filli.

Vernet almost screamed when his legs were released and his buttocks sprung together. He lay unmoving, his eyes tightly closed as the numbness gave way to feeling, then pain, and he sucked air through his clenched teeth, with every two or three of the hisses turning into hoarse, barking noises. He sounded like a puppy with its new-found voice, yelping as the waves of agony swept over him, and when they released his hands his arms wouldn't move and he had to leave them dangling on either side of the table like two dead eels.

Filli allowed him two minutes' ecstasy, then tapped his head with the barbed wire. The shock brought Vernet back to earth; he caught his breath and held it. But he stayed as he was, still as a corpse, listening to the silence and waiting for instructions.

'Sit up.'

With difficulty he dragged himself to a sitting position on the table. The rough wood rasped against his bare bottom.

'Can I . . . ?' He glanced to his left at the other two men. 'My pants . . . ?' He pressed his thighs together and stretched his shirt down as far as it would go.

Rosso studied him through narrowed eyes but said nothing. His expression didn't change. Pietri shrugged his shoulders. Filli tapped the edge of the table with the length of barbed wire as a reminder, then crossed his legs and leaned back in his chair. It only needed glasses of champagne all round to give a slightly clubby atmosphere to the gathering. He shook his head. 'In a minute. Would you like a cigarette?'

Vernet nodded. This was more like it. But he didn't trust himself to speak. When the cigarette was alight and the first ambrosial lungful of smoke had dispersed with a whoosh, he too crossed his legs and then eased his back by leaning on his arms. He was going to live. His brain began to race again. He was going to live! He wasn't going to have that bloody length of barbed wire rammed up his arse. He was going to live and he didn't give a bugger what they wanted him to do – he would do it, and smile while he was doing it. He raised his eyes to the ceiling and closed them. Nobody hurried him. They all knew the after-effects of fear and merely stood around, watching the trembling knees and arms.

But fear is a temporary emotion, like pain easily forgettable, and as the feeling slowly edged to one side, Vernet's agile brain took in the new possibilities. The Corsicans had had him on a plate. They could have hurt him, but they hadn't, not even for fun. They hadn't even pushed before sitting him up. They were all talk; they could be used. And they were on the right side . . . The shaking and the twitching stopped and he opened his eyes. Filli nodded to him encouragingly. He stared back, expressionlessly. And a grateful Corsican capo like this dark bastard must lead to better things. Rosso's 'lie-detector' had clicked Vernet's opportunist's brain into top gear; his fear had changed to a cocky optimism. He'd spotted a chink – a chink to be exploited. But still, a little continued abjection . . .

He tugged another lungful off the cigarette, savoured this one a little longer, and waited.

'When are you meeting Monsieur de Guy-Montbron?'

He told them.

'Where are you meeting Monsieur de Guy-Montbron?'

He told them. No hestitation. Legal assassination – right up his street. Philippe de Guy-Montbron, the smug, sophisticated, aristocratic fucker, lying face down in the gutter and Paul Vernet, the poor little ragged-arsed bastard who wasn't good enough to be called Montbron, standing with the good guys, making the decisions, looking after number one.

'La Taverne in the Place de la Contrescarpe. Just above the Rue Monge. We met there once before. It's safe and secure. You can sit up there all night without being bothered.'

Filli's lips parted. 'You *used* to be able to sit up there all night without being bothered, Paul. But not any more. Not after tonight. And Montbron'll be alone, no backmarker, no friend?'

'He'll be alone. I was his marker.'

'Poor bastard!'

'Leave it out, Félix! OK, Paul, that'll do for a start.' Filli moved away from the table. 'Put your trousers and other things on and come over here. Bring your glass with you and show me on the map where this Place de la Contrescarpe is.'

Vernet did as he was told. Fully dressed he felt comfortable, relaxed and part of the team. The trousers made all the difference. He joined Filli and stared at the large-scale map of the 5th arrondissement. After a moment he stuck his finger on the Place de la Contrescarpe and glanced confidently at Filli's profile.

Filli didn't look up. 'OK, I've got that. Now, what's the name again of that café?'

'La Taverne.'

'All right. Here's paper and a pencil – make a drawing of the square. OK, that's good. Let's have a look at it.' Filli bent over the rough plan, stuck his finger on the right-hand side and said, 'This is La Taverne?'

'Yes.'

'And this, opposite,' he traced a line to the other side of the square, 'is the Café de la Place?'

'That's right. Can I have another brandy?'

'In a minute.' Filli moved his finger to the right. 'And on this side of the square?'

'Le Match.'

'And the time?'

'Half-past eight tonight.'

Filli straightened up and stared at each of the men in turn.

'Got the picture, guys? Good. This is how we'll do it . . . Rosso, you'll be in Le Match, where you can keep an eye on La Taverne. This is Le Match. Point it out to him on your drawing, Paul. OK, Rosso?'

'OK. Parking?'

'Your car and driver'll be tucked away in the Rue Monge. You'll have a runner who at a nod from you will stick on the red flasher and shoot up the road and into the square to pick up our body . . . Let me rephrase that. Our *live* body. I don't want the bugger ruined – only damaged. We've got a lot to talk about, so I don't want the bastard brought home with his throat hanging on to his chest. Have you got that?'

Rosso don't look up. He stuck his tongue in a hollow tooth and sucked. Filli understood; he spoke the same language. He nodded and turned to Pietri.

'Now you, Félix, you'll take a seat in the Café de la Place . . .' He jabbed his finger on to the rough sketch, tapping it as he spoke. 'It's dead opposite so you'll have no difficulty watching it. At twenty-five-past eight you move across the square and grab a chair as close to the target as you can get. Rosso will stroll out of Le Match, walk in front of the target and then turn and draw him. When this happens you'll move in beside him, stick something in his gut and tell him not to move. Lift his weapon, take him over to the kitchen of Le Match, and if necessary do a bit of preliminary work on him so that he won't make too much fuss while you're waiting for your runner to fetch the car. Is that nice and clear?'

'Where will you and the snout be?'

'Don't call Paul a snout, Félix . . . He and I'll be where we can see everything that's going on. Our car'll be nearby, like yours, and I'll have Bachala standing just behind me in case you two need a hand. He'll also be standing next to Paul in case Paul forgets whose side he's on . . . Just a precaution, Paul – insurance – nothing to worry about.' He folded up the paper, stuck it in his pocket and glanced at the blank faces regarding him. 'That's about it. I can't see anything going wrong – can any of you?'

Nobody moved; nobody spoke. Rosso sucked his tooth again.

Filli nodded his satisfaction. 'OK. Anybody fancy a bite to eat?'

23

GABY VIOLLE DROVE slowly to the other side of the square that made up almost the entire centre of Buc village and turned down the same track-like road he'd seen Monique take. He followed the high wall that bordered the road for two or three hundred metres and arrived at a typical château entrance flanked by two miniature towers in front of a tree-lined drive. He glanced along it as he drove past. It seemed to disappear into infinity.

He made a difficult turn, returned to the village centre and parked his car pointing towards Paris, then walked back to the only café in the village. It was a scruffy-looking place with a couple of decrepit metal tables and chairs on the dusty gravel pavement outside. The curtain, three-quarters of the way up a window that looked as though it had last been cleaned on VE Day, concealed the interior far better than a set of heavy metal shutters could have, but Violle wasn't concerned about the state of the place, he wasn't going to spend the night there.

He opened the door to the café. It squealed in protest, but there was no one to suffer it. The empty interior was dark where the crusted window kept out the sunlight. The proprietor was nowhere to be seen. Violle lit a cigarette, then leaned against the marble-topped counter and studied the meagre selection of bottles on the shelves. The café's bad time must be now; normally it would probably have been humming with at least three local drinkers. The choice was pastis, pastis, or pastis. He turned away just as a tousled head appeared round the wooden-bead curtain at the side of the bar.

She was pretty in a Leslie Caron sort of way, but very young. She parted the curtain and walked along to where Violle was standing, unconcernedly doing up the top of a full-buttoned, slightly soiled dress. Her unconcern was understandable. Her breasts were hardly noticeable beneath an apologetic undergarment, and, like her features, were immature. She couldn't have been more than fifteen. The gently growling, satisfied snore from behind the curtain showed how the early afternoon was being spent. They weren't expecting custom, so there had been no need to lock the door.

'Pastis, please,' said Violle. When she stood opposite him he caught the whiff of sex – recent, unwashed sex – but he kept his findings off his face. He flushed lukewarm water into the drink, sipped it and, resisting a grimace, gave her a ten-franc note.

'It's all right,' he said as she fiddled with the old-fashioned till, 'keep it. But tell me . . .' He leaned forward confidentially, his arm on the counter, and jerked his chin in the direction of the window. 'The big house . . .' He paused.

She obliged. 'Château d'Arleaux.'

'Yes. Fabre, I think the name is?'

'Mademoiselle Fabre.'

'Is it very far down that road?'

She thought about it for a second or two and then raised herself on to her tiptoes and tried to see over the curtain at the window, as if to remind herself exactly where the road was. She stayed like that for a moment, then said, 'The entrance is about two hundred metres on the left, with a long drive to the house – about two kilometres. If you want to go and sell something, I wouldn't bother – they're Paris people, they don't buy on the doorstep.'

'Thanks.' Violle took another sip of his pastis. 'If I go just to look at the house, can I carry on and go out another way?'

She shook her head. 'Only if you want to walk across the field. The big gate down there's the only way in and out. And you can't go left, the road only goes as far as the pond. Is there anything else?'

He smiled; it made her day. 'Thanks, I'll try and think of something while I'm waiting for my friend.' He poured another drop of water into the pastis, picked it up and moved away to go and stare out of the window. She waited to see if anything else was going to happen, then gave a half-smile to the back of his head and wriggled her way through the curtain.

Violle took off his jacket and hung it on a chair at a window table. He slipped the MAB PA-15 out of his belt and tucked it into the inside pocket, then loosened his tie and sat down. He sipped again from the glass. It was warm and muddy, how the locals liked it. Ice only came in the winter and then only on the road after it had been raining. Pulling a face, he propped his elbows on the table, then parted the grubby, unwashed curtains a couple of fingers' width and gazed out at the little square and the inevitable 1914–18 war memorial with its four sides crammed with rows of names and enamelled pictures of men who looked as if they came not only from a different generation but from a different planet.

He blew smoke at the gap in the curtains and watched it spread across the dirty glass. It didn't make any difference. All the wars were over – theirs and his – and what a bloody waste of time it all was. He lit another cigarette from the stub of the old one, thought about another pastis and decided against it. He'd better ration them. God knew how long this was going to take. He studied his watch: thirty minutes since he'd seen Monique's car crawl up the narrow lane. It seemed like thirty hours. He sat back in his chair and stared at the wall and the indecipherable, faded advertisements that graced it and blew more smoke at the smoke-stained ceiling. Then he gazed into the square again. The scenery was unchangeable. Nothing would happen to make it more exciting. It was going to be a long wait, a very long wait. He went to the counter again and tapped on it with a coin. There was a confused, hurried scuffle, a muffled curse, a few grunts and a long delay. He resisted tapping again. When the girl came out he ordered half a dozen hard-boiled eggs – 'Don't take the shells off' – and gave in to another pastis. She also gave him a newspaper. He made it last three hours.

For the seventh time he got up, stretched, and did another tour of the café. Once the proprietor had stumped through the curtain, stared at him without speaking and then withdrawn. The only time he saw the girl was when he ordered another pastis. He sat down again and stared at the unchanging scene. Three hours and the only thing that was different was the length of the war memorial shadow. He turned his head away, leaned back in his chair, allowed his head to loll back and closed his eyes. But it wasn't sleep. It was pure boredom. And then something jerked him upright. Eyes open, he turned towards the window, parted the curtain and gazed at the square.

The unchangeable had changed.

A single-decker country bus had pulled up in the shade on the opposite side of the square, on the corner of Monique Bonnet's road to Buc. He widened the gap in the curtain fractionally so as not to miss any of the excitement.

Three people got off, two men in their going-to-market best clothes and a woman with a small child on one hand and a cluster of loaded heavy-duty raffia shopping bags on the other. She was sweating already and she'd only got as far as the memorial. She walked briskly past it as if it didn't exist. It didn't in her mind, or vision; she'd seen it every day for the past forty years. The men from the bus were heading for the café. So was she.

The activity brought a rush of interest from behind the counter. Violle didn't take his eyes off the square but he could hear the wooden beads flicking and flacking behind him to the sound of the male voice and the squeaky consonants of Leslie Caron. Then the woman and child came in through the creaking front door and the girl suddenly appeared at Violle's side, busying herself picking up his glass and wiping the table. The woman with the shopping bags gave her a brisk, suspicious glance and an even more suspicious one to the man behind the counter, his elbows propped on the marble top as he studied the non-existent polish on an empty glass. He looked as though he'd been in that position for the past three hours. Violle hoped her nose wasn't as sensitive as his. The two men who'd got off the bus sat down at one of the outside tables and lit their Gauloises. They were in no hurry. It was just as well, since there was no rush to find out how much water they wanted with their pastis. One of them banged the table with a coin. Violle went back to his gap in the curtain – just in time! He'd almost missed it.

The nondescript black Peugeot slowed and moved at walking pace past the stationary bus, then changed gear opposite the café and headed out of the village. Violle hadn't seen where it came from – he'd been too busy watching the café owner's wife – but he had a clear view of Harry Metcalfe, and beside him the driver, recognizable even from a tiny passport photograph.

Philippe de Guy-Montbron looked neither right nor left. He wasn't expecting watchers. And Violle wasn't expecting to see Montbron – not cruising past a shabby café on his way to Paris with his target, H. Metcalfe, sitting in the passenger seat looking as relaxed as if he was on his way to a picnic. Violle had time to note the car's registration – there was nothing else he could do, other than run out into the square and pump 9mms fruitlessly in the direction the car had taken. That would take Madame's mind off what her husband had been up to while she did the shopping! The set expression on Violle's face didn't crack as he stood up and took his jacket from the back of the chair. The weight of the MAB dragged it down but he left it where it was, in the pocket, paid for his eggs and final pastis, moved stiffly out into the bright sunshine and then hurried towards his car. He caught up with the Peugeot just before it filtered on to the autoroute to Paris.

Montbron stayed on the autoroute until it ran into the Place d'Italie and then turned down the Avenue des Gobelins.

'Hold tight, Harry!'

Montbron jinked through the orange traffic lights, skipped round an indecisive bus, passed on the wrong side a wavering female in a new Renault and, against the traffic, shot across the Rue Monge.

'Jesus!' Metcalfe closed his eyes.

Violle watched the manoeuvre, crossed the lights carefully and pulled into the side of a road a short distancc into the Rue

Monge. By twisting in his seat he could keep the Peugeot in sight. It was just a question of gauging what Metcalfe and Montbron were going to do next. Montbron didn't make it easy for him.

'Just in case anybody liked the look of us!' grinned Montbron. The grin sat awkwardly on his normally sombre features but he seemed to be enjoying himself; either that or he was as nervous as Metcalfe. He pulled into the side of a café-lined corner and opened the door. 'Park the car anywhere round here, Harry, as long as it's easy to get at and pointing in that direction.' He frowned for a moment at the traffic in the Avenue des Gobelins. 'An orderly retreat, no squealing tyres. You might be driving. When you've parked, go up that road there.' He pointed in front and to the right. 'The Rue Mouffetard. Carry on until you get to a small square surrounded by restaurants. That'll be the Place de la Contrescarpe. I'll be sitting outside the café on the south side of the square. It's called La Taverne. Make your way across the square so that I can see you. Don't approach me – just keep your eye on me. OK?'

'Sure. Who else am I looking for?'

'Vernet. About five feet five, cropped black hair, jet-black eyebrows that meet over his nose. He's got a round chubby face and a bit of a belly. He's going to be fat if he doesn't watch it. He should be sitting beside me. I'll give you the nod if I need help. Otherwise, if we get up and walk away and I haven't got his arm screwed up round his ears, just follow and make sure we're clean. You happy about that?'

'So far. Have you got any other enemies in town other than Gérard Neurie?'

Montbron looked at Metcalfe searchingly. 'I think you could bet money on that, Harry. But now's not the time. Perhaps over a drink later . . . ? See you up there in the square.' With that he slipped out of the Peugeot, cut back to the Rue Monge and began walking, fairly briskly, north.

Violle cursed when Montbron and Metcalfe parted company. He jammed his car at an angle between two others – they were going to have a very interesting time working their way out – and eased himself out of the driving seat. He stayed on his side of the road and moved in Montbron's wake. He had difficulty keeping him in sight. When Montbron turned left at the Rue Rollin, Violle stayed on his side of the Rue Monge until he was level. It was just as well. Montbron was standing idly staring into a corner-shop window; he hadn't gone to sleep. When he was satisfied he wasn't being followed he moved off, up the sloping Rue Rollin towards the Place de la Contrescarpe.

There were a lot of people about in the square. It was a warm evening and dinner-time. Violle, jacket draped casually over his arm and tie rolled up in his pocket, melted into the crowd, but there wasn't much for him to do. Philippe de Guy-Montbron had vanished. He stood for a moment near the side wall of a shop and gazed about him. He wasn't too worried. He had an instinct for this part of the act. Montbron's car had been garaged, he'd walked the last part of his route covering his rear, though not very effectively, so he wasn't all that worried, and had come to the Place de la Contrescarpe – he had to be around here somewhere. He'd turn up. Violle turned back, stepped into a small bar and pointed to the phone at the end of the counter.

'Help yourself,' grunted the barman.

'A glass of red while I'm using it . . .'

Violle dialled Neurie's contact number. He didn't say who he was. She didn't ask. 'Tell Neurie that his Pigeon has joined up with Diderot,' he said, 'and they're both in the vicinity of the Place de la Contrescarpe, near the Rue Monge. Tell him I've made Pigeon second choice and that I'm concentrating on Diderot. Tell Gérard to join me here and we can either roll him and his contacts up together or let them all continue to run, but under control. He can decide on the spot.'

'Where will he meet you?' she asked.

Violle put his hand over the mouthpiece and pointed his chin at the barkeeper. 'What's the name of the café on the far corner?'

'The Café de la Place.'

Violle repeated the name into the phone. 'I'll meet him there when I find out where he goes to ground. Tell him to wait if I'm not there.'

'Just a minute,' cautioned the voice. 'This Diderot . . .'

'Yeh?'

'You know Gérard wants him kept upright?'

'Yes, I do. What about it?'

'There's a clear directive here – nobody must be allowed to push him over. You know what that means?'

'I initiated the bloody thing! But don't worry, you can tick it as having been passed on. I'll look after him.' He drank his wine in a gulp, thanked the barman and walked slowly back into the square. Starting at the Café de la Place, he began looking for Montbron.

Félix Pietri, sitting in the second row of tables on the café pavement, continued sipping his glass of Ricard. He didn't give Violle a second glance.

Violle stopped and studied the menu on the glass door of the Café de la Place as he peered inside. It made him feel hungry. He'd only eaten boiled eggs since breakfast, but any thought of food vanished when again he saw the photograph of Philippe de Guy-Montbron come to life, this time walking towards him on the opposite side of the road. He continued staring at the menu as, from the corner of his eye, he watched Montbron turn past the Café Le Match, cross the square and work his way among the outside drinkers in the other café – La Taverne.

Violle moved away from the menu and walked slowly back the way he'd come. He waited for a minute or so on the corner, from where, by turning his head only slightly, he could see that Montbron had made himself comfortable at an empty table on the far end of La Taverne's pavement area.

Violle nodded to himself in approval. Montbron had thought it out, he'd done it properly. If he didn't like the company, or the atmosphere, all he had to do was step over the trough of knee-high greenery and disappear into the crowd on the corner of another narrow access road. Easy! And he had the view covered as well. Nothing was going to happen in the tiny square without his seeing it. The man knew exactly what he was doing. He was offering no chances.

Violle continued round the perimeter of the square, crossed the road on the far side and gazed into the window of a shop selling tourist rubbish. He looked up and down the narrow street. There was no sign of Metcalfe, just an awful lot of flower people, students with only peace and pot on their mind. He didn't linger but wandered with them. On the other corner of Montbron's café two straggly-bearded youths with unwashed hair down to their waists made acceptable noises on a couple of Spanish guitars. Stopping to watch for a minute, he caught the eye of one of the players, who winked at him and then smiled an invitation. He stared back blankly, then dropped a couple of shiny new franc pieces into the guitar case and moved on towards the entrance to the café. He stood for a moment and studied the crowd sitting at the tables on the pavement. He didn't look directly at Montbron, but he didn't avoid him. Montbron had a whisky in front of him with a small *pichet* of water. He didn't give Violle a second glance, but picked up his glass, sipped from it, and continued his discreet but systematic quartering of the area.

After a moment's apparent indecision on the corner for the benefit of anyone watching, Violle made his way casually among the occupied tables and sat down in the row behind Montbron, just beyond his left shoulder. Montbron didn't turn round; his eyes were locked on the activity around the square.

Violle waited a moment, then raised his finger and when the waiter appeared at his shoulder ordered a cognac and a black coffee. It was now a question of waiting to see what Montbron was doing in the Place de la Contrescarpe; who he was meeting and what his next move was going to be. Or . . . ? He re-arranged his coat lying on the chair beside him so that the MAB wasn't caught up in its folds. Or, if he looked as though he was getting restless, sticking the MAB in his left ear and telling him to hang around until Gérard Neurie arrived to take him home for a quiet chat over the other half of his whisky and water.

He sipped from his glass of cognac and rubbed the stiffness

from his thigh. It was instinctive. In a moment he was probably going to be throwing himself around like a full back. There wouldn't be any thoughts of stiffness then – or boredom. The cognac was helping. It had almost met the medicinally warm pastis he'd had in Buc, and thinking about medicine, he picked up the glass and threw the contents straight down his throat. He stared at the back of Montbron's head, still and unmoving, and could almost see the eyes swivelling. There was no relaxation in the set of the shoulders; the man was like a coiled spring. But there was something missing. Violle raised his finger for another cognac. Where the bloody hell was Neurie's English ex-friend Metcalfe? He glanced across the square at the Café de la Place and ran his eyes down the row of tables outside. He wasn't there. Then the other cafés in turn – not there either. If he was covering Montbron he was making a bloody poor job of it. He allowed his eyes to return to the back of Montbron's head. Maybe he'd just come to the Place de la Contrescarpe for his dinner after all!

Violle took a mouthful of coffee, replaced the cup and picked up the small brandy glass. He held it to his nose and sniffed gently as he studied Pietri picking his way through the people hanging around the centre of the square. Nothing suspicious – Pietri meant nothing to him – but for a second or two he stood out among the wandering tribes as a man who had a definite place to go. Violle lowered the glass to his lips and sipped as Pietri sidled round the table next to Montbron and lowered himself into the vacant chair. The other occupant of the table said nothing. Montbron glanced at him casually but nothing registered except a man with a swarthy complexion, shifty eyes and a navy-blue coat over a white open-neck shirt, its collar folded over the outside of the jacket. He looked just like 50 per cent of the crowd. Violle hadn't lost interest in him.

Vernet and Filli, along with a bulky, fair-haired gorilla named Bachala, watched the square from the inside of La Taverne's glass front door. They were concealed from view by the neck-high lace curtain that covered the entrance. But it wasn't enough for Vernet. With both hands in his trouser pockets and head hunched into his neck, he crouched as far back as Filli's grip on his arm would permit. He was frightened.

Filli's eyes didn't miss a thing. He hadn't missed the movement of Violle's head as he inclined slightly to study Pietri's profile, and he pinched his fingers into Vernet's neck as he urged him forward to study the man sitting behind Montbron. He could feel the shivering in Vernet's body even as he moved his grip and tightened it on the back of his neck.

'That guy sitting behind your Guy-Montbron,' murmured Filli out of the corner of his mouth, 'is he one of your team?'

'We d-don't h-have a t-team,' stuttered Vernet. 'It's l-like I told you, it's j-just him and me.' He was reluctant to move out of the safe anonymity of the café curtain; he didn't want to take the risk of having to look into Montbron's eyes. The only move he would have welcomed was a quick dash downstairs where he could empty his bursting bladder and press his face against the rusty cistern behind the locked door of the primitive lavatory until it was all over.

'Look!' insisted Filli. 'He's just to the left of your friend and almost behind Pietri.' He tightened his grip on Vernet's neck. 'Bloody well look!'

'I don't know him. He's nothing to do with us.'

'Fuck it. I don't like him! Watch Paul, Bachala. If he tries to run for it shoot him in the stomach.' Filli moved through the door like a whisper and, with his back pressed against the glass front of the café, slipped along until he was level with Violle and Pietri, about five rows of occupied tables behind and about eighteen inches of pavement gradient above. His automatic was cocked and in his hand. Nobody seemed to have noticed him.

At twenty-five-past eight, Rosso came out of Le Match, turned left and started towards La Taverne. He spotted Pietri in position and allowed his gaze to slide over Montbron. There was a lot of animal instinct working in the square. He didn't stop. He glanced upwards over Montbron's head and made eye contact with Violle. It was momentary, just a flicker, but enough. Violle read his mind. Then Rosso caught sight of Filli standing in the background. This wasn't part of the plan. His surprise showed and Violle's MAB was out of the folds of his coat in the same second as his own appeared in his hand. Pietri turned in his chair and jammed his short-barrelled Special into Montbron's side. 'Don't mo—' The rest was drowned out by the explosion of Violle's automatic. The bullet thudded into the side of Pietri's head, the force of the impact propelling him out of the chair to flop in a confusion of arms, legs and blood at Rosso's feet.

Violle sensed the danger from behind and moved sideways, but his leg caught in the angle of the chair and delayed him. He was moving, but he was a fraction of a second too slow.

Filli's single shot into the back of his head killed him instantly.

Montbron's reflexes didn't let him down. He too had seen Rosso's change of expression and the scent of danger almost blocked his breathing. His hand was already on the butt of the Browning and his thumb had automatically hauled back the hammer from its half-cock when he felt Pietri's weapon gouge into his side and heard the unfinished guttural sentence, broken off by the explosion of Violle's automatic. He was on his knees when Filli's second shot rang out. Scrabbling past Pietri's twitching body, he crashed unintentionally into Rosso's legs, throwing himself off balance. He hadn't considered Rosso. He thought all the danger was behind; it was only when he partly recovered that he saw Rosso's arm straighten and begin pumping bullets from the heavy automatic in his hand. He fired once, upwards into Rosso's stomach, and Rosso's scream as the .45 tore through his body rose several pitches over the pandemonium echoing round the once tranquil square. As he straightened he fired again into Rosso's doubled-up figure and then heard the repeated shots coming from the back of the café. He didn't stop to work out who else was in the act. He couldn't see Filli, whose bullets were howling off the hard pavement, zinging with high-pitched whines around the square, but he knew where they were coming from and that he had to run through them. There was only one thing he could do: stay low, and get out.

Ignoring the screams and shouts of people still ducking for

cover, Montbron leapt over Pietri's body and at a crouch dived for the corner of the square.

Harry Metcalfe watched him come.

He'd tried each of the little side-streets without luck. He'd eventually settled for the car park in Daubenton but had had the long walk back up the Rue Mouffetard to get to the Place de la Contrescarpe. He'd just reached the corner of the square when the first shot rang out. Pressing hmself against the wall, he'd inched his body round until he could see the whole of the square. The two hairy musicians were flat on the ground with their faces pressed against the pavement. Other people were scrabbling round in the centre of the square looking for a place to hide, and in the three or four cafés there was chaos as people who one minute earlier had been sipping aperitifs, relaxing, now threw themselves amid the crashing of tables and chairs into the doubtful security of the bars and restaurants. Two more shots sent the pigeons flapping off their new perches on the rooftops and the only ground activity now was in the far corner, on the side of La Taverne.

Still pressed against the wall, Metcalfe opened his jacket and slipped his hand inside, easing the Sig/Sauer out of his waistband. He didn't bring it out into the open, but kept it concealed in the fold of his jacket. One of the bearded guitar players watched with one eye, but when he caught sight of the butt of the weapon he quickly turned his head and pressed his face into his arm. He didn't want to know.

Metcalfe watched Montbron's progress. There was nothing else he could do. His hand still rested on the stubby Sauer and he hadn't seen Violle go down, but there was no question about the man under fire, crouching almost double, and heading directly for him.

He stepped back, edging round the corner as he hauled the Sauer from under his jacket and held it at his side. As Montbron turned the corner and straightened up, he grabbed his arm and pulled him into safety.

Montbron was out of breath – exertion and fear – and he scrabbled for his balance on the slippery cobbles as Metcalfe snapped, 'Keep running, Philippe. I'll join you. Go on! I'll catch you up . . .' He peered round, then leaned back as another bullet thudded against the wall.

'You stupid bastard – you're going to get your bloody head blown off!'

'Bugger off, Philippe! I'll catch you . . .'

The screaming was still coming from the square, where Filli's voice was making itself heard over the pandemonium as he crashed among the upturned tabes and chairs outside the café. As they gathered themselves to bolt down the road, Montbron lost his footing and staggered against the wall.

And then Filli arrived. He hurtled round the corner, saw Metcalfe first, then Metcalfe's automatic, and without hesitation fired two wild shots at him. Metcalfe ducked, sent a quick unaimed shot over Filli's head, and as the Corsican disappeared back round the corner, he grabbed Montbron by the collar of his jacket and pulled him into the road.

'Quick! Where?'

'Follow me!'

Scrambling to his feet, Filli poked his head round and fired twice before ducking back out of sight. One bullet splattered on to the pavement by Montbron's foot and whistled off down the narrow street, sending more pedestrians scampering for cover, and the other thumped into the wall beside Metcalfe's head. If Metcalfe hadn't already got the message he got it now. Close proximity to Philippe de Guy-Montbron had served him with a death sentence. He waited until Montbron was scuffling down the Rue Mouffetard before scampering to the other side of the street. Filli and Rosso's runner danced round the corner together, but before they could aim their weapons, Metcalfe sent two quick shots in their direction.

Rosso's runner walked into both and stopped dead as one of the bullets caught him in the throat and tore through his jugular. He hung there for a second, surprised, then dropped his weapon and crashed into Filli, dragging him down with him. Metcalfe aimed at Filli's head. There was nowhere for Filli to go. The runner died and collapsed on Filli's arm, trapping the automatic under his body. Metcalfe and Filli stared at each over the sights of Metcalfe's Sig/Sauer. Filli didn't flinch, but stared, unblinking, as if memorizing a new enemy for the next world. Had it been the other way round there would have been no hesitation, Metcalfe would have been dead, one in the heart, one in the head, and then he'd have worried about who the hell he was.

But Metcalfe still hadn't sorted out the argument. He was there to act as back-up to a friend who'd come to collect a little man with dark hair and a tendency towards fat – a little man named Vernet. He hadn't bargained on war. He shook his head, lowered the Sauer and turned and ran, skidding and slipping on the smooth cobbles in Montbron's wake. Filli watched him go, then closed his eyes briefly and let out the breath he'd been holding. He pushed the dead man off his arm, rolled over and crawled back round the corner into the confusion of the square.

By the time he got back to Vernet and Bachala, curiosity was slowly overcoming fear and people were timidly getting to their feet and forming a crowd around the pavement in front of La Taverne. Filli ignored them. In the immediate distance he could hear multiple sirens as police vehicles converged on the Place de la Contrescarpe. He let the morbid have their moment – they'd earned it – and crooked his finger at Bachala, who had remained where he'd been told to with one hand firmly grasping a pale and sick-looking Vernet by the arm whilst the other ostentatiously held a police MAB automatic. He didn't let go of Vernet as he approached Filli.

With the two men following him, Filli pushed his way through the ring of people silently studying the different aspects of death. He glanced briefly at Pietri. He was lying face downward and there wasn't a lot left of the back of his head. He looked peaceful enough. Rosso had suffered. He'd ended his death dance squeezed up against someone's scooter with both hands pressed into his body in an unsuccessful attempt to keep his stomach from falling out of the hole made by Montbron's soft-nosed .45. His face showed the agony, and the fear. His death hadn't been a nice one.

'Cover him up,' said Filli to no one in particlar as he turned his back on him and elbowed his way to the tables. He lit a cigarette, flicked the match into the gutter and said to Bachala, 'Get rid of these morbid bastards.' He looked at Vernet. His face was blank, there was nothing to be read there, but it was no consolation to Vernet. 'Let go of him,' he ordered Bachala and jerked his finger at Vernet. 'Come with me, Paul.'

Bachala waved his pistol and the crowd around Violle's body edged back. But not far enough for Bachala. 'Go on! Fuck off! The whole bloody lot of you . . .' Nobody moved even when the square began to fill with flashing blue and red lights. The police were arriving in strength.

The first car skidded into the square and disgorged four seriously armed Special Action Police who rapidly fanned out into the square. The crowd melted away to the far pavements and watched. One of the new arrivals pointd his machine-pistol at Bachala and let go of the safety-catch.

'DST,' said Bachala cautiously.

The policeman's face was like a wood carving, and his finger was on a hair-trigger. 'Put that weapon on the ground.'

'I said I'm DST.'

'Do as he says,' said Filli without looking round.

'You turn round as well.' The policeman's eyes flicked briefly at Filli, then he raised the machine-pistol to his shoulder and aimed it at Bachala's face. Without taking his eye off the policeman, Bachala bent at the knees and placed the revolver on the ground in front of him.

'And you.'

Filli did the same.

More police were arriving, bigger cars, higher ranks. One of them recognized Filli and relieved the armed policeman of his responsibility. By the time the square was cleared of sightseers Filli had emptied Violle's pockets and placed the contents on one of the small tables. There was nothing there to associate him with the Élysée or with any of the intelligence services. Filli had already formed a conclusion. 'Have a good look at him, Paul.' He lifted Violle's head and turned his face upwards. 'He's got to be a friend of your friend Montbron. He was covering for him, and by the way he brought that piece out of his coat he was expecting trouble. Tell me about him.'

'I told you, Monsieur Filli—'

'Call me Georges.'

'Georges – I've never seen him before in my life. Montbron only came on to the streets for the Gautier job, and he came alone. That's why he recruited me as his back-up – he knew he could trust me. He didn't want to go public . . .'

'All right. You've told me all that before.'

'I did say—'

'OK. Shut up!' He turned to Bachala. 'Hang on here, Claude, and tell the *flics* anything they want to know about Rosso and Pietri. Keep your ears open about this bugger—' he jerked his chin at Violle '—just in case somebody does an on-the-spot ID. I've already spoken to the cheese there. If he says anything to you, tell him that the DST expects a full identification when the report's completed – my name on the cover and it comes to Montmorency. OK?'

'OK, Filli.' He wasn't invited to call him Georges.

24

MONTBRON WAITED AT the bottom of Rue Mouffetard until Metcalfe drew level with him. He kept his eyes about him whilst in his jacket pocket his hand maintained its tight grip on the Browning. He glanced sideways at Metcalfe, but Metcalfe was looking straight ahead; he had other things on his mind.

They were both walking, not rushing, a casual movement matching the lack of urgency of the people around them. They had become part of the evening crowd, but walking in a different direction to most, who were heading towards the shooting as part of the evening's entertainment. Neither man spoke until they were in the car and moving, with the rest of the slow evening traffic, along the Avenue des Gobelins, towards the Place d'Italie.

Metcalfe lit two cigarettes and passed one to Montbron. They'd both recovered their breath, the adrenalin had receded. 'You didn't say it was war, Philippe.' He didn't look at Montbron as he spoke. 'I don't think you've been altogether straight with me.'

'You sticking around?'

'Have I got a choice now?'

Montbron shrugged. 'You killed a *barbouze*, a Corsican one. They take that sort of thing very seriously. I think you've got a choice of staying with me or taking your chance on trying to get out of the country. They'll be looking at you with very serious intent, Harry – you could become a liability. But by the way, thanks.'

'A liability to whom?'

'Me. But let's get out of here. We'll talk about it later. I might have to pay you off.'

'Perhaps I ought to thank you for allowing me to very nearly get my head blown off!'

But Montbron wasn't in the mood. 'That was a set-up. They'd got the bloody place pegged out . . .'

'Vernet?'

'No! He may be a bloody madman, but he wouldn't put my head and his arse into a bag by stupidity. He's no reason, no opportunity, and besides, he wasn't due until half-past eight. The excitement started before that.'

'I wasn't implying an on-the-spot ambush from a follow job.'

'What are you implying, Harry?'

'That he was responsible for the set-up, that he's gone over – or been turned.'

'That's bloody stupid! He's got more to lose than I have. No, this is something else.'

At a traffic light Metcalfe wound down his window and flicked out his half-smoked cigarette. He lit another one almost immediately. His nerves were still tingling. He gave up the Vernet theory; at least he gave up expounding it. 'How'd it go wrong, then?'

'Like I said, I think they moved in on the spur of the moment. They hadn't closed the door properly. There was a guy who must have been sitting just behind me – he wasn't on their side. He helped me out and got this head blown in for his trouble. The last I saw of him he'd gone to sleep on the table. He looked very dead.'

'Perhaps he was a good Samaritan.' Metcalfe blew smoke at the windscreen. 'Or an interfering bugger who couldn't duck out of the way in time.'

'He was Trade, Harry. He killed the guy who shoved a gun in my side. It's been worrying me. I don't suppose he was that friend of yours, Neurie, by any chance?'

Somewhere behind them, but a long way off, a police siren howled and then faded. Metcalfe glanced quickly over his shoulder. He saw nothing to upset him and turned back. 'I didn't see him, there was too much going on. What'd he look like?'

Montbron gave a rough out-of-the-corner-of-the-eye-glance

description of Gaby Violle that received a definite shake of the head from Metcalfe, and then continued. 'All the people I saw up there were Corsican. The stranger wasn't, and he wasn't part of their business. He killed one of them,' Montbron glanced at Metcalfe again, 'but they got their money back on him. You go in their ledger as a debit. That's why I think you might as well stay here and take your chances with me. They'll find you in England once they get down to working out who owes what. The Corsicans love a good vendetta!'

Montbron turned his eyes to the front and concentrated on the road. He wasn't smiling; he wasn't joking either. 'I didn't see what happened back there. I don't even know how he got in place behind me. I didn't notice him, or the bugger he killed, until a gun was jammed in my side and a voice garbled something in my ear. All I know is that that stranger opened the war. He fired the first shot, but there was someone in the background, behind us both, who joined in. That's where his came from – the back of the café. The guy with the little moustache who charged round the corner after me is a nasty bit of work named Filli. I knew him in Algiers, though he didn't know me. You've heard of the Mafia?'

'Who hasn't!'

'He's of the Corsican variety. He tends to stick with the official side of the murder business. I won't bore you with the different organizations he's been involved with, but we're like that, us French, we work on the beehive principle, dozens and dozens of little units, all independent and nearly all with the same object in mind. At the moment it's cut the throat of the OAS. Next week it'll be cut the throat of those who cut the throat of the OAS. Know what I mean?'

'Where does the Corsican Mafia fit in?'

'They've been chosen as the least-principled bastards for execution work. They don't give a bugger who, or how, they kill just so long as they have the authority to do it. The French, being pragmatic about these things, reckon the best way of putting down a rebellion is to kill as many of those rebelling as they can before they get the chance to excite sympathy from the masses by a public trial. The *barbouzes* are winkling out the naughty boys and putting them down, and the people who should be jumping up and down and screaming barbarity are sitting back with smug smiles on their faces. That's how many hands have been washed of the problem. When it's all over and the casualty lists appear, these are the people who'll be the noisiest, and in the forefront of condemning the method of crushing the revolt. They're called politicians.'

'D'you want another cigarette?'

'Thanks. Light it for me, will you. The man I mentioned – Filli – runs a murder squad, all Corsicans, all the same type. They made good soldiers, but they're unprincipled bastards. If the fellow who helped me out was what I think he was, he would have known all about them. He'd have known what sort of ground he was moving across.'

Metcalfe lit two cigarettes and passed one across to Montbron. After a moment he said, 'You've got ideas about this stranger then?'

Montbron nodded vaguely. 'Yes, but nothing definite. I've got a nasty feeling he might have been put in the field as back-up to stop me falling over, which is exactly what I didn't want.' He paused for a few moments and then said thoughtfully, 'But it's more likely he's DST or SDECE, in which case he shoud have known of Filli's existence and his mandate. Of course, he might not have known him by sight—' He stopped again and took the cigarette from between his lips. 'And that's the more likely explanation and explains why he hadn't covered his rear. He marked two of the others, killed the one who was down to putting me out of the game, and was getting ready for the other one before taking me on. It sounds as though he'd got it all worked out. And it wasn't the *barbouzes* he was sitting there waiting to take, was it?'

Metcalfe still made no comment.

It didn't stop Montbron from settling his nerves by talking. 'And we're all Frenchmen. You wouldn't believe it, would you? I wonder how you English would behave in similar circumstances? Would you be happy to kill each other for politics?' He shrugged.

He didn't want a reply. He knew he wasn't going to get one. 'Both the guy behind me and Filli seemed to have the thing worked out. They'd marked their target, they'd laid their plans, and the whole fucking thing blew up in their faces. They should both have gone for the kill instead of being too greedy . . .'

'What d'you mean?' Metcalfe's curiosity got the better of him.

'I don't know how much your friend Neurie told you about me, but both wings of the anti-OAS faction – that's Filli's people and Neurie's people – want to take me home and screw my arse. They wanted me alive, Harry, because they thought I could lead them to bigger and better things. The stupid bastards! In this business you can only run up one rung at a time. I couldn't have led them anywhere except to the man they probably already know about. I'm just a soldier, a cog, I'm not running the bloody show! Neurie and Filli should have put their money in the bank, they should have played the numbers game. Kill your targets one by one, that's the only way you win this sort of argument. What you don't do is bugger around hoping that the bloody idiot's going to take you to the rest of his playmates. It doesn't work like that. Killing the other side out of the game's the only answer. They had the chance. The silly bastards ballsed it up. They should have killed me when they had the opportunity.'

'Very neat!' said Metcalfe cynically. 'You ought to listen to yourselves talking sometime. You bloody people have gone back to the Middle Ages.'

Montbron didn't even shrug. He probably hadn't heard what Metcalfe said. It didn't seem to worry him. It didn't worry Metcalfe either. He didn't give a damn about the French; they had never behaved like other people.

'What are you going to do now?' he asked.

Montbron glanced sideways, then back to the road. 'I'm going to stop at the next café and make a phone call. Then I'm going to drink a very large cognac. What about you?'

'I wouldn't mind a cognac either. In fact, several!'

'I didn't mean that.'

'I know you didn't. Tell me about your phone call.'

'Can I trust you?'

Metcalfe shook his head. 'Of course you bloody can't – I'm an Englishman.'

Metcalfe had drunk his cognac and ordered another by the time Montbron came out of the phone cabinet.

'There's been no official reaction so far,' said Montbron as he sat down.

'Is that what you went to phone about?'

'No, I'll tell you about that later. We've got to do something about you, but first I think we'd better have a closer look at your immediate prospects.'

'I don't like the sound of that!'

'It's probably worse than you think. Filli would have marked you, particularly as you pointed your gun at him. As far as he's concerned, you're one of his enemies. You helped get me off his hook, so he's going to pull out all the stops to find you and work you out of his system.'

'So if he catches up with me I'll tell him exactly what my role was.' Metcalfe knew that wouldn't do him a lot of good, but it helped a bit saying it. Montbron didn't interrupt; it probably sounded just as silly to him. Metcalfe ploughed on. 'That I was helping Gérard Neurie and SDECE run you into the net. I could ring Neurie now and tell him I uncovered you at Buc and was following you for a new trace but got involved in a gun fight and had to defend myself. Neurie can't prove evil intent on my part,' he stared at Montbron over the rim of his glass, 'unless somebody tells him otherwise.'

Montbron emptied his second brandy and raised his finger for the waiter. When the two empties had been replaced he said coolly, 'First of all, do you seriously think Filli'll buy that? I've just told you he's a Corsican. He wants blood. He's not interested in who set you on the road and who your handler represents. Filli and his *barbouzes* want you because you helped me out of their basket. He thinks you're part of my team. He won't take no for an answer when he sticks a hook into the back of your neck and hoists you up to the ceiling for the initial chat – and that's only part of your problem. They'll want you to tell them what you, an Englishman, were doing with me in the middle of our private and domestic little squabble. You English are not trusted, but you know that, of course, and being English won't stop you from being put through the wringer. A session with our wringers, just in case you've never come across them before, usually leaves the guest flat on his back for a few years while his bones knit together. I'm sorry to rub it in, but your screams won't be heard in Whitehall. They won't even be heard outside the walls of the Fort d'Ivry dungeons. You're dead weight, Harry. If they catch up with you, they'll sink you like a bag of rusty nuts.'

'Thanks for those comforting words.'

Montbron almost smiled. 'Don't mention it. I'll be on the same length of string with you.' He became serious again. 'And the other people, SDECE and their associates, the official hunting party – who do you think they're going to blame for that guy's head ending up on the table? Not Filli. They're going to blame you and me. We're the ones who killed the man from the Rue des Saussaies; we're the—'

'Just a minute, how do you know he was DST?'

Montbron clenched his fist and carried it to his ear. 'They're already talking about it. He was a senior DST executive, but actually, at the moment when he got himself killed, he was very special, with a capital "S". He could have been of, or working with, Department Maurice, though they're not saying, in which case his death's more serious than it seems.'

'You mean that your entering the field as a senior OAS assassin is receiving recognition beyond your wildest dreams?'

'It's not a laughing matter, Harry, not for me, or for you. Corsicans and *barbouzes* are one thing, Maurice is another. They normally keep aloof from this sort of domesticity. But you're committed. You were there, and they too will want to know who the stranger was with the English haircut, last seen waving a gun in the Place de la Contrescarpe and running down the hill behind the man on the wanted poster.'

'Neurie would have told them.'

'Told who? Don't count on it, my friend. I've already told you about the French way. The beehive? You've forgotten already? Neurie wouldn't have told a soul. You were his little trump, the boy from outside brought in to snuggle up against an old friend who'd gone in with the wild boys. You were a lead, and it was all very convenient –' Montbron suddenly stopped and stared hard at Metcalfe. Metcalfe knew what was coming. 'Monique—'

Metcalfe shook his head. 'Neurie's operation. She was in the dark, he said she wasn't to know. She's not in the business – she doesn't even know my status here or in the UK. In Singapore she thought I was a rubber planter.'

'What *is* your status, Harry?'

'Don't ask, Philippe. I helped you, not the other way round. I'm telling you this because I don't want any trouble for her.'

Montbron glanced over the rim of his glass. He was no fool, but he was a Frenchman. 'Your professional veneer slipped a bit there, Harry. You're not taking this woman seriously, are you?'

'Forget it. Just keep her out of it – she's nothing to offer. About Neurie. He doesn't like me—'

Montbron's lips curled in an imitation grin. 'I'm not surprised if you're knocking off his wife!'

'She's his ex-wife.'

'Some people never let go. But I think you've got an added problem with this man Neurie, Harry. The same source suggests he too might be with Department Maurice. If that's the case, he'd carry an awful lot of clout. I'm not too happy with the thought that your buggering around with his wife has brought him close to me . . .'

'He was already on to you.'

Montbron didn't look smug; if anything he looked slightly concerned. 'It doesn't matter now. At the moment we've got more problems than we can handle, since bloodletting on the streets of Paris brings another department into the works to make life difficult for us, and they can be a bloody nuisance when they put their minds to it.'

'Who are they?'

'The Sûreté. They'll also be after you when they make their investigations into the murders in the square. Somebody will have seen you. Somebody always does.' He raised his glass to his lips and tipped it, staring down its side into Metcalfe's face. Metcalfe stared back, expressionless. When he'd drained the small glass, Montbron smiled sadly and said, 'With all that lot coming at you with bared teeth, I think the first thing I've got to do is to get you out of Paris. You'll have to stay with me until the dust settles, but then we'll wriggle you out of the country.' There was no answering smile from Metcalfe.

'What do you say, Harry?'

'I'm considering the alternatives.'

'And what are they?'

'That's the trouble, I've just considered them. There aren't any. What's the next move?'

Montbron sighed inwardly. 'Have you any idea when Neurie pulled the curtain back on the Buc place?'

Metcalfe told him when and how. Montbron tried not to shrug his shoulders. It had been a shot in the dark, but a lucky one; it had hit something. Metcalfe continued. 'But he wouldn't have spread it around, he—'

'What d'you mean he wouldn't have spread it around? You're talking about his suspicions of Buc?'

Yes. I know how he works. Inviting me to hook little fingers with him was unofficial, it was a bit of personal blackmail. All he wanted was for me to have a look inside the house on Avenue Beauchamp. If you'd been there still I would have been out of the game and back on my little holiday. Getting invited to Jeanette Fabre's place at Buc wasn't on the itinerary. They'd lost you. It was just your bloody hard luck that Jeanette got sociable.'

Montbron shrugged Jeanette Fabre's motives aside. He didn't tell Metcalfe that if Jeanette hadn't invited him when she did he would have had her do it. He'd needed someone in place of Vernet. He'd chosen Harry Metcalfe – and got him! But something else caught his fancy. He sat forward on his chair and stared into Metcalfe's face. 'Did you get the impression that Neurie was sure I was at Buc?'

'No, I think he was certain you weren't. Putting me in to sniff out the drains was pure and idle speculation, the result of his suspicions of Marie-Claire being transferred to her sister. At this moment he's probably sitting with his feet up waiting for me to ring in with a blank return.'

'Unless that chap in the Place de la Contrescarpe was someone from Neurie's wing put in by him to follow you, and you led him there. He might have phoned Neurie and told him you'd flushed me and that it looked as if we'd gone in together. If that's the case, Neurie won't be too pleased with you either. For someone who came over for a quiet session with an old girlfriend, you're building up quite a following of folks who'd like to see your head in a bucket, Harry!'

Metcalfe stared at him blankly. Montbron shrugged. 'But that's neither here nor there now. If your assessment of Neurie's reactions is anywhere near the mark, then Buc is still safe. Neurie'll ignore it. Nobody in his right mind would go back there after Contrescarpe.'

'He'd be right.'

'But I'm not in my right mind, I think it's still safe. Except for . . .' He hesitated, and felt the thin ice underfoot. Metcalfe felt it too.

'Except for what?'

'Monique. We're going to have to do something about her.'

'No we don't. I just told you, she's uninvolved – all the way through. She doesn't know you, me, or anyone else in the pit.' Metcalfe's lips tightened. 'What had you got in mind for her?'

Montbron didn't reply. He avoided Metcalfe's eyes.

It wasn't good enough for Metcalfe.

He leaned across the table and put his face near Montbron's. He kept his voice very low. It didn't disguise the menace in it. 'She doesn't get hurt, Philippe. I'm prepared to run with you on this one, but I'm giving you fair warning. How you play politics and soldiers is your own business, it's nothing to do with me. You can bloody well kill who the hell you like and I'll cover you so far, but . . .' He paused for a second to make sure Montbron was taking it all in, then said, 'If you as much as look cross-eyed at Monique, I swear you'll have something on your back that'll make your Corsicans look like garden fairies! That's a promise, Philippe!'

Montbron temporarily rearranged his plans. It didn't show on is face. 'Harry, for Christ's sake! What the bloody hell d'you think I am?'

Metcalfe knew what the bloody hell he was. 'Just keep it in mind, Philippe. OK. What now?'

'We go back to Buc and check that you're right about Neurie not telling anyone, then we go under the blanket for a couple of days while the country gets bombarded with bullshit about Contrescarpe and then forgets it. You can make arrangements about keeping Monique pressed tightly against you. When the storm dies down we'll see what can be done about getting you both out of the way. That's if you haven't lost interest in her by then!'

Metcalfe didn't acknowledge the Frenchman's suggestions, or his cynicism. He gazed about him. The lights were just going on. There were a few people using the outside of the café and a few more inside. Some were eating. It was all very normal. They knew what they were going to be doing tomorrow; he wished he did. He emptied his small glass and met Montbron's eyes. 'Come on, Philippe, drink up. I've had enough of this bloody day. Let's bugger off and get ourselves out of sight.'

25

'YOUR FRIEND GUY-MONTBRON has got a lot more than most of that OAS scum to answer for, Paul.' It was a strangely subdued Filli who sat in his swivel chair in the operations room on the Boulevard Montmorency and stared suspiciously at Paul Vernet. Filli felt a heavy sense of loss. He had been close to his fellow countrymen, Rosso and Pietri particularly. Someone was going to have to pay a heavy price. That someone was Philippe de Guy-Montbron and he didn't even want to talk to him now. It was going to be first peak into the gunsight and the bastard's head goes into a bloody pulp. There was going to be no more pissing around with thoughts of him talking about his friends. But talking about friends: 'You said Guy-Montbron was a loner. You said you were his only contact. How do you account for all these other buggers appearing in Contrescarpe to back him up?'

Vernet stared back at the thin, black eyebrows above the cold, black eyes, but he didn't wilt. Yesterday was a different life ago. He'd come off the kitchen table and there was no way they were going to nail him back on to it – not now, not ever. Filli needed Paul Vernet far more than Paul Vernet needed Filli if the little Corsican peasant was set on playing lie-detectors with Philippe de Guy-Montbron. There was no other way he was going to find him. But careful – Filli still pulled the strings! Vernet brought his shoulders away from the wall he'd been leaning against, crossed his legs and casually folded his arms. He allowed a little anxiety into his voice to show who was still master.

'What other buggers, Georges? I only saw one and I'd never seen him before in my life. I swear to God, Georges, he was no part of our business, a total stranger – I told you that when you pointed him out. If I'd known him I would have said so.'

'So you did. Shall I tell you who he was?'

Vernet shook his head. He didn't want to know.

'He was a top-grade fuckin' DST excutive who got in the way. Why don't these bloody ponces stick to the only bloody thing they're any good at, carrying de Gaulle's handbag, instead of getting in the way of people who know what they're doing . . .' Filli's sombre expression didn't change as he wound himself up. 'Either they want me to clear up these bastard OAS people or they want every bugger who knows how to shoot a gun getting in on the act.' He brought Vernet back into the conversation. 'What about the bastard who killed Richet? Who was he and how did he come to join the party?'

Vernet shrugged his shoulders. 'I didn't see him, and I didn't see Richet go down. I've no idea where he sprung from or what his game was. Maybe he was DST too – or SDECE?'

Filli fixed Vernet with a disbelieving stare. The rush round the corner of the square into the Rue Mouffetard was as clear as a crisply focused still picture. He was never going to forget the tall, blond, hard-looking bastard standing there with a gun in one hand and hauling Montbron up from the deck with the other. Without him he'd have had Montbron like a snared rabbit and he'd be lying face downward on that bloody couch with just the handle of Rosso's lie-detector sticking out of his arse. But that had gone; that was yesterday. This was different. He closed his eyes and studied the face and repeated the words, first to himself, then aloud: '*Quick – where?*'

'Pardon?' Vernet frowned into Filli's closed eyelids.

'*Quick – where?*' repeated Filli and opened his eyes. 'That's English, isn't it?'

'Yes,' said Vernet without hesitation.

'I thought it might be. You sure?'

'Yup.'

'That's all we need! Now we've got bloody *rosbif* in on the act! Why would *rosbif* be helping Guy-Montbron?'

'No idea. Just a minute . . .' Vernet's head jerked up. 'He

was with the British Army at one time – Singapore, Malaya, somewhere like that. Maybe he's brought some English friends over to help out?'

'I'll send the bastards back in boxes.' With that off his mind, Filli got back to work. 'OK, Paul, since it looks as if you and I are the only members of the team still standing up, I'm promoting you. Not much bloody opposition for Guy-Montbron, is it?' His lip curled under the thin black line of hair above it. 'The best man they've got. And against him, me and a fuckin' renegade!'

'I've already shown—'

'Shut up! What was the fall-back plan between you and Montbron if the rendezvous failed? How would be make contact? You've closed up your safe house – he knows that. When does the place at La Chapelle come into operation? Has he got the phone number?'

'Which d'you want first?'

'Don't get bloody smart, Paul. Give me the fall-back plan.'

'I don't go near the old or the new place after a misfire. That's cover for me in case he's rolled up and is made to give addresses.'

'He would be that all right! And you're still insisting that it's only you he'd need to be worried about?'

'I keep telling you, Georges . . .'

'Yeh, I know you do. OK, go on. So you abandon the unused new pad. You've got a third lined up?'

'Right. I don't go to it for forty-eight hours after the misfire, and then I don't leave it until he makes contact.'

'By phone.'

'That's right. He has the phone number only, no address. Just in case . . .'

'I know, you told me – he's looking after your welfare. Straightforward talk is it, no messing around?'

'There's no need to piss around, is there! He says, "D'you recognize my voice?" and then he goes into the act.'

'That's what I mean, Paul, by messing around. That's messing around. It shows he's a free agent. If I had the bastard in chains with his teeth hanging out and he said, "Hello, Paul, this is Guy-Montbron" instead of "D'you recognize my voice?" you'd know immediately that all was not the way it should be and shove the bloody phone down the *lavabo* and run like bloody mad, wouldn't you, you stupid bastard! Didn't he tell you that?'

Vernet shrugged again. It sounded logical put that way. He changed the subject before Filli did. 'Maybe this guy helping Guy-Montbron was with the fellow from the DST, a back-up to help put the body in the bag.'

'Forget it. The DST doesn't run to Englishmen to help them out with their problems. *Rosbif* aren't liked by them any more than I like them here. But the bugger's cut himself off a thicker slice of the *jambon* than he knows, and he'll realize it when he comes face to face with Georges Filli again. Now let's get back to today. This reserve place of yours—'

'Stalingrad.'

Filli ignored the interruption. 'I'm not going to bugger around having an empty gaff tapped and people hanging around in the bloody doorways. What's going to happen is this. You and me, Paul, are going to move in tonight. I'm going to lay down on the bed and you're going to hover around waiting for the phone to ring. When someone comes on the line and says "D'you recognize my voice?" you'll go through all the motions he expects of you, and your excuse for not hanging around the Place de la Contrescarpe is that you bolted at the sound of gunfire and thank God he got away all right. Then you'll agree to his new rendezvous, which you and I will attend. The coffin box for the late Guy-Montbron will be waiting just round the bloody corner. The bastard's going to die, Vernet, preferably by gut or spine shots. No soddin' mercy.'

'Just you and me?'

'That's right.'

'I'd like my gun back, please.'

'Why not? And to show you how much I trust you, you can collect it on your way out. It's now a registered DST weapon and when you've signed this you'll have authority to carry and use it and to kill people who upset Charles de Gaulle.'

'What is it?' Vernet moved away from the wall and stared

down at the official-looking form that Filli had placed on the table. He didn't pick it up, or read it.

'That, Paul, is an application form in your new name.'

'New name? What do I want a new name for?'

'You want a new name, Paul, because one day, when we've hung all these OAS people from the lampposts, the good guys are going to start looking around for the criminal bastard who helped the man who killed our beloved Minister of Special Affairs. They're going to say let's hang that bastard Paul Vernet along with the rest of them. I've taken you under my wing. I don't want that bastard Paul Vernet to hang with the rest of them. Due to my kind nature, you're going to live to a ripe old age. So, forget Vernet. He doesn't exist any more.'

'What's my new name?'

Filli tapped the form on the table. 'It's in there, along with all the details required by this bureaucratic jungle we live in for you to apply for a position with the Direction de la Surveillance du Territoire, and that', he produced another sheet of paper, 'is your acceptance of the rules and conditions and your appointment to this department. All this means, Paul, that if you try crossing over the road again to join up with your good friend Philippe de Guy-Montbron in his war against the State, you will be deemed to have committed treason and you will go to the plank. Got it?'

'The plank?'

'The guillotine.'

26

IT WAS PAST two in the morning. Jeanette Fabre didn't scream; she didn't have hysterics. When she opened her eyes she thought she was still in the dream. Without moving her head, she studied Montbron's figure standing beside her bed. Her face, still full of sleep, was without expression.

A short time earlier Montbron and Metcalfe had slipped over the wall and through the overgrown copse. In silent and almost invisible single file they had made their way into the house through Montbron's concealed entrance and then up into the attic room, where Montbron had left Metcalfe with the remains of a large bottle of Bell's and a couple of spare blankets.

When he saw that she was awake, Montbron switched on the bedside lamp and crouched down beside her.

'Trouble,' he said simply.

'Place de la Contrescarpe?' Her voice was muffled by the pillow.

He nodded.

'The radio's been full of it. That was you, was it? All those people killed. What happened, Philippe?' She still hadn't moved. She looked comfortable and cosy, her head deep in the large feather pillow, her eyes full of sleep. At that moment she didn't look as though she was interested in anything but getting on with the dream; she was asking questions by instinct.

Montbron steered her along gently. 'It's too complicated,' he said softly. 'I've brought Metcalfe with me. He's upstairs.' He made himself comfortable on the edge of her bed and directed the lamp's soft glow on to the wall away from her face. He lit a cigarette.

'Give me one too.'

He passed her the cigarette and took another from the pack. Her hands were shaking as she carried it to her lips and drew heavily. It did some good. It calmed her nerves, though it didn't improve her voice. 'They said four men were killed,' she hissed. 'Near the Rue Monge. Was one of them your Vernet?'

More questions. He frowned at an uninvited train of thought, then smiled sadly. 'Nothing for you to worry about, Jeanette. You're clean, there's nothing to connect you and nothing's going to happen to you . . .' He paused and re-worded the lie before uttering it. 'Or Marie-Claire. There are no tracks leading to you. If you sit quietly and do nothing stupid—'

'Stupid? Like what?' Jeanette's senses were sharpening.

'Like suddenly changing colour. Becoming de Gaulle's greatest fan overnight; standing on an empty barrel in the centre of Concorde and screaming to the world what a great fellow our leader is. That sort of thing. Just behave normally. Be your usual indiscreet, bitchy self . . .'

'How unkind!'

He smiled to show he didn't mean it. 'I want a favour.'

'I can hardly wait!'

Montbron waved the gust of smoke away from his head. His eyes were cold and calculating. 'Actually, two favours. First, I'd like somewhere to ride out the storm, somewhere safe, out of the way. A couple of days – a week at the most. Just Harry Metcalfe and me.'

'And you're thinking of the Camargue?'

'It's your decision.'

Jeanette's sleepy complacency was deceptive. 'Surely, Philippe, that'll be the first place they look when they find you're no longer in Paris?'

'Jesus! I don't think you've heard a word I've said.' He shook his head with mock impatience. 'I think I'd better climb in there with you and wake you up properly.' Then he smiled thinly to show it was the last thing on his mind. 'For God's sake, Jeanette, I've just told you, there's nothing to connect me with you, or with this house. There's no reason why you should come into anyone's thinking. You're clean, this is clean,' he waved his arm to encompass the room, 'and that means the Camargue is clean too.' He stopped and frowned, then said sharply, 'You've got somebody staying there?' His nerves were reacting. The relaxation of tension was having its effect. She got the message.

'Only the servants and the two *gardiens*. Don't worry about them, the servants are Spanish and the *gardiens* are interested only in the bulls and their horses. None is political. They know nothing of our problem, nor do they care. They've probably never even heard of the OAS, and de Gaulle is something out of an Asterix comic! Can you trust Harry Metcalfe?'

He didn't reply, instead said, 'Will you tell the people at Saintes-Maries to expect a couple of your friends from Bordeaux?'

'Bordeaux?'

He put his hand under her chin, raised her head and kissed her lingeringly on the mouth. 'Just do as I say, Jeanette, there's a good girl, and don't keep querying things. It won't make you any the wiser. And yes, Bordeaux. Don't, whatever you do, mention people coming from Paris.'

'OK.' Jeanette smoked in silence for a few seconds, then raised her eyebrows.

'Yes?'

'You said two favours.'

Montbron nodded. 'Get in touch – not by phone – with Monique Bonnet and tell her that Harry Metcalfe has had to go urgently to Marseilles and is going to have to stay there for ten days or so. Tell her he's stopping for a couple of days in Nîmes, but he won't enjoy the bouillabaisse unless she's lapping it up in bed beside him, that he can't go that long without seeing her, he's in love, all that sort of thing. You know what to say.'

'I know what I'd like to *hear*.'

'Don't be romantic, Jeanette, this is serious. Tell her to take the Inter flight to Nîmes. She's to let you know when and what, and you'll pass it on to Metcalfe, who will meet her at the airport. Tell her not to spread it around, but on the other hand not to make a big secret issue of it if anybody gets really nosy.

Don't mention my name to her. Tell her just to get on an aeroplane and leave. Can I trust you with that?'

Jeanette pouted. She envied Monique's romance. 'I've trusted you, Philippe, with things more sensitive than that.' She gave him a cool and-don't-tell-me-you-don't-know-what-I-mean look directly in the eyes and spread her legs widely under the bed-sheets.

Montbron wasn't in the mood. 'I said this is serious.'

She studied his face for a moment, then raised herself on one elbow and crushed out her cigarette.

'You going now?'

'No. One car hurtling through the night on its own is a guaranteed target for police mobile patrols, even coming from the wrong direction. We'll go tomorrow. We'll be ready to move when the working traffic starts blocking the roads. Most Paris exits'll be covered, but they'll have to relax for the morning surge otherwise they'll have a bigger problem than they've already got. Which brings me to another point . . .'

'Another favour?' Jeanette was reading minds. She got in ahead of him. 'Take the Mercedes, it's—'

He shook his head quickly. 'Thanks, but too conspicuous. Even those evil bastards on motor bikes have an envious streak in them, and those that don't harbour animosity. How about the Peugeot?'

'Being repaired. Take the DS, and try to look poor and working-class! It's in the garage. What about money?'

'No problem.'

'When shall I see you again?'

Montbron pulled a face. 'Don't ask. A week, three weeks? Never? I can't say. Maybe it'll just fade. But don't sit around waiting.'

Jeanette stared into his face for some time, then shrugged and without taking her eyes off him pushed the bedclothes to one side. Her short white silk nightdress was rucked up around her waist as she offered her small, exquisite body to him. 'Then you owe me, at least, a proper goodbye.'

Montbron leaned over and gently kissed the delicate join of

her thigh and body. She lay back and closed her eyes. For once their lovemaking was silent, but it was intense and fierce. It was a very serious business saying goodbye, perhaps for ever.

He left her bed at first light. She didn't stir. Her eyes flickered and opened and she watched him dress and then move like a shadow through the door. When she closed her eyes again, they were wet. But she didn't sleep.

27

JEANETTE FABRE'S CELLAR was as well stocked as everything else in her sprawling farmhouse in the Camargue, but it was still a wicked way to treat a 4th growth Beychevelle.

Harry Metcalfe had no qualms about it. He wrapped his lips around the top of the bottle, tilted it and filled his mouth with the splendid wine. Holding it for a moment while he savoured the quality, he decided it was too cold, and swallowed. He took another mouthful for effect, wiped the top of the bottle with the palm of his hand and passed it to Montbron.

Half-past four in the morning. It was damp from the heavy suspended dew, and the chill, still night air caused the two men to fasten their stiff oiled jackets to cover their open-neck shirts. They were sitting in silence, their backs propped against the semi-solid wall of a well-constructed permanent hide overlooking the large expanse of silent, brooding black water that stretched sideways and lengthways as far as the light from the stuttering stars allowed them to see. And it was all owned by Jeanette Fabre: the water, the hides and the land that abutted the depthless, still marshes.

Philippe de Guy-Montbron was comfortably and proprietorially at home. It wasn't the first time he'd sat as Jeanette Fabre's guest shivering in the early hours waiting for the first glimmer of dawn to disturb the thousand or so ducks slumbering a few hundred yards away.

He accepted the bottle from Metcalfe and treated it with the same lack of reverence. In his other hand he held a three-quarter length of crusty baguette loaded with butter and half-inch slabs of local cured ham; in between each gurgle of the bottle he bit off a large lump and chomped noisily. Jeanette's Spanish housekeeper expected men to have appetites; this was her idea of a snack between meals. An hour ago she'd woken them up and put before them dinner-plate-sized portions of *pipérade* and pint bowls of thick black coffee and scalding milk. At twelve o'clock they'd have to do justice to a bath-sized dish of Camargue-style paella. But they weren't arguing.

Harry Metcalfe stared up at the night sky. There was a light blue tinge behind the stars and by stretching, then raising his head fractionally over the rim of the hide, he had an unrestricted view over the flat land to where the new day's sun would make its appearance. There on the horizon, with just a touch of imagination, he could see the outline of distant trees. Dawn was on its way. He turned his head towards the marsh. There was a definite reflection and somewhere in its depths a duck brought its head out of its tiny armpit, twitched its wing feathers experimentally and gazed around before sticking its head back into the quiet feathery dark again. It too had sensed the dawn. A tiny ripple from its movements disturbed the mirror-like surface. Metcalfe lowered his head, eased his shoulders against the hard wall and stretched his legs out in front of him.

'Half an hour?' he murmured.

Montbron answered through a mouthful of baguette. It was a distorted whisper. 'Forget that. There's something I want to tell you.'

'The last time you said that I couldn't sleep!'

Montbron took two more swallows of wine and passed the bottle back. He wasn't amused. 'What was your friend Neurie's assessment of my position?'

'I thought *you* were going to tell *me* something?'

Montbron didn't exactly sigh. He reached into the bag at his feet and brought out an unopened packet of Gitanes. He carefully stripped the Cellophane, took out a cigarette and placed it between his lips. He didn't light it. 'I'm not OAS,' he said bluntly. He couldn't see Metcalfe's eyebrows rise. Not surprise – scepticism. 'I'm Army Intelligence, or to be exact, GLI – Light Intervention Group.'

'Doesn't mean a thing to me.'

'How about B3, Inter-Army Coordination Centre?'

'Neither does that. What does it mean in English?'

'There's no equivalent. The British Army doesn't have a hundred different intelligence groups. You rely on the civilian Five and Six for your main source of information. Your intelligence corps interviews captured prisoners during wartime and makes sure their cups of tea are made with the right amount of milk and sugar. We, on the other hand, like to confuse ourself with dozens of military intelligence organizations all doing the same thing, sometimes in the same place, but never in cooperation, and never telling anybody, not even branches of the same organization, exactly what's going on. We have an obsession with secrecy; we trust no one, and we spy on each other. Your friend Neurie is a typical example. It'll be our downfall.' Montbron's flagellation was taking a torturous a route as the intelligence systems he was criticizing. Metcalfe thanked God he was British.

'Neurie wasn't the first to trip over his own wire,' said Metcalfe.

'What do you mean?'

'He had you marked almost within hours of your ducking into your hole in the ground at Marie-Claire's. They had cameras and watchers on you. Why didn't he pick you up? I think there's a lot more known about you than you imagine. Who put you into the field? And how many others have gone in without back-up from other units? Your OAS Central Committee is probably run entirely by implants and infiltrators from the French intelligence services and Army organizations, none of them knowing that they're all on the side of the good! What a bloody laugh! And they all think you're the evil one because you knocked off a Government Minister. I reckon somebody inside the OAS structure split on you to Neurie and his "funny" team.'

But Montbron wasn't listening. He was thinking. Metcalfe was laughing by himself, but it wasn't funny; it was a bit too near a distinct possibility. Montbron shook his head, but Metcalfe couldn't see it. 'It's the balls-up again.' He was talking to himself, trying to work out the route and the method. He was hovering very close to something he didn't want to think about. But it wouldn't stay out of the way. 'Xavier,' he breathed.

'Pardon?'

'Sorry, Harry. Did Neurie mention the name "Xavier"?'

Metcalfe didn't even have to consider it. 'Nope. The only name he mentioned to me was yours. I told you he'd gone off me. He wasn't telling me anything else, he was just making threats.'

Montbron held his hand above the parapet for a few seconds and decided that what little breeze there was about was coming off the water. He lit the cigarette that had been dangling between his lips and exhaled with a whoosh. *Would Xavier's people pinpoint me for testing? Not possible. I covered my tracks; no one followed me from Fouquet's. Besides, why would Xavier's OAS troopers want to know where my safe house was? I was already contracted. If they were doubtful, they could have picked me up on the rendezvous. Scrub Xavier. What about Neurie's people? Would they kill their own man? No point. They were already watching. Besides, Jeanette said they'd left the fat girl intact. It doesn't make sense. Another group? No doubt about it. But how? And what about Contrescarpe? That, Montbron, is what you're trying to avoid thinking about. Whoever it was, followed me from Buc – but the bloody Corsicans were already there. Paul? Where was he? Don't even think it . . .* Metcalfe's hissed question came at the right time.

'You haven't told me anything yet, Philippe.'

Montbron remained silent, drawing on his cigarette in tiny puffs and dispelling the smoke in a thin stream, watching closely the direction in which it dispersed.

'If you expect me to continue to cover your back,' urged Metcalfe, 'I want to know more than you've told me. Go back to your B3 for starters and let's have the name of your coordinator.'

Montbron considered it for several seconds then made up his mind. 'OK, Harry, this'll confirm your worst fears.' He said it almost jocularly, but it was deadly serious. 'It's a two-man shaft. You won't have heard of General Lemercier. He's my ringmaster, and head of the Rhine Army's intelligence centre at Elm. The reason he's head of the Rhine Army intelligence centre is that he's untouchable and, as if such a thing existed, incorruptible.'

'A rare animal in these strange and unpredictable times,' murmured Metcalfe.

But Montbron wasn't interested in sarcastic observations. He shrugged the interruption aside. 'And he's all those things because he's de Gaulle's cousin. Not only that, he's the great man's close friend – probably his only friend! The unkind or envious say that one military genius in the family was all they could afford, so Lemercier was deprived of a chance at St Cyr and, come the London adventure in 1940, went across the Channel to start his military career as batman to his cousin, the Grand Charles. They say genius will out! It seems the young Lemercier could plan intelligence missions into France from London better than he could press the old man's trousers!'

'Very romantic! So we've got a loyal French general in the frame – one who knows how to press trousers! Whatever next?'

'Have you finished, Metcalfe?'

'Go on.'

'Lemercier's brief – it was a personal one, face to face with his cousin the President, no witnesses – was to bring out of the woodwork *by any means*, and to deal with them in any manner he felt appropriate, the leading players in the OAS/Métropole Central Committee in mainland France. Lemercier gave me the ferret job.'

'Why bring a show in from Germany? De Gaulle has enough intelligence and security people around him to start a Third World War. Why start thinning out his border troops? It doesn't make sense to me.'

'You're just a simple Englishman, Harry. You're missing the thrust of the game. De Gaulle doesn't trust the intelligence services. He thinks they're all swimming around in the same pond with the people who want him out, one mind, one purpose: his nose in a split and his arse as a rallying point for the unwashed! But try not to be too smug, your time'll come.'

'What d'you mean?'

'I can't see it, but I can visualize the pained expression on your face. These bloody Frogs! What a bloody mess they've got themselves into! But wait, Harry. It's not beyond the realms of possibility that one day Englishmen might question the intentions of their leaders and drag them out on to the streets to explain their actions under the lampposts with ropes hanging from the crossbars.'

'Wishful thinking, Philippe. We don't do things that way.'

'I'm happy for you. But let's wait and see.'

Metcalfe said nothing for a moment, then took a long intake of breath. 'OK, let's get back to your problem.' He scrabbled about in the bottom of his own bag for cigarettes, lit one, then picked up the almost empty bottle from where he'd carefully placed it on the dirt floor and nudged it into the crook of Montbron's arm. He leaned back against the wall of the hide again and savoured the pungent smoke of the Gitane. 'Are you asking my advice on what you ought to do next?'

Montbron didn't reply. He knew what he was going to do next. He didn't need an Englishman to tell him.

Metcalfe listened to the silence for a moment, then said, 'OK, so no advice. But tell me, why did your General Lemercier pick you for the hatchet job?'

'Lemercier didn't trust many people, quite rightly. Why me? Lemercier and I fought side by side for eight years in Indo-China. Eight years under the hammer you get to know your right hand. We went into Dien Bien Phu together and when it went under we were tied together like a couple of cart bullocks and dragged to the prison camp they'd prepared for us. Yes, it was there waiting for us long before the battle had been decided. But Lemercier had had enough humiliation. Sitting in a prison camp was for the others, not him, and not for me either! He and I escaped, and went through a worse hell than the last days at Dien. But we made it. Promoted to colonel, he raised the Troisième Régiment Étranger Parachutise – Foreign Legion paratroopers – and called for me as a company commander. But de Gaulle wanted him for other things and before the real battle died down in Algeria he was promoted again and sent to Germany to raise the standard of the Army's Intelligence Service. I was also promoted and sent to Cercottes – a training centre for the 11th Shock Troops – as a senior instructor. That was Lemercier's doing. He wanted someone standing by, someone who could be transferred without question, somebody he trusted should the day ever arrive.'

'I've got the message,' murmured Metcalfe. 'So now they're making room on Joan of Arc's plinth for two more legends!'

Montbron brushed aside Metcalfe's sarcasm; he was getting used to it. 'You asked. I'm telling you how. When Lemercier briefed me we became the only two people in on the act.'

'Three,' said Metcalfe.

'What d'you mean?'

'Lemercier, you – and now me!'

Montbron shrugged. The darkness gave the hide the anonymity of the confessional; shrugging and self-recrimination were between him and his maker. How much more to tell this sceptical Englishman? 'I explained the brief,' he continued in a low monotone. 'To infiltrate the Paris OAS Central Committee. I couldn't volunteer. At this stage of their game they've become as shy as little convent girls. They clench their chubby thighs together very tightly when new boys, particularly new boys from Germany and ex-Cercottes graduates, decide to jump on to the already creaking revolutionary bandwagon. So I had to come in the hard way.'

Metcalfe's scepticism showed. 'You mean your friend General Lemercier said, "My friend and cousin Charles of the Élysée has told me he doesn't mind if you go to Paris and kill the odd Minister or two, plus, of course, carloads of ministerial bodyguards and a mixed bagful of DST Government intelligence agents if they get in your way? But don't worry about it, old boy, we use Corsicans nowadays, and we've got plenty more of those waiting to pop up to provide target practice! Come off it, Philippe!' Metcalfe puffed on his cigarette. For a brief moment the glow lit up the lower part of his face, but there was no taut, angry expression to go with his words; it was a relaxed face, a face that had heard all sorts of bizarre explanations from all sorts of people trying to prove that they were something they patently were not. He removed the cigarette from his mouth and with it went the temporary illumination. 'And what about Gérard Neurie? He's not a street-corner operator, or a wild boy from the pampas. How come he latched on to you so quickly?'

'I thought you'd already sorted that one out?'

'No one's ever going to sort this lot out, Philippe.'

'You could be right there, but as you said, Harry, it shows that he wasn't a street-corner boy. Neurie and people like him were essential to my credentials. The fact that the serious intelligence people wanted my arse added to the authenticity of my application as assassin-in-chief to the OAS. None of our civilian intelligence agencies are pure. They all have within them OAS sympathizers, and some have active participants. That they could pass on the information that I was on a genuine wanted schedule for a genuine OAS atrocity was the cornerstone of my cover. It all helped fulfil my brief,' Montbron explained patiently, 'which was to get myself in front of the OAS Central Committee and identify them. De Gaulle suspects three senior members of his Government are involved, but they'll only crawl out to pronounce on a major policy decision – a major policy decision meaning ace, king, queen, jack for the chop. Lemercier's plan was to show the OAS Committee how I'm a man they can't possibly manage without, how I can kidnap and spirit away a well-guarded Government Minister . . .'

'So you went one better and killed the poor bugger!'

'That's a different story. Gautier, the Minister of Special Affairs, was known to Lemercier as an OAS adherent. Taking him out for a walk was a double-double. I was supposed to have chosen him for his position; I wasn't supposed to know that he was actively supporting the OAS. The fact that I went after him showed I was working on my own account. That was what the OAS Committee was expected to think.'

'So why the carnage?'

Montbron took his time answering. 'The best-laid plans . . .' he recited. 'Don't forget my intention was kidnap, not massacre. Unfortunately, as I've already told you, Vernet had a rush of blood to the head and ran amok. There was nothing I could do once the shooting started.'

'Philippe, I think I've heard enough about this Billy the Kid running with you. You didn't like my idea that he might have dropped you in the shit and gone over to your Corsicans or their mates, but take this for another suggestion. I don't like the sound of the bastard, and I don't trust him. I haven't got that sublime faith you seem to have in blood and if you want me to stand beside you, or behind you, in this caper, you'll cut the bugger adrift. No contact, no more of this idiocy about getting away from the fire and into the country. By the sound of him he's quite likely to start knocking off the cows just to listen to the poor bloody creatures scream for help. You want my help, Philippe? Get rid of the bastard!'

Montbron didn't respond. 'Pass the bottle, Harry, and shove the advice.'

Metcalfe gave him both – the bottle and the advice. 'You're on a bloody hiding to nothing, Philippe. You've got to close down this paper-chase and get out of the country until your people, or theirs, resolve this bullfight. You stick your head back in Paris, or anywhere near your crazy relation, and you won't have one to stick your hat on. They're all after you now: Neurie's lot; little short-arse's lot, whoever they may be; and your new-found OAS chums as well. I'm giving you this advice free, Philippe. Contact your General Lemercier and tell him to wave a white flag for you now. Tell him you're coming in and going back to being a soldier again. Have him clear your face quickly with Central Intelligence and make sure everybody knows, right down to the lady who pushes the croissants trolley along the corridors, that you're one of the good guys. But above all, Philippe, disown this fucking brother of yours. He's very, very bad news . . .'

'I'm carrying on.' Montbron pinched the burning end off his cigarette and ground it out with the heel of his boot. He didn't elaborate.

'Then you're bloody mad.'

'And I'd still like your help.'

'As long as this madman remains in the frame, Philippe, you can forget it.'

'I'm clearing him as soon as the dust settles.'

'Not good enough.'

'Bugger you, Harry!'

'And fuck you too!' Metcalfe meant it.

'Not so loud – you'll frighten the ducks!'

28

THE EDGES OF Georges Filli's patience were beginning to fray.

Thirty-six hours after installing himself in Vernet's foxhole there had still been no contact with Montbron. He was bored with ham sandwiches, with Vernet's pathetic attempts at making coffee and with his continual whining. Filli wanted action. He wanted a decent meal, he wanted something to happen, but above all he wanted to move out of range of his new chief assistant. He missed Pietri. He missed Rosso. He was becoming maudlin.

'I'm changing the script,' he told a disinterested Vernet. 'I'm moving a team of technical people in with you. You'll stay with them. There'll be a watching crew opposite.'

'No need for that,' grunted Vernet through a mouthful of buttered baguette. That was another thing that got on Filli's nerves; the bloody man was always eating. 'Montbron doesn't know the address. He only knows the phone number.'

'Shut up and listen. Just in case, there'll be a watch opposite and some phone people sitting in this shithouse for as long as it takes. The bastard's got to ring sometime. He's got to get in touch with you, he can't just leave you squatting in this bloody tenement for ever.' He gazed around the small room: dirty crockery on a dirty Formica-topped table, dirty bedsheets on a smelly bed that would have been over-large in a room three times the size. A whore's workshop. It looked like it, and smelled like it. He couldn't keep the look of disgust from his face. 'You know what to say when he rings?'

'If he rings!'

'*When* he rings, *con*! So get it right. It's "Where are you,

Philippe? When can we meet? Where can we meet?" You want those bloody questions answered, in any bloody order, but for Christ's sake don't ask them like that! Sprinkle 'em around the conversation, and don't forget: act natural. You're shit-scared, you need money, you need him. Just remember, catching the bastard is your passport to the rest of your life. If he gets away by your stupidity, I'll have your balls in place of his! Have you got the picture, Paul? I want something out of this. Think about it!'

Vernet carried on munching his sandwich; he appeared more interested in its butter content than in what Filli was saying.

'I said, have you got it?'

Vernet swallowed and cleared his mouth ready for another assault on the baguette. He hesitated, the chewed end of the baguette just short of his open lips. 'You worry too much, Georges.' He wagged the lump of bread at Filli and bared his teeth. There were still pieces of masticated bread fringing the corners of his mouth; it wasn't a pretty sight. 'I'll have the bastard made up into a sandwich for you and delivered to Montmorency.' *And when I've done that I'll give some thought to what's going to happen to you . . .* but he kept the grin going even as he munched. It distracted Filli from looking too deeply into his eyes.

Filli stared at him in disbelief. 'Jesus Christ! I don't believe this!' He watched the bread, helped by a shove with the palm of his hand, slowly disappear into Vernet's mouth, then turned his back and closed the door behind him.

Filli felt much better after a bath, several cups of thick black coffee and a very large glass of Rémy Martin. He dressed slowly, his mind at full stretch. He knew he was being obsessive, but he couldn't help it. He wanted Montbron. He wanted the bastard so badly it made his gut ache and threatened to dislodge the meal he'd just enjoyed. He lit a cigarette to dull the gnawing pain, then picked up the holstered Petter automatic that had killed Violle, slipped it out of its pouch and dropped the magazine into his lap. He emptied the round from the breech and weighed the automatic in his hand, studying it all the time with a thoughtful expression.

The decision made itself.

He fitted the magazine back into the butt, slammed it home and walked over to the chest of drawers by the door. He pulled the bottom drawer right out of its housing, stuck his arm into the empty space and pulled out an identical Petter M50 automatic. He dropped the one that had been used to kill Gaby Violle in its place, replaced the drawer and went through the same checking procedure with the new weapon. When he was satisfied, he slipped it into the holster and attached it to his belt. He poured himself another glass of cognac, drank it in one swallow, as if it were medicine, then phoned the Boulevard Montmorency.

'This man, Gabriel Violle,' he said when he was put through to his operations centre, 'logged as DST Central—'

'Not run-of-the-mill. Killed the day before yesterday by unknown, possibly OAS, murder squad. It's all been documented like that and fed into the system.'

'OK. Where was he operating from? Who was directing him? What was his current mandate?'

'Like I said, not run-of-the-mill. He was a fancy operator, had his own cloud. He walked across the road a short time ago to head a special unit, a possible Department Maurice outline, but that can't be confirmed. The Maurice Bureau never acknowledges death in the family; it doesn't even acknowledge the use of humans. In fact the bloody place doesn't exist. Violle came out of DST's E2. But just a minute, you know all this about Violle—'

'I want it official, on paper, on record. Now how about answering my questions?'

'As far as we know he wasn't being directed. The word is that he was running the show. That squeak came from a mouse in the cupboard, and the same squeak suggests that he was arm in arm with a guy named Neurie, of unknown pedigree, who's doing a very special song-and-dance act against a specific OAS assassination group.'

'Violle was working from the Élysée Palace. How about this man Neurie?'

'It doesn't say anything about that, except that Violle hadn't been clocking in at the Rue des Saussaies or the Élysée for some days.'

'OK,' yawned Filli, 'submit to the D-G a request to go to Ministry of the Interior. Suggest he goes high, possibly Matignon. I want a meeting with this Monsieur Neurie concerning the death of Monsieur Gabriel Violle. It's to be open, above board and official. Not indoors. Neurie can name the field; I'm not choosy where. Ring me back here when it's been arranged. Oh, and before you ring off, get a team to this address.' He gave Vernet's address in the east of the city. 'Surveillance. Use Patrice and one other. There's a room opposite that overlooks. Also a telephone watch from inside the address – full, twenty-four-hour clip-on on incoming traffic. Nothing on the line going out. Tape indoor conversation, but for my ears only. Got it?'

'Got it.'

'OK, ring me when you've arranged the other thing.'

He lit another cigarette and raised the dark-coloured bottle up to the light and saw that there was enough for another glass. He poured it out, sat down in the only soft chair in the room, the cigarette in one hand, the glass of cognac in the other, and without touching either went to sleep.

29

BY THE TIME Gérard Neurie had arrived at the Place de la Contrescarpe the post-mortems and the arguments had been in full flow. He kept out of the way, watching from the fringe of the audience. He was particularly interested in the attitude of Georges Filli. The man looked cool and calm, with an unexcited professionalism. He had barely glanced at the crumpled, wrapped bodies being unceremoniously loaded into the back of a dark blue police mortuary van as he listened to the raised voices around him.

Neurie had watched Gaby Violle's body join the others in the back of the van and then departed as inconspicuously as he'd arrived. Filli had impressed him. He marked him down as a very dangerous man, one you didn't turn your back on unless he was lying in the gutter with a hole in his head.

Which is why he was intrigued when, on calling on Maurice a few days later, he was given an official-looking note, a wry smile, and: 'I see you're still mixing with these strange people.'

'Which strange people, Maurice? They're all bloody strange in this business.'

'Corsican gangsters, Gérard. But not ordinary Corsican gangsters. This one has access to the Ministry of the Interior and wants to meet you and shake your hand. Somebody named Filli. Watch your silver if you invite him home for dinner! Read the note.' Maurice busied himself with a very long whisky and water and studied Neurie as he read the note. He'd listened to Neurie's commentary on the hunt for Gautier's killers in silence. His reaction had been typical but his assessment short and to the point.

'Help yourself to a whisky and whatever you put into it, then tell me why we are losing this fight, Gérard.'

'We're not.'

'Ah . . .' Maurice's exclamation could have been caused by the strength of the whisky. He sipped again, then, peering over the rim of the glass, said, 'Is that all? "We're not"? Marc Morel, a promising young man – I know his father – into the bucket. A bloody waste. Violle, a senior DST executive, shot in the back of the head doing a labourer's job. It's beginning to sound like bloody Verdun. You sure we're not losing?'

Neurie didn't reply immediately. He wasn't prone to self-recrimination. Regret was something else, but he'd got it all off his back and into perspective last night. There weren't any more friends left. Violle had been the last. The others were screwed up in graves among the sand-dunes, in the abandoned rubber plantations and the silent jungles, and, nearer home, where the shadows were always darkest. Self-flagellation was a solitary occupation and he'd enjoyed his agony as the evening had turned into night, sitting full length, his feet resting on the glass-topped coffee-table and the windows to the balcony wide open allowing in the night-time Paris smells and the muffled sounds of the still bustling traffic below. He'd got over the initial shock of Gaby Violle's death. It had been replaced by a numb, hard-to-cool anger and an almost despairing feeling of frailty. Shot in the back of the head – that caused the anger. Frailty? Gaby Violle had been proved fallible. He had been like the rest; he'd fallen flat on his face in the mud when hit. Bullets in the back of the head made no distinction between age and experience, youth and impetuosity. Gaby had proved to be as vulnerable as Morel. It was unforgivable. But he refused to allow it to turn into a wake.

He treated death with contempt. He'd been too close to it too many times to respect it. Gaby Violle was dead; tears and recrimination weren't going to bring him back. Unhappiness? That was a different thing, nothing to do with getting your head blown in. The bottle of whisky and the small jug of water on the table had remained unpunished. For Neurie it had been just an evening drink, with no more significance than that.

But today was another day and Maurice saw it differently. Was he right? *Were* they losing?

Maurice saw the shutters come down over Neurie's eyes. He knew Gérard Neurie; there was nothing coming along that track. 'I'm not sure it was such a good idea using people outside the family. They get known, they get killed. Are you known?'

Neurie didn't answer. He folded the Ministry of Interior note and tapped it on the edge of Maurice's desk. 'This man Filli wants to know me. I'm inclined to show my face to him. I want to lose some of this arrogance, to have him looking over his shoulder occasionally, but above all I want to show him that I know who killed Violle.'

'Is that a good idea?'

Neurie took two long sips at his whisky and water, then placed the glass carefully on the edge of the desk. 'I'm going to cripple him, Maurice, and put him out of the show. I think it's just as well that when the time comes he knows who's doing it.'

Maurice didn't wince. He studied his protégé for several seconds. Neurie didn't look like a killer. He had an almost gentle face, no occupational characteristics, and soft brown eyes. It was a face totally lacking in aggression, but Maurice knew better. Real, professional, killers never did look like killers. After a moment he said, 'Tread carefully with him, Gérard. Look at the signature at the bottom of that note. Somebody in the Matignon loves him, although that shouldn't be too much of a surprise. The present Prime Minister's office has little affection for any of the intelligence services, Department Maurice included. They wouldn't be totally unhappy if a spot of internecine face-slashing took place due to mistrust and suspicion, and who better to reorganize the intelligence system when the blood has stopped flowing than the much-loved and ever-loyal Corsican faction?'

Neurie shrugged. 'That's political fantasy, Maurice. You've forgotten what it's like peering round the brick wall at the real world. There's no time out there for pros and cons, people are getting their heads kicked in while you sit here wondering what's going to happen to the soft jobs when the war's over.' He smiled evenly to show he wasn't committing blasphemy, then opened the note again and glanced at it. 'But he does seem very sure of his ground. Listen to this: '. . . the Director-General of the DST has submitted to the Ministry of the Interior a request that a meeting be arranged between Monsieur Filli of the Action Association (Special Services) branch of the DST and the senior officer of the anti-terrorist group of which Monsieur G. Violle (deceased) was a member, the object of which is an exchange of information on overlapping OAS activities and to define limits of departmental responsibility in the prosecution of these activities . . .'

Gérard looked up into the cool grey eyes of the old man. 'In other words, the Corsican wants exclusive rights to clearing the streets of the OAS. Either that or he's got a guilty conscience – not an emotion normally attributable to Action Association – and wants to say sorry! Very doubtful. But he might have something to offer. I know he's concentrating his resources on the OAS's new assassin-in-chief and wants a clear run. He's not going to get it. It'll be salutary for him to know he's not running barefoot through the jungle alone.'

'I still don't see—'

'At the moment, Maurice, Filli and dozens like him are roaming the towns and countryside settling old scores with the approval of the Government. All they have to say to justify murder is that the corpse was OAS and nobody gives a bugger. They are killing anyone who walks across their track regardless of whether he's a disgruntled soldier, an OAS killer or a member of any other organization – legal or illegal. I can't kill them all, but I can have a bloody good look at the most dangerous of them.'

'With this Filli obsession, and obsession is what it sounds like to me, aren't you in danger of losing sight of the reason you were put into the field, Gérard? Your objective was to bring down the killers of Jean Gautier – that was all. It was not to become embroiled in a vendetta. Are you anywhere near bringing these people home?'

'Philippe de Guy-Montbron,' said Neurie, 'as we have already discussed. One man with one pack-carrier, probably a picked trooper from the old days. Montbron has brains as well as audacity, but he can't run a war on his own and he's going to slip up badly, particularly if Filli gets to him first. But it's not enough just to kill Montbron, because thirty-six hours after we've buried him they'll have another equally bright, equally war-experienced character to take his place. We've got to strike off the head of this bloody snake, Maurice, and it's somewhere in Paris. Montbron, when we bring him home, can be persuaded to point us to the centre of OAS/Métropole operations. That must be the bonus of our strategy against him and the reason why he must not be allowed to fall over. Violle had this objective in mind, which was why he took on the job of watcher, and why he died. He stopped Filli from knocking Montbron into the gutter. That's another reason for making Filli a target. He wants to kill Montbron; I want him alive.'

Maurice nodded his head. It all made sense to him as well. 'It's your show, Gérard, and I'm not going to cry over a dead Corsican, but I think you'd better have another A/12 agent, someone to pick up Violle's pieces. How about—'

'No. I'd rather continue this alone now. I've got one or two safe pairs of hands from Violle's E2 for sweeping up and watching. I don't want Department Maurice people jumping through the hoop with me. We'd get in each other's way.'

'Fair enough.' Maurice seemed to have been waiting for this admission. 'Then tell me, Gérard, why have you been enquiring of British MI in London the whereabouts of one Harry Metcalfe?'

Neurie stared across the table into Maurice's pale grey eyes. There was no trace of mockery. *Christ! Is there anything going on that this crafty old bugger doesn't know? Or is that equally crafty old bugger Michael in London allowing his curiosity to get the better of him? It's quite true, you can't trust these bloody Englishmen. But play it straight. Look him in the eye . . .*

'Metcalfe's a chap I've worked with in the past. He's trustworthy and discreet. I thought it might be an idea to use him on a ferret job and try and move him close to Montbron. He knew him as well.'

'Any success?'

'I think he might be running with him.'

'Be careful about playing English cards, Gérard. That's just about all it would take to have steam shooting out of the Élysée chimneys. Englishmen are not welcome in the sort of games we're playing at the moment; they're purely domestic, foreigners not welcome. Don't let it get out of hand.'

Neurie said nothing.

Maurice had another go. 'I don't suppose this Harry Metcalfe is the same one whose name featured on your divorce decree three years ago?'

Neurie stood up. He still said nothing.

Maurice understood; it had been uncalled-for. But there was no repentance. 'Keep me in touch. Let me know when you've got this Montbron man in chains. Oh, and by the way, the report on Violle's death showed that he was killed with a 9mm parabellum, fired from the new-model Petter – the M50.' Maurice picked up his glass again. 'I thought you might like to know.'

'Very interesting.'

'It's not general issue.'

'Thanks.' Neurie left without shaking the old man's hand. There was no goodbye either.

30

NEURIE ARRANGED THE meeting with Filli on unconsecrated land. It was Neurie's choice – the third bench on the south-side promenade of the Lac Daumesnil in the Bois de Vincennes.

Neurie arrived first. His sweeper, unconcealed, stood well out of earshot feeding the ducks from a bag of stale cake.

Filli made his approach obvious. He was alone and traversed the lake from some distance, walking on the hard shoulder. Filli played no set rules. You said one thing and did another. There were no honourable people in this game; it was the gutter, not the field at Agincourt. His team, three plus one, arrived separately, checked their areas, and as soon as the principals were settled, they dispersed, staying out of sight, out of range and totally anonymous. The team was led by Jean-Baptiste Pecotti. His brief was clear and concise: 'Look at this man. His name is Neurie. Remember his face, but don't commit yourself – looking at him is enough. He's a dangerous man to trip over. If you have any doubt, back off . . .' Which Pecotti, being Corsican and proud and stubborn, had no intention of doing.

Neurie didn't move when Filli sat down beside him. He continued to stare out across the flat, shallow waters of the lake, its surface disturbed only by the ripples raised by the ducks as they fought for more than their fair share of the DST's stale cake. There were no handshakes, no introductions, no preliminaries. Filli started the auction.

'I wish to know everything about the activities of Superintendent Gabriel Violle leading up to his death in the Place de la Contrescarpe, along with anything else concerning him and your organization that has happened since.' Then he made another mistake. 'And then we can get down to serious matters . . .'

Neurie didn't react. Neither did he turn his head. His interest appeared to be centred entirely on the squabbling ducks.

Filli took the lack of response in his stride; he remained cold, calm and calculating. 'I know that you and a team from E2 are engaged in a special operation against the OAS/Metropole. I know that you are the controller of that team . . .' Filli waited for a moment, studying his companion out of the corner of his eye. He learned nothing from Neurie's expression. 'And that you have been granted special powers to find the people responsible for the death of Minister Gautier. I have also learned that you are a senior executive of Maurice. I know—'

Neurie opened his jacket. He felt Filli stiffen beside him as he reached in a pocket and brought out a packet of cigarettes. Filli didn't relax; he was like a spring. Neurie studied the packet. He didn't open it, nor did he look at the man beside him. Filli, it seemed, had no qualms about revealing the existence of what had to be a fairly comprehensive network of spies within the domestic intelligence organizations. Neurie kept his feelings from his face. He left Filli's revelations unacknowledged and turned his head, still tapping the unopened packet of cigarettes on his knee. Filli seemed mesmerized by it.

'You were in Contrescarpe yourself,' said Neurie. It was an accusation. Filli accepted it with a little jerk of his head but he didn't answer. He too had found something interesting to look at on the lake. Neurie gave him a few seconds, then continued. 'Were you in front of or behind Violle when he was killed?'

Again Filli didn't answer the question. 'I had a very elaborate ambush laid on at the Place de la Contrescarpe. It was foolproof, and the result of a great deal of very serious preparation. I was about to spring it in the face of one Lieutenant Colonel Philippe de Guy-Montbron, for your information the killer of Minister Gautier. Your Violle not only ruined the ambush by killing my deputy but through his interference cost the lives of two more of my men and allowed the Minister's murderer to escape. That, Monsieur Neurie, was a lot of bloody hard work down the drain. Not only that, it sent Guy-Montbron scampering back into the undergrowth, Christ only knows where. That's what your Monsieur Violle caused, and I presume he did all that with your help and the connivance of your department . . .' Filli was beginning to bubble, but it was only inside, and in his voice; nothing showed on his face or in his manner. 'So don't sit there, Monsieur Neurie, with a righteous look on your face, and ask where I stood while my men were being gunned down.'

Neurie stuck a cigarette in his mouth and flicked his lighter under it. 'What did you want to see me for?' he asked.

'The elimination of the OAS rabble in Paris is my designated responsibility,' said Filli. 'I agree the success of this campaign is your department's interest as well, but it's a personal matter for you. Yours is a purely passive involvement, a question of identification, of quarantine until the war is over, of tidying up the mess when I've finished the work. You have nothing to do with the end-game. You have my meaning?'

Neurie turned his head and looked into Filli's face for the first time. He carried his cigarette to his mouth again but kept his hand covering the lower part of his face. He didn't take his eyes off Filli's.

Filli stared back. He wasn't expecting answers. The fact that the questions were getting home was enough for him. He turned his head away and continued. 'By arranging to meet me and listen to what I have to say you have already accepted the authority that I can attract. That authority could go higher.' He glanced out of the corner of his eye to see how Neurie was taking it, but learned nothing. 'The operation directed by you could be closed down at the flick of an intercom switch.' Neurie let him have his head. 'But for the time being I believe it could serve a purpose, in conjunction with Action Association, in running down again' – he underlined the word 'again' by spitting into the dust at his feet, a gesture he'd brought with him from the Algerian *bled* – 'Lieutenant Colonel Philippe de Guy-Montbron.' He turned fully on the bench so that he faced Neurie square on. 'I want two things from you, Monsieur Neurie.'

Neurie raised his eyebrows.

'Firstly, that you send me a complete list of operatives working on this project and give me an assurance that information concerning Guy-Montbron be passed immediately to my department in the Boulevard Montmorency, and that you play no part in the eventual taking of this man.'

Neurie grunted noncommittally.

It was enough for Filli.

'You said two things,' prompted Neurie.

'Ah, yes. There was an Englishman at Contrescarpe offering back-up to Guy-Montbron. He killed one of my men. There's some confusion about this Englishman's role in the affair. Was he holding Violle's hand and became disorientated by all the shooting, or was he for Guy-Montbron, which offers the interesting supposition that *rosbif* is backing the overthrow of our Government?' He paused to allow Neurie a moment to work out the implications of that, then narrowed his eyes. 'Which, in your estimation, Monsieur Neurie, is the more likely of those two suppositions?'

Neurie removed the cigarette from his lips and flicked it into the lake. He watched it fizzle and float and then suffer the inspection, and rejection, of a hungry mallard. It gave him time to think about Metcalfe. Not that Filli raising it was any surprise. The bigger surprise was that the Corsican country boy could tell the difference between an Englishman and a Rhodesian bushman! But Neurie kept his expression blank and watched the disappointed duck splutter back to the DST's stale cake. Metcalfe had jumped into bed with Montbron. It wasn't a surprise; it was the first lesson in the opening game: never trust an Englishman when there's intrigue and killing in the air.

He turned in his seat for a better inspection of Filli's eyes, two flat, inexpressive buttons, and wished he hadn't bothered. 'Englishmen?' He shook his head lightly. 'They don't play in this sort of game – there's nothing in it for them. You've made a mistake. It sounds as though someone's been feeding you horse shit.'

Filli's eyes narrowed for a brief second as he glanced back into the recent past. 'Horse shit be fucked! I looked the bastard in the eye as he shot my man. If he'd had any sense he would have killed me too, but the stupid bastard lost his nerve. He had me to rights, he only had to pull the trigger! Bloody Englishmen!' He spat into the dust at his feet to show what he thought of Englishmen. 'He's going to pay for it.'

'Have you finished, Filli?'

Filli's chin jerked up at the tone of Neurie's voice.

'What d'you mean, have I finished?'

'Right. When you get back to your dispensary get on the phone and ask your D-G to spell out to you the significance of a Presidential "K" authority. I operate under such an authority, so let's not have any more talk of flicking intercom switches but more of how long you and your people are going to be allowed to occupy the streets of Paris. I don't like you, Filli, or your methods. The reason I agreed to meet you was so that the next time you and your people go on the rampage, mine is the face you will see when you look over your shoulder. Bear that in mind, particularly when the names Violle and Morel are mentioned. To borrow your earlier question, you have my meaning?'

The calm, matter-of-fact manner in which the words were delivered took Filli unawares, but he rode the punch. Not a man to frighten easily, he nevertheless felt a familiar chill at the back of his neck. He stared hard into Neurie's cold, expressionless eyes and read the message. Neurie was making a serious threat. He was talking death, and Filli had no doubts that he was quite capable of carrying it out.

Filli kept his feelings hidden. He stood up and buttoned his coat, but before he moved away Neurie uncrossed his legs and said, casually, 'What sort of gun do you wear, Filli?'

'Petter M50, 9mm.' Filli's expression didn't alter as he began unbuttoning his jacket again.

'D'you mind if I have a look at it?'

Filli slipped it out of its holster, removed the magazine and pulled back the slide, allowing the round in the breech to flip into his hand. He held the weapon out, butt first. He knew what it was all about. 'Send it over to Montmorency when you've read it!'

Neurie didn't move. It didn't matter now. He stared at the automatic for a moment, then shook his head. 'Never mind.' He waved the pistol away.

Filli reversed it, reloaded and slipped it back into its pouch on his belt. He didn't look like a man who'd won an interesting point; he'd forgotten about it by the time he closed his coat on it. 'I do not intend giving up the search for Guy-Montbron. It's more than national interest – it's personal. I suggest you bear that in mind if we find ourselves lying in the same ditch. The same applies to the Englishman. Goodbye.'

Neurie didn't respond. He continued staring back at the ducks, who, having exhausted all other sources, had come to his part of the embankment and were gazing slit-eyed at him with the vague expectation of some more stale bread and cake. But Neurie wasn't seeing them. He was wondering how nasty little bastards like Filli had got themselves into what had always been something of a gentleman's profession. But then, he decided philosophically, when times were bad, street corners, even in the best of districts, attracted a very untypical sort of whore.

Neurie waited until Filli was out of sight before getting to his feet. He took the long route round the pond, through the Bois de Vincennes and out on to the Boulevard Poniatowski via the Route des Fortifications. He spotted, in quick succession, two of Filli's team and wandered down Poniatowski towards the Porte Dorée looking for the third. The three-man team – the infallible watch crew. But this lot were dopey. He left all three staring at the bushes in the gardens behind Charles de Foucauld, as he was intended to, and carried on back to Picpus. He climbed into the car and closed his eyes. The driver, waiting under the awning of a nearby café, waited until Neurie's E2 cover man slipped into the passenger seat before joining them. He didn't spot the fourth man, Pecotti, either.

Neurie's reserve safe house was in the Rue Bonaparte, a narrow street between the Boulevard St-Germain and the Quai Malaquais. Every other shop in the dark, overshadowed street sold antiques; if antiques weren't your thing, there were one or two interesting, or different, nightclubs. Pecotti watched Neurie go to ground and waited for the next move. He was in no hurry; his patience was inexhaustible. He was doing what he did best and he settled down, philosophically, for however long it was going to take.

31

THERE WERE TWO Japanese in the antique shop peering through thick-lensed glasses over a 1930s blonde half-nude painting. They looked up guiltily when the door opened and a broad shaft of morning sunlight cut through the gloomy interior. They studied Neurie surreptitiously as he walked through the shop and waited until he'd gone through the curtain at the back before resuming their inspection. Neurie ignored them.

He sat back in his chair in the large but gloomy room and closed his eyes and twiddled his thumbs – an unconscious gesture. Behind his closed eyelids his mind was ticking over in time with his twirling thumbs. It was Filli's commentary on the Englishman. It had to be Harry Metcalfe. Gaby Violle had said on the phone to Control that Montbron and Metcalfe had got together. *What a bloody combination. Five minutes after they shake hands four men drop dead in a square in Paris. But let's hope they stick together – Englishmen are much easier to find in France than Frenchmen. And there's another interesting little factor . . .*

Neurie's eyes opened. He gazed around him, then leaned back and reached for the orange folder on the shelf behind him. He opened it and flicked through the wad of pictures of the comings and goings at the Massotte house on the Avenue Beauchamp. He didn't dwell on the bulk, he knew exactly what he was looking for and when he found them he put them to one side. There were several, and not one would have got beyond a chorus of belly-laughs at the most amateur of photographic competitions. He spread them out before him, grainy, out of focus, too dark or too light. Harry Metcalfe featured in all of them, but he was interested only in the other figure: Mme Monique Bonnet, one-time nursery playmate and, briefly, wife. He picked out one, a very poor best, and stared hard at the image, the attractiveness and obvious sensuality undisguised by the poor quality of the print.

But attractiveness and sensuality weren't what he wanted. Here was the interesting factor: Harry Metcalfe was back in the saddle. He hadn't been pushed off, he'd gone of his own – or was it Montbron's? – accord. And Monique was still there – waiting? Where? Metcalfe wasn't going to enjoy sleeping with Montbron. His legs were too hairy to start with, even if he was that way, and Metcalfe certainly wasn't. *So, Monique, has our old friend, the lecherous bastard, told you where his tongue's hanging out? If he hasn't yet, he bloody well will . . .* Neurie bundled the pictures back into the file and reached for the phone. Then stopped. *Let's do it the hard way. Let's make ourselves as sick as a bloody pig on heat . . . Let's give it the personal touch.* Monique would find it hard to refuse a cup of coffee and a little gentle probing to a familiar face standing with his finger on her doorbell. The phone dropping back into its cradle has a touch of the definite about it. He was right.

Monique's flat was a mess. There were clothes all over the place, draped across chairs, spread over the dining table, hanging wherever a coat hanger could hang. The bedroom door was ajar. He glanced in. The bed had its share too, but jutting out of the curtained window recess was an expensive leather suitcase that seemed to have been hurriedly shoved there, out of sight. It looked as if he'd struck gold. Monique was about to do a bunk.

'I was walking past and wondered how you were getting on?' It was a strange business; a one-time unforgettable intimacy at its most raw reduced to a forced, embarrassed shyness. She was unnatural too. Perhaps the regret was mutual? Two strangers in an empty flat. Gérard felt slightly gauche; that remembered funny feeling when he came back after the war and found his spotty playmate had grown up. She was a woman, an attractive woman, not one of the chaps. That first open-mouthed kiss, her breast warm and live, and the feel of her tongue on his . . . *And what's it like to be still in love and wave her off on her honeymoon with the bastard who broke it all up? Fuck you, Metcalfe! Jesus, Neurie! For Christ's sake cut it out, you're behaving like a bloody schoolboy. Get on with it!*

'Any chance of a cup of coffee?'

A slight reluctance? She was on edge. Nothing to do with entertaining an ex-husband.

'Going away?' He waited until she'd gone into the kitchen before settling himself down on the sofa. A silly question. He was still gazing about him when she came out and leaned against the doorpost. Silly or not, she considered his question seriously and nodded absently. 'Yes, I want to get away from Paris for a bit.' *Don't make a song and dance about it . . .* Jeanette Fabre had passed on Montbron's instructions as bluntly as they'd been given. *But don't make a pantomime of secrecy either if anybody gets seriously nosy . . .* 'I get restless this time of the year – don't you remember?'

He didn't. But shrugged. He remembered lots of other things. This wasn't the time or the place.

She took up the conversation again. 'Are you busy?'

'So so. Where are you going – south?'

'More or less.'

'That's nice.'

She gave a nervous laugh; it was more of a snort, but he knew what she meant. 'I'm not so sure about nice. Depends how well you know the place. Marseilles?' *Oh my God! Should I have mentioned that? Careful! Don't be secretive. This is Gérard, ex-husband, ex-boyfriend, ex-childhood sweetheart, ex-everything you can think of. He's not the Gestapo!*

Neurie smiled disarmingly. They were getting on famously. They sounded as natural as a couple in a Mauriac struggle, and as casual. But he wasn't ready to go yet. 'Even Marseilles has its charm.' He didn't believe it; the Marseilles he knew wouldn't know how to spell charm. 'Perhaps I could call round when you get back? Just to make sure everything's all right. Nothing complicated . . .'

He stuck with it as long as he could. But they were running

out of small talk. Her mind wasn't on it, she was somewhere else. She didn't exactly push him out, she just stopped talking. He gave up and began sorting himself out on the soft, low-slung sofa. 'I've taken up enough of your time. I think I'd better let you get on.' She didn't try to stop him as he stood up, placed his coffee-cup on the table and held out his hand. She ignored it and tilted her cheek towards him. 'Have a nice trip. I'll let myself out.' He turned for the door. She hadn't moved. He stopped with his hand on the doorknob, turned his head and offered her a quizzical smile. 'Any idea where I can find Harry Metcalfe?'

She stared at him as though he'd hit her under the ear and moved back a pace so that her shoulders had something to rest against. She recovered quickly. 'Harry Metcalfe?'

Neurie's smile didn't shift; he locked it into place. 'That's right. You haven't forgotten him already?' She didn't appreciate the joke. He kept his hand on the door-catch and his eyes on hers. 'Is he still in Paris?'

She didn't nibble. Jeanette Fabre's warning hadn't included *. . . and don't mention Harry Metcalfe to anyone, least of all Gérard Neurie or any of his friends*, but it all seemed part of the same script. She decided to repair the breach. 'I don't know, Gérard. Perhaps he's gone back to England. He didn't tell me. He just left. He could have gone back, but if I run across him, shall I ask him to get in touch with you?'

'No, don't bother, it's not important. It was just a thought. Well . . .' He unclipped the smile and nodded. 'Enjoy your trip.' He didn't mean it.

She remained where she was for some time after he'd left. Neurie's parting words had left an uncomfortable feeling. Nothing definite that she could put her finger on or her mind to, nothing tangible, just a gentle, warm massage of warning near the pit of her stomach. But it was nothing sinister and she shrugged it aside. Harry had said he'd seen Gérard the other day, perhaps they were friends again, though it was hardly likely, knowing Gérard! But why was Jeanette being so mysterious on Harry's behalf? Maybe he was in trouble, in which case the last person he would want help from was Gérard. She stared at the door as if wondering whether Neurie was standing outside, listening to her thoughts. Unconsciously she was getting into the dark side of the grey game and something was rubbing off; she was thinking furtively, she was covering tracks. But Neurie's gentle interrogation had vanished from her mind by the time she had retrieved her suitcase from its inadequate and futile hiding-place and finished selecting a wardrobe for the unlikely holiday resort of Marseilles, via the salt-marshes of the Camargue's Nîmes.

And Neurie had got what he came for.

Two hundred metres from the entrance to Monique Bonnet's flat stood the Café Raspail. Nothing elaborate, it was only a bar with the one item on the menu, hard-boiled eggs, piled in a wicker basket on the counter. Outside, under a no-frills canopy, were six metal tables, each with two uncomfortable metal chairs placed with their backs to the café window so that the drinkers could watch the girls walking by on the pavement. All the tables were occupied.

At the end nearest Monique's flat, sitting on his own with a tulip-shaped glass half-filled with diluted Pernod and reading *L'Équipe*, sat Georges Filli's invisible man, Pecotti. Jean-Baptiste Pecotti came, for Filli, from the right part of France. A Corsican – he couldn't have been anything else – he was a thickset, bull-necked peasant from the Filosorma *bocca* who hadn't pulled on his first pair of shoes until his twentieth birthday. With short legs shaped like the stumps of felled oaks, he had the gut of a sumo wrestler hanging over his belt like a sack of water. But he suited Filli's purpose. He was a Corsican of the old school. He was good at watching, but he was also a man for the occasion, provided the occasion was a one-sided rough house and he was on the dishing-up side. A man with the instincts of an orang-utang, his fear ducts had yet to be tested. There was nothing in Filli's briefing that offered the slightest suggestion that this was going to happen now. Georges had mentioned that Englishmen had come into the business on the other side; what Pecotti thought of Englishmen showed as a glint of malice in his Neanderthal features. This was the work he liked best, and being told how to do it by Georges Filli was the added bonus. Finding Englishmen and kicking their balls into a pulp was right up his street.

As he sat waiting, the smoke from a dark-papered Gauloise hanging from his limp lips wriggled its way past his screwed-up eyes. But he didn't remove the source of the irritation; he read better with his eyes screwed up like that. When he saw Neurie leave the entrance to the apartment he paid his bill, folded the newspaper, and with the cigarette still smouldering between his lips, prepared to leave. He showed none of the surprise he felt when Neurie strolled towards him and turned into the café.

He opened his newspaper again, turned slightly in his chair and leaned back. Glancing through the thin lace curtain behind him, he saw Neurie establish himself at the counter with a *demi-pression*. He watched for a few seconds longer, then settled back in his earlier position. He ordered himself another Pernod, adjusted slightly the position of his chair so that he could see Neurie's outline without turning his head, and went back to the sports pages of his newspaper.

He'd barely settled down when Neurie was on the move again. But it wasn't enough to panic him into activity. A lowering of the newspaper, a slight incline of the head and he saw Neurie put down his half-drunk glass of beer and make his way to the telephone cubicle at the other end of the café. It gave him no concern. The target was visible. What he was saying on the phone was another matter, but it wasn't his problem. His brief was to watch, not listen.

In an upstairs room of the antique shop Neurie's new assistant, a specialist seconded from the Department Maurice secretariat, allowed the phone only one sequence of rings.

'Find Roger Bineau,' Neurie told her, 'and tell him to come to the Café—' he glanced over his shoulder and read the name backwards from the glass front of the café '—Raspail. It's about three-quarters of the way down the Boulevard Raspail from Sèvres Babylone, on the right-hand side. I'll be in the bar.'

Pecotti, watching Roger Bineau park his car in a side-street opposite, tucked himself further behind his newspaper when Bineau came across the road and entered the café. He knew him by sight, but that was all. It was doubtful whether Bineau knew him.

Pecotti allowed himself a confirmatory glance through the window. Neurie and Bineau were perched on stools at the counter, their heads close together as they concentrated on peeling hard-boiled eggs. It looked as though they were settling in for the rest of the day. He stuck his head back into his newspaper and decided to wait for further developments before ringing Filli. He tapped the window again for the waiter. Watching the two men stuffing eggs into their mouths had given him an appetite. He ordered four.

The wait was a lot shorter than he'd anticipated.

Ten minutes and two eggs each later, Neurie and Bineau left the café and walked back towards the building housing Monique Bonnet's apartment. Pecotti didn't move; he just peeled another egg and watched.

As they passed the entrance he saw Neurie jerk his head towards the door and Bineau take a sideways glance. They walked a little way further, then crossed the boulevard and retraced their steps until they were almost opposite where Pecotti was sitting. They stopped in front of a larger café, a proper one with a restaurant, outside tables and a glass-protected veranda for diners afraid of getting their heads damp, and stood talking for some time before parting. Neurie headed towards the taxi stand by the Sèvres Babylone Métro and Bineau, after a moment's hesitation, entered the restaurant and found himself a table behind the glass protection. He sat down in full view of his watcher, facing squarely in the direction of Monique Bonnet's apartment entrance.

Pecotti waited until he'd settled, then made his way to the telephone.

The car sent from the Boulevard Montmorency found Filli in one of the restaurants in the Place de la Contrescarpe with a large dish of *boeuf bourguignon* in front of him and an almost empty carafe of the red *ordinaire*. It was the morbid part of his brain – 90 per cent of his character – that had inspired the visit. He wasn't recognized. But the publicity had been total; the restaurant was doing good business. He wasn't the only person in Paris with morbid tendencies.

He left his plate half finished. He was glad to leave. He hadn't enjoyed his lunch or his second visit to the Place de la Contrescarpe. Even the wine left an unpleasant after-taste.

'Pecotti rang from a place on the Boulevard Raspail,' the driver told him. 'The message is that his friend paid a visit to an apartment block there and spent some time in one of the flats.'

'Name?' growled Filli. It was a muffled question and came round one of his fingers, which was busy inside his mouth dislodging pieces of *boeuf bourguignon* from between his teeth.

'Sorry, I didn't get that, boss.'

'What was the bloody name of the person he was visiting!'

The driver shrugged. Filli was behaving almost normally again. He nearly smiled in anticipation of Filli's reaction to his reply. 'One of three, apparently.'

'For Christ's sake! Can't these useless bastards do a simple thing like follow somebody to a bloody door and read the name? Am I running a sodding playschool?'

The driver went on as if he'd heard nothing. 'Two couples and a woman living on her own. The other three flats were empty at the time.'

'That's something. Go on.'

'Monsieur and Madame Rosiers, an old couple in their seventies. He's a retired tailor. The other couple are Monsieur and Madame Bosquet, newly-weds, not long back from their honeymoon in Martinique and still giving the new bed a hard time. They rarely come up for air according to—'

'Why the hell are you telling me all this?'

'Pecotti offered it as a sort of elimination process. I think he was trying to show you that you're not running a sodding playschool!'

Filli lit a cigarette. 'Have you ever considered that one day you might find yourself strolling up and down the Faubourg-St-Honoré in a peaked cap, picking up dog shit with a little barrow?'

The driver was unperturbed. 'Shall I go on with Pecotti's words?'

Filli blew smoke against the windscreen by way of assent.

The driver continued. 'Nothing happened when these names were put through the wringer. No connection with anything. The whole lot were anonymous!'

'Why do I get the feeling you're saving number three for something?'

The driver pulled up at a red traffic light, stuck his fingers in his top pocket and pulled out a crumpled strip of paper. He tilted it towards the light and read from it: ' "Madame Monique Bonnet. About thirty. A looker who does nothing except make herself look beautiful." The concierge's words, according to Pecotti.'

'On the game?' Filli had down-to-earth opinions of attractive women in their thirties who did nothing except make themselves look beautiful and live in posh apartment blocks.

The driver shook his head. 'Not according to the concierge.'

'Then why the bloody hell have I given up half my soddin' lunch? Is that the sum of Pecotti's report on the job I gave him?' Filli unloaded another burst of smoke against the windscreen. 'My bloody granny's pussy-cat could have handled this!'

The driver shrugged again and pulled away from the lights. He stuck his hand out of the window and poked a single finger into the air at the impatient youth in a souped-up, battered *deux chevaux* behind. It was an automatic gesture that meant nothing to either of them. The boy didn't follow it up and the driver continued with what he'd been saying. 'Although he did say she'd had an Englishman staying with her for a few days.'

'How could he tell he was an Englishman?'

'That's exactly what Pecotti asked. Apparently the concierge was in London during the war with de Gaulle and the man said "good morning" to him.'

Filli had a sudden flash vision of a hard-faced killer and a pair of cold eyes lining up the barrel of an automatic on his face. That was an Englishman. Would that grim-faced bastard say good morning to a concierge? Bloody unlikely. He'd be more likely to kick the old bugger in the crotch for getting in his way! 'Did he say anything else?'

'I don't think Pecotti asked. They ran the woman's name and address, along with the other two, in a routine profile just for the hell of it. She was born in Normandy, Monique de Cantenac. Married twice, first to one of our non-monarchial aristocrats, a Baron Neurie, and second to—'

'Neurie? You sure about that name?'

The driver had another quick look at the scrap of paper. 'That's the name I wrote down. That was her first, and then—'

'Forget it! Put your foot down and get me to wherever Pecotti's deposited his fat arse, as quick as you can. Break the bloody law if you need to!'

Pecotti, in good watcher manner, didn't stay in the same place too long. He'd moved to another café further down the pavement. Still sitting outside, still well out of sight of Neurie's man, he continued to command a clear view of the comings and goings of both the restaurant and Monique Bonnet's apartment-block entrance. He had in his hand the inevitable small glass of cloudy liquid, from which he continued to sip as he followed Filli's approach. He caught the eye of the waiter hovering in the doorway. Pointing to his glass, he raised two fingers and with his foot kicked a chair out from under the table.

'Anything moving?' murmured Filli as he sat down and dropped a packet of Gauloises on to the metal table. He waited for Pecotti to help himself and light one before doing the same, then sat back in his chair, legs out in front of him, hands in his pockets, and listened, with apparent disinterest, while Pecotti brought him up to date.

It didn't take long.

Neurie's man, Bineau, was still in his greenhouse, still alone, still eating. Nobody had gone into, or left, Monique Bonnet's place. But something was going to happen. Filli could feel it in his Corsican toes. He sipped his Pernod thoughtfully. Pecotti stopped talking and did the same. Pecotti, in true Corsican peasant-stock manner, had no party chit-chat. He and Filli were on the same social roundabout; they could have been two foreigners thrown together at an empty table in a crowded restaurant. Filli glanced at him briefly, met his eyes through the spiral of cigarette smoke and then looked away. A pity it wasn't Rosso sitting there knocking back his Pernod. It wouldn't have lasted a second with Rosso – he drank the bloody stuff as if it were cold tea. But it wasn't Rosso, and Rosso wasn't going to drink any more Pernod; he wasn't going to drink any more cold tea either. *Forget bloody Rosso. Let's see what we've got here!*

He drew on his Gauloise, removed it from his lips and allowed most of the smoke to escape through his nostrils before inhaling what was left.

This is what we've got here . . .

Just up the road there is the ex-wife of Gérard Neurie, a senior officer of SDECE, or, worse, possibly Department Maurice, one of whose close associates, Gabriel Violle, by accident or design became involved in Montmorency business. Result: the aborting of a perfectly laid ambush and the deaths of three Montmorency agents, plus his own. We also note the involvement of an Englishman in the game.

Gérard Neurie, who had been controlling Violle, suddenly decides to pay a visit to his former wife, who apparently has a close friendship with an Englishman! The coincidence is that it happens only hours after being put in the picture by yours truly of Montmorency's version of the balls-up at the Place de la Contrescarpe. Is there a connection between Neurie's ex-wife and the bloody Englishman? Is it the same Englishman? Possibly.

The coincidence is too strong, particularly as Neurie, after visiting his ex-wife, sticks a watcher on the job to mark her movements. So how do all three tie up? What did she tell him, and what the bloody hell's going on? And what about this fucking Englishman? Where's he gone?

A sucking of teeth from the other side of the table brought Filli out of his reverie.

'The sniffer's left his table.' Pecotti swung his eyes from the restaurant's glass frontage and half rose from his chair to get a clearer view of Monique Bonnet's front door. A taxi had pulled up and double-parked. After a short wait the driver got out of his cab and walked towards the door.

'Pay the bill and follow me to the car,' growled Filli and moved quickly on to the pavement. He was in time to see Roger Bineau start his car up and manoeuvre it so that he covered the main stretch of the boulevard. It didn't worry Filli as he clambered into his own vehicle. The driver was already pointing in the right direction. They all sat and watched Monique come out of the building, a small, hard bag in her hand, followed by the taxi-driver with a large suitcase in each of his. Filli sniffed as he watched the driver stuff the heavy bags into the boot. There was plenty of time for everybody to get into position.

'If you bugger this up,' Filli warned the driver, 'and we end up driving around Paris with nobody in front of us, I shall spread you across the front of this car and personally blow your bloody bollocks off!'

The driver took it in his stride. Pecotti lit another cigarette. Then the three vehicles moved down the Boulevard Raspail, traversed Paris, and, in convoy, headed north.

Half an hour later, as they drove under the north autoroute and continued on the N17, Filli broke the silence he'd imposed upon himself.

'Jesus Christ!' he hissed. 'Le Bourget! She's going on a bloody aeroplane!'

'Local, boss,' said the driver without turning his head. 'That's the Air Inter terminal they're going in.'

'Thank Christ for that! Pecotti, come with me. You' – Filli touched the driver's shoulder – 'stay with the guy. Watch him park and follow him. Quick, as he moves away, have a good look. Do either of you two know him?'

Pecotti said he knew him by sight. Probably the DST. The driver shook his head. Filli said, 'OK. Keep your face away from him, Pecotti, don't let him catch a glimpse. Stay in the background, one eye on him and one on me, and be ready to move when I twitch my finger. Right, where's that bloody woman going?'

He soon found out.

'Nîmes. She's going to bloody Nîmes!' Filli sidled up to Pecotti. 'Get over to the counter, quick! I want two seats on that bloody aeroplane, you and me. Here—' he shoved a wad of notes into Pecotti's hand '—pay with this. Just a minute!' He grabbed Pecotti's arm. 'That other bastard's doing the same . . .'

'No he isn't, he's going to the phone.'

'OK, right, be quick! I'll be with the woman. She's going to the bar.'

Filli found an empty table in the corner of the bar and lit a cigarette as he watched Monique settle at a table and order a glass of champagne. He glanced at his watch. The aircraft for Nîmes wasn't due to leave for another three-quarters of an hour. He ordered the same for himself and settled down for a long wait.

Pecotti's agitation showed even from a distance. His normally sombre, laughless face was, for once, suffused with animation. It stopped Filli's glass reaching his lips. 'The bloody aeroplane's full,' he spat. 'Not a seat to be had.'

'Go back and tell them who you are.'

'I did. It didn't help. They told me to bugger off when I started swinging the stick. Friggin' peasants!'

Filli didn't panic. But he wasn't far off it. 'Where's Neurie's dog?'

'He's gone. Your driver's gone too.'

Filli gulped down his champagne and burped noisily. There was no one in his corner to show disapproval, but it wouldn't have mattered anyway; Filli in a worried state of mind had no time for the niceties of convention. He crumpled his half-smoked cigarette into the ashtray and moved briskly towards the Air Inter departures counter.

'What have you got going to Nîmes?' he demanded from the girl with the sweet smile.

'Why does everybody want to go to Nîmes this afternoon?' she asked without moving the smile. 'You're the second last-minute application—' She was about to offer more observations but was brought up short. The smile vanished as well.

'D'you know what this is?' Filli flicked his DST authority card on to the counter so that it rested by her hand.

She glanced down and studied it. She wasn't very impressed. 'The other fellow had the same thing.' She produced another smile and fixed it into place the way she'd been taught; there was no warmth in it. 'And I have to tell you the same as I told him.' She continued to stare at the card, then looked up into Filli's jet-black eyes. 'It's not a very good likeness. Where do you people get these done, from a vending machine?'

He didn't shoot her. He just wished he had Rosso's lie-detector in his hand and her pink little bottom bared and winking up at him. But he kept a grip on his usually volatile temper and gave a suppressed 'Ffff – ! Never mind about that.' He picked up the card and put it back in his pocket. 'Is there anything going somewhere near Nîmes?'

It took her three minutes to glance at an itinerary. Filli's toes were beginning to itch. 'I can offer you two seats on the 17.05 flight to Perpignan.' She flipped a page. 'Boarding in . . .'

Come on you stupid bitch!

She took her time as she studied the tiny watch on her wrist. 'Twelve minutes.'

'I'll take them!'

He picked up his tickets and change and stuffed them into his pocket. At a brisk walk he made his way across the International

Flights concourse and then to the Security Division on the far side.

They showed more interest in the DST credentials than had the girl at Air Inter. They agreed to arrange for Nîmes Security Group to hold Monique Bonnet and another half-dozen passengers for a snap security check, but couldn't guarantee delaying her for more than half an hour without arousing suspicion.

'How long does it take to drive from Perpignan to Nîmes?' he asked.

'About three hours,' suggested the Senior Duty Officer, then glanced at Filli's twitching hands. 'Say two and a bit.'

Filli stared expressionlessly at the officer and muttered his own calculation. 'Two hours. Still doesn't give me enough bloody time! How can the Nîmes flight take-off be delayed for two hours?'

'You've got to be joking!' The DST official looked into Filli's unsmiling eyes and quickly changed his observation. 'You're not joking! But there's no way, my friend. Nothing'll stop internal flights. It'd take the threat of the bloody thing being structurally unsound to do that.' He pulled a face and thought for a moment, then added, 'The report of a bomb on board would jerk the schedule off balance.'

'There's a bomb on board,' reported Filli.

The DST man blanched and shook his head. 'It'd have to be a warning over the phone, recorded, and logged in here . . .' He pointed his finger delicately at the recording equipment in the corner of the office and avoided looking Filli in the eye.

'Stand by for a bomb report!' advised Filli.

32

MONTBRON DROPPED HARRY Metcalfe at the Fabre house with twenty-two unlucky red-billed Spanish marsh ducks they'd shot, and, with a casual remark of 'Something I've forgotten', turned the jeep round and drove into Saintes-Maries-de-la-Mer. Just before reaching the centre of the town he turned off towards the sea and parked outside an old-fashioned café with a long open veranda that faced the salty acres of l'Étang dit l'Impérial. It was anonymous and secure, and as a spot to build a café, guaranteed to fail. The state of the place showed the owner had reached the same conclusion. With nothing in its favour, even the view had to struggle; flat, almost without horizon, it was totally uninteresting. Only the odd, perverse local came here to drink, no one to eat. Nobody came to enjoy the scenery. Montbron certainly hadn't.

He ordered coffee and drank it as he sat and looked around him. He was the only person there. He left the cup of coffee half drunk and made his way into the back of the café and locked himself into the telephone cabinet.

'D'you recognize my voice?'

Vernet nearly jumped out of his skin.

'Jesus Christ!' His eyes darted round the grubby room and rested on the two expressionless faces studying him. He took the phone from his ear, pointed furiously at it and made whirling signs with his finger. The two technicians shrugged their shoulders at each other and then at him. Neither made a move. After a stagnant moment or two, one of them pulled a face and pointed at the recording apparatus on the trestle-table. Its light glowed a bright green and beside it a large tape spool turned silently and lazily on its spindle. 'Talk, you stupid bastard!' he mouthed at Vernet.

'Are you all right?' asked Montbron, his voice edged with suspicion.

'Sure! Sure! Where are you? What happened? I went to the Place de la Contrescarpe like you told me and there was all bloody hell breaking loose – what happened? I bolted . . . I got out of it, and I've been having the shits ever since! What happened? Where are you?'

The man who'd waved his hand at Vernet slowly uncurled from the ground-level armchair he'd been lounging in and pulled himself to his feet. He glanced professionally at the recorder. The tape was still gliding from one spool to the other. He leaned over it and studied the volume meters. They flicked jerkily within their limits and he nodded to himself as he straightened up, then caught Vernet's eye. 'Stop asking him where he is, you silly sod!' He'd pitched his voice low enough to escape the zone of audibility. He knew what he was doing; zones of audibility were his speciality. It was the sort of people who got in his way that he wasn't sure of. 'But don't stop talking, *couillon*!'

'Listen,' said Montbron. 'I don't want to go into detail at the moment. I got caught in the fracas at Contrescarpe and had to bolt. Did you get away all right? You weren't spotted? You weren't followed?'

'Nothing happened. But you? But—'

Montbron cut in on what was going to be another hysterical outburst, 'I'll let you know all about it when we meet. I'll be back in Paris in a couple of days. Get ready to move out.'

'OK. I'll stay here until you make contact. Where are you now?' Vernet glanced automatically at the man by the recording equipment. No facial rebuke this time, but a nod of encouragement. 'And where shall I meet you?'

'I'll be in touch. In the meantime, check your surroundings. Make sure you can move about in the open. You know all the tricks – use them!'

'Sure, sure—' Vernet began to panic. It sounded like the goodbyes were about to be said. 'Phi—'

'Watch it!'

'It's all very well for you to tell me to watch it, you're out there, you've got things to do, but what about me? Phi—' He cut off the name, but started again before Montbron could interrupt. The technician at the recorder made a slight adjustment, nodded to Vernet and went and sat down on the edge of the bed. Vernet turned his back to him. 'I've got to have something to do. I'm bored. I'm going round the bloody bend! I can't just sit here all day and all night with my thumb stuck up my arse, staring at the wall. I want some action! Give me some work, give me something to do. Let's get together . . .' He glanced over his shoulder at the technician and looked for approval. There was nothing, just a blank look, not even a shrug of the shoulders. He stopped talking into the mouthpiece. He'd said enough. He was learning fast.

Montbron said nothing for several moments. It worried Vernet. He glanced at the machine, then at the technician again. The silence was pressing down; it was like smoke. 'Are you sti – ?' He cut the query in half and waited again.

Montbron made up his mind. Give him something to do, something to keep him quiet, something to keep him in the game. It wouldn't do any harm. 'OK, listen, I want you to find out as much as you can about Jacques Bouchard, but don't stick your neck out and don't do anything silly.'

'Who's Jacques Bouchard?'

'Minister of the Interior. Go to the library. Read all about him, look for flaws in his screen – you know the sort of thing. I'll fill you in in detail when I come to Paris.'

'When's that?'

'I told you, I'll contact you when I get there.'

'We going to ki—?'

'Shut up. Don't say anything! I'll be in touch.'

The phone went dead in Vernet's ear. He held on for some time, listening to the buzz of the instrument in his hand, until the technician took it from him and replaced it on its cradle.

'Looks like you and your mate are going to knock off the Minister of the Interior,' said the man who'd been listening through earphones. He stared at Vernet with new interest. He hadn't been told what he was dealing with; he didn't even know Vernet's name, his real one or his new DST identity. To him and his records Vernet was simply 'the subject'. It was Filli's way of looking after the welfare of his new recruit. His brief had been to 'listen and record', but now 'the subject' was suddenly cloaked in a new personality. Vernet had begun to gain status.

'Get Filli on the phone.'

Vernet bubbled with new confidence; it was all becoming very natural. Filli no longer frightened him; nor did Montbron. He was beginning to feel very sure of himself, that this was his destiny. But he had to be careful of going over the top, he wasn't through the wire yet, and if he didn't watch his step he'd be like the blind man walking a crumbling parapet: a bottomless drop on one side, a pit full of angry snakes on the other. It brought him back down to earth when the man at the phone said, 'Filli's out – no contact number. They'll pass the word when he calls in. They said you'd better stay put. Us as well.'

Montbron remained in the phone box. He replaced the receiver and stared at it, unseeing, for half a minute. Something was wrong. Paul Vernet didn't sound right. He sounded nervous, not a frightened nervous, a worried one. *I've got news for you, Paul – we all are.* Frightened? He wasn't the only one. But there was something else, a scent of fear spiced with the suggestion of arrogance. Paul Vernet's enquiring whine had had an edge of interrogation . . . Montbron raised his head and frowned at his taut expression in the cabinet's small mirror; he didn't like what he saw very much and after a second or two pulled a face at the eyes looking back at him. *He's got to go, and it's got to be done tomorrow – one way or the other.*

He felt a lot better having made the decision.

He dropped more tokens into the slot and dialled.

'Diderot,' he grunted when it answered.

'. . . *moment*,' came the response, and a few seconds later Xavier's fruity accent tickled his ear. Xavier didn't waste time. The Place de la Contrescarpe wasn't mentioned. With the daily toll of indiscriminate killings mounting in Paris, and the casualty figures from Algiers beginning to get to the people, he probably didn't connect Montbron with the episode. 'Are your plans completed?' he demanded.

Montbron allowed the question to hang in the air for a moment, then, hedging, replied, 'The day after tomorrow. Please arrange your committee and decide on a rendezvous for you and me to meet. I think you'll be satisfied.'

'That remains to be seen. Ring this number at ten thirty-five precisely, Tuesday morning. Goodbye.' He put the phone down without waiting for Montbron's acknowledgement.

Montbron made one more call. It was brief and almost one-sided. 'Diderot. Can you have a plan drawn up for the assassination of a very senior Government Minister. Plenty of detail – Paris and country home – to take place within the next ten days and to appear the assessment of a one-man surveillance operation on the Minister's routine movements. Can it be ready for Monday night and dropped at Montparnasse station? You have the other key.' He glanced down at the otherwise unidentifiable key in his hand. 'Number seventeen?'

'Target's name?'

'Jacques Bouchard. The full committee meets to approve his assassination on Tuesday. I shall make my last report to you Tuesday p.m., then close down. Is that OK?'

'Perfectly. Oh, and Philippe—'

'Sir?'

'Well done.'

Harry Metcalfe showed no curiosity about where he'd been when Montbron returned from Saintes-Maries.

Relaxed in a deep armchair in the conservatory at the end of the main building, he had a tray of interesting-looking bottles on a low coffee-table on one side and a dish of cashew nuts on a table on the other. He was drinking from a long glass of almost black liquid, the outside frosted with condensation from its chilled contents.

'I'll have the same,' said Montbron and reached down to fill his hand with nuts as he sat down opposite Metcalfe. 'Anything in the paper?'

Metcalfe folded *France-Dimanche* and tossed it into an empty chair. 'The usual guff. Jeanette Fabre phoned.'

Montbron appeared comfortable and at ease as he watched Metcalfe prepare his drink. But it was a wasted effort. Metcalfe wasn't interested in Montbron's state of mind. Montbron waited. It could only be good news.

'Is she well?'

'She didn't say. What she did say, though, is that Monique Bonnet is coming down tomorrow. She's catching an afternoon flight to Nîmes and she asked if we could meet her. I said we'd be there with roses. Is this your doing?'

Montbron was noncommittal. 'I mentioned it.' He waited a second. 'I won't be here when she arrives. I'm going back to Paris tomorrow. That unfinished business . . .'

'You're crazy!'

'Maybe. I'm leaving early in the morning. Will you come with me?'

'No.' Metcalfe turned and put a glass in his hand, then looked him in the eyes and slowly shook his head. 'Because there's nothing I can do to keep you on your feet. You've lost this one, Philippe. Forget it and get out.'

'You're wasting your breath, Harry.'

Metcalfe shook his head again. 'I think you've got a death-wish, Philippe. I think you've got a yearning to end your days in some scruffy Paris gutter. I also reckon your wish is about to come true, and I don't want to be there when it happens, watching, or lying alongside you! How long can I stay here?'

Montbron managed a crooked grin. Somewhere in Metcalfe's words he felt a prophecy. It gave a chilling feeling of fear and almost brought with it the shiver that started somewhere behind the navel. He'd had shivers before, bone-shuddering, teeth-chattering shivers of pure funk, nothing delicate about them. They'd been almost pleasurable. Now, however, he shrugged the feeling aside.

'You can stay as long as you like. Jeanette has no plans for the place. She comes on the spur of the moment, on a whim, and she hasn't got any whims just now. But take my advice . . . ?'

'Some other time.'

Montbron shook his head. Metcalfe was going to get it anyway. 'I'll manage on my own, Harry, but don't forget, you're committed, you've been logged, so don't go to sleep. Another thing for you to worry about: if I go down, you'll go too. When they start backtracking you'll be one of their first stops, and they won't pause for first-name introductions. You'll go straight on the rack, and if Monique's here with you she'll go too, so as soon as you get the strength back in your legs, start running – anywhere. Take her too, and if all goes well you won't have to leave anything behind.'

'Like what?'

'Your balls. Our friends picked up some very nasty habits playing with the *fidayine* in the Aurès mountains. Drop everything and run if you see anyone walking towards you with a sharp blade in his hand and his eyes staring at your crotch!'

Metcalfe wasn't in the mood. 'Can we be serious for a minute?'

'I am being.'

'The other sort of seriousness. This guy in Paris, this relation of yours, Vernet. I've been doing some serious thinking about him. I think that business in Contrescarpe was too elaborately set up to be an instantaneous ambush. It was planned, Philippe. Nobody followed me to the square. The bloody fighting was already going on when I got there. You were done, and your bloody half-brother helped them build the set . . . I warned you before. I'm going to do it again and then wash my hands of you. The bastard's been turned, Philippe. It's fucking obvious! Don't trust him. Drop him – or shoot the bastard on sight in the back of the head before he does you.'

Montbron shook his head. He knew what he was going to do. Words weren't necessary. He almost smiled, only his lips were too stiff to accommodate it.

But Metcalfe wasn't finished. With a look of exasperation he said, finally, 'OK. If you want to be pig-headed about it! But whatever happens, tell me what you're going to do next – just in case.'

Montbron's smile vanished. 'Forget it, Harry. If you're not going to help out, you don't get to see any more of the pictures. What you don't know can't harm you when they start breaking your fingers and looking at your tongue.' Montbron suddenly smiled. It was exceptional, not forced. For once this was a real smile. 'I'm going to take your advice.' He drank from his glass and then lowered it. Metcalfe waited. 'I'm retiring from the Paris scene on Tuesday night and slipping back to Germany. I shall become legal again by Wednesday morning. You and I'll meet again when the smoke lifts – if you haven't fucked yourself to death over the next couple of days! D'you know how to get to Nîmes Airport?'

33

GEORGES FILLI DREW into Nîmes Airport car park a good twenty minutes before the delayed Air Inter flight from Le Bourget touched down.

It had been a nightmare journey from Perpignan; the car was never going to be a good second-hand buy after Filli's cross-country treatment. Filli wasn't feeling too good either. His knees felt as if they'd been operated on with a hammer and chisel and his nerves cried out for a drink, but he was here now and there were more fun and games waiting round the corner – enough to take his mind off shaky knees.

He sat for a short while longer staring at the open car park, but there was nothing to interest him there. Taking Pecotti by surprise, he threw the door open and dragged himself out of the seat and into the evening sun. By the time he felt the ground under his feet his system was almost back to normal. Pecotti's was already there – it hadn't been anywhere else. Pecotti hadn't enough imagination to suffer from a break-neck race on a cross-country course with a madman who knew only one gear and only one position for the accelerator pedal.

Filli enjoyed his third cigarette as he stared at the main arrivals indicator board. It told him that the delayed Air Inter flight from Paris was now scheduled to land at 21.15. He glanced at his watch, then at the main hall clock; both agreed. He was feeling quite relaxed now. He turned towards the arrivals gate and studied the passengers from the recently landed flight. They all looked happy enough, but it wasn't obvious whether the happiness was derived from landing in one piece or the prospect of a warm night under the mosquito-netting listening to the unhappy bulls. He followed them with his eyes as they made their way towards the baggage-retrieval lobby, then moved his gaze to the main entrance and studied, in all his ugly glory, the heavy figure of his partner lounging with a cigarette in his mouth against the wall of the telephone area.

Filli caught his eye for a second, then glanced away. He didn't dislike Pecotti, but he wouldn't go out of his way for his company. He wouldn't let you down, he was solid and sure and reliable, but he was a bloody poor substitute for Rosso or Pietri. He shrugged to himself. Yesterday was the past; today was something else . . . And talking about something else, what the bloody hell had this woman come to Nîmes for?

He had this question on his mind when, half turning back to the indicator board, he spotted Harry Metcalfe.

Harry Metcalfe had a face Filli was never going to forget, and here he was, at Nîmes Airport, sitting comfortably and relaxing at the airport bar with a glass of something in one hand and a cigarette in the other. Filli ought to have been surprised; instead all he had was just a cool feeling of the inevitable. The little nerve just below his left eye began to twitch. Wasn't inevitability what the game was all about? He had another cautious look.

The *rosbif* looked very much at home. Which, thought Filli, was very good news, because this was where the bastard was going to be buried. He had seen enough. He tried not to smile his happiness. *God favours the honest and hard-working among his flock!* He turned his head away. He didn't rush, but casually gave another glance at the indicator board so that only the back of his head was visible to the area of the bar, if anyone there was interested in a dark-haired, shortish man looking at aeroplane arrival times. He stayed like that, studying the board, until he became almost a permanent fixture, then, resisting the magnetic pull of another long glance at the bar, he moved slowly in a time-to-waste stroll across the imitation-marble concourse to the line of telephone booths.

As he walked past Pecotti he inclined his head slightly. After a brief moment the fat man straightened himself up, glanced at his watch and moved off in the same direction.

'Three people at the bar – d'you see 'em?' said Filli when they joined up.

Pecotti gave it a sidelong glance and grunted.

'A man and a woman together, and a man on his own,' continued Filli. 'The man – light blue trousers, dark blue shirt, fawn jacket—'

'Got him.'

Filli sat in one of the uncomfortable fixed bench seats with his back to Metcalfe. Pecotti sat opposite, smoking and reading a crumpled newspaper he'd found stuffed in the side of his seat. He didn't appear to have looked across at the bar. 'OK,' murmured Filli, 'that's one of the reasons we're here. He's our new target, the Englishman. He's the guy you keep your eye on, and if he as much as wipes his nose on his sleeve I want to know, OK?'

'I thought it was a woman we were looking for?'

'It was. She was going to lead us somewhere, but she's just done it. We're there. She can bugger off now for all I care. Christ! Don't look at me, keep your bloody eyes on him.' Filli stubbed his cigarette out and lit another. 'He's got to be waiting for the woman. When they leave they'll take us to the bastard I've been looking for. Have you got all that?'

Pecotti's eyes swivelled and met Filli's; it was a very brief encounter. 'Yeh, why? What's the next move? You want me to roll that number up and take him home?'

Filli stood up. He didn't look at Pecotti. 'Do nothing until I say. Get that into your bloody head and keep it there. I've waited too fuckin' long for this to have it slip down the bloody drain. Now listen. I'm going to the car. When she gets off the plane, follow the woman and the guy and check them into their car. Then join me. We'll go wherever they go. OK?'

'OK.'

'Don't lose them.'

Metcalfe wasn't expecting that sort of company.

He behaved like a man in love. He wrapped his arms round Monique Bonnet and barely took his eyes off her except to look occasionally, and unseeingly at the road ahead as he drove the car back to Jeanette Fabre's sprawling farmhouse. Filli had the easiest follow job he'd ever had. He couldn't believe his luck, he told Pecotti. Nobody deserved to have things made this easy for them.

It took three-quarters of an hour and, then, after a long stretch of straight road where Filli let Metcalfe get well ahead, the brake lights of Metcalfe's car flashed brightly and he disappeared. Filli wasn't worried. He put his foot down and took off, and at the point where Metcalfe had disappeared cruised past the entrance to the Fabre property just as Metcalfe and Monique Bonnet walked arm in arm from the car to the house entrance. Filli was a contented man.

He drove on meditatively and, after another three or four kilometres of featureless *vaccares*, stopped at a roadside ranch that had been converted into a tourist centre. Fronted by a corral full of subdued miniature black bulls, it was an untidy collection of wooden buildings under a huge plastic sign offering 'Café – Snacks – Drinks – Horses – Souvenirs'.

Filli pulled in.

'We'll go and have a look around later,' he told Pecotti over a plate of Camargue paella. He was in a happy mood and the food was quite good, considering.

'What'll we do till then?' mumbled the fat man.

'I'll think of something.'

34

MONTBRON STAYED ON the A6 to Paris, avoided turning off to Buc and drove straight to the Gare Montparnasse, where he collected from left-luggage locker number 17 a plain brown envelope. It was quite bulky. He retraced his route down the Avenue du Maine, joined the *périphérique* and drove into Buc an hour later. Nobody had noticed that Philippe de Guy-Montbron was back in town. Probably nobody cared.

Apart from Jeanette Fabre. And she was confused. There were a lot of questions and no answers. But she knew the form. By now she was quite used to Montbron's comings and goings and knew better than to press him for explanations or reasons. He'd said he wanted three weeks; he'd been away three days, his explanation unfinished business. To Jeanette that meant more killing somewhere in Paris; more trouble; more fear. But she shrugged them off. Treason was a very serious business.

Montbron locked himself in his attic room and opened the envelope.

It was all there. General Lemercier had been more than efficient. It was a most comprehensive outline for the assassination of a top dignitary, a model of detail, of fall back, of restrike. It was a two-man military gem, and infallible. And so it should have been. Six of the Army's top security and intelligence and counter-terrorist experts had individually been set an all-night project on a hypothetical killing. It was a high-powered version of 'to catch a thief . . .' and General Lemercier's amalgamation of their plans had produced the impossible-to-fail assassination.

As he turned the pages and studied diagrams, drawings, angles, weapons, weapon positions, Montbron's lips pursed in a soundless whistle. It was frightening. Six anonymous soldiers had between them devised a foolproof method of breaking some of the best physical protection in the world and a security system developed, tried and tested over seven years of internal strife. It was a dangerous document. Why stop at the Minister of the Interior? This pointed to the very top of the heap; it was the ultimate destabilizer. If they could do it, why couldn't their brothers in the OAS?

Application. Montbron began tearing the precious sheets of paper into shreds. The grey-faced masters of the revolution were too intent on the result, and predetermining the effect of that result. They were playing to a world audience and expecting applause every time they struck out at the leader. It didn't matter that every attempt ended in failure. The world is a fickle audience. Toppling a giant meets with more approval than disapprobation, and great powers have more enemies than friends – particularly among their friends! But the OAS, the military minds, should have known better; they should have realized that they'd always fail because they couldn't keep their eye on the ball long enough to hit it properly. Because they were too busy wondering what they were going to do with the result. Thank God!

But with Lemercier's plan they didn't need the splash of a Minister of the Interior's death to show that they now had brain as well as muscle. With this they could take out de Gaulle. If the men who'd drawn up this plan, and the man who'd put it together, had been seduced into treason like many of their, and his own, contemporaries, they'd have been renaming the streets, squares and airports by now and Charles de Gaulle the First would be lowered into the ground with pomp, circumstance and crocodile tears and *Algerie* would remain *française*. Montbron tried to smile but nothing would come. His lips were too tight and his mouth had dried out like a dead camel's ear.

He flushed the fragments of paper down the lavatory. It took several flushes before the last square inch of potential dynamite disappeared from sight. But he'd got it all in his mind, memorized – a very dangerous situation to be in. He was about to satisfy the blood-lust of a group of military fanatics who wanted the President, via his Minister of the Interior, in bits and pieces. It was a more than dangerous game. He was not dealing with men of ideals, he was dealing with soldiers, practical men who'd seen blood, and tasted it. They were not fools, and misguided didn't equal idiocy. He was under no illusions about what he would be handing the OAS Central Committee. The main point was that in doing so he would be handing them their own death sentences – provided, of course, he didn't get his first.

35

THE MESSAGE THAT came up with a plate of sandwiches and a bottle of Vosne-Romanée was short, concise and cryptic. It had come over the telephone and was in his real name. Only two people connected the name Guy-Montbron with the Château d'Arleaux at Buc – Harry Metcalfe, and General Lemercier. It wasn't from Harry Metcalfe. And it wasn't scheduled.

From the start the edict had been definite: *no* personal contact, none whatsoever. No allowance, no latitude, as simple as that. It couldn't have been made clearer: no contact. Something must be desperately wrong.

He stared grimly at the five words on the sheet of paper, the sandwiches and wine ignored.

Versailles. Coq d'or. 1900. Lundi.

Jeanette wasn't curious. She'd taken the message, written it down, and passed it on. Montbron didn't query its contents; there was nothing hidden in the words. *Be at the Coq d'Or restaurant in Versailles at 7 p.m. Monday.* Code or not, it meant nothing to Jeanette. He glanced down at his watch. 'Can I borrow the car again?'

'Can I come with you?'

'Sorry, Jeanette.' She understood. 'I'll tell you all about it in a few days.'

'It'll be over then? We'll have won?'

He smiled sadly. 'It'll take a few more weeks. I'm going now, I don't know what time I'll be back. Leave the door open, please.'

'I'll wait upstairs.'

'Don't count on it!'

'I thought soldiers at war were perpetually horny, spent all their spare time raping the cowed citizenry? What's going wrong here?'

'This horny soldier's saving it all up. You might get lucky!'

'I think you're all talk, Montbron!'

From the outside the Coq d'Or was an ordinary little restaurant in a backstreet in Versailles. It wasn't easy to find. Nor was it easy to lose the shadow that moved in on him when he left the main car park on foot. It could have been a friendly shadow, or one from Paris. Montbron was taking no chances and managed to slip him off his back between the Boulevard de la Reine and the Avenue Debasseux. He then cut down the Rue Maréchel Foch and turned back to the restaurant he'd already passed. His follower had got there before him and was standing just inside the door with his elbow on the small bar. He didn't smile.

'Monsieur Mercier will be with you in a moment,' he said gruffly. There was nothing about him to say what he was; he could have been a well-scrubbed motor mechanic or a cashier at the Crédit Lyonnais. He couldn't possibly have been an Army intelligence officer. 'That table in the corner has been reserved for you.'

Montbron didn't argue. He sat down with his back to the room and left the other chair against the wall for 'Monsieur Mercier'. He moved his own fractionally and glanced out of the corner of his eye. The motor mechanic had seated himself at a table against the window and facing the door. None of the other diners gave either of the two men more than a cursory glance. The food looked and smelled good enough for them not to concern themselves with new arrivals.

Montbron ordered a bottle of red wine and started on the basket of bread. After the second thick chunk he realized how hungry he was. Lunch had been a long time ago, a rushed affair somewhere between the Camargue and Paris. It hadn't left a great impression.

He was on his second glass of indifferent wine and the third piece of baguette when the door behind him opened and closed.

After a second's pause a hand touched his shoulder and a voice said, 'Don't get up.'

He didn't move as General Lemercier squeezed past him and settled in the chair opposite.

'I'd apologize for this,' said the General, glancing round the room, 'if it mattered. But we're not here to appreciate the décor of a second-rate Versailles café, or test the food for a rosette . . . We'd better order something—' He broke off as a young waitress stopped at the bar, collected two menus and came towards them.

They both ordered. The General demanded another bottle of wine, a better one than Montbron's house wine, which he studied, frowned at and nudged to one side as if it were a badly dressed soldier. When it came, the food was very good. The place must have been recommended by the motor mechanic. Montbron glanced casually over his shoulder. The boy looked at home; he was obviously a man who enjoyed his dinner. It certainly couldn't have been what the General was used to.

'I've decided it's time this thing was finished with.' Lemercier put down his knife and fork and touched his moustache with his napkin. 'I'm closing in on this Secret Army rubbish and folding the whole bloody rag-bag up once and for all. They're finished in Algeria, they're going to be finished here. It's gone on long enough.'

'When did you decide this, General?'

'After we spoke yesterday. I think it's bloody silly pussyfooting around with these people, identifying them, tracking them for their contacts and gently rounding them up for a show-piece trial. It does the Army no good to have its people shown as a revolutionary, treacherous rabble. We're going to cut the head off this OAS thing as soon as you've gathered them together.' He pulled a face as if mentioning the OAS had brought a rise of bile into his throat, then reached for his glass and washed the taste away. 'So far, Philippe, it's been just you and me – for obvious reasons. I'm now enlarging the circle for a major offensive.'

'But it was agreed that your intentions were dictated by the exigencies of security, sir. I haven't heard of any mass denial of the revolt by the bulk of the Army, and the threat of sympathy action still exists. Nothing's changed that I've heard of.' He paused for a second and watched Lemercier refill their glasses. Lemercier didn't rebuke him, so he continued, his voice even lower than the barely audible tone he'd used before. 'If you swamp the field, even with men you trust and who've proved their loyalty, you'll scatter these people far and wide. At the moment they feel safe, their base is secure and they pick and choose when and what they want to hit to further their cause.'

Montbron leaned across the table to meet the cool grey eyes opposite. 'Let me carry on. Gain their trust, join their inner circle. Then we can pick them off all together without having to look over our shoulder for a sympathetic reaction from the Army in Germany. At the moment the Army's neutral, it's waiting to see how far the OAS can carry the ball, but if it finds that the General Staff, represented by you, is playing the same sort of underhand game, then there's always the likelihood that it'll come into the field to even up the odds. In keeping to your original plan, sir, allowing me to infiltrate, there's nothing to upset anybody until the whistle's finally blown. When my cover's laid bare it'll be too late for any rally – there'll be nobody to rally to. The OAS will have no head, no leaders. They'll be gone – dead.'

Lemercier had listened patiently but it was obvious his mind was made up. 'It's too slow, Philippe.' He stopped, swallowed two large mouthfuls of wine and stared into Montbron's eyes as if debating whether he was secure enough for the next bit. 'Since I last spoke to you I've had a long and enlightening session with the President. It worries me, Philippe. Charles de Gaulle is a frightened man. Don't shake your head – it's true. He's not afraid of death. Good God, the man's survived over a dozen attempts on his life. But he is afraid for France. He feels that sooner or later even one of their bungling attempts is bound to succeed, and when that happens the country will sink into a darker abyss of oppression and indecision than in 1940. He's one of the few Frenchmen living who has a decent record of being right. In fact, according to him, he's one of the few Frenchmen in history who has never been proved wrong!'

For a moment Lemercier's lips twitched. They almost softened into a smile, but it didn't quite get there and the thin line reformed itself. 'He wants those elements of the Army whose loyalty is unquestioned to move into Paris in force. He wants an undeclared martial law, with everything that implies, curfew, control of movement, the lot. He thinks this will kill the Organisation de l'Armée Secrète, and then, when he's had them all shot, he can slowly hand back power to the civil authorities. It's frightening. He really feels this is the answer. He cannot see that this would test the Army and throw it one hundred per cent behind the people he must destroy. Not only that, but the people would take to the streets as they've done before, and then heaven help us all!'

Lemercier paused. 'You realize, of course, that three-quarters of the Army's made up of national service conscripts, totally unreliable in war and even more useless for anything else! They'd throw away their uniforms at the first whiff of organized rebellion and join the rabble on the barricades. De Gaulle doesn't understand that revolution in France is unacceptable to the masses unless it's carried out by the working-class Frenchman – and the working-class Frenchman's taste for the blood of the bourgeoisie and civil disorder hasn't diminished one iota over the past two hundred years! They'd take him for a start! Charles would find himself swinging from one of the lampposts in the Place de la Concorde, and the rest of us would be strung up like little wooden dolls down the Champs-Élysées – very untidy! If he carries out this idiotic plan he'll have played right into the hands of the OAS, and it'll give them exactly what they've ineffectually been striving for. That, Philippe, is why I've changed my mind. That is why we must strike now and not let this thing drift on. Have I made myself clear?'

Montbron stared into the General's eyes for several seconds, then slowly shook his head. It wasn't a negative gesture; it was the action of a man recovering from a heavy blow to the head. That was what it felt like. Lemercier had destroyed his appetite, and he pushed his unfinished meal a few inches away with his finger. He no longer felt hungry. It was wine he wanted. He emptied his glass under Lemercier's disapproving eye, then lit a cigarette.

'Have you any idea how many people are involved?'

Lemercier shrugged his shoulders. 'I'm concerned only with this so-called OAS/Métropole Central Committee. We take this lot in, lock 'em in the dungeons and the rest of them – the minions – will have their names on paper within days.'

Montbron pulled a face. 'Their screams will be heard.'

'I don't give a damn,' growled Lemercier. 'And it won't matter. By the time the screams have died down and the people ask what's happened it'll all be over and we can go back to playing soldiers with the traditional enemy on Lüneburg Heath. And de Gaulle can stop worrying about black abysses and start worrying about the price of bread! Now this is what's going to happen. You see that boy by the window – the one who brought you here?'

Montbron didn't tell him that the boy had botched the job, but nodded without looking round.

'He's one of a team. Good, hard men, no question about their loyalty.' He shrugged slightly and wrinkled his nose. 'Only about their ability. They're none of them my first choice for the job in hand, but loyalty, not brains, is the first essential at the moment. But they're good – I picked them myself. Right, that one by the window's the only one who's going to talk to you. The others'll take their mark from him. He's been briefed and he knows exactly what's expected of him. You will put him in the picture as far as your movements are concerned, then leave it up to him. He's going to track you to your meeting. Don't worry, he's good at the job.'

Again Montbron didn't disillusion him. He was going to have to make things easy for the 'boy'.

'He will be in two-way radio contact with the rest of his team and as the "Committee" leave the rendezvous he will identify them one by one, pinpoint their vehicles and direction, and the team will pick them up as they enter the ambush areas. There'll be two centres for photographic identification. Telephoto and special systems will be operated as they break from the rendezvous. We want all this material to be used as proof of complicity, and just in case any slip through the net and end up in somebody else's backyard. I'm not giving any chances, Philippe. I want these people out of circulation, either permanently, or for as long as the youngest Frenchman's memory lasts. It's not to happen again.

'Now, the success of the operation depends on your gathering the people under one roof. Which is what your story has been all about. Having got this bunch of treacherous bastards together, your safety will depend on being able to convince them of the integrity of your plan to kill the Minister of the Interior for them. You have no worry once you've done that. You leave the meeting to slide back into your hole until the operation's completed and then you can come out, point your finger at them and stand back until Charles de Gaulle calls you into the parlour for kisses and ribbon. Erm . . .' He frowned as he studied the bottle of wine, holding it at an angle over Montbron's glass before refilling it. 'What about this civilian team of yours?'

'One man,' Montbron reminded him.

'Of course, the mad bastard with the blood-lust. What did you say his name was?' He poured the wine. 'Have you got rid of him yet?'

Montbron shook his head. 'It's been taken care of, but, in any case, I'd rather keep that off the record, at least until the celebrations are over. I don't want him exposed – not yet.' He paused and watched Lemercier carefully empty the last of the wine into his glass, then changed the subject. 'There's going to be a lot of clearing up to be done when these people are safely shackled to the wall, a lot of explanation, many brows to be soothed, and I'm afraid, General, it's all got to come from you. You're not going to be very popular in some areas of the Establishment when the shooting stops and the talking begins.'

'What d'you mean?'

'The murder of Gautier, the death of a special Presidential agent, the killing of several DST people . . . I'm fairly bad news with SDECE's people at Tourelles; the DST want my skin for their tom-toms; and there's an Action Association group dedicated, I believe, to hooking me up like a side of pork in their abattoir. They might not take kindly to the suggestion that we were all on the same side. They won't take my word for it, that's for sure. They, particularly the last lot, might even say, "Sod it, we'll have the bugger anyway!" That's why I don't want other names mentioned until the embers have died down; I don't want my helper hanging on a hook alongside me – he doesn't deserve that.'

'Leave it to me, Philippe, you've nothing to fear. I'll sort it all out. Shall we drink to success?'

'Don't you think that might be a bit premature, General?'

Lemercier's optimism wasn't to be dampened. He raised an eyebrow. 'General? We might be calling *you* that before long, Philippe. Success!'

Montbron kept his feelings from his face; they wouldn't have pleased General Lemercier.

Montbron remained where he was for several minutes after the General left, then got up and joined the man by the window.

He was quite a good-looking young man in his mid-twenties. Nobody would have thought he was Army and his rank could have been anything from sergeant to captain. There was a self-assurance about him that came from being Special Forces. Montbron recognized it. It wasn't arrogance, but an inner conviction that stemmed from being 'Special'. He was drinking a small glass of cognac, no coffee.

'D'you know who I am?' asked Montbron. He didn't bother whispering. There was no one within earshot.

The young man didn't remove the glass from his lips. '*Le Duc de Bordeaux*?'

So things weren't all that bad, thought Montbron. 'You call me Diderot. What's your name?'

'You can call me Denis,' he said after a moment's thought. Montbron held his gaze for a second. There was no hint of humour in the young man's eyes; no cocky superiority to show that he knew the original Diderot's name had been Denis. Perhaps it was a guess. Perhaps it was his own Christian name. Montbron let it pass.

'OK, Denis, this is how it'll happen. At half-past ten on Tuesday morning I shall lock myself in a phone box at the Invalides terminal. That's where you'll mark me. I don't want to see you, so start as you mean to go on. If at any stage I spot you, you can bet your balls that they will too, and that'll be the end of you – and me. I don't care about you. The dangerous part will be when they direct me – that's where the real surveillance begins. And, Denis—' he reached across the table and gently but firmly pushed down the young man's hand holding the cognac glass to his mouth so that he could see all his face '– these men know what they're doing. Their lives depend on knowing what's going on. Remember that when you join in, because yours will too. OK. I shall go to another phone box – public – and then they'll direct me somewhere else. At this point they'll move in behind me and they'll be looking for a tail; they'll be looking for you. If they make you, you might as well go back from whence you came. That's if they don't kill you. They might save me for later.'

'You don't have to keep on about the danger, Diderot. I've got the message. You don't want the flatfaces to see me. They won't.'

Montbron shrugged. He felt more like screaming. He always did when his life was placed in the hands of youngsters who wanted to show him how tough and resourceful they were. Paul Vernet behaved like a dodgy fuse at times, but he was no child and Montbron knew what to expect of him, or thought he did. Denis was a bit too sure of himself. But better get on with hammering the nails into the door. 'I'm glad to hear that, Denis. I'll try not to hold it against you when I'm lying face down in the gutter. Just don't get cocky about this, all right?'

'Whatever you say. What next?'

'After the second phone call I'll be directed to a rendezvous where I should be collected by a man in his mid-fifties, thin moustache, hair dark, probably black, dyed. He and I'll have a little run-around, maybe by car, probably by Métro or RER, possibly by taxi, but whatever it is, and regardless of what your high-ranking friend told you, for this sort of tracking you're going to need at least one mate standing by with a car. Don't overdo it. When my conductor has decided the only people following us are his, he'll move on to the rendezvous and the door will close very firmly behind us. You won't get within a thousand metres of it, but that's not my concern – it's yours, and the rest of your crew's.'

Montbron watched the young man carefully. 'If you're still around – and upright – when the meeting ends, they'll come out one by one, heads of the different branches of the organization, bodyguards, the lot. The bodyguards will be killers, probably better at it than you, most of them ex-Legion paratroopers. Shoot yourself if you make a mistake and they move in on you! If it all goes according to your boss's wildest and most optimistic dreams, when you regroup for the closing scene – the shadow game and the kicking-the-door-down bit – I'm to be taken in as one of them. I don't want anybody clicking his heels and patting me on the back. Have you got that?'

Denis held Montbron's gaze steadily, then nodded his head. 'I'll make it my personal business to see that your arse's kicked down the front doorstep as hard as the man standing next to you.' He was too nonchalant for Montbron's liking, but there was nothing he could do now. If this boy's part in it went wrong there was always the original fall back – his own identification of the group's leaders and his expectation of becoming one of them himself. That was the original plan, and it stood a much greater chance of success than Lemercier's sudden desire for rapid action and the introduction of a boy-scout group to close down the game. It smelled of the heavy hammer from the throne room of the Élysée Palace being dropped squarely on Lemercier's highly polished boots. It sounded as if de Gaulle was losing patience with his rebellious colonels.

Montbron left the restaurant on his own. Denis made no effort to leave with him, but instead ordered another cognac, lit a cigarette and sat staring at the wall. He was quite looking forward to tomorrow.

36

As NIGHT APPROACHED Filli and Pecotti left the café and propped themselves against the corral fence to watch the small black bulls eat their supper. They stayed leaning on the fence for some time, until the late-evening sun turned orange and began its downward journey beyond the seemingly endless plains around them. Filli ground out yet another cigarette, looked at his watch, and then at the sky as he straightened up from the fence.

'Meet me in the car,' he grunted to Pecotti and walked across the dusty space to the souvenir shop stuck on the end of the café like a temporary lavatory. It contained the usual expensive, useless, low-grade rubbish. But it also had a selection of large-scale maps of the area.

Filli left the passenger door open to gather in the rapidly cooling air and spread the map out on his knees. It was an easy map to read: the main road to Saintes-Maries-de-la-Mer, two or three secondary roads intersecting vast areas of pale blue with little symbols of tufts of grass, and no other features except salt and water and . . . His eyes followed his finger. And the names and locations of the country properties and converted farm-houses – *les mas*. His finger found the Mas St Justin and he lowered his head to study it.

Pecotti wasn't interested. Squashed into the driving seat, he'd pushed it as far back as it would go. But it wasn't enough. The bottom of the steering-wheel gouged deeply into his fat gut. It would have been unbearable to the normal person, but Pecotti ignored the discomfort and dozed, albeit fitfully, with his mouth wide open and his head on the backrest of the seat. His sleep was short-lived.

'What do you make of this?' Filli moved the map so that, supported by the steering-wheel, it rested on Pecotti's stomach. He kept his finger on the Mas St Justin.

Pecotti opened his eyes, stared at the map, then closed them again. 'You're the boss. Tell me what you want to make of it.' Pecotti was never going to be anything other than a temporary member of Filli's team; Filli would make sure of that. He stared at the fat belly, then at the bristly roll of chins and took back the map. It was at times like this he realized the value of Pietri and Rosso. He was even having kind thoughts about Paul Vernet.

'OK, listen.' He kept his head down over the map and traced a jerky series of lines with his finger. 'This road,' he raised his head and pointed back the way they had come, 'which is that one, goes to Arles. It also passes our pig's hidey-hole.' He glanced down at the map, measured his bent thumb against the road, then looked up again. 'About three kilometres along there is an unmetalled road that leads to nowhere, but at one point as it wriggles around to nowhere it runs fairly near our pig's house. We can drive along it, park the car somewhere and with a little walk across the swamp get close to the back part of the spread. You can count the number of people who're likely to get in our way while I work out a plan of campaign.' He folded the map roughly and slapped Pecotti on the knee with it. 'So, wake up and pay attention, Pecotti, otherwise I'll throw you out of the soddin' car now and do this thing on my own.'

Pecotti got the message.

As their car pulled out of the rough car park, one of the tourists who'd been watching the evening round-up of playful bulls by the show-off Camargue cowboys detached himself from his place on the fence and walked briskly into the café. When he got inside he glanced over his shoulder and watched two other cars pull out at the same time and form up behind Filli at the exit. Filli took his time before pulling out on to the main road and studied the procession through his rear mirror. It wasn't suspicion, it was habit, and he saw nothing in the two cars to trouble him.

The car immediately behind him went towards Saintes-Maries.

The other waited until Filli was well down the road, then followed. He overtook Filli's car and shot straight past when Filli turned up the rough road. But he didn't go far. Just out of sight of the turn-off he made a skidding four-point turn and returned to the car park, where he joined the other man inside the café. He too had a map of the Camargue.

The first man, dressed in a Camargue cowboy shirt, locked himself in the telephone cabinet and rang Roger Bineau, now installed in a temporary operations room in a private house near the airport.

Between them, Bineau and two local attached SDECE agents had done a very good job on Monique Bonnet.

Easily throwing off Filli's dogs at Le Bourget, Bineau had had none of the trouble that had bugged Filli and Pecotti at the airline reservations. Different approach, nicer personality and stronger credentials. She hadn't liked Corsicans. Bineau's mandate from Neurie had been a simple one: follow Monique Bonnet, log her progress, and when an Englishman joined in the game, make contact with Neurie in Paris, but let the two of them run as far as Montbron. Neurie hadn't swallowed Marseilles; nobody went to Marseilles for rest and recuperation. Bineau's two local contacts had met him at the airport. Filli's enforced delay of the aircraft had served everybody's purpose and whilst his two men had been turned loose on Monique Bonnet, Bineau, after hovering in the background, had made himself comfortable by the telephone.

Filli's arrival by car at the airport had taken them all by surprise. As for Filli, confident that Bineau had been shunted out of the picture long ago by his own men, he failed to look over his shoulder and thus missed Monique Bonnet being marked at the counter by Bineau's two locals. But the Nîmes men, after their initial shock at finding two other vaguely official-looking Rottweilers also doing a sniffing job on Monique Bonnet added Filli and Pecotti to their list and followed them to the ranch. Bineau could feel content.

But Neurie had a different set of emotions. The agents' description of Filli took him by surprise. He'd slipped up and there was nobody to blame but himself. He'd underestimated Filli's tenacity. He thought he'd frightened him off and the realization that he'd led him to what was probably his most vulnerable asset, and through her to Metcalfe, and then to Christ knew what, filled him with an impotent anger as he commenced the time-consuming indent for the use of a military aircraft.

He was still awaiting its approval when the second call came through from Nîmes.

'It's a dead road,' he was told by Bineau, 'used only by duck-shooting parties. It has a couple of cut-offs but apart from that doesn't go anywhere. They can't get out except by coming back, but at one point it runs within half a kilometre of the boundary of the place where the target went to ground. My people on site reckon the two spooks are on a watching brief and have gone in close to observe movement.'

Neurie thought about it. 'Roger, can one of your men get near enough to control the comings and goings without disturbing those two, or the people inside the house?'

'Yes, but—'

'Do that. Cover the front door. Let the two dogs have their heads. If they want to go in, don't stop them, they might cause a minor bolting and then you'll be in a position to follow whatever comes out of the hole. The man and the woman you picked up at the airport are bait. The one I want is a clever, shifty bugger and I think he's probably somewhere in that house. I want him out of there and back in Paris with his other friends. If he gets a whiff of those two Corsicans it'll persuade him to make that move. Just a minute, hang on . . . OK.' Neurie acknowledged with a nod the man who poked his head round the door and whirled his finger over his head. 'I'm on my way,' he said into the phone. 'Get the other guy out of that café at Saintes-Maries and have him meet me at Nîmes Airport in . . .' He glanced at his watch, then looked up quizzically at the man still waiting by the door. 'Two to three hours,' mouthed the man. Neurie nodded again. 'Tell him to be there at half-past eleven.'

37

FILLI LEFT PECOTTI sleeping in the car and went on his own across the shallow swamp to the point where the Fabre property began. He clambered through the ranch-style fencing and made himself comfortable squatting on the remnants of a hay bale, his back against a water trough. The only noise coming from the building was from the extreme left, where raucous chatter and subdued laughter indicated that the Spanish cook, servants and *guardiens* were eating and drinking as well as, if not better than, the two honeymooners and were well into their late dinner. The rest of the house was quiet, with dim lighting showing through the curtains of a middle room. At the extreme right, a large extension that looked like the master suite was in total darkness.

An hour passed. Darkness was complete. The lights were on in the extension and after a time one of the servants must have dragged herself away from the festivities and tidied up. The lights went out in the middle room. But the activity still continued in the servants' quarters. Filli eased his stiffening joints and continued working things out. He wasn't concerned with the servants; he was wondering why only one room was lit up in the posh part of the ranch. One of them was working his way into the woman, and OK, you needed a bit of light for the third or fourth exercise, but what was the other bugger, Montbron, doing in a dark room? He hadn't even switched on the light to clamber into his nightshirt. Filli shook his head. Like everything else in this friggin' episode something wasn't quite right.

Half an hour later the Spanish finally wound down and one by one the lights in the left-hand side of the house went out. A few minutes later the honeymoon suite closed down again while they got their strength back. The place was now in total darkness. Filli had got it all sorted out.

He sloshed quietly back to the car. Pecotti was still dozing on the back seat. He didn't disturb him as he slid into the front and drew the Petter M50 from his waistband and began screwing on a custom-built six-inch suppressor. It made the weapon feel unbalanced and awkward and it was too long to fit back into his belt, but he wasn't troubled by it. He kept it in his hand and in the dark touched the hammer. It was cocked. Filli's weapon was always cocked. He laid it in his lap and turned his head. 'OK, fatso, you can wake up now, we're going inside. Have you got a baffle for that cannon of yours?'

Pecotti grunted from the back. He sounded disappointed; one of the pleasures of being legal was the healthy sound of unsilenced gunfire. A simple man, Pecotti; simple pleasures. He crawled out of the back of the car and sucked salt-laden air into his lungs. It was sharp enough to wake him up.

'Stay close, and don't make any noise,' growled Filli. 'You're going to get your feet wet but don't give me any bloody complaints, 'cos I'm not in the bloody mood. When we get to the house you go to the left-hand part of it. By the noise coming from it, it's full of servants – Spanish, by the sound of them. Check 'em out one by one. I don't want them interfering.'

'What'll you be doing?'

'I'm going to take the right side and end up on the wing. You can join me there when you've finished. Before you move in I'll show you exactly where we meet so we don't frighten the piss out of each other. You've seen the woman and you've seen the man – the Englishman. They're both in the house, and they've gone to bed. Apart from them there's supposed to be one other guy in there somewhere, but he's lying low. We might have to winkle him out room by room, but we'll play that game when the time comes. Are you ready?'

'Sure. Move on.'

For a man of his massive size and shape Pecotti moved like a ballet dancer.

After Filli had sprung the inadequate lock on the back door and vanished into the shadows of the house, Pecotti moved silently to the left. He waited inside for a moment until his eyes settled down, then made his way through the kitchen, which still retained in its warm atmosphere the aroma of strong Spanish peasant cooking, rough wine and the pungent scent of Spanish tobacco. He savoured it for half a minute, then moved out into the stone-floored corridor. The squelch of his wet shoes and socks seemed to echo off the wall. He stopped, knelt down and removed them, then rolled the wet bottoms of his trousers half-way up his massive calves. His bare feet felt at home on the cold stone.

The first door on his right showed a thin pencil-line of light at the bottom. He put his ear to the wooden door and listened: no voices, just the gentle, shuddering breathing from an open mouth. He turned the knob. It wasn't locked. He slipped through the door and stared into the startled eyes of a middle-aged woman who had just lowered a dog-eared paperback with a lurid cover on to her chest as she stared at the door. Her mouth opened. Pecotti squeezed the trigger and the bullet thumped solidly just to the side of her eye. He leaned forward and fired up into the open mouth of the man lying beside her. He died in his sleep without opening his eyes. The book still twitched in the woman's hands as Pecotti replaced the two rounds and edged his way back into the corridor.

'What was that?' The door opposite opened just wide enough for a head to appear, a shadow made vaguely solid by the light from under the cook's door.

Pecotti's bullet sounded like a lump of dough being slapped on to the board ready for kneading. He stepped over the body, a girl's, into the room and ran his hand down the wall until he found the light switch. It was a dormitory. Two other girls – eighteen, nineteen – raised tousled heads and bleary, light-shocked eyes at the disturbance. Pecotti shot them both, without expression, without feeling. He was doing a job of work; Filli had said he didn't want any interference from the servants. He switched off the light and closed the door behind him. There was only one more room. It was at the end of the corridor. The silence was oppressive. No movement, no talking, no crying, no laughing. He raised himself on to the balls of his feet and glided along the stone floor. He stopped outside the room and listened. The heavy breathing wasn't his. He strained his ear against the solid-wood door and began opening it, slowly. He paused and listened again. The only sound in the room was a slight gasp and the sweaty, silk-like movements of two bodies slithering together. They didn't hear the door open; they wouldn't hear anything.

The room was bathed in a dark red light from a red shirt draped over the far bedside lamp, and the two bodies were locked so closely together in a tight sexual embrace that it was hard to tell them apart. Their little gasps showed that they weren't far away from what they'd been striving for. Pecotti watched for a second and felt his stomach and groin react with envy, then he moved to the bedside and shot one in the back of the heart and the other in the head. They began to die without a whimper. It took a moment and they came apart as one of them arched his back in protest, but it was momentary and silent, and with bulging eyes and teeth clamped tightly together he relaxed back inside his dead partner.

Pecotti studied the two dead men for a moment or two, then lowered himself to the edge of the bed facing the door and replaced the spent rounds. He flicked the refilled cylinder back into place, switched off the subdued lighting and continued his inspection of the property. There were several more rooms but they were empty. At the extreme end of the building, tacked on as if an afterthought, was a solidly built kennel. He switched on the light and peered through a crack in the door. Two Dobermanns stared hungrily back at him, their teeth bared, their eyes shining, but making no sound. They only made noise when they were outside on the loose, and they'd been locked up for peace and quiet; *Guardiens* can't make love with Dobermanns growling and snarling all over the place. Pecotti shot them both through the crack in the door.

Filli also took his shoes and socks off.

He avoided the master bedroom. He knew who was in that – or at least he had a damn good idea who was in there – and what they were doing. He went silently to the first of the other doors and stuck his ear to the panelling and listened. An empty room, even through the wood of a door, has a distinct character. He opened the door a few inches and slid in, then went down in a crouch before reaching up and switching on the light. The bed was made up, the room was tidy, but it was dead. He did the same with the other four rooms. They told him nothing other than that they had been cleared and cleaned. There was no trace of anyone having stayed in them recently. He came out of the last one and moved on his tiptoes to the master bedroom. Maybe they were having a threesome? Filli stood in the dark passageway and ran the idea through his mind, but it didn't provoke a smile or serious consideration. He moved a few more steps and waited outside the door.

He bent down and studied the room through the keyhole.

The main light and the bedside lamps were switched off, but the room was bathed in a diffused and indistinct light that filtered through the partially opened bathroom door. Very sexy, very seductive, with just enough of a ghostly glimmer to see the anguish and the ecstasy in each other's eyes. Filli's lip curled. His instincts were more primitive and he liked as much light on the subject as in an interrogation confessional. The woman had no choice.

He continued moving his eye round the room, allowing it to get used to the dim interior. There was no movement. The bed was still, and by twisting his head and straining his eye through the tiny orifice, Filli could just make out a single mound in the middle. That was enough. Standing up, he opened the door and silently moved into the room, stepped to one side, and stood with his back to the wall. He didn't close the door behind him, and he didn't put on the light. Not yet.

Harry Metcalfe and Monique were wrapped together in an exhausted sleep. They could have been dead. They should have been; the novelty of the shared bed hadn't yet worn off. But something must have stirred deep in Metcalfe's subconscious.

Causing a little animal-like whimper from a dead-to-the-world Monique, he unravelled his arms and legs from hers and, still in a deep sleep, turned away, paused for a moment on his back, then rolled to the other side of the bed. The side nearest the door. Filli let him settle, listened to his breathing, and then switched on the light.

Metcalfe's reaction was instinctive. His eyes shot open, he threw the thin bedsheet aside, and was half out of bed when his eyes locked on to Filli, the Petter held rock steady in his hand pointing at his face. A moment's hesitation, then recognition, and both feet thumped on to the thick carpet as he prepared to throw himself across the room. Filli shook his head in warning. Metcalfe's change of mind was almost too late as Filli's finger tightened on the trigger. It was automatic for Filli. It would have been a mistake. Metcalfe stopped dead, his hands open, palms upwards like a Muslim supplicant at morning prayers. But Metcalfe's eyes were not pointed towards heaven; they were still locked on to Filli's.

'Stay like that,' said Filli softly, then, frowning in recollection: 'You do speak French?'

Metcalfe said nothing and didn't move.

Filli continued staring, and for a brief second allowed his hard black eyes to flick towards the mound on the other side of the bed. Except for a tiny subconscious squeak of annoyance at the light, and a lowering of her head under the sheet, Monique hadn't moved. She continued sleeping, deeply. It would take a bomb to disturb her. And that wasn't too far away.

Out of the corner of his eye Filli sensed the arrival of Pecotti and relaxed slightly. 'Everything all right?' he asked. His voice was still low, a hushed tone as if he was in the presence of the dead.

Pecotti came into full view without distracting Filli. He stood to one side and studied Metcalfe.

'Is this *rosbif*?'

'I asked you a question.'

Pecotti nodded. 'All cleaned up. Seven, and a couple of dogs. They won't trouble us. What about him?'

'He's not going to trouble us either, are you, English? Unless, of course, you want to die.' He jerked his chin, very slightly, to the other side of the bed. 'And her as well. Pecotti . . .' He didn't take his eyes off Metcalfe. 'Throw those clothes on the floor and bring that chair over here to the middle of the room. Good. Now, you, English, stand up very slowly. Pecotti, pass him those pyjamas. I don't want to stand here looking at his cock! Right, now go and look under the pillow and bring his gun out. Good. Give it here.' He glanced at the Sig/Sauer, then stuck it into the back of his waistband. 'Go and stand over there, Pecotti, and don't wake that bloody woman! Right, you, English, put your pyjamas on and come and sit in this chair – slow-ly! OK. Put your left arm up . . .'

Metcalfe did as he was told. His brain was numb from the shock of waking to find in front of him the evil face he'd last seen lying on a pavement in Paris. He should have shot him there and then . . . *But what's the point crying about it? I didn't, and the bastard's here. He's obviously come for Montbron, and there's no bloody Montbron here for him to work on. There is somebody else, though, somebody he can work his frustration off on . . . I don't like the look of the little bastard standing up any more than I did when he was on the ground! And he's got a darker face here than he had in Paris. Maybe it was the fear that made him look paler. You'd better look in the mirror yourself, Metcalfe!* But Metcalfe knew what he felt. If pale was the yardstick of fear, his face must be the colour of paper. So, was the man what Montbron reckoned he was? Or was he one of the others who'd found out that Montbron was playing the double game? He had to be OAS. Or did he?

Metcalfe's quick communion with himself ended when his upstretched arm was grabbed by Filli and brought down with a cutting force on to the sharp backrest of the chair. His bottom rose automatically from the seat to relieve the pressure on his arm but the cry of pain that bubbled into his throat was muffled into a gurgle by the bulbous silencer on the end of Filli's automatic being rammed into the side of his open mouth. He swung round, following his arm, so that only one buttock was resting on the seat. The pressure on the arm was eased fractionally as, at a nod from Filli, the fat man came to his side, grabbed his elbow and threaded the arm through the stretchers so that the elbow rested on the middle bar of the backrest.

At that point Filli took over again. He rested his other hand on Metcalfe's wrist and pressed down. It was only a gentle, experimental pressure, but Filli had perfected the technique in Algiers. It worked. With the slightest touch of the hand the victim was paralysed with agony. He dare not move. A bit more pressure and the arm came apart at the elbow. Filli tried another tentative touch. Again Metcalfe's bottom rose from the seat. Filli nodded with satisfaction and removed the barrel of the Petter from Metcalfe's mouth, staring critically as Metcalfe sucked in air and tried to shake the tears from his eyes. He brushed Metcalfe's eyelid with the muzzle of the automatic and rested it lightly on his cheekbone.

Those were the formalities.

'Is your ladyfriend deaf?' Filli lowered his mouth to Metcalfe's ear and stared at the unmoving mound on the bed.

Metcalfe made no reply. He was too busy gritting his teeth.

'Never mind,' said Filli, and straightened up. He'd got the pressure exactly right on Metcalfe's elbow. 'Where's Guy-Montbron?'

'Who's he?'

The pressure was infinitesimal. 'Ssssss!' It was like a knife cut.

'Again?' suggested Filli.

'I don't know anyone by that name.' *What the bloody hell are you playing at, Metcalfe? Tell the bastard everything. You owe Montbron fuck-all! D'you want to walk around for the rest of your life with your arm inside out!*

A fraction more pressure and Metcalfe fainted. Filli wasn't surprised. It was normal; they all started like this. He released the pressure but kept the dead hand in his. 'Go and get one of those servants,' he said to Pecotti as he studied Metcalfe's bowed head. 'Let's find out when the bastard left, then, when he wakes, this one can tell us where he's gone. What're you waiting for?'

'You mentioned the servants,' grunted Pecotti.

'That's right.'

'You told me to check 'em out, clean up . . .'

'Yes,' said Filli suspiciously.

Pecotti stared back, his eyes dull, hooded, expressionless.

'Oh Jesus Christ! You haven't . . . ?'

'You said—'

'I know what the fuckin' hell I said! Oh, Christ! I don't believe this.' He stared into Pecotti's sweating face, then let go. It was made more threatening, more ominous, by the slightly off-pitch whisper. 'You homicidal, moronic bastard! You've killed them! You've killed the whole bloody lot? Jesus Christ! How many?' But Pecotti was spared the full weight of a force-ten Filli-style haemorrhage of anger – not that Filli's anger had the slightest effect on him; he knew he was on a short string, although he didn't realize he was also on a short life-expectancy graph – when Metcalfe's nodding head brought both Corsicans back to the matter at hand. The muzzle of the automatic returned to its original position against Metcalfe's cheek and Filli relieved the pressure on his wrist. But only enough to allow Metcalfe back to consciousness.

'OK, you stupid bastard,' hissed Filli to Metcalfe, 'you've got one more chance to end up in credit. Where's Guy-Montbron?'

'I don't—'

'OK.' Filli's voice had a resigned note to it. This sort of pain was all right for the *ratons* in Algiers – those buggers would shop their mothers at this stage – but it obviously wasn't the thing for a *rosbif*. They had different priorities, he'd been told. So, he'd just have to try one of these other priorities. 'Pecotti . . .' As he addressed the fat man he looked down and stared into Metcalfe's face, then slowly shook his head. This the Arab would have laughed at as a form of persuasion, but he'd see how the English viewed it. If nothing else, Filli was always open to new methods.

Pecotti had ground to make up. He was waiting for anything, eager to please.

'Boss?'

Filli jerked his chin at the mound on the bed and spoke in the Corsican dialect. 'See if you can raise a happy smile on her face.'

Pecotti stared at him, first in surprise, then in disbelief.

'And don't take all bloody night over it!'

Pecotti came to life. He stuck the stub-barrelled revolver into the clip on his belt and with two paces went to the foot of the bed. No hesitation, no finesse, he grabbed the sheet covering Monique and with a flick of his wrist whipped it off her as if it was a handkerchief. She was naked, and suddenly, brutally, wide awake. She turned her head. The scream was already well developed when Pecotti grabbed her ankles and pulled hard. She slithered and ended face upwards, half on and half off the foot of the bed. The scream choked and died of shock.

'Leave her alone, you bastard!' Metcalfe tried to rise from the chair and bellowed in pain as the cartilage in his elbow tore with an audible crunch. 'Oh, Christ! OK, OK, I'll tell you. Guy-Mon—'

But Filli wasn't listening. Neither was Pecotti, who, with Monique's wriggling legs under his ample armpits, calmly and methodically undid his belt and allowed his trousers to slip over his enormous gut to his ankles. He pulled his underpants down to his thighs and then let go of Monique's feet and moved his hands to her tightly clenched thighs.

'Get off, you bastard!' she screamed. 'Leave me alone! *Harry, Stop him! Help me*!' Still screaming, she lashed out with both feet, now suddenly free. One caught Pecotti a solid blow in the stomach, another caught him high up in the groin. He didn't complain – he wasn't feeling pain – and his expression remained set. There was only one thing on his mind. He took his hands from her thighs, dropped his arm on to her flailing legs and leaned forward and hit her, open-handed, across the face with all his strength.

Metcalfe bellowed again, a wounded animal, pain and anguish competing for first place. 'Leave her alone!' He managed to turn his head and appeal to Filli. 'Call him off! For Christ's sake, stop him! Get him off! What d'you want to know? Quick man!'

Filli actually smiled. They could stand pain, these Englishmen, but they were like children with women. He was very interested, he wished there was more time to develop the process. He wiped the smile from his mouth. 'Sit and watch, English. We'll have our chat in a minute.'

'I said, I'll—'

'I know you did, and you will. Now sit quietly or I'll break your arm.' He pressed again, fractionally, and Metcalfe felt the welcome red mist coursing into his brain. But it wasn't to be, not this time. Filli had timed it to perfection. He was impotent. He couldn't move an inch.

And then Filli signalled to Pecotti, removed the automatic from Metcalfe's face and leaned forward slightly. 'Take a good look, *rosbif*. You know what comes next. But you can relax, not too much, just a little. One bit of hesitation, one lie, one wrong word, and it won't be "You've got one more chance". There'll be no chance for you, my friend, or for her, so have a good look. I'm going to ask you some questions and you're going to answer them truthfully and honestly. Pecotti there will be standing ready with his cock in his hand. Remember, no chances. OK?'

Metcalfe nodded and closed his eyes. He was never going to forgive himself, not for what he was about to tell but for not having told earlier. He was never going to be able to look himself, or Monique, in the eye again.

'Open your eyes,' snapped Filli.

Metcalfe did as he was told but he avoided looking towards the bed.

Neurie's calculations on his arrival time hadn't taken into consideration a very strong head wind. He was a good twenty minutes later than his estimate, but in his mind twenty minutes made no difference at all. Metcalfe would have argued that with him.

The driver slid the car close into the side of the hedge just behind his colleague's car and joined Neurie and Bineau as they walked silently up the road towards the Mas St Justin. The watcher detached himself from the shadows and led the party through a side-gate he had discovered, then drew them into the even deeper shadow of a large garage and outbuilding.

'No guards?' queried Neurie. 'No dogs?'

'It struck me too,' whispered the watcher. 'Bizarre. I've only watched. I didn't take a closer look in case I ran into something and started a stampede. But I've got it all worked out. Everybody in the house is asleep – or dead.' The man who'd collected Neurie started to say something, but he never finished as the watcher continued: 'It's been like a morgue, except for a short time ago when I thought I heard a woman screaming. But I wasn't sure. It could have been the horses on the other side of the house. They've been bloody noisy. Whatever it was, it didn't develop into anything interesting.'

'What about the servants?' asked Neurie.

'Haven't seen a thing, but they'll all be on the far side, round the back there. Besides, look at the time – way past the working classes' bedtime . . .'

Neurie stared at the dark mass of sprawling buildings and then touched the watcher on the arm. 'No sign of the Corsicans?'

'Nothing.'

'OK. You stay here and cover the front. Roger and I'll go and have a look round the back. We'll poke around inside if we can find an easy way in. When we've got the place tied up Roger'll find the outside lights and you'll be able to see what you're doing. If anybody tries bolting past you, grab 'em, but don't take any chances. There are some very nasty people in that house, and they'll blow your bloody face off if you get in their way. Shoot first, shoot low, and try not to kill. I'm here to talk to the buggers, not bury them. OK?'

'Whatever you say, sir.'

'Come on, Roger.'

By a circuitous route the two men arrived at the door forced earlier by Filli. It was closed but not locked. They didn't enter but stood in silence for several minutes, listening, then continued checking the outside. The house looked and sounded empty. No noise – not a sound. No light anywhere until they turned the corner of the servants' quarters and saw the main bedroom, its light barely visible through heavy curtains.

'Can you get to that window without making a noise?' breathed Neurie, then touched the shingled surroundings, in warning, with his foot.

Bineau got the message. One man walking across that lot would sound like the Roman Army on the move. But he must have eaten his carrots as a boy. 'There's a concrete apron all the way round. Give me a couple of minutes.'

'Don't hurry.'

Bineau was away for some time. Suddenly he reappeared alongside Neurie. Neurie hadn't heard or seen him. It was a sobering thought. 'There are voices in there. Sounds like one of those TV programmes, one voice asking the questions, a different voice giving the answer. There's no conversation – just question and answer.'

'OK, let's go.'

'Er, one more thing.'

'Be quick.'

'There's a terrace on the other side of that room. The windows, or doors, open out on to it. I just touched it with my hand. I wouldn't swear that it's locked . . .'

'What're you getting at?'

'Why don't I go in that way and meet you in the room?'

Neurie thought about it for less than ten seconds and dismissed it. 'We don't know how many people are in the room. With bullets flying in all directions we'd probably end up in a blood bath. Stick with me until I say otherwise. Got a torch?'

Roger Bineau placed his hand over a thin black pencil torch and flicked it on. He opened his fingers fractionally and allowed the edge of the beam to splash against the wall in front of them. Neurie's face was long and drawn and his eyes wide as he drew close to the younger man. His whisper was barely audible.

'The kitchen is there.' His finger moved vaguely in the dim light. 'The servants should be on the other side. Go and see what's happening there. If they're sleeping, don't disturb them, but there's something funny going on and I don't like the feel of it. Anyway, I don't want them rushing around in the dark. Lock 'em in their rooms if necessary. I'm going along there.' He jabbed his finger in the opposite direction. 'I'll make my way round to that bedroom. Join me there when you've checked all this out. Don't forget to switch on the outside lights so that we know what we're shooting at! Off you go.'

Neurie took the same route that Filli had taken. Filli had made it easy for him; he'd left the door to each of the other bedrooms open. Neurie didn't bother looking in them; people didn't sleep with open doors. The door to the main bedroom was also ajar. Its light, glancing down the corridor, made it easy for Neurie and he moved as far as the door, where, with his back to the wall, he stopped and listened.

Filli was saying, '. . . OK, so we've got the Buc connection and the alternative hideaway in the Avenue Beauchamp. Now tell me about the other things – his meeting places, his drops, live and dead – and then we'll get on to—'

'*Boss*!' bellowed Pecotti and his hand stabbed for his revolver. But his belt and its stubby holster were on the floor where he'd dropped them in preparation for his rape, and his trousers were still round his ankles. He staggered and fell, staring wildly at Neurie's head, which had now come round the corner of the door.

Filli was quick. That's how he'd stayed alive so long. But this time he wasn't quick enough, and he made the wrong move. He let go of Metcalfe's wrist, swung round in the direcion of Pecotti's terrified stare and fired without looking, without aiming.

The bullet splattered into the door-frame's woodwork chest-high. Neurie knew what he was dealing with. He didn't hesitate. His first bullet, an explosion that assaulted the eardrums of everyone in the room, caught Filli in the neck. The force of it picked him off his feet and threw him across Metcalfe's shoulders. The second heavy bullet hissed past Metcalfe's ear and caught the staggering Filli under the armpit, ploughing through his ribs, penetrating both lungs and splattering against the left-side ribs. Filli's automatic dropped out of his nerveless fingers into Metcalfe's lap.

Metcalfe didn't need a second invitation.

He grabbed the Petter with his right hand, shoved Filli on to the floor and with his left hand dangling uselessly at his side stood up and pointed the automatic at the fat man still scrabbling on his knees for his belt and revolver. Metcalfe was oblivious of Neurie. He didn't want to know him; he didn't care. There was one thing in his mind. He knew what he wanted to do and nobody was going to stop him. His brain was suddenly cold. There were only two people in the room, one an obese, obscene lump of filth lying on the lush carpet, its trousers rucked round its ankles, a revolting, hairy mass below a bulging, flopping gut. He aimed, took his time, and fired. The popping of a cork. There was no satisfaction from the noise of retribution. Pecotti screamed as the lead-nosed bullet splashed the bones of his right wrist into a bloody gore. And as he screamed he began to scrabble away on his bare bottom, his one good arm trying to lever his body out of range of the man staring at him over the ridge-sight of Filli's silenced automatic.

Phluttt!

The next bullet drilled straight through his kneecap before shattering the joint into tiny fragments, the blow and his own impetus literally picking him up and hurling him through the double doors on to the terrace and into the blessed dark. Under the open sky Pecotti's screams sounded louder as they rent the air. And then the outside floodlights went on and turned the surroundings into daylight. Seconds later Bineau burst into the room, his automatic waving about in front of him as he sought the source of the hideous noise.

'Jesus! What the bloody hell's going on? What's happening out there?'

Neurie caught him out of the corner of his eye as in two strides he was across the room and by the bed. 'Forget it,' he snarled over his shoulder. 'Let him get on with it. Just watch that bastard on the floor there!'

Bineau boggled at Neurie, and then at Filli. Filli's deathbed was a little less heavy on his stomach. 'Keep your eye on him,' repeated Neurie. 'Don't let the bastard move. If he does, shoot him!' He picked up the discarded bedsheet and gently wrapped it around Monique before gathering her in his arms. He held her close, whispering, his mouth by her ear as she struggled to consciousness. Her eyes opened. And she cried, sobbing as he held her close and stroked her head. She wouldn't let him go. Her arms around his neck, she clutched him as her body was convulsed and racked with heavy, anguished sobs, repeating his name over and over again. Neurie, looking almost content, spared only a sideways glance outside as another muffled shot came through the broken doors, and another louder, more anguished scream came from the fat Corsican's distorted face as his ankle-bone disintegrated. Bineau took another horrified look at Metcalfe, his bare, sweat-soaked chest glistening under the exterior floodlights, cold-eyed and oblivious of everything except the screaming man at his feet.

'Stop him!' yelled Bineau. 'You've got to stop him. It's bloody inhuman.'

Neurie looked at him briefly. 'You go and stop him then.'

'I bloody will!'

Bineau left Filli, but there was no danger, Filli wasn't going anywhere, ever again. The Frenchman bounded across the room and through the doors to the terrace. Metcalfe was standing, still staring down at the howling Pecotti. There was no more anger in Metcalfe's face; he looked as calm as if he were an undertaker sizing up a corpse for its box.

'For God's sake, you sadistic bastard,' bellowed Bineau, 'leave him alone now! You've almost killed the poor fucker! Get back inside.'

Metcalfe studied the young man for a second, said 'OK,' then straightened his arm and shot Pecotti twice in the pelvis. Pecotti didn't feel the second bullet; he'd lost consciousness. Metcalfe didn't look at the Corsican again. He turned his back on the bloody mess, handed the automatic, butt first, to Roger Bineau and turned into the room. He ignored Neurie, glanced embarrassedly at the bundle in his arms, then moved slowly across the room to stare down at the dying Filli.

'Roger,' said Neurie, calmly, 'get on the phone. I want an ambulance.' He glanced at Metcalfe quickly. 'Is that creature out there dead?'

Metcalfe shook his head.

'Two ambulances. Quick as they can. And a doctor – female. Quick! OK, you, Metcalfe, stay where you are and watch that Filli doesn't do anything smart—'

'He can't, Gérard,' broke in Bineau. 'He's falling out – going fast. If you want anything from him you've only got a couple of minutes.'

'Get those bloody ambulances. And you, Metcalfe, just watch him. Don't touch – I want him alive.' He looked down and stopped stroking Monique's head, gently turning her face from his neck so that she could see him. But she refused to open her eyes and kept sobbing his name, over and over again. He stopped her by gently placing a finger over her mouth. 'It'll be all right, darling. I'm here. I'll look after you. But listen, I'm going to lie you down, only for a moment . . .' She clutched him closer. 'Just a moment. I'm going to lie you down. I'll be back in a second.'

Moving towards the man crumpled on the floor, Neurie elbowed Metcalfe to one side. 'Get out of my fucking way, Metcalfe, you irresponsible bastard! If you as much as look at Monique again I swear I'll blow your bloody head in! Now get out of my fucking sight before I do you some serious damage. Go and put some bloody clothes on – I'll want to talk to you in a moment.' He turned to Roger Bineau, standing by the door. 'Roger, get someone to go with this bastard and tell him to keep an eye on him. Then come back here.' Neurie turned his back on Harry Metcalfe and bent low over Filli's body to stare into the dying Corsican's face.

Filli forced the red mist from his eyes and focused on Neurie crouching on one knee beside him. He could see Neurie's lips moving. With an effort he could hear what he was saying, but there was nothing he could, or wanted to, say in reply. Neurie tried again.

'Did you kill Gaby Violle, Filli?'

Filli stared back and opened his mouth, but no words came. It had filled with blood that dribbled out thickly and slowly, working its way down his chin and trickling into the wound in his neck that was already dyeing his white shirt into a rich and expensive shade of red. Filli could feel his life rushing away from him; it was pouring out of the hole in his throat and searing like a red-hot poker in his chest, though the thought of dying was enough to remove the excruciating pain from his brain. But there was no sympathy in Neurie's eyes.

He made no attempt to answer Neurie's question, but Neurie must have mistaken his shudder for a shake of the head.

'If you didn't kill him, Filli, who did?'

But Filli was going fast. His brain took one last trip. *So now we've all gone. Pietri, Rosso, Richet. That fat screaming bastard Pecotti must have got it too. And now me. We were a good little bunch. So who's left? No one. Yes there is . . . He's the cause of all the good ones going, and he's the one who gets away with it. And he wasn't even one of us. That snivelling bastard Paul—*

'Who killed him, Filli?' Neurie's voice was getting fainter.

'Vernet . . .' It came out with blood and bubbles.

'Who's Vernet?'

'He's dead, Gérard,' said Bineau.

'What's that?'

'No point shaking him. He's dead.'

'Fuck it!' said Neurie.

'I agree with you. It sounds just about the right word for it. But he's still a lot better off than that fat sod out there! And, er, Gérard . . .'

'What?'

'I think you'd better come and look at the servants' quarters.'

'Why?'

'Just come and look.'

Neurie stared at him. 'Oh, Jesus Christ!'

38

ROGER BINEAU OPENED one of the spare rooms and dropped into the bed. He was tired, but he didn't sleep. He tried but found that all his brain would allow him to do was stare at the ceiling and watch images of young girls with bullet-holes in their faces; *guardiens* dead and locked together like some gruesome Epstein sculpture; and flicking across that, the more realistic images of an agonized Jean-Baptiste Pecotti on his sick-bed.

But for Pecotti in the end death was the better option. He watched the sun come up and died in Nîmes General Hospital before it was strong enough to cast a shadow. Georges Filli got a cheap temporary wooden coffin. There were still traces of its last occupant stuck to the side of the box but nobody took any notice, least of all Georges Filli. For Neurie and Metcalfe it was too late to go anywhere, and too late to sleep – if either of them had had any thoughts about sleep.

Neurie accompanied Monique to a private hospital on the outskirts of Nîmes and watched until the nightmare, drugged from her mind, faded into an all-embracing grey mist and, with his name still bubbling incoherently from her bruised mouth, she descended into a dreamless sleep.

By the time he returned from the hospital, Neurie had drained some of the bitterness he felt for Harry Metcalfe from his mind. Apart from the tragedy of the situation, things for him and Monique had moved in the right direction. Monique was back where she belonged – with him. She knew it. He knew it, and he made bloody sure Harry Metcalfe knew it. Metcalfe accepted the situation. He was more interested now in the salvation of Harry Metcalfe and the hope of seeing, very soon, the back of

Gérard Neurie's head disappearing over the horizon while he returned to gentle civilization across the Channel. But there was a lot of ground to cover first.

They sat in the main drawing-room with the level of a bottle of Johnny Walker Black Label moving rapidly towards its base. Having already bared his soul to Filli, Metcalfe had no qualms about sharing Montbron's confidences with Gérard Neurie. He told him, almost word for word, of the conversation he'd had with Montbron at the duck shoot. Neurie listened impassively. When Metcalfe finished Neurie's reaction was hardly muted.

'If what he told you is halfway to being somewhere near the truth then I'm not bloody surprised that the Army doesn't know whether it's coming or going! By the sound of it, half of them don't even know whose bloody side they're on. They don't know whether to salute each other or pull a bloody gun out of their trouser pockets and start shooting! What a fucking cock-up! And the stupid bastards have allowed Montbron to stick his head in the bloody oven. He'll be cooked. Somebody'll want it on a bloody platter! And I'll tell you something for absolutely nothing, he's not going to be able to walk away from it and go back to some sterile little army base with his only worry the quality of the shine on his boots.' Neurie had little admiration for the peacetime French Army.

'What about this General Lemercier and the Élysée connection?' asked Metcalfe. 'Won't they get him off the hook?'

Neurie pulled a face. It was a possibility that he viewed with no optimism. 'Sounds too bloody far-fetched to me. The whole bloody story could have been pinched from Dumas *père*, except he wouldn't have written anything quite so silly!'

'So you're going to do nothing?'

'I didn't say that – and I don't need you to prompt my actions.'

Metcalfe didn't take umbrage. He was technically Neurie's prisoner. He was an Englishman who'd consorted with the enemy, even if the enemy had now proved to be one of the good guys. He'd stuck his nose into French affairs and the bastards, in the shape of Gérard Neurie, had every right to lop the bloody thing off. But now that Neurie was making up lost ground with his ex-wife, perhaps a certain amount of old friendship would be rekindled. He wasn't terribly hopeful, and took some solace in the recollection of the punishment he'd meted out to the fat Corsican. He shrugged his shoulders, poured another generous measure of whisky into his glass and left Neurie with the choice.

Neurie relented. 'I've already decided. I'll get in touch with this Lemercier at first light and tell him the thing's blown up in his face, that his Diderot operation is no longer a private affair. If it's as you say Montbron told you, he'll be the only person who can cramp Montbron's style and pull him out of the game. But you know how these top-level bastards react to disaster. It's the same in England . . .' He emptied the glass he'd been nursing against his chin. He seemed to be speaking from personal experience. 'At the first sign of a balls-up heads start retracting into their shells. The bastards who put Montbron up to it will only admit it if his mission is of great political significance and advantage. So far he's done nothing to convince anyone of that. They'll want his head. We already want his head. Filli's people want his head. The poor bugger's got nowhere to go.' He held out his empty glass. 'Put some more whisky in that, please. We might as well get pissed while we think about it!'

Metcalfe emptied his own and refilled both glasses. No water – this was not for pleasure. At this stage of the night whisky was purely therapeutic. He swallowed a large mouthful but kept the glass near for another one. It was performing miracles. 'Won't everybody be pleased when he points out all these OAS people who're running the thing in Paris?'

'No,' said Neurie, 'becuse the bloody politicians want to do it their way. The Army, whether you like it or not, has the right answer. If a soldier commits treason, they put him up against a wall and shoot him. End of treachery! Politicians are different. Something has to be gained, bargained for, and if unpleasant, swept under the carpet until it can be usefully employed to their advantage, when it will be brushed off and brought back into play. They don't want heads or bodies. They just want the bloody thing tucked out of the way, which is why they want the OAS dealt with by civilian agencies over whom they wield total control. So it becomes trials, minor sentences and later, when some other political hoo-ha has taken everybody's mind off it, forgiveness and carry on, all is now well!'

Neurie paused briefly before continuing. 'Of course, as is usual with this sort of rebellion, a lot of OAS support comes from politicians, overt as well as covert. If their involvement in ending the Fifth Republic has gone deep they'll be quietly put to one side instead of letting the Army shoot them. Then, when the chopper falls, they'll all close ranks. They'll look after themselves and be happy ever after, and we'll never know who was who – they'll see to that. And that's why Montbron's efforts are more likely to find him an unmarked grave than a place on the podium beside the President at the next 14th July parade.'

'This is all bloody silly!' rasped Metcalfe. 'According to Montbron the President wanted the army to move in.'

'Of course it's bloody silly,' snapped Neurie. 'If it's true! De Gaulle does a lot of bloody silly things. Sticking his nose in intelligence affairs is only one of them. He's obviously encouraged this other silly bugger in Germany, his cousin, to imagine that they're the only two people in France who have any new ideas on intelligence and anti-terrorist matters.'

'So where do you come in?' asked Metcalfe.

'You know bloody well where I come in,' replied Neurie caustically. 'Things haven't changed all that much. In fact, things don't change at all in this bloody business. I've had enough of it!'

Which was a surprise to Metcalfe. If anybody was going to be the oldest intelligence operator in the world he would have put money on Gérard Neurie. But still . . . 'So who are your masters?' he asked.

'I don't think it matters to you, Metcalfe.'

'Department Maurice?'

'How do you know of Maurice?'

Metcalfe shrugged. 'Only the name, not the principle. I've known of Maurice for years. The name has cropped up from time to time. I had a vague idea that it was part of the Élysée, hovering somewhere between de Gaulle and God. When a President has that sort of intelligence structure at his fingertips, why the bloody hell can't he leave things to the experts and not to do the job himself?' Metcalfe looked askance at Neurie. 'Or perhaps I've read it wrong and the famous Maurice is only a word in the wind.'

Neurie shrugged the main part of the question aside. 'Oh, it exists all right. There's no argument about that. But it also poses the big problem.'

'What's that?'

'The department doesn't share information. It has no friends outside the broken-glass-topped walls of the Palace – and doesn't have any inside, either!'

'But Montbron was sent by the President himself,' insisted Metcalfe. 'So why wasn't de Gaulle informed by his own intelligence praetorians of the state of play as it stands?'

Neurie shook his head. 'I've not yet accepted Montbron's bona fides, but with regard to the other thing, de Gaulle's head rarely descends from the clouds of world statesmanship. He's not normally interested in domestic intelligence matters; he's only interested when international affairs intrude. Besides,' Neurie lifted his glass from the table and sipped tiredly, 'there are a dozen different agencies with different heads. Like that bloody snake, every time you lop a head off, another grows. That's what happens in the French Intelligence Service! And since each one of them refuses to divulge information outside its own four walls, you have the makings of a monumental balls-up. You've seen the result of one such balls-up at the Place de la Contrescarpe. Nevertheless, sometimes there are good reasons for keeping cards very close to the chest. Revolution's one of them. We are in that state at the moment, so, with the sort of atmosphere hanging over Paris where you have no idea who you trust and who you don't, it's better you keep things to yourself until you know for certain who has safe ears. That's what Department Maurice is doing – making sure who has safe ears and who has the other sort.'

'But de Gaulle did bring his head out of the clouds and interfere,' insisted Metcalfe.

'Quite. And look what a bloody mess he's made via your friend Lieutenant Colonel Philippe de Guy-Montbron!'

'What are you going to do about it then?'

'After I've spoken to General Lemercier I'm flying back to Paris to clap your bloody friend Montbron in irons before he undoes any of the work that has been done by Maurice. Montbron's going to put the finger on them; but he won't succeed. What he'll do is disperse the top putschists to the four corners of the continent. And when that happens our list of their contacts and sympathizers becomes so much waste paper. You can't prove anything without having the heads of the organization in the box, even if they only get their knuckles rapped. It's the small fry, as always, who'll pay the bill.'

Neurie was becoming tired and bad-tempered. He was fed up with educating Englishmen on the intricacies of the French intelligence maze. 'So, that, briefly, is why at this point of the game we don't want private interference from people like Montbron – and least of all from you!' He emptied his glass with a gurgle and tapped it on the table. Then he looked into Metcalfe's eyes. 'So you're coming to Paris with me.'

'Pardon?'

'You heard what I said. I want you in Paris standing right beside me when I start talking to Montbron and the people running with him. And I do mean beside and not behind me! I'm still not happy with you, Metcalfe. I stopped trusting you years ago, and as far as I'm concerned, you've done nothing since to make me alter my opinion of you. There're a lot of questions about your activities still to be resolved, and that doesn't include my own personal argument. You're not a bloke I want to be friendly with any more. Keep that well in mind. We'll leave for Paris at first light.'

'And if I don't want to go?'

'Don't tempt me, Metcalfe.' Neurie stared at him with red-rimmed eyes. 'Does the name Vernet mean anything to you?'

Metcalfe stared back, then closed his eyes for a second; they were beginning to sting. Like Neurie, not enough sleep and too much whisky, as well as the throbbing of an arm that was never going to feel right again. 'Vernet?' he repeated, then shook his head and tried to look honest. 'Nope, nothing. Why?'

'Montbron never mention the name?

Metcalfe started to shake his head again but stopped under Neurie's hard stare. Lying for Montbron had become distinctly unprofitable. It wasn't difficult to jump sideways. 'Oh, what the hell!' He tightened his lips. 'He's part of the Montbron family.'

Neurie's eyes opened a little wider. There was no satisfaction in them; his expression remained cold and unfriendly. He waited.

Metcalfe reached instinctively for his empty glass and manoeuvred it towards the lonely whisky bottle, but Neurie forestalled him.

'What d'you mean, family?'

'His half-brother.'

'And you were going to keep that to yourself?'

'I don't owe you a damn thing, Neurie. You get that as a bonus becuase I'm fed up with the whole bloody lot of you. Perhaps now I can go home?'

Neurie ignored Metcalfe's outburst and sat back in his chair. 'You've still got a lot to answer for, Metcalfe. You could have told me this earlier, it would have saved a lot of trouble.'

Metcalfe emptied the remains of the bottle of whisky into his glass. He wasn't contrite. 'Not for me it wouldn't. What's he done?'

'Filli said he's the guy who killed Violle. I'm making him my life's work. I'm going to kill him.'

'If you find him,' said Metcalfe caustically.

'I shall – eventually,' Neurie said firmly.

Metcalfe raised his glass before emptying it. 'Very dramatic, very French!'

'And if I have much more of that, I'll nail you to the wall beside him!'

Neurie dragged the telephone away from his ear and ran his hand over his unshaven chin. He'd been hanging on for ten minutes. The only sign that he hadn't been cut off was the faint hum of an international connection and the occasional sound in the background that could have been a voice, or a cow mooing for its breakfast. Neurie pulled a packet of cigarettes from his coat pocket and tapped one out on to the small telephone table. He stuck it between his lips, then swallowed. The inside of his mouth was crusted with too much whisky, too much talking and too many cigarettes. He lit it and added to the foul taste at the back of his throat.

'Hello?' The phone came tinnily to life near his ear.

'Go on.' He fumigated his nostrils with smoke and dragged again. He seemed to have infinite patience, even after ten minutes.

'We've just spoken to the Senior Intelligence Directorate at the Élysée Palace. He confirms your status.'

'Then perhaps you'll now pass me to General Lemercier.'

'That is why I needed to confirm your status, sir. General Lemercier died last evening.'

The silence seemed to go on for ever. Neurie stared staight ahead. He was looking at nothing; his mind had gone to sleep. The cigarette smoke curling into his eyes brought him back. He still said nothing.

'Hello? Sir? Are you still there?'

'Yes. You said died? What did he die of?'

'It was a car accident. He overturned on the autobahn between Saarbrücken and Völklingen. Witnesses say his Mercedes went out of control. It seems to have been a burst front tyre. The car went into flames.'

'Was there anything suspicious about it?'

'Like what, sir?'

'Never mind.'

39

PHILIPPE DE GUY-MONTBRON pulled the curtains to one side and stared at the flailing rain. Above the downpour was a grey-brown sky that showed no gaps and cast a gloom that would have been ashamed of itself on a mid-January late afternoon.

Jeanette didn't move. She kept her head low in the pillows and pulled the duvet over it. She knew what was going on outside. She'd seen and heard it at dawn while Montbron was twitching his way through a close-quarter nightmare and she was twitching through a wide-awake horror of the coming day. She'd climbed back into bed beside him when the Mogadons had begun to take effect.

Montbron turned away from the window. Without looking at her, he quietly opened the bedroom door. He hesitated for a brief second, then slipped out. He didn't say goodbye and she didn't hear him go. She could have been dead.

He parked the car in the underground car park that stretched, damp, gloomy, echo-resounding and almost without limit, under the Esplanade des Invalides and walked from catacomb to catacomb until he mounted a set of narrow concrete steps and surfaced by the side of the Aérogare des Invalides building.

The run-around started from there.

At the third telephone rendezvous, after taking the Métro to the Gare St-Lazare and the bus to the Place de la Nation, he was collected by two grim-faced and uncommunicative ex-Legionnaires and taken by taxi back to Invalides, where he was dropped off at a small hotel off the Rue de Grenelle. He withdrew his earlier misgivings about the tracking abilities of Denis; he hadn't caught sight of him once. But, he grimaced wryly to himself, perhaps he hadn't turned up. He had, however, picked up on a double team – Xavier's people, they had to be – who were very good at their job. His escort from Nation had also spotted them and made no attempt to worry them.

His escort left him in the hotel foyer. It must have been a very safe house. Nobody came rushing up to find out what sort of room he wanted. He was left severely alone until from a door on the business side of the foyer appeared the ever-immaculate Colonel Vaucoulet – Xavier.

And it still wasn't finished.

Xavier's greeting was brief and without warmth. After a casual glance at the main entrance, he turned on his heel and indicated to Montbron to follow him out through the door by which he'd entered. They cut across an open-ended office, along a narrow corridor, then through a swing-door into a kitchen that carried a heavy aroma of fine coffee but nothing else, and out into the street by way of a heavy metal door. The street was deserted, except for an anonymous dark blue Peugeot 303, its nose just poking out of a short cul-de-sac about a hundred metres away.

Still no sign of Denis. Montbron mentally gave him up. He couldn't be that good.

Xavier took the wheel of the Peugeot himself and, without conversation, drove back into the Rue de Grenelle. Joining the one-way system, he filtered round the Hôtel des Invalides, down the Avenue de Ségur and turned off into a largish road with grand houses off the Place Cambronne. He parked the car, left the key in the ignition and walked towards one of the large houses. he must have been very confident; he'd taken no evasive action, no precautions to discourage a follower and hadn't looked over his shoulder once. Montbron did. As he closed the door on his side of the car he glanced up and down the road. He hadn't expected anything less. One car moved briskly towards Xavier's and at the top of the road, where it joined the Place Cambronne, the nose of another vehicle edged round and stopped on the bend while the driver got out and went through the motions of checking a non-existent puncture. A man approached from another car, ignored Xavier and Montbron, slid into the driving seat of the parked car and drove it away.

Montbron followed Xavier through the door of the house, opened by an unseen hand, but he didn't look round again. He knew what was happening outside. The road would now be empty, and heaven help anything that came down it without a definite purpose.

Montbron had been wrong to worry about Denis. Denis knew exactly what he was doing. He'd got it sewn up beautifully. But his lead watcher team, led by his number two, code-name 'Richard', had floundered and at that moment Richard was dying, slowly, in a battered old Panhard in a lonely corner of the underground car park just off the Boulevard de Picpus. His partner was already dead, curled up on the back seat with his throat cut.

Richard had done well at Invalides. Led by Denis, he'd picked up Montbron and followed him on the Métro to the Gare St-Lazare, unseen by either Montbron or his other followers. But it was there, at the station change-over, that he had made his mistake. It was the only mistake he'd made all day, and it was the only one allowed. There were no seconds with Xavier's people.

If he'd been alone Richard would have made it. But he'd taken time out to bring his partner into play with the car. It was the use of the vehicle that had blown them; the joining-up was badly done. A hesitation, then a move too quick, and they were marked by Xavier's second group. By the time they'd followed Montbron's bus to Nation they'd been spoiled. Xavier's people were extremely efficient. Their lives depended on it.

Whilst one OAS team continued shadowing and covering Montbron, the second took Richard and his friend quietly to one side and held them while one of their number spoke on the telephone to Xavier.

Xavier's reaction was predictable. 'Find out who they are, where they're from, how they got on to Diderot and what their interest in him is.'

'And then?'
'They're no friends of ours.'

One of their number drove the Panhard down the ramp into the car park. Richard and his partner followed in the back of the other car. When they met up Richard was taken to one side and allowed to watch his friend's throat being cut. The dying man was then thrown on to the back seat of the Panhard. They left one of the doors open, leaving his feet to dangle outside and jog up and down as he died. It was known as the tongue-loosener. Richard watched without expression.

They then spoke to him, unthreateningly, and he told them everything he knew about Diderot, which wasn't very much, and as little of the operation as he thought he could get away with. Gaining confidence, he played down Montbron's role and indicated him as a minor player of undetermined allegiance in an Army probe on the OAS/Metropole, with the whole operation being directed from the Germany Intelligence Centre at Elm. As far as he, Richard, was concerned, his mandate covered only the logging of Diderot's activities in Paris. He told them that as a serving officer, Montbron, ostensibly on accrued leave before posting to England, had excited the attention of Rhine Army Intelligence. Richard was quite pleased with himself; it sounded convincing.

But not to them.

He'd overplayed a very bad hand. They didn't believe a word of it, and they told him so.

But they didn't give him a chance to change it. There was a moment when they all stood looking at each other, nobody saying a word, then, suddenly, one of them hit him hard in the stomach. He gagged. They hit him again, the same place, and when he doubled forward they pulled his head up, stuck a rolled-up newspaper into his mouth, hoisted him on to the bonnet of the car and held him there while another of the men grabbed his foot and straightened out his leg. One of the others, a swarthy, three-quarters Algerian renegade with a bored expression, moved lightly to one side and without warning rose on to his toes and brought a heavy, thin-edged steel jack lever over his shoulder in a round-arm swing, whacking it just above Richard's knee. The flesh split like a soggy orange and the crack of the thigh-bone snapping sounded like a pistol shot. The Algerian stepped back, still bored, his expression unchanged as he watched Richard's eyes bulge out of their sockets. He was about to scream into the newspaper but before it reached his throat he managed to faint.

They gave him no time. The scream was still where he'd left it when they slapped him back to life, but the wodge of paper held and absorbed it. The scream showed only in his face.

After a moment the leader of the team indicated for him to be sat back on the bonnet as his other leg was grasped. Richard nearly fainted again. The Algerian moved back into his earlier position and crossed his arms. He'd cleaned the lever on Richard's good trouser leg and it now shone like a crusader's sword as it rested on his shoulder. The leader reached forward to grasp the end of the screwed-up newspaper and began pulling it out of Richard's mouth. It seemed endless and kept coming, wet and soggy, like a conjuror's opening trick. When his mouth was empty, Richard tested the scream but it had finished, replaced by the dryness of fear. He tried lubricating his mouth with spittle but nothing came, so he gave a dry, hawking spit instead.

'D'you want the other leg done?'

It was a silly question. It didn't require an answer. It didn't get one.

'Let's start again. What's this Diderot's play?'

Richard gave it to them, chapter and verse, everything he knew about Montbron's project. He held back on the Lemercier connection but had no hope that they wouldn't go deeper. While they exchanged glances with each other, he lowered his head and studied his ruined leg. He wondered if he was going to have anything left worth making a bolt for. He kept his head bowed for the next set of questions.

'The guys waiting for the shadowing brief,' said the leader, conversationally, 'are they reporting to you, or is there a central group in town collating –' He stopped at the sound of a car door slamming and cocked his head warily, but didn't let up. 'Don't worry about that – go on.'

Before Richard could answer a car engine started up round the corner. All eyes turned and the Algerian dropped the tyre lever, which clanged an echo round the dank concrete walls.

Richard thought he had a chance. A stupid thought, a stupid action with one leg. Forgotten for that brief moment, he shrugged off the hands holding his arms, lashed out with his one good leg at his questioner, swung a sharp, hand-edge cut at the Algerian and threw himself off the bonnet of the car. It was a hopeless attempt, and he knew it. But it was all he was going to get and shouting at the top of his voice, with his useless leg trailing behind him, he hopped for the sound of the car engine. It wasn't far away, just round the corner, but it could have been a thousand miles. And it went in the opposite direction, away from him. But he was never going to make it anyway.

The Algerian, already on his knees from Richard's wild blow, moved his hand smoothly to the inside of his jacket and with a clean, habitual movement straightened his arm and pointed a long-barrelled Mauser at Richard's back.

'Aim low!' screamed his leader.

But it was too late. His finger had already begun to squeeze the trigger and two 7.6mm's thumped into Richard's back. The impact lifted him off the ground and propelled him another two metres before he crashed face down into the powdered concrete dust.

The car engine revved noisily as it mounted a ramp somewhere in the hollow distance, and faded. The silence in the car park and around the Panhard was total.

'Why'd you shoot him? He wasn't going anywhere.'

The Algerian shrugged. He was already replacing the two spent cartridges. He said nothing.

'You stupid bastard. You could have thrown that friggin' gun at him and stopped him!'

'Gutty bugger, though,' observed the man who'd been holding

Richard down. He was busily rubbing life into his arm where Richard's cutting blow had numbed a nerve. 'I'll give him that.'

'Go and get him. Stuff him in the car and let's get out of here.'

'He's not dead,' said the Algerian as he turned Richard on to his back with his foot. 'D'you want to have another go at him?'

'Can't be bothered. Shove the bastard in his car and lock the door.'

'What about this Diderot?'

'Fishy. Decidedly fishy. I think Xavier'll want to have a good long look at that bugger.' He glanced down at his wrist. 'We'll have to move fast. I can't trust the phone. I think I'm going to have to break in on their little tête-à-tête and give them the good news that they've got a winkle sharing their high hopes.'

'Goodbye bollocks!'

'Shut up! Get that bloody car started and let's get out of here.'

40

MONTBRON HAD EXPECTED something like a court martial or a selection board, with all the important people sitting along one side of a green baize table, the details of the applicant, or supplicant, in a pink folder in front of each judge. He couldn't have been more wrong.

The gathering was like after-dinner brandy-time, except there was no brandy. They were relaxed, or so it would have appeared to anyone not used to sensing the forced air of relaxation employed by brave men on the fringe of danger. They stopped talking among themselves when Xavier led Montbron into the room and studied the tall Army officer, whom most knew by reputation.

There were ten of them, six obviously military. They spurned the use of code-names. The only one Montbron recognized was a man he'd met in happier days in Saigon. Now a leader of the new order, he was not a revolutionary by choice but had nevertheless accepted more than a figurehead role. Lieutenant Colonel Jean-Marie Rostand-Bercy was a man of action, an airman and self-appointed leader of the 'Old General Staff'. He was the first to greet Montbron.

The others generated the natural suspicion of plotters in the presence of a new member to the conspiracy. The fact that Rostand-Bercy had broken the thin coating of ice around Montbron went some way to lightening the atmosphere, but it was obvious they were not keen to hang about and were there under sufferance.

'Let's get on with it, please.' The man who called them to order was not Army. He could only be one thing – a politician, and a senior one. He was, in fact, the Under-Minister for Transport in the present Government and he'd booked himself a very important role in the new order, when it came. And he had no doubt that it was 'when' rather than 'if'. 'Vaucoulet . . .' He frowned at the man at Montbron's side and then said, 'Instruct, er, Monsieur, er, Colonel Guy-Montbron to explain his actions in the Boulevard St-Germain . . .'

'That's all been gone into,' one of the other officers explained patiently. He spoke as he would to a new pupil starting kindergarten. 'It's all been explained. Colonel Guy-Montbron is not here to go over past actions but to put before us a plan for the execution of Jacques Bouchard. And I'm sure that like the rest of us, he doesn't want to stand around talking. He wants to get on with it and get out of here.' He turned and looked Montbron full in the face. 'To somewhere where he doesn't have to keep one eye on the lavatory door.'

No one laughed. Everyone stood and stared at Montbron.

'Why don't we sit down?' Montbron felt comfortable and at ease. The Army people were younger than he was and, with the exception of Xavier and Rostand-Bercy, junior in rank. He was not concerned with the politicians, but their faces were etched in his mind.

Whilst they arranged themselves in chairs around the room he moved to the window and perched his bottom on the thin metal radiator. It was easier this way; he could look down into each face as he told them of Lemercier's plan to kill the Minister of the Interior. It was almost unreal to watch the nodding heads of approval from the graduates of St Cyr and the almost gloating pleasure of the politicians as the infallible plan for the murder of one of their colleagues was laid out in detail by Montbron and then explained to the politicians in comic-paper-like terms by the studious-looking ORO – Organization Intelligence Operations – executive, Dr John-Pierre Perigot.

Then came the questions. Montbron had done his homework, he'd memorized General Lemercier's plan of action, and with every question asked and answered, the group's estimation of him rose. By the time the questions had dried up, he'd become a fully paid-up member of the club; one of them. All it needed was the invitation to join them at the top table. But it never came.

A hesitant knock at the door that led deeper into the house killed the conversation, the speculation and the self-congratulation. All heads turned to the man leaning round the door. He looked for Xavier, and when he'd found him, jerked his head sideways apologetically and disappeared. The heads turned to Xavier. He shrugged his shoulders and drooped his mouth at the congregation, then went through the door and closed it behind him.

He was gone almost ten minutes and returned to the room without fuss, passing from one delegate to another. A brief word, head to head, a nod, and after a slight pause a ripple of movement as the conspirators slipped away. No rush, no panic, no goodbyes. One minute they were there, the next minute the room was empty except for Rostand-Bercy, Dr Perigot, Xavier and the guest of honour, Montbron. It was then that Xavier's mask slipped.

He'd already spoken to the other two. There was no mistake; Montbron didn't need to be paranoid to realize that he was the only one not to have received Xavier's mouth to his ear. And that it wasn't going to happen that way.

It happened quickly, without warning, as if it had been rehearsed to perfection. One second they were spread around the room, the next they were in a little group with a man on either side of Montbron and the friendly expressions replaced by dismay on the face of the bespectacled Perigot, and by curiosity on Rostand-Bercy's part.

'You're blown, you bastard!' hissed Xavier. Montbron hadn't noticed the stubby automatic in Xavier's hand, but he felt it as it was jabbed into his waist. 'I'm not going to ask your reasons. You fooled me, you fooled us all, but that's as far as you go. You're finished – you're dead.'

'I'd like a question,' said Rostand-Bercy.

'One,' replied a tight-lipped Xavier. 'And then the bastard's going to be taken outside and have his head blown off.' He looked hard at the Air Force colonel. 'And I'm surprised there's anything *you* want to say to the treacherous bastard – unless it's "Let me pull the bloody trigger"!'

'That would be a request, not a question,' answered Rostand-Bercy, 'and that comes after I've asked: why, Montbron? For God's sake, why? You're one of us. You're already more than halfway along our road.' He stopped and stared into Montbron's face. 'Or was Gautier's killing a put-up job?' He looked at Xavier. 'Is that possible?'

Xavier shook his head. 'They've been clever – bloody clever. I can read them now. They pulled a double-double. They marked Gautier down as one of ours and got him out of de Gaulle's way by the use of this *escroc*, which allowed him to tell us he killed him because he thought Gautier was loyal. Don't you get it? We were patting the bastard on the back for doing such a good job. We didn't think for one moment Gautier had been exposed.' Xavier was getting over his initial anger. He'd only just noticed that Montbron hadn't yet said a word.

But before he could start interrogating, Perigot spoke for the first time. 'So why the charade over Interior? Why should he and his people go to all these lengths to give us a first-rate plan to kill Jacques Bouchard?'

'It was never going to get that far,' Xavier told him without taking his eyes off Montbron. 'His mission is complete. He made it this morning. He's marked everybody in the OAS/Metropole Central Committee—'

'But they already know that,' interrupted Perigot. 'Why go to these lengths?'

Xavier raised his eyebrows at Rostand-Bercy, an unspoken, almost imperceptible mark of impatience with civilians embroiled in military matters. 'They say they do, my dear doctor, but the bastards are bluffing. They don't know you, they don't know half of us. They know him—' He nodded at Rostand-Bercy. 'But he doesn't care. They know me, and I don't either. But that's not the point. This bastard's come to gather the evidence so that if we fail – which is not likely – he's going to point the finger and pronounce the charge. That's what the treacherous bastard's doing here. And he's also broken into our chain of command.

He knows our houses.' He jabbed the automatic into Montbron's stomach again, but it wasn't enough to settle the bile of anger inside him. He raised the gun and without warning cracked it across Montbron's face. As Montbron's head went back, he followed it up with another glancing blow across the side of the temple. 'Don't you, you double bastard?'

Montbron straightened up, blinked away the trickle of blood that was starting to course down his face, then shook his head. He shrugged his shoulders and very nearly smiled, but his mouth refused and it became a grimace. 'I don't suppose there's any point in saying I haven't got the foggiest idea what you're talking about?'

Rostand-Bercy *did* smile. It seemed that he was the only one left in the room with a sense of humour. He addressed Xavier. 'What arrangements have you made?'

'Arrangements?'

Rostand-Bercy jerked his head at Montbron.

'Oh, those arrangements. I'm going to have the bastard taken out, shoved in a dustbin and a bullet fired into his head. The *boueux* can take him away and tip him on the dump with the rest of the day's rubbish. Why, have you got a better idea?'

Rostand-Bercy stopped smiling. 'Philippe de Guy-Montbron is an officer and he's a gentleman. He's proved himself in the field for France; he deserves to die in the company of a fellow officer and with dignity. I will not allow him to be mishandled by one of *les ordures* that we have the misfortune to be leading. I will go with him and make sure he is executed in the proper manner.'

'I don't think—' began Xavier.

'Then it's arranged,' snapped Rostand-Bercy. 'Call in your thugs and tell them that Colonel de Guy-Montbron is in my custody until we reach the killing ground. Instruct them accordingly.'

'Can I ask a question of Colonel Vaucoulet?' Montbron dropped the Xavier name play and brought a tiny sense of pride to the renegade colonel. He addressed no one in particular, but it was Xavier who nodded his head.

'I'm not admitting any of the things you accuse me of,' said Montbron evenly, 'and I don't expect you to reconsider your intention to murder me—'

'You're not being murdered,' snapped Xavier testily. 'You're being executed as a spy.'

'However you wish to salve your conscience, Colonel, is your own business. What I would like to know is how you decided, without giving me the opportunity to refute these allegations, that I am not with you and your organization?'

Xavier was slow in responding; it was as if he was considering the wisdom of answering questions. But he couldn't resist the opportunity. He hunched his shoulders and allowed a disdainful droop of his mouth. 'The people you had in place to shadow you were below average. One of them, it seems, knew more about you than was good for him . . .'

Poor Denis. The useless, cocky sod! He sounded like bad news right from the beginning at Versailles. Loyalty has never been a substitute for ability! Montbron kept his face blank. There was no need to ask what had happened to him.

Xavier hadn't quite finished. 'You can have a word with him about it shortly when you meet him in the dustbin.' He actually smiled at his own sense of humour; he must have been a hoot in the mess when the port was circulating. 'But that's enough. You tried, Montbron, and you failed. Goodbye.'

He didn't offer to shake hands or attempt any of the other civilities. He walked to the door and opened it. There were two men standing there. One of them was the leader of Richard's execution team. He studied Montbron with interest. He had an undertaker's commercial expression: how big the coffin, how many to carry it, how many to hold him down while the shot went in. As far as he was concerned, Montbron was already dead.

'Colonel Rostand-Bercy will go with you to ensure the thing is done properly,' Xavier told him in a voice inaudible to the people in the centre of the room. 'Just make sure you carry out my orders and nobody else's,' he added pointedly. Xavier was no fool. A field-commissioned officer, he had an unhealthy mistrust of the St Cyr brotherhood. He hadn't taken to the instant camaraderie between Rostand-Bercy and Guy-Montbron, but he wasn't going to discuss his feelings with an ex-para sergeant. 'Administer the *coup de grâce* yourself, Delguarde.'

'I don't need—'

'You'll do as you're told!'

'*Oui, mon Colonel!*'

41

GÉRARD NEURIE LED Metcalfe down the steps of the military Falcon turbo-prop aircraft at Le Bourget and escorted him across the tarmac to the waiting dark blue Peugeot. The car dropped them off on the Avenue de Maréchal Fayolle and they walked, withut speaking, across the park to the building housing the apartments and unofficial command centre of Maurice himself. The business was getting to 'Maurice'. Totally out of character, he'd told Neurie, after he'd been brought up to date on the affair in the Camargue, to 'bring the Englishman with you. Don't sign him in – I'll leave instructions downstairs.'

"Downstairs" looked like all the other downstairs of the impressive apartments of the wealthy that dominated the perimeter of the Bois, but there was a difference. The concierge was not a nosy old pensioner who'd had a lucky break and was sharing his curiosity with a gossipy old woman behind a curtained window inside the entrance hall of the building. This concierge was a cold-eyed individual of twenty-five who had one hand permanently wrapped round a 9mm automatic that he held behind him just out of sight. His partner occupied another part of the entrance hall. Unseen, armed with a lethal H&K machine-pistol, he controlled the buttons. Along with the rest of the team they were changed regularly in case of corruption or persuasion, and Department Maurice special agents such as Neurie were as anonymous to them as they were to any other members of the traditional, or orthodox, intelligence organizations. These guards took their duties very seriously. There were no stairs. Visitors came through the heavy-duty, explosion-proof glass doors only at the invitation of the concierge, and the lift doors opened only after an inaudible electronic signal from the man behind the curtain.

Neurie and Metcalfe were expected.

'Sign here please, sir.' The young man watched very carefully and checked the name Neurie had written. He stared hard at Metcalfe and asked him to move to one side to make sure he wasn't holding a gun to Neurie, then unapologetically and inexpressively pointed his chin at the lift doors. They opened as the two men approached. The concierge was still watching carefully when the doors closed on their faces and they began the upward trip.

There were two more men on the landing when the lift came smoothly to a stop and the doors opened with a gentle hiss. One of the men was sitting on a hard high-backed chair, his knees crossed, the inevitable machine-pistol resting on his thigh, its muzzle pointing steadily at the open lift. The standing man studied them for a moment, then pointed to a door where the thick-carpeted hall narrowed to a small cul-de-sac. There hadn't been much friendship shown; not a single smile from beginning to end. But it was a striking show of security. Metcalfe was impressed.

Maurice didn't rise when they came into the room. He was sitting behind a partner's desk that was as large as a small mountain plateau and covered with well-aged, maroon-coloured leather. Maurice, not a small man, was dwarfed by its magnificence. Two chairs were placed strategically on the opposite side of the desk, but there was no recess for jutting knees. It was not meant to be comfortable – not that side of the desk.

'Does this Englishman speak French?'

Maurice didn't wait for a reply. He stared at Metcalfe for several seconds, then, as if having considered these the niceties of introduction, dismissed him for the time being from the conversation and settled his eyes coldly on Neurie. 'Let's get to the point quickly, Gérard. Tell me about the man who murdered Jean Gautier – what's his name?'

'Philippe de Guy-Montbron.'

'And how this Englishman comes to be involved in our affairs.'

He didn't look at Harry Metcalfe and made no attempt to bring him into the conversation. He could have been referring to some other Englishman. But it was water off Metcalfe's back. He knew the French; their rudeness didn't trouble him. He turned sideways, crossed his legs and gazed at the scenery through the picture window as Neurie answered the question.

When he got to the conversation between Montbron and Metcalfe in the duck hide, Maurice stopped him with another wave of the hand and turned his eyes to Harry Metcalfe. He studied him for a moment, then said, making no allowance for Metcalfe's grasp or otherwise of the French language, 'Tell me exactly what this Guy-Montbron told you.'

Metcalfe swung his chair back so that he faced Maurice head-on and the old man listened politely as he went through the conversation he'd had that early morning overlooking the Camargue water. When he'd finished Maurice said one word.

'Crap!'

'Pardon?' said a surprised Metcalfe.

'I said, crap. The man's trying to dig a hole under the wire for himself. I've never heard such a cock-and-bull story in all my life!' He stared long and hard at Metcalfe, then, after an exchange of glances with Neurie, continued: 'Of course, he chose the right person to unload this pile of rubbish on. If he'd tried it on a Frenchman he'd have laughed in his face.'

But Metcalfe didn't have to remain on his best behaviour; he was a guest. If this old bugger wanted a whipping-boy he'd chosen the wrong one. 'That's only your opinion, sir,' he said with an edge to his voice. 'I came into this act not of my own choosing. I owe no allegiance to you or your adversaries and I have no axe to grind.' He turned and stared at a blank-faced Neurie for a second, and said, 'Neurie knows who and what I am. He started this game and I had to go along with it. The reason's of no interest to you, it's purely between him and me. But whether I believe what I was told by Montbron is neither here nor there. Your opinion on what I've told you is your own business. I did as Neurie asked and I've passed on additional information to your people. Again, what you think of that information doesn't concern me. My only interest now is to step off the roundabout and let you get on with it.'

Maurice stared at Metcalfe, unimpressed. He didn't appear to have heard a word he'd said and continued where he'd left off. 'I believe this gangster, Montbron, has used you. He's given you an interesting story to bring to us in the hope that it will make us stop and think so that he can get on with whatever he's been programmed to do. He was run to ground by Neurie's man Violle, which cost Violle his life, then the Action Association people almost slipped him in the bag, and again he slipped away after causing the death of several men. Ask yourself, Monsieur Metcalfe, why he'd take you, an Englishman, into his bolt-hole and tell you things that he must have realized you had no obligation to withhold if pressure was exerted. As indeed it was, by all accounts. You've told the peole from "AA"; you've told Neurie here, and you've told me – which is exactly what he wanted you to do. Everything is closing in on him. He wants time. He chose you to buy that for him.'

'I can't answer for his motives in choosing my company, but surely he's not so silly to doubt that your first action would be to break his story through General Lemercier. Don't forget, when he told me these things the General was still alive. Montbron couldn't have foreseen a car accident on the autobahn.'

'But he could foresee the murder of the General. What do you think he was doing when he was out of your sight? They have telephones in the Camargue, don't they? He was arranging the murder of the General so that his story couldn't be refuted.'

'You have evidence of this, sir?'

Maurice shrugged his shoulders. It could have meant yes, no, or it's no bloody business of yours. Harry Metcalfe took it as the latter. 'Then can't you confirm his statement with General de Gaulle?'

'Hardly. Even if there was a remote possibility of a modicum of truth in Guy-Montbron's story, do you think there would be minutes of the business? D'you think for one second that the President of France would be prepared to discuss some private arrangement he made with his cousin to interfere in the intelligence operations of the security services of the country? Or that he would even remember such a conversation? No,' said Maurice emphatically. 'Forget it! So thank you, Monsieur Metcalfe, for your assistance in this matter. I don't think we'll need any more help. We can manage this on our own now, I think.' He actually smiled, but it didn't stay very long. He didn't offer Metcalfe the opportunity to reply, neither did he stand up or shake hands; his dismissal was as abrupt as it was unexpected. 'Perhaps you will allow me to have a word with Monsieur Neurie?'

He must have worked a private signal. No sooner were the words out of his mouth than the door opened behind the two visitors and a man in a black and yellow striped waistcoat, white shirt and black trousers stood to one side of it and waited for Metcalfe to leave the room.

'You haven't yet said what you think about this ridiculous story, Gérard.' said Maurice after the door had closed. 'Can you see anything in it?'

Neurie shook his head noncommittally. 'I don't think I'd like to offer an opinion just yet. Perhaps later.'

Maurice raised his eyebrows. 'How much later?'

'When Montbron's nailed against the wall in the Santé and I've prised open his eyes to see how deep his convictions go.'

'So you continue to treat him as a criminal?'

'As I said, Maurice, for the time being.'

'D'you think he'll try to get in touch with the Englishman?'

Neurie stared at the old man for a moment, then shook his head again. 'He'd be a bloody fool if he did, but when you're short of friends, who knows?'

Maurice kept his own counsel. He said, 'I think I can safely leave that sort of thing to you. You know what to do if he does. My advice . . .' His heavy eyebrows clinched together and his eyelids dropped, though whether through boredom or tiredness, it wasn't obvious; maybe it helped him think. Neurie knew him. He waited. 'Is to keep this Metcalfe under your wing until the thing's finished, just in case contact is attempted. If he tries to bolt back across the Channel, break his legs. He's got to stay here until it's finished. No arguments.' Maurice opened his eyes again. He didn't appear to be joking. Neurie didn't laugh either.

'In any case, take his passport off him and make sure he's logged for detaining wherever passports are needed. Now, you probably haven't seen this yet?' He slid a sheet of paper across the desk, but it only reached halfway. It stayed there for a moment, like a wounded soldier in no man's land, both men looking at it, neither man prepared to help it to its destination. Neurie gave in first and stood up to retrieve it. He started reading before he resumed his seat.

It started with a DST (department origination unspecified) submission that a top-rank political assassination was being planned (source of information unspecified). The target (hypothesized): the Minister of the Interior. The assassinators: an élite murder unit of the OAS. Suggested leader: ex-Lieutenant Colonel Philippe de Guy-Montbron. Timing of attempt: no estimation, but would follow a full meeting of the combined heads of the political and military cadres of the OAS/Metropole.

That was the first part.

Maurice watched Neurie's expression as he read it for a second time. It told him nothing.

'What's the source?' asked Neurie after a moment.

'Group Filli at Montmorency.'

'They'll have to change their name,' said Neurie without expression. 'Where did *they* get it?'

It was Maurice's turn to shrug his shoulders. 'The whole of the Montmorency Action Association team set up for the prosecution of those responsible for the Gautier assassination has been closed down. There are only two of the active unit left: a woman undercover agent and one other man, an unknown. He's a special agent personally recruited by Filli who's now gone so far underground that he's untraceable, according to the Montmorency cut-out line. No name, no shape, no identification, not even from the female survivor, who never met him. But he's got to be the one who brought the Interior target information to the surface. That's a thought for you, Gérard: you're both on the same side, both looking for the same man. Make sure you don't bump into each other in the dark.'

Neurie was thoughtful. 'According to Metcalfe, Montbron had a helper.'

'So?'

'Could that helper be twisting? Doing a turn for both Filli and Montbron?'

'I've never credited you with a lively imagination, Gérard,' said Maurice testily. 'I wouldn't spend too much time thinking along those lines. You're getting into the realms of impossible coincidences! Things don't work like that.' Maurice jabbed a finger at the sheet of paper in Neurie's hand. 'Forget that for the moment. Whether it has credence or not, I've got Jacques Bouchard tucked up in a bomb-proof holiday home for the next week or so. It was a hell of a job; he's a pig-headed bugger at the best of times, but he is at least intelligent. He can also read a real threat better than most, so there's no need to worry about the attempt succeeding. All you have to do is concentrate on finding Montbron. Anyway, read the rest of that – the bit at the bottom.'

Neurie glanced down at the sheet of paper. It detailed the forthcoming meeting of the OAS/Métropole Central Committee and indicated that among the Committee were three members of the Government (unnamed). Army insurgents were not named, but code-names and suspected safe houses indicated. Neurie ran through them quickly. He was looking for one, Buc, but it didn't feature. Another interesting omission was the name of Philippe de Guy-Montbron. But Xavier's name featured prominently. 'This is the first time they've been together under one roof,' he said cautiously as he slid the paper back across the desk. 'But there's no date indicated, or estimated. Could be any time.' He stared across the desk at Maurice's blank face.

Maurice raised his eyebrows. 'Could be today!'

'Are you keeping anything back, Maurice?'

Maurice shrugged. That was all Neurie was going to get. He tried another direction. 'If we can believe Metcalfe, this is exactly what Montbron's operation was aiming for.' He stared into Maurice's face.

Maurice looked sceptical, but didn't dismiss the suggestion out of hand. Neither did he agree. But he nodded.

It was enough for Neurie. The crafty old bugger had been inside the Paris organization almost since its inception. So what was he waiting for?

'I think when names have been put against all these players we might as well bring the revolution to a halt,' said Maurice after what appeared to be a lengthy private communion. 'It's finished in Algeria. We can bring in those misguided bastards who opted for Spain as a safe haven for waging war. The Spanish'll look the other way when we slip in and drag them out; they don't want to be involved. The same for those who chose Austria and Germany. This Paris lot have made such a balls-up of winning the hearts and minds of the people that they've lost any chance they might have had of setting up a new guillotine in the Place de la Concorde. It'll give the treacherous bastards quite an interesting little surprise when our people come knocking on their door with an invitation to a private room over at Vincennes or d'Ivry . . .'

'Do you know all of them?' interrupted Neurie.

Maurice thought about it for a moment. 'The answer to that's a reluctant no. But as you remarked, and according to our man, if it's today, this bunker meeting puts them all together for the first time. Some of them don't even know each other, but by this afternoon they will – and so will I! So, all in all, I think what we'll do is let this little rabble have their afternoon gathering, and then, when they've all gone home and put on their carpet slippers, we'll go in and pick them off.' Maurice shook his head sadly; it could have been contempt. 'All in a bunch. Pick up one, pick up the lot. No cells, no cut-outs according to that memo. They've behaved like amateurs. You wouldn't have thought we had five years' German occupation of this country not so long ago. Didn't these stupid bastards learn anything from the Resistance or the Gestapo? Or are memories that short?'

Neurie had no answer for him. Instead, after a brief moment of silent gratitude for the short memories, he said, 'Your man on the inside, will he be able to pinpoint Montbron so that I can walk in on him while he's in his bath?'

'No,' said Maurice bluntly. 'My man's going to have to go the way of the others. I'll even have him on trial with them, though he'll get off. After a short time we'll have an amnesty and all these bastards'll be out on the streets again, though they'll never get another job – I'll see to that. What you've got to make sure of is the rounding-up of this new hot-cock, Montbron. Get him inside somewhere, Gérard, and find out who made him tick in the first place. I don't accept Lemercier; it's got to be somebody I should know about. Also, somebody's head's got to go for Gautier; it could be his. Violle, too. I want something in return for him. So do you, don't you?'

I want a man called Vernet. But Neurie kept the name to himself; one day that was going to be his own personal satisfaction. 'I'll stay outside then, Maurice, and concentrate on Montbron. Will you keep my "K" authority active?'

'Certainly. By the way,' Maurice looked keenly at Neurie and brought his hands level with the top of the desk, allowing them to hover like two shaky helicopters, 'I think in the interests of possible doubt over Montbron's motivation, it might be politic to have something to show at the end of the day – something with blood flowing in its veins, that can stand up, eventually, before his masters and maybe prove us wrong. I wouldn't like to go to my grave with the death of a very brave man on my conscience.' He lowered his hands into his lap. 'And of course, neither would I like the thought of a traitor and a murderer sitting by the lake in the Bois feeding the ducks. D'you get my point?'

'Your points, Maurice, are never obscure!'

'Then it's all in your hands. But there is something else I'd like.'

'What's that?'

'This Filli man who's still in the tunnel. He sounds like somebody I could do business with.'

Neurie's eyes narrowed as he stared at the old man. But he said nothing.

Maurice stared back. 'A good man. The sort I need, on his own, a shadow. He sounds like the best type of agent, good Department Maurice material. I want to see him when he comes out.'

42

Montbron's assessment of Denis's ability was miles out. Richard was expendable. Denis had decided that before the game of watch-him-watch-me started. It was the old game of attrition, or now you see me, but you don't see them watching me watching you. Even Xavier's hotshots had dropped their guard once they'd caught the snoop. They didn't mark the backup – or that backup's backup – which allowed the second and third watching crews, unaware of Richard's problems, to go all the way and hand their target to Denis, who quickly tucked himself among a row of trees in the École Militaire and dispersed the remaining teams into rapidly arranged covers in the side-streets off the Rue Cambronne.

Having waited for Richard's report, and after repeated abortive attempts to contact him, Denis stared blankly at the handset of the two-way radio, shook his head at his partner behind the wheel of the car, and removed Richard's wavelength from the security band.

'Maybe his set's busted,' suggested the driver. There was no conviction in his voice. Denis felt the same. He didn't bother replying, instead lowered his head for the umpteenth time and studied the area road-map of the 15th arrondissement. He'd got it sealed up, but there was something niggling, something not quite right, and there was no one to share the misgivings. Richard, who'd have been worth a suggestion or two, had gone up the spout, the bloody fool, and it was bloody inconvenient of old Lemercier to take the jump before the show was over. The stupid bastard ought to be there, sitting in the back of the car telling them all what to do. But Denis had had his orders, in writing, and they couldn't have been clearer or more concise.

And if there was one thing that settled Denis's conscience, it was clear, concise orders in writing. Absently, he took a cigarette from the packet on the dashboard, lit it and flipped the packet into the lap of the driver. He glanced down at his watch and studied it at length. It looked as if he was learning how to tell the time from it. Eventually he looked up.

'That makes twenty-eight minutes since the targets disappeared into the house on Croix-Nivert.' He was talking to himself. 'Both ends covered and watching parties in reserve spread around the place. Can't go wrong.'

The driver grunted an obscenity, but when Denis, unamused, stared at him, he coughed the curse into a snort and flicked his cigarette ash out of the window. Denis's sense of humour had gone into limbo for the duration. He went back to his map and litany. 'So, if they come out of there,' he followed his finger, 'Group Two'll have them; and out of there, the smart boys'll be on to them. There's no other way out for them.' He stared at the map and shook his head. 'Another fifteen minutes and we'll go and scare the buggers into the open . . . What the bloody hell's that?' The two-way radio emitted a squawk and then crackled into life.

'Six to Denis . . . Come in.'

'What?' Denis touched the map with his finger where a pencilled number six sat in a black ring.

'Delguarde . . .' crackled the set.

'What about him?'

'He's just driven past and turned into Frémicourt. There's a hold-up at the lights, a bit of a jam—'

'Fuck the traffic report!' interrupted Denis. 'What the bloody hell's Delguarde doing out of his cage? He's top minder, he should be hanging around waiting for the brass to move. Anybody else in the car?'

'A driver and two in the back.'

'Christ! How the bloody hell did he get out?'

'No idea—'

'Forget it! You've got a motor-bike backup?'

'Roger!'

'A talking one?'

'Roger!'

'Get him behind Delguarde and I'll join him shortly. Put him on line one.'

'That's Richard's. They'll cross—'

'Do as I say. Get the bike out and clear.'

'Roger!'

Denis threw his cigarette out of the window and lit another. He flicked the switch on the handset. 'Can anybody see or hear anything from the target? Somebody's got out without being seen. How did that happen?'

Nobody replied.

'Will some fucker answer me!'

After an embarrassed pause a reluctant voice said, 'There's no noise coming out of the place. We're not in tight enough to make out any words, but there was plenty of noise earlier. For the last ten minutes it's like the Western Front—'

'What the bloody hell does that mean?'

'It's all quiet!'

'Stop being fuckin' clever. If it's quiet it's empty – the bastards have bolted under your fuckin' noses. For Christ's sake move in! *Now!* Bernard, take over, I'm going after a bolting rabbit.' Denis raised his finger from the button and said, 'Move!'

As the car screeched to the Avenue Duquesne exit of the École Militaire, Denis slowed the driver down and searched through the wavebands for Richard's old slot. It was noisy, primitive and almost unintelligible, but sounded like, '. . . We've joined the Boulevard Montparnasse.'

Denis and the driver looked at each other. The driver pulled a face. Denis looked back at the road-map. 'Make for the station.'

'. . . de Vaugirard,' crackled the set.

'Fuck it! Go for Boul' Mich'.'

'. . . he's turned into the Boulevard St-Germain . . .'

'Lucky bugger, Denis!'

'He's going for the bridge.'

'Which bloody bridge?'

'Sully, I think. Oh, Christ! Bloody lights. He's gone.'

'Bugger the lights! Go with him.'

'Can't, *flics* all round me. Tournelle and St Bernard are full. I can't make it. He's gone . . .'

'Direction?' Denis was as cold as ice, and as cool.

'Bastille.'

'Go as soon as you can. Just keep in that direction. I'll cut across the Pont de la Tournelle and try to catch you up. Keep in touch.'

'Roger!'

'Just a minute. Did you get close enough to see anybody in the car?'

'One of the two guys sitting in the back was Rostand-Bercy.'

'Who was the other one?'

'Couldn't swear. Looked like the number Richard was tagging.'

'Can you give it a name?'

'Does Diderot mean anything?'

The driver and Denis exchanged glances again. Denis smiled gently, without humour, then flicked the switch again.

'Find the bastards!'

43

THERE HAD BEEN no goodbyes for Montbron. The two ex-paras led him through the back of the house to the kitchen, then down a narrow stone stairway to a dank cellar lit by a low-wattage bulb set into the arched ceiling. Montbron looked about him. There was nothing extraordinary, it was a cellar like any other cellar in a house this size, but to Montbron it had a special significance – it looked like a cellar where he was going to die. It made a mockery of everything he'd done with his life to end up dying in a Paris cellar, shot by a fellow Frenchman.

'Come on, get a bloody move on!' Delguarde jabbed him in the back with his fist and urged him deeper into the cavern until they were stumbling along, bent double. The other ex-para was in the lead and after a few more stumbling steps grunted for them to stop. Montbron straightened up as far as possible and stared ahead. The leading man had stopped at what appeared to be the end of the tunnel and was rolling a five-hundred-litre barrel to one side to join another he'd already moved. He was making light work of it. They must have been empty, probably on springs. Montbron bent his knees again and found a more comfortable height. He judged by the progress they'd made that they must be somewhere under the middle of the road where he'd been dropped off with Xavier. He hadn't seen Rostand-Bercy since they'd entered the cellar.

'Move!' Delguarde's fist thumped into his spleen again.

They entered a similar cellar to the one they'd started in and after another damp walk went up a flight of stairs and through a door into a second kitchen. Deserted. Montbron sniffed silently. Not abandoned; just deserted for this afternoon to allow egress for a condemned man. They were led out of the back door of the house and into a narrow passageway at the end of which stood a large three-car garage. There was only one car in it.

'OK, Delgado,' said Rostand-Bercy.

'Delguarde,' hissed the ex-para sergeant. His name seemed to be a sore point; he'd obviously had this treatment before.

Rostand-Bercy smiled easily. 'OK, *Del-guarde*.' He enunciated the word deliberately, as if testing the man's sensitivity. 'You get in the front and tell the driver where to take us. I'll sit in the back with the traitor.' Montbron glanced sideways at the Air Force colonel. Had he caught a hint of mockery in his tone? So what if he had? There was nothing there for him. Rostand-Bercy leaned forward and tapped the ex-para on the shoulder. 'And hand me your automatic in case he tries to take a flyer.'

Delguarde hesitated for a brief second, then opened the front door and clambered in beside the driver. 'Don't worry about him, Colonel,' he grunted, and pulled a heavy Colt automatic from its holster under his right arm. He held it in his left hand so that the two men on the back seat could see what he was doing, and with his thumb eased back the half-cocked trigger.

'Put your hands in your coat pockets,' he ordered Montbron, 'and if you as much as sneeze without my say-so, I'll blow a hole in your knee.' He transferred the automatic to his right hand, to show that he was ambidextrous, and folded his arm so that the muzzle, out of sight from anyone poking their head in the car window, rested on Montbron's kneecap.

'Where are we going?' asked Rostand-Bercy.

'The usual place,' replied Delguarde without looking round. He didn't elaborate. Rostand-Bercy didn't press him, but sat back in the seat and gazed out of the window as the car moved east through Montparnasse before filtering into the Boulevard St-Germain and crossing the Seine by the Pont de Sully. Avoiding the Place de la Bastille, they worked their way north towards République before turning on to the quay running alongside the Canal St-Martin. Delguarde and the driver knew the route intimately; it wasn't their first trip to this particular abattoir.

'Is this all right?' said the driver to Delguarde after he'd turned into an open space bordering on the edge of the St-Martin locks. 'Looks nice and quiet.'

'Go further across there.' No reason. Delguarde chose his spot from some inner preference. Perhaps the smell of blood and the aura of fear were more pronounced in the still-deserted area where his finger pointed.

'That's where we did those *melons* last week. It was your birthday, remember?' The driver was on a high. So was his voice. The prospect of a killing had raised his adrenalin and he sounded breathless.

But Delguarde was unaffected. 'Shut up! OK, this'll do.' He half-turned his head and looked mockingly into Rostand-Bercy's eyes. 'This won't take long. You can wait in the car if you like, Colonel.'

Rostand-Bercy ignored him and reached for the handle, by which time Delguarde was already half out of his door, the heavy, unsilenced Colt pointing at Montbron's side of the back seat.

'You, shithead! Out!' He moved the automatic in the direction he wanted Montbron to move and stood back. Montbron studied him carefully. There were no chances on offer. Delguarde knew exactly what was going through Montbron's mind; it was exactly what would be going through *his* if the positions had been reversed. 'Start walking to the lock – slowly – and when I say stop, stop.'

'I think you're enjoying this, Delgado,' said Rostand-Bercy. He'd left the car and strolled behind the two ex-paras, his hands in his pockets, a look of distaste on his thin aristocratic features.

'Of course I'm fuckin' enjoying it,' grinned Delguarde. 'It's what it's all about, isn't it? And if you're not enjoying it, get back in the soddin' car and put your hands over your eyes.'

Rostand-Bercy bridled. 'Just remember who you are talking to, Sergeant. You've got a job to do – do it! And do it bloody quickly and without fuss, or you might find yourself being brought down here for a spot of the same in the not too distant future.' He stared hard at the ex-para, then returned to the car.

Delguarde shrugged and turned away from Rostand-Bercy. He

touched the back of Montbron's neck with the muzzle of the Colt. 'All right, bastard, kneel. That's right. Now, move on your knees to the edge of the lock . . .' He looked round and grinned at the other ex-para. He didn't include Rostand-Bercy in his fun-sharing.

Montbron stared at the swirling water. It had a reputation, this gently moving canal. Everybody – the Paris Algerian factions, the FLN, the MNA – used it to dispose of their real, and imaginary, enemies. The FLN had their special execution plot, taking the trouble to wrap their victims in sacks and float them towards the Bastille. There must be a moral there somewhere. Delguarde wasn't of that school. A couple in the back of the head, a splash to disturb the serenity of the surroundings, and the corpse could make its own travel arrangements. Montbron waited his turn with equanimity. He'd always accepted that his end would be by the bullet rather than in a warm bed with the duvet pulled up round his ears, but somehow even his wildest nightmare couldn't have produced the unlikely scene of that bullet being shot into the back of his head by a French paratrooper.

He had contemplated running for it when he'd left the car, but with three marksmen waiting for it, it would have been death by inches rather than the quick red flash and everlasting sleep. As he looked at the water he wondered whether a sudden dive would put them off their aim. But where would he go? As far as the lock gates, and then they could stand on the concrete lip and blow bits off him at their leisure. Much better wait quietly and hope that ex-Sergeant Delguarde's hand was as steady as his sense of humour.

The Colt was removed from the back of his neck.

He didn't have to look round to know what was happening. Delguarde would take half a step back; there was nothing he could miss hitting from a metre's distance. Montbron closed his eyes. He knew it would be quick. No pain, no noise. He'd be dead before the explosion caught up with the bullet.

BANG!

He felt his bladder loosen. He shouldn't have heard that.

BANG! Pause. BANG!

Montbron nearly passed out. Delguarde was having his fun. But where were the bullets going? *Come on, you sadistic bastard, get it over with!* He dearly wanted to piss, but his pride refused his brain's request. *Sod it!*

He opened his eyes and began to turn his head. A hand touched his shoulder.

Denis sat in the car and tried to look cool and patient. His toes tingled and there was a slight feeling of looseness around his groin. It was an unusual sensation for Denis, one he didn't recognize. More experienced men could have told him that it was a fear and time-running-out sensation, but it was the first time he'd come across it. He gave up trying to control his feelings and leaned forward, beating his fist hard on the dashboard and accompanying each thump with the most vile language he could muster. The driver, an ex-special operations airborne commando with four years' unbroken front-line and behind-the-lines action in Indo-China and another three years' special duties in Algiers, looked at him out of the corner of his eye; he was hearing things he'd never heard before. He nodded admiringly, but wisely kept out of it.

'Where is he? Where is he? Where is he? Where the fucking hell is he?' Denis was calming down. They were heading slowly up the Rue du Temple towards République. They'd already cruised three times round the Bastille waiting for a marker from the motor bike, who so far, in spite of Denis's repeated calls, had remained obstinately silent. 'Why would an alley cat like Delguarde be heading in this direction?' said Denis to the driver. 'What the bloody hell would he want around Bastille or République? And what the bloody hell does he want to bring Rostand-Bercy and Diderot with him for? And where's that fucking motor bike?' He pressed the tit again and without preliminaries grunted into the handset, 'Where the bloody hell are you?'

He closed his eyes in supplication. Nothing. He tried again. Noth – *Christ!* His eyes shot open like rat-traps when the crackling took on a new note and something solid interspersed the atmospherics. 'Jesus!' he said quietly. 'Come on, you bugger! Come on!'

'. . . nothing doing!' said the voice. 'Can I make a guess?'

'You might as well. We've fuck-all else.'

'I'm going to whip along the Quai de Valmy. Just a feeling . . .' Then silence, and the motor bike was gone, off the air, before Denis could query his feelings. The driver frowned and shook his head slowly.

'If you've got anything to say, say it now,' rasped Denis. 'We've lost the bugger!'

The driver banged the side of his head like a swimmer clearing his ears of water. 'Jesus! The bloody Quai! He's right . . .'

'Tell me about it.'

The driver had already jammed his foot on the accelerator and swerved across the traffic into the broad Faubourg-du-Temple. Behind them a whistle blew from an irate policeman, but by the time he'd got his second breath there was nothing to whistle at. 'Delguarde,' grunted the driver. 'He's the head hatchet man. He's killer-in-chief, and loves every minute of it.'

'Get to the bloody point.'

'The canal is known as the butchers' gutter. It's like a fuckin' abattoir, where all the scores are settled. They've probably got a priest permanently on duty in one of the ruins. Delguarde's on a murder job. Your pal Diderot's had the back of his head shaved and Delguarde's going to top him. And I know where.'

'Can't you go any faster?'

'Jesus Christ!'

But Denis wasn't watching. In his hand had appeared a very large Browning automatic – a .45. He brought the slide back a quarter of an inch and checked the round in the breech. He didn't look up. 'What have you got?'

'MAB.'

'Better let me get the first shot in. Are you accurate?'

'Reasonably, but I don't think we're going to make it.' He swung into the Avenue Claude Vellefaux and increased speed. 'We lost him twenty minutes ago. He'd have come direct. We'll be just in time to fish the body out of the lock.'

'Don't be so fuckin' depressing. If you know where we're going, get us there and get me into a shooting position. I don't want a slanging match with Delguarde – I just want to kill the bastard.'

'It's here.' The driver braked the car quietly and got out. 'Follow me.' He ran at a crouch, followed closely by Denis. After fifty metres he stopped, put out his arm to hold Denis back and flattened himself against the wall. He peered round the corner. There it was, an open derelict area bordering on to the canal. Denis took in the tableau with a fleeting glance: Montbron on his knees; Delguarde standing above him; Rostand-Bercy leaning against the side of the Peugeot, his arms folded and his ankles crossed, as if he was in the paddock at Longchamp watching the parade; and Delguarde's partner standing between the two, with a pistol in his hand, hoping to get one in himself.

Denis steadied himself, then took a deep breath and let it out slowly. He pressed himself into the wall and jammed his arm against it for support. 'Seventy bloody metres,' he hissed. 'No go. Come on. Follow me. When I fire, run for the guy by the car and put a bullet in the bastard's back. Don't fuck around with his head . . . Watch it, the bastard's moving!' With that he took off and loped across the open ground, his arm before him, bent at the elbow, the Browning pointing at Delguarde's head. He had a strange feeling of slow motion as if he wasn't getting any closer, although his feet were moving and his heart pounding against his ribs. Still no one looked round. Delguarde and Montbron were the centre of their attention, the imminent murder of a helpless victim all-consuming, mesmerizing. They heard nothing and they saw nothing as they waited for Montbron's head to explode.

Delguarde touched the back of Montbron's neck with his Colt and with his arm outstretched stepped back two small paces. Denis was twenty metres away, but there was no more time. He stopped, wrapped his other hand round the Browning, steadied the foresight into the rear recess, emptied his lungs and squeezed the trigger.

BANG!

Delguarde's head almost left his shoulders as the heavy .45 bullet thudded into his face between his eye and his ear. He vanished from sight in a welter of arms and legs. It was a marvellous shot, but Denis didn't gloat. He fired again and caught the second man high in the chest as his driver's MAB thundered in his ear and Rostand-Bercy, moving across the open ground, stopped as if he'd run into a brick wall. Unbalanced, he staggered backwards under the force of the bullet and collapsed across the Peugeot's bonnet.

Denis moved forward and glanced quickly at Delguarde's body. He wouldn't be troubling anybody any more. His partner looked as if he'd dropped off to sleep. Lying on his back, his eyes closed, blood was bubbling under his chin. Denis ignored him – he wasn't going anywhere. But Rostand-Bercy was having trouble. He slithered off the bonnet of the Peugeot and went down on his knees with both hands clasped to his stomach. Denis nodded to his partner, pointed at Rostand-Bercy and moved towards the still-kneeling Montbron.

'Stand up. Move backwards, away from the edge . . .' Denis's voice was close to his ear. He did as he was told and was gently steered to one side by the hand on his shoulder.

He nearly tripped over the pair of legs just behind him. Delguarde, on his face, his teeth dug into the grassy soil and the top quarter of his head missing. The one eye left intact was wide open and staring at nothing. He hadn't even heard the explosion. Montbron turned to face Denis, who stood comfortably relaxed, feet apart, the .45 Browning at his side.

'That was close,' said Denis.

Montbron stared hard at him and tried to focus his wavering vision on the young man's serious expression, then looked down. His hands were shaking uncontrollably and the shock was still evident in his face. He swayed slightly, stuck both hands in his pockets, and closed his eyes. He hadn't said a word. Denis tried not to look embarrassed; this sort of fear was new to him. He looked down at Delguarde for a moment to allow Montbron to recover, then offered him a cigarette. Montbron opened his eyes and stared at him. Denis got the message. He took one from the packet, stuck it between Montbron's lips and lit it. He did the same for himself.

'Sorry it got that far,' he said. 'We lost you.'

'One day you'll tell me how you did it,' said Montbron. The cigarette was doing wonders for his nerves. 'But, er, thanks. I think I'm getting too old for this sort of game.' He stared down at his hands, still shaking, and back into Denis's face. He mentally apologized for doubting the young man's ability. But there were other things to do. The game hadn't run its course yet. He glanced over Denis's shoulder. 'Have you killed Rostand-Bercy?'

Denis shrugged. 'That was the intention. Let's go and have a look.'

They stepped round the body of Delguarde's driver. Denis's second bullet had blown most of his throat away. There was not much holding his head on, but his fingers still twitched, as if he was trying to reach the pistol that lay a few inches from his hand.

Montbron looked back at Denis and shrugged. His throat was too dry for words. His brain, numb from shock, hadn't caught up yet. 'Good shooting,' he rasped.

'Luck,' said Denis. 'I was aiming for his crotch.' He bent down and peered into Rostand-Bercy's face. 'He's not dead – yet. If you want to talk to him, I think you'd better hurry up. I'm going back to my car for a chat with the dustbin men.'

'Give me a few minutes.'

Rostand-Bercy had been propped against the Peugeot's front wheel by the man who'd shot him. His eyes were focusing, but he wasn't seeing much. Montbron kneeled beside him. His hands were no longer shaking, at least not so violently, allowing him to smoke comfortably and luxuriously as he studied the dying man. It was good to be alive. He didn't offer Rostand-Bercy a cigarette; he wasn't going to live long enough to finish it. But he sounded remarkably lucid.

'Not quite the way I intended this to end,' he said haltingly. 'You've rather buggered us all up . . . Who are you?'

Montbron hesitated.

'Come on! Quick! We haven't got time. We're both blown now. Who's your master?'

Montbron stared at him, then shrugged. It didn't matter now; it wasn't going any further. 'Army – Germany. B3, Inter-Army Coordination Group. You're . . . ?'

'Department Maurice. I've been inside OAS/Métropole since they set up in Paris . . .' Rostand-Bercy gritted his teeth and reached out for Montbron's arm as if grasping something would help him hang on to life, but his eyes weren't focusing and his hand fell short. He took a deep breath, then coughed. Blood and spittle dribbled over his lip but he ignored it. Montbron just stared. He didn't like what was about to come out with the blood and spittle. 'So you've well and truly buggered up my side of the game. Everything's gone up the spout . . . Why the fucking hell didn't someone tell you to lay off?' It was a silly question, and he knew it. He paused and refocused on Montbron's face. 'I didn't realize you had friends coming up behind you, otherwise I'd have ducked.' He was almost rambling. Montbron didn't stop him; he couldn't last much longer. '. . . was just about to take Delguarde out when I got this one. I couldn't stand by and watch your head fall into the canal, so for your sins, you interfering bastard, you're going to have to carry my post for me to Maurice himself – you do know of Department Maurice?'

'Yes, but—'

'Forget the buts, and forget your people in Germany. Go to Maurice. You got a pencil?' Rostand-Bercy's voice was becoming laboured. His face had gone a dark grey colour, as if someone had stuck a tap into the back of his head and was emptying the blood out of his system. Without intending to, he tipped forward on to his knees, but something was holding him together. 'Take down this number. It's a one-off. It'll serve as identification and tie you in with me. You've marked the palefaces on the OAS Committee.' It wasn't a question. He didn't wait for a reply. 'They're the ones. Don't bother with the Army, they're known. Write these others down. They're all Government and civilian admin—' He stopped talking, lowered his head and coughed.

Something solid came out with the blood and splashed over his knees. It almost finished him.

Montbron, on his ankles beside him, grabbed his arm to stop him toppling forward on to his face, but Rostand-Bercy summoned something up from somewhere. He pushed his hand away and dragged up his head.

Three more names gurgled out of his throat. He seemed to gather strength from having got them out. 'These three didn't come out, not even for you and your fancy plan! They've got to be put down. They're the money. They want the power, and the country. Without them the whole OAS fabric crumbles – for ever. It'll never be a menace again without these people. Get their names and the names of the Government people to Maurice himself. Don't talk to anyone else . . .'

Rostand-Bercy's eyes glazed over and he stared, unseeing, at Montbron, then doubled up again. Another, fatal, stream of blood gushed from his mouth and splattered on to the sandy soil. Montbron didn't move. Denis's driver had done his job well. It hadn't been simply a lucky shot at a moving target; he'd aimed for the chest and got something good. Rostand-Bercy's head dropped as if for a closer look at the blood on the ground, and as he moved forwards, he exposed his back. Montbron leaned over and stared at the huge exit wound just below his shoulder-blade. He'd been hit with a split .38, a dumdum. There was a small entry hole in the chest, but it'd had come out of his back like a dinner plate, bringing with it anything that got in its way. Rostand-Bercy was minutes away from death.

'Get yourself under cover quickly. They'll have all the OAS dogs in Paris after you when this gets out. You've no time, Montbron. Don't hang about. Do Maurice when you've crawled into your hole. Stay there . . . They'll find you. Don't come out until he . . .' More blood gushed. There couldn't have been much left in his body, but he was still thinking. 'Take my gun, and take his – the one that got me. It'll look as though you got the better of us. Leave my cover intact until Maurice can close in on them . . . Tell him about Metz . . .'

'What about Metz?'

'When Métropole breaks up they'll regroup at Metz. Tell Maurice the Army at Metz is with them. Don't let . . .' He didn't try any more. He toppled forward and died on his knees with his forehead resting on the ground in front of him.

Montbron left him as he was. He picked up the driver's gun and kicked Delguarde's heavy Colt as far as it would go into the lock. It hurt his toe, but that didn't trouble him. He felt almost light-headed as he forced his shaking legs to carry him to the car, where he leaned on the open door and unashamedly threw up the contents of his stomach.

Denis dropped his cigarette and ground it into the dust. He gave Montbron a few more minutes to sort himself out, then walked across the open site and joined him by Delguarde's car. Montbron had made a good recovery, but Denis didn't comment on it. 'I'm afraid we buggered up our side of the job,' he said bluntly. 'We marked the big nobs and pegged them down, but they were too good for us.'

'It's not important now,' said Montbron absently.

But it was to Denis. He shrugged aside the attempted consolation. 'I've just been talking to my man at the Place Cambronne. They had a superb escape system – bolt-holes going in every direction. The bastards are probably eating their paella in Barcelona by now.' He pulled a face. 'And so they should – they were Army people organizing it.'

Montbron looked askance at Denis. Cocky? Maybe, but you couldn't really fault him, and you couldn't keep on thanking him for abandoning the round-up to look after the welfare of an ageing colonel who seemed to have buggered up his side of it as well.

Denis saved him the embarrassment.

'So, what now, Diderot?' he asked lightly.

'Call your men off. Go home, wherever that is, and I'll sort your future out with Lemercier . . . What's the matter?'

Denis was shaking his head. 'Where've you been for the past twenty-four hours?'

Montbron stared at the young man's grim expression. 'If you've got something to say, say it. And quickly!'

'Lemercier's dead. Last night. A car accident in Germany.'

'Shit!'

Denis nodded sympathetically, but wisely said nothing. What could he say? He offered Montbron another cigarette, lit it and then his own, and leaned against the car, arms folded. He had no idea how bad it really was.

Montbron swore again. His elbows on the roof of the Peugeot, he stared across the space, unseeing, as he smoked his cigarettes. Denis didn't disturb him.

'Who's taken over?' he said at length.

'No idea.'

Montbron scowled. It didn't matter. Whoever was going to take over Lemercier's responsibilities wasn't going to help him. Lemercier had insisted, and continually emphasized, that he was on his own until the carpet was finally rolled up. He wouldn't have left notes. That wasn't his style. He certainly wouldn't have expected to end his life before the final curtain. Montbron was on his own – in more ways than one.

'Shit!' His vocabulary was suffering. How about Denis? But Denis couldn't help; his new boss would probably have him under the microscope purely because he had been close to Lemercier and was operating in Paris. He'd have to hope Lemercier had made Denis's operation legal . . . 'Get yourself back to HQ as soon as you can. Today. Don't bugger around with this any more. Did Lemercier give you orders?'

'Of course.'

'Written ones?'

Denis thought about that one for a moment, then nodded his head reluctantly. 'Yes. Personal – handwritten. But they're not for general consumption.'

'They bloody well will be now, unless you want to end up in the same bucket as the guys you've just been trying to net. Cover yourself, Denis, until you know what colour handkerchiefs your new boss uses. Was I mentioned in these notes?' He tried to keep the hopeful tone out of his voice. Just as well.

'Only as Diderot, and as a target figure for surveillance. He doesn't mention any contact he had with you.'

'OK. Keep it like that. Don't change your story. Let them come to their own conclusion, don't make any suggestions. Do you know my real name?'

Denis met his eyes unblinkingly, held them for a second, then shook his head. They both knew what he meant.

'What will you do now?'

Montbron flicked his cigarette over the top of the car. 'Don't even think about it, Denis. I'll finish this job and vanish. What you don't know . . .' He held out his hand. 'I'll take this car – you won't need it.' He jerked his head at Delguarde's body by the lock edge. 'And he certainly won't. Take care of yourself.'

'And you, sir. Good luck.'

44

MONTBRON LEFT THE Peugeot in a parking-lot behind the Gare du Nord and made his way into the main concourse of the station. His dark suit had taken a battering, but nobody seemed to offer him a second glance as he went unhurriedly towards the washrooms. He looked and felt much better after a wash and the use of a stiff brush on his navy-blue stripe and walked with a confidence he didn't feel towards the bank of telephones.

Vernet nearly did it again.

'Where the bloody hell have you been Geor – ?' He realized his mistake and slammed down the phone. The two men in the room stared at him. He was ashen-faced and his hand shook as it hovered over the handset. He refused to meet their eyes. Then it rang again. He took a deep breath and did what he should have done the first time – he picked it up and listened.

'D'you recognize my voice?'

'Jesus! What's going on? I've been waiting at the end of this phone like a bloody damp fart since the last time you rang! Where are you?'

'Did you answer the phone just now?'

'The bloody phone hasn't rung since the day before yesterday when you said you'd be in touch. What d'you mean, did I answer it just now?'

Montbron's nerves were still raw. It would be a long time before they recovered from the battering they'd undergone by the Canal St-Martin. He was slow, his instincts suffered accordingly; he must have rung the wrong number. 'Forget it. Get ready to move. I'm getting you out of there and taking you somewhere safe. Then we'll get you home. Stay by the phone.'

'What about the—'

'Nothing. It's finished. I'll ring you back. What's your nearest Métro?'

'Nearest Métro? I'm not sure. Just a minute, let me think . . .'

'Danube,' mouthed the technician.

'Danube,' repeated Vernet, 'but wh—'

'OK. Don't move until I call back.'

'But—'

Montbron had put down the phone and Vernet was left with a dead buzz in his ear and an enquiring look on the face of his technician.

'Try Filli again,' he snapped.

Vernet's voice had gone up an octave and it stayed there when the man on the second phone replied, 'Same as before. He's nowhere. He's out of contact. Looks like you're the boss now. What do you want us to do?'

'Bloody hell!'

'I couldn't agree more!'

Vernet was trying to think, but nothing was happening; he wasn't programmed to think, he was there to be told what to do. *Christ! What would Georges do? What would Philippe do?* 'OK.' He bared his teeth and sucked in air. It helped calm him down a little. He jabbed his finger at the second man in the room. 'He can stay here to watch the phone and keep trying for Filli. You come with me and cover my back. We'll find out where Montbron's hidey-hole is, and if we can't take him ourselves we'll at least know where to direct Georges and the troops . . . What's the matter?'

The technician was shaking his head. 'Not me, brother!' He waved his hand at the equipment spread around the room. 'I'm technical affairs, I listen to things on the phone. What I don't do is chase around Paris after homicidal maniacs or get involved in gunfire. Forget it!'

'Jesus Christ! I could have you put away for that.'

'Try it! But would you like a bit of advice?'

Vernet jumped at the offer.

The technician lit a cigarette and strolled across to the

window. He parted the lace curtain and invited Vernet to look down the shabby road. His finger tapped against the glass as he spoke. 'There are two of Filli's guys in that room along there. They're probably staring at us now through their power scopes. Now, they're into the violent part of the business, into the head-bashing game, so if you just tinkle the bell and flutter your eyelashes at them you might be able to persuade one of them to look after your back. Shall I get them on the phone?'

Vernet nodded. 'Be quick.'

They must have been waiting. The phone was picked up before the bell had got into its full stride. The technican handed the receiver to Vernet.

He told the man on the other end his new DST name. The man wasn't interested; it didn't mean anything to him. 'So, what d'you want?'

Vernet took a deep breath, then swallowed; the other two men in the room stared at him from their comfortable positions. They were both smoking now, coarse Gauloises in heavy, dark maize paper. The heavy pungency just about dispelled the strong, garlicky body odour that had built up in the unventilated room. The technician allowed a tiny flick of an eyelid to his mate. He had a good idea what the reaction over the road was going to be.

Vernet looked up and locked eyes with the technician as he told the man on the other end of the phone what he wanted.

The answer was immediate. 'Sorry, mate. Filli put us here, Filli's going to have to give the word to move us. Get him on the phone and tell him your problem. When he rings me back and tells me what to do, I'll come back to you—'

'I can't get in touch with him,' interrupted Vernet.

'Tough. Keep trying.'

'Look,' yelled Vernet, desperation taking over diplomacy. 'Just listen, you bastard! This whole soddin' operation is about to take off. Filli put me in charge, and that means in charge of you too, so just get your bloody arse out of that room and down on to the street or you'll be out of a bloody job!'

The technician pursed his lips and blew the ash off the end of his cigarette, then shook his head slowly. He'd have bet money on the response.

'Fuck off!'

Vernet took the phone from his ear and stared hard at it. It was dead.

'What did he say?'

Vernet dropped the phone back on its cradle. 'He said he can't leave his post without Filli's say-so. Try Filli again.'

And then the phone rang.

'You recognize my voice, so move out now, exactly as you are, no bags, nothing. Danube – Gare de l'Est. When you get there, take the direction Châtelet les Halles. Got it? Don't look for me, I'll find you and cover you. OK?'

'OK.'

'The very best of luck,' said the technician as he replaced the earpiece. His mate said nothing.

'Piss off!' Vernet was a very worried man.

But the technician wasn't offended; he understood Vernet's state of mind. 'I'll keep trying for Filli,' he said. 'Maybe you'll be able to ring from the Métro and let me know the form so I can pass it on to him.'

Vernet didn't answer. He checked the magazine of his HK4, jammed it back in the butt, gave it a nervous slap and slid a round into the breech. He flipped the safety on and tucked the automatic into his waistband. Without another word to the two men, he slipped on his jacket and went out of the door. Further down the road the two watchers smiled to each other as he came out of the building and walked towards them. They'd set the camera on multiple exposures and it clicked away merrily as he passed beneath their window and out of sight.

45

HARRY METCALFE DECIDED it was about time he took an interest in what was going on. He turned his head and studied Neurie's set features from the right-hand seat of the car and said, 'Are you going to tell me where we're going – and why?'

Neurie didn't take his eyes off the busy road. 'You've got somewhere else you'd rather be?'

'You know bloody well I have,' growled Metcalfe.

'It'll keep.' Neurie glanced sideways. There was no sympathy in either his voice or his expression. 'Give me one of your English cigarettes. Light it for me.' He took the cigarette from Metcalfe and stuck it between his lips, but he didn't smoke it, he just left it there and forgot about it. 'I want you with me until your friend Guy-Montbron has been brought out of the woodwork and spread, legs apart, across the bench in my workshop. You know him, he knows you. That's enough for me. Who knows . . .' He almost smiled behind the cigarette. 'You might just be able to bring him out on his knees with his thumbs stuck firmly in his ears.'

'Not much chance of that,' said Metcalfe grimly. 'He doesn't like many people, and trusts almost no one. Nor would I after listening to that cantankerous old bastard back there.'

'There is someone he trusts.'

'His family?'

'Right. Vernet. And I know where this Vernet has stuck his head in the sand.' Neurie rolled the cigarette from one side of his mouth to the other and helped himself to a shallow drag from it on its way past. 'So we go and pick him up and sit on his head until your chum comes to join him to talk about all these new problems he's suddenly found.'

'How did you find out where this guy's hiding?'

'Resources currently out on the streets on surveillance programmes against the OAS include an indent for a technical listening team on an unspecified detail in the north-east of the city. It's a scruffy address, but the originator of the indent authorized his own request with the initials "GF".'

Metcalfe raised his eyebrows. Nothing connected. He didn't interrupt.

'GF,' went on Neurie, 'Georges Filli . . .' He glanced sideways. He'd got the effect he wanted. Metcalfe's casual, slightly bored manner was replaced by a white, tight-lipped face. The anger was still bubbling away somewhere inside.

'When Georges Filli wanted to keep things out of general intelligence consumption he used an unknown, irregular source for the application. Maurice's Élysée office pushed it down the tube and I recognized the initials of the initiator. It's easy when you know how to work the system.'

Metcalfe continued to look straight ahead. The taste of Filli was still very strong in his gullet. 'Good. Then I've no doubt', he said drily, 'that you've already considered the possibility that this team of organ-grinders could have been sent out to stick their wires into the phone of some government Minister's girlfriend.'

'Why would they want to do that?'

'Well, for starters, to see how indiscreet he's been when the lights have been turned down low.'

Neurie grimaced and glanced out of the side-window, then lowered his head and stared upwards at the sad, drab neglected buildings on either side of the road.

'Look around you, Metcalfe,' he said, without turning his head. 'Would you fancy anything coming out of one of those?'

Metcalfe shrugged. He didn't fancy anything from anywhere. He'd lost his appetite following Monique's defection to Neurie. Neurie hadn't laboured the point, there was just quiet satisfaction, with an underlying threat for Metcalfe to keep well out of her way now that she had abandoned the Boulevard Raspail and moved into his place overlooking the Seine. It seemed the cement was setting very hard on the repaired marriage. Neurie gave him a quick glance.

'I don't think even you would. Neither would French Government Ministers. They don't work the girls in this part of Paris. Algerian clap's not something you'd want to take home to the wife after an evening out with the boys—' He stopped talking suddenly and began to manoeuvre the car into a narrow parking space. It was nowhere near Vernet's place, but Neurie seemed to know exactly where he was, and where he was going. Before he got out of the car he opened the glove compartment, reached in and brought out a solid Czechoslovakian CZ Mod52 automatic. He studied it for a moment, then handed it to Metcalfe. 'Unregistered,' he told him. 'The guy who came here waving that about left with a bad taste in his mouth. Don't shoot it without discussing it with me first!' Metcalfe stared hard at him. Neurie wasn't smiling. But Metcalfe knew what he meant. They'd been in this end of the business together before. It didn't mean a friendship was being renewed, it meant expediency – for Neurie.

Neurie led the way to the top of the road, then turned left and after about two hundred metres stopped outside a corner café. 'D'you fancy a glass of wine?' He was already sitting at one of the outside tables.

Metcalfe wasn't given an option. 'The place we're going to visit', said Neurie as he sipped his red wine, 'is down there.' He jerked his chin sideways at the road branching off to their right. 'Going by the number on that place opposite, I reckon it's about three-quarters of the way down on that side of the road. We'll sit here and have a little look for a while, perhaps another glass of this, and then we'll cross over and approach it from that side. They'll have to hang out of the window if they want to see us coming.'

'And if they've gone the whole hog and got a watcher team opposite?'

'Let's not make life more complicated than it already is. Don't forget we're all on the same side.'

'Oh, that's good! I thought you said they were Filli's people?'

'You English always see the dark side of a situation. Have another glass of wine.'

'Thanks.'

'And while you're drinking it, I'll just go and make a little phone call.'

Harry Metcalfe didn't know Paul Vernet from Adam. Even if he had it was unlikely from that distance that he'd have spotted him as he came out of the building, turned left, away from the corner café, and headed towards Danube Métro station to meet Philippe de Guy-Montbron.

Neurie's little phone call appeared to have turned into a big one. Metcalfe finished his wine and ordered another. He seemed to have been sitting there for hours. The café inside was dead. There was no rollicking laughter or clink of glasses, and the only wine going down seemed to be his. He frowned, looked down at the watch on his wrist, then tried to see the inside of the café through the curtains. They were made so that people couldn't. He drank his second glass of wine with a gulp, strolled into the café and ordered two more. Neurie was nowhere to be seen. He went back to his table and lit a cigarette. There wasn't much else he could do.

He was halfway through Neurie's new glass of wine when he saw him coming from the direction of Vernet's safe house.

Neurie carried on walking past the table until he was out of sight of Vernet's window, then doubled back and rejoined Metcalfe. He absently picked up the half-glass of wine and sipped.

'A few interesting facts.' He grimaced. 'A strange sort of shooting match over at St-Martin's canal. I don't know whether it concerns Montbron, but I have a funny feeling about it. Three bodies, newly killed, all identified as OAS. Two leg-breakers, Foreign Legion people, and the third a big shot – a very big shot indeed. Central Committee, no less.'

'What's the story?'

'There isn't one, other than what I've just told you. Work it out for yourself. How do three hard men who know their way around go under the hammer?' He drank a mouthful of wine and held the glass close to his lips ready for another one. His eyebrows were pinched together as he studied Metcalfe's face. 'You know something, Metcalfe? I'm beginning to get a nasty twitch in the gut about Montbron. I'm almost getting to the stage of believing what he told you.'

'Steady there, Neurie, remember what the man in the clouds said – that what Montbron told me is a load of crap. You'd better watch out for the disloyalty clause in your contract!'

Neurie brushed aside Metcalfe's sarcasm. He was thinking very hard as he spoke. 'We've got your story, and we've got another story about a top meeting here in Paris. They tie together. Montbron got himself invited. One of the men shot near the canal was head of their tactical think-tank and indispensable to that meeting. It would have had no teeth without him being there to assess Montbron's contribution . . . Are you following me?'

'Montbron killed him and his two bodyguards?'

'It doesn't make sense, but I can't think of anything else. We'll sort that one out later. At the moment we've got other problems.' He gestured to the street he'd just been down. 'You were right about the watchers along there. They've got a crew at number 74, almost opposite Vernet's hideaway. I made out a camera and a fixed telescope on the place and there'll be a hand line between the two bases. I wanted to pinpoint the building they were using as an observation post.'

'Why?'

'I've got some people coming to persuade them to terminate their little operation. I don't give my best when somebody's looking over my shoulder – particularly people from Filli's side of the hill – and I don't look my best when I'm breaking into somebody else's game. Pictures can be a bloody nuisance at the inquest! This way we can go in through Vernet's front door without bothering to pull stockings over our faces! Would you like a sandwich while we're waiting?'

Metcalfe stared hard at Neurie, then shook his head. Neurie

must have felt he was winning; he was almost being friendly. But Metcalfe didn't let it go to his head.

Neurie's two-man team led by Roger Bineau moved into number 74 with quiet efficiency. They knocked lightly on the door of the flat overlooking the road and made their introductions from the safe end of a police 9mm MAB PA-15. Filli's men didn't argue. They recognized the weapon and the specially issued DST authority card; they had exactly the same. Same weapon, same card.

'You're closed down,' said Bineau. 'Everything – operation, job, department. Your boss's dead, you're all surplus. They'll tell you about that and where to sign on for unemployment pay when you get home. What've you done so far? OK, let's have the film. Like you, it's superfluous now.'

Whether Filli's men believed him or not they didn't show it. They weren't worried. There'd be another Filli round the corner. The leader dismantled the camera, broke open the back and removed the partially used 35mm. He held the exposed end and shook it. The unexposed portion slid out of its canister and the whole film waggled up and down like a dying yellowy-green snake as he offered it to Neurie's man.

'It's dead now. Throw it in the can on your way out.'

He did.

On it had been the only images ever recorded of Paul Vernet.

Across the road, Metcalfe held up the corridor wall, his unfamiliar Czech automatic prominently displayed, whilst Neurie knocked lightly on the door.

Vernet's technician friend was taken by surprise. He'd only just settled down. He thought Vernet had come back. 'What the bloody . . . ?' Whatever it was going to be died as his throat dried up and he looked at Neurie's automatic, a few inches from his face.

'Can we come in, please?'

The technician should have been very worried by the polite

tone, but he misinterpreted the signal; politeness wasn't a normal function in his life. 'Who the fu—'

Neurie's pistol thumped into his stomach and he reeled backwards. His friend, still lying half on, half off the ruined sofa, tried to get out of the way as he crashed in a heap across his legs. Neurie followed him in, indicating to Metcalfe to shut the door, and before the technician had time to recover, Neurie's pistol scraped across the side of his face, forcing him to turn his head so that he could see the card in Neurie's hand.

He peered at it through streaming eyes. It was blurred, but it made sense; he almost laughed as his hand went snaking towards his inside pocket for his own. It didn't get there. The automatic in Neurie's hand barely moved as it cracked hard across his wrist. He couldn't stop the bellow of pain, but he managed to stop the movement of his hand. His friend could have been dead, or a cast-off statue. He hadn't moved an inch or a muscle since the technician had crashed on to him, but his eyes were all right; they were flicking from Neurie's automatic, to Metcalfe standing by the door, to his bleeding mate.

Neurie let the technician have a little wave of his damaged wrist and waited for him to get his breath back.

'Which of you two's Vernet?' he asked.

'Jesus! You rough bastard! You didn't give me a chance—' The technician stopped with a hiccup and held his hands out to Neurie to show that he had no ill intent; the one damaged wrist couldn't quite keep up the prayer and he had to help it in place with the other hand. 'We're DST, from Montmorency. We're official technicians on a job.' It didn't placate Neurie.

'I asked you a question; none of those were the answer. I'll ask it again, once. Which of you two's Vernet?'

'Neither. We're Georges Filli's people from Watching. There's another team from Watching across the road. We're the listening crew.'

Neurie took his eyes off the man for a second and glanced at Metcalfe. Metcalfe, arms folded, tightened his lips and shrugged. The Czech automatic rested comfortably in the crook of his arm. He didn't disturb it.

'So, where's Vernet?'

'Who's Vernet?'

Neurie kept the frown from his face. Metcalfe's cynicism was on target again. Montbron's family had gone over – or been pulled over. Or was he playing an interesting game, ducking with Montbron and running with Filli? Was he that good at doubles? And if he was, was he good enough to have convinced Filli he was playing straight with him? Either way, Filli had been playing his Vernet card very close to his chest. He glanced again at Metcalfe. Metcalfe's face was expressionless. He turned back to the technician and studied him. The man didn't seem capable of lying. 'Forget it. Who was your body?'

'We only knew him as "the Subject".'

'And where is he now?'

'Gone.'

'Gone where? When?'

''Bout half an hour ago. I don't know where.' The technician was getting his strength back – and his confidence. They were developing into truculence. Neurie got the message.

'D'you like your job?' It was a mild, polite question, more effective than a bellow of rage. It was Neurie's way.

'Pardon?'

'I said, do you like your job? If you don't it won't take me long to arrange a little traffic-warden beat for you.'

'I'm happy with the telephones.'

'I thought you might be. So, shall we stop trying to be clever and talk seriously about what's been happening here?' His eyes settled on the other man, who was trying to keep out of the conversation. 'And perhaps you would like to start thinking as well. Both of you, talk to me about the Subject and what he's been doing since you came on the scene.'

'I can do better.' The technician didn't fancy traffic wardening. 'There are some phone calls wrapped on to that—' he pointed to his recorder '– which'll explain why he's no longer here. I'll fill in the gaps if the conversation lapses.'

'Play the music.'

Whilst the tapes were being rewound, Neurie handed Metcalfe

a cigarette and lit it for him. He ignored the other two men and leaned against the door beside the Englishman. After a few minutes Montbron's voice came hollowly through the flat, inadequate speakers.

'Stop that there for a second,' said Neurie. He turned to Metcalfe and in a voice too low for the technician and his mate, hissed urgently: 'D'you know that voice?'

Metcalfe exhaled cigarette smoke and muttered, 'Guy-Montbron.'

Neurie's expression remained unchanged. 'And the other one?'

Metcalfe shook his head. 'Dunno.'

'Which one's your Subject?' Neurie asked the technician.

'The scared one.'

It was a clear picture. 'Run the tape.'

'You sure he didn't drop a name?'

The technician thought about it for a moment, then shook his head, but it was only a half-hearted shake that shuddered to a stop as he frowned in thought. 'Funny, he did once call himself something, when he was talking to the guys across the road. They told him to get stuffed!'

Neurie allowed himself to be diverted. 'Why? What did he want from them?'

'Backup. I think he had ideas about taking this guy who phoned on his own. He was going to make a big mark for himself with the DST.'

'And the men over the road didn't want to help?'

'That's right. Not without Filli's say-so, I understood.'

'You taped that conversation?'

The technician's jaw dropped. 'Er, well, no. We were only doing calls coming in.'

'Inefficent bastards!' murmured Neurie to himself. 'OK, so what's the name he used?'

The technician stared back at him, mesmerized.

Neurie didn't rush him.

After a moment the technician managed to shake his head. 'I can't remember.'

'Jesus Christ!'

'But the people opposite will have his picture. Their brief was everything in and out. I was there when Filli charged them. Is that any help?'

'Get 'em on the phone.'

The technician looked quite pleased with himself; he considered that that little touch of sound advice would just about save his quality of life. But his face gave him away.

'Well?'

'They've gone. They've taken their equipment.'

'Give me the phone.'

Neurie's face was without expression as he dropped the phone back on to its cradle. He stared at it for several moments while he thought about what he'd just been told, then turned to Metcalfe. Metcalfe raised his eyebrows. He looked like a man used to hearing about cock-ups.

'They took half a dozen shots of the last man to leave this building. You know who that was.'

Metcalfe nodded. This was going to be good.

'They stripped their cameras before they shoved off and tossed the film into the can. They were told to empty the cameras before they left because I didn't want our entry here on record.'

Metcalfe smiled. 'You did say—'

'Forget what I said. It's a bloody balls-up, Harry!'

'Nice to know that major balls-ups are international! What now? D'you think he'll double back here and bring our friend with him, or has Montbron taken the lead again and taken them both home? Where's home?'

'Christ knows! Let's get rid of these two clowns and start thinking.' He turned to the two clowns. 'OK, you two, get this gear out of here and take it back where it belongs. Report to whoever's running the circus at Montmorency and tell him or her I'll want to talk about you two sometime in the near future. Close the door quietly behind you!'

When they'd left, Neurie picked up the phone again and spoke to Roger Bineau on the other side of the road. 'Get over here, Roger. Leave Louis there. Tell him to stay put and ring if anybody comes through the front door – anybody. Don't put the bloody phone down – wait until I say goodbye! Just a minute, you wouldn't have a Métro plan in your pocket, would you?'

'Funny you should ask that . . .'

'Bring it with you. Be quick.'

'Danube . . . Gare de l'Est . . .' murmured Neurie as he studied the Métro plan on the end pages of the new arrival's diary. 'And then Châtelet les Halles . . .' He looked up. He seemed to have lost interest in Harry Metcalfe as he stared blank-faced at the Frenchman. 'What happens at Châtelet les Halles, Roger?'

Roger Bineau didn't have to look at the plan, he knew exactly what happened there. 'It's a main RER junction.' He stuck his finger on the black dot and moved it north, south, east and west. He looked as if he was a priest baptizing a baby's red vein-lined head as he recited the names of the limits of the RER system. He was quite content with his contribution.

Neurie turned slowly and gazed into the younger man's eyes. 'I asked you what happened at Châtelet les Halles; I didn't ask for the name of every bloody railway station in Paris!' But he wasn't displeased. 'Where does this one go?' Bineau had missed out the south-west corner.

'Versailles, St Cyr, that sort of place.'

At the mention of Versailles, Metcalfe moved round the table and joined the huddle. 'Buc is near Versailles,' he said.

'So what?'

'Jeanette Fabre's house.'

'Jesus Christ! Is it as easy as this?'

'No, it's not,' joined in Bineau. 'Châtelet connects RER A, B and D. Versailles is Line C. You have to go to St-Michel-Notre Dame to join that one.'

'Thank you. I might have known.' Neurie, his head bowed, stared at the plan for several seconds. The silence was total; he could have been standing over an open grave, but he was shaken out of his obsequies by the explosion of a match as Metcalfe lit a cigarette. 'Give me one of those,' he muttered, then turned to the Frenchman. 'Roger, have you got a road-map of that area?'

'What area?'

'South-west of Paris, Versailles, *Buc*! Come on Roger, wake up for Christ's sake. We've all had a hard day! Don't start a bloody conversation and then go to sleep! Have you got a map?'

'In the car.'

'Go and get it, and be quick! Where's that cigarette, Harry?' Metcalfe looked at him sharply. Things must be going well, he was calling him Harry again. It was getting more like old times by the minute – but then perhaps things were going badly and he wasn't thinking what he was saying. Metcalfe passed him a cigarette. It was received without thanks; he didn't even notice it. There were no more "Harrys". Neurie stuck a match to the end of the cigarette and inhaled noisily. 'D'you think he'll make for the Fabre house at Buc?' he asked.

'Eventually,' said Metcalfe. 'I think he's made it his Paris base. It's safe, or at least it has been up till now. Your people never penetrated it.'

'Violle did.'

'Violle didn't – I did. And it was by accident. But I don't think Montbron's going to stick around very long. I think if he's heading back to Buc it's to collect the essentials, his tools and get-out papers.That's if he's heard the little bit of unhappy news about his erstwhile leader.'

'And then?'

'Haven't you got an opinion?'

'I'm asking yours.'

Metcalfe didn't even have to think about it. 'He's going to have to go underground until the smoke disperses. He'll take his man Vernet with him and fade into the scenery – new names, new things to do. He might even try another country. In fact he must try another country, because when this lot dies down and the public's forgotten what it was all about, there are still going to be some people with very different ideas about punishment for those who went on the scruffy side of the line. You for one.'

'What d'you mean?' But Neurie knew what he meant. The response was instinctive; he didn't think it had showed.

'You want somebody for Violle. Filli wasn't enough. He

wasn't enough for you to be able to look yourself in the eye every morning and watch yourself grow old. People like you are a bloody menace to society. You want a bucket of blood to wash away a doubtful debt. Somebody like Montbron to cleanse your conscience.'

Neurie laughed. It was a barking, cynical laugh that covered the chink Metcalfe had opened. 'A bloody pontificating Englishman! Whatever next?'

Metcalfe had had his say. He smiled and said nothing more.

Neurie hadn't finished. 'But you're right – and wrong. It's Montbron's bag-carrier Vernet I want. Montbron's going to be there, anchored to him, though, so that every time the bastard grunts a reply to my question Montbron will nod his head in confirmation. I want them both, preferably today, but if not today then tomorrow, and if not tomorrow I'll have the pair of them in ten, twenty, or thirty years—' His diatribe was cut short by the arrival of Roger Bineau.

'The car radio was on a permanent blip,' he said as he handed the map to Neurie. 'There's an urgent top-priority call out for you. I went above myself and asked them what it was about. In your name, of course.'

'So what was it all about?'

'They went coy on me. You're to take a public line and ring this number without delay.' Bineau pulled a scrap of paper from his pocket and handed it to Neurie. 'They wouldn't say who was at the other end.'

Neurie stared at the number. He knew exactly who it was and what it meant. 'I'll be back shortly.' He left the other two, Bineau curious, Metcalfe indifferent, and made his way back to the café on the corner. It was as safe a means of phoning as any. Neurie dialled the number. He recognized the voice. He'd last seen the owner of it in a yellow and black striped waistcoat. But he didn't sound like a footman now. 'Are you clean?' he asked.

'Get on with it.'

After a short pause Maurice's voice replaced striped waistcoat's. He didn't announce himself; he expected people he rang to know who it was. 'Gérard, we've got a problem.'

Neurie grimaced to himself in the small mirror. Not another one . . .

'In our conversation early this morning,' said Maurice, 'I told you I had a high-wire act in OAS/Métropole. He was scheduled to come through when the meeting broke up, but nothing happened, he went quiet. I've just found out why.'

Neurie's expression didn't alter. He knew very well why infiltrated agents go quiet. 'They lifted his cover and killed him?'

Maurice ignored him. 'The Army mounted an operation in Paris today. They didn't warn anybody and without an inside line got the result I'd have expected – a total botch-up. All they've managed to do is scatter the OAS Central Committee—'

'Can't this wait, Maurice?'

'No.'

'Then who reported this to you?' Neurie was getting impatient.

'It came through as a routine Army communiqué. They broadcast the good news that another OAS big-head has rolled into the dust. They claim credit for it—'

'Rostand-Bercy,' interjected Neurie. The conversation was getting nowhere – most unlike Maurice. Normally incisive, something had shifted his foundations. Neurie hurried it along. 'And two listed OAS gunmen shot and killed at the Canal St-Martin. It sounds like a good day, Maurice. What's the problem you rang about?'

'Jean-Marie Rostand-Bercy was my man.'

Neurie frowned. That's why Maurice was upset. He said nothing.

Now Maurice was impatient. 'You still there?'

Neurie shrugged. 'Maurice, it's the luck of the game. If the Army killed him, your structure is still intact. A dead Rostand-Bercy will smell all the sweeter to the Métropole lot, and any friend of his'll get a free pass. Have you got anybody else in there?'

'No. But that's not what I'm getting at. The Army didn't kill him. Rostand-Bercy was spotted by E1 in the back of a dark blue Peugeot near the Pont de Sully today. Sitting in the back with him was Philippe de Guy-Montbron. That means only one thing to me: Rostand-Bercy was blown and Montbron was detailed to take him out for execution. That removes any doubt about which side he's on and lays bare that stupid story the Englishman brought us. The man's what we've said all along – a top-grade assassin.'

'How do you account for the killing of the two OAS bodyguards, Maurice?'

'Simple. Rostand-Bercy somehow got hold of a weapon. He killed the two guards before Montbron finished him. A fourth man was reported by an Army intelligence unit leaving the area where the bodies were found. No identification, but we don't need identification, we know it was Montbron. The other point is that he killed our man after the meeting, which means he'll know the composition of that meeting. He'll be able to put names to familiar faces and stand up and point them out across a crowded room. Rostand-Bercy mentioned a group of political people who hold this thing in their hands; they were going to be there. I want their names. That means I want Montbron. I want him alive and in a position to talk to me at great length. Bring him to me – today.'

'That might be a tall order.'

Maurice didn't budge. 'Then tomorrow at the latest. Another thing—'

Neurie interrupted. 'Can you get someone into General Lemercier's HQ and monitor all personal calls made for the General?'

'It's already done. You want to know whether your target's reported in?'

'That sort of thing. It'll tell us whether he's—'

'I know what it'll tell us,' snapped Maurice acerbically, 'but don't count on it. I know he's a leper and ought to be put down, but I want him first – he's all we've got to help us put this bloody lot to bed. So go and find him . . .' He paused before continuing: 'I was about to say, before you interrupted, that two people were found dead on the back seat of a car in an underground car park off the Boulevard de Picpus. It had all the makings of an OAS *opération ponctuelle*. They've just been identified as special intelligence executive from Elm. That's Lemercier's command. Make of it what you will.'

There were no goodbyes. The phone went dead and Neurie was left staring at the instrument as he absorbed the last few words from the man at Neuilly.

Neurie and Bineau studied the large-scale map spread out on Vernet's Formica-topped dining table.

'From Châtelet the RER goes to St-Rémy-les-Chevreuses,' said Bineau tracing the line with his finger. 'You were interested in Buc?'

'Right,' murmured Neurie.

'It's there.' Bineau underlined the village with his fingertail. 'A fair walk, but not silly.'

'What about that place . . .' Neurie followed the line with his finger, then stopped and lowered his head to read the small print. 'Robinson?'

'Same line, but it branches off. It's nearer.'

'OK, then that's it. They're going to Buc via the RER to Robinson – and so are we.'

'I brought the car to the door.'

'I've got my own,' snapped Neurie. 'And you're not coming, anyway. You stay here in case all this bloody train- and mapwork is superfluous and the bastard has doubled back and is waiting in a café until we all bugger off—' He stopped in mid-sentence and gazed about the scruffy room. 'Give this place the once-over, stick anything that doesn't look right for a shithouse in a bag and take it back across the road with you. Put a lock on the door and watch the front until I give the word.'

'You don't really think they'll come back here?' said Metcalfe.

'Harry, I don't know what the bloody hell I think at the moment. Let's worry about things on our way to Buc.'

Metcalfe interrupted Neurie's thoughts. 'You know, Gérard,' he said when they were on their way to Neurie's car, 'what you ought to do is have a message broadcast over the Tannoy at that railway station – what did you call it?'

'Châtelet les Halles. What the bloody hell for?'

'To tell Montbron that he's got his little finger entwined with a guy who's gone over to another side. Filli wanted him dead. No conversation, no argument, just a bullet in the back of the head. It was something to do with hate and a Corsican debt of honour. That's what he said in the Camargue. So, what did he offer Montbron's faithful follower to persuade him that the grass was greener, or at least thicker, in his corner of the maze? And why didn't he run when Montbron appeared on the end of the phone?'

Neurie kicked himself. He'd seen no threat to Montbron from Vernet. Quite the opposite. It hit him across the bridge of the nose and almost made his eyes water. Montbron had the heart of the OAS/Métropole in his hands. If he was on the right side, the war was over; if he wasn't, they could squeeze him and still win, provided he remained on his feet. But Vernet was going to kill Montbron – that was the deal he'd made with Filli. But what was he getting out of it? First things first. Montbron had to be warned, and Vernet had to be taken out.

'Bugger you, Metcalfe, I think you've put your finger on it again. But stop bloody talking for the next half-hour, and if your disposition hasn't improved since the last time you were in a car chase with me, close your eyes. You're about to experience the fastest crossing of Paris ever!'

46

MONTBRON WATCHED AND followed Vernet, but didn't approach him until he reached the top of the escalator that ran into the main departure area at the Gare de l'Est. Vernet was clean. Montbron walked alongside him for a moment with no sign of recognition, then, without turning his head, murmured, 'Go back down to the Métro and go for the Châtelet les Halles train. I'll be right behind you. Don't look round. I'll cover your back.'

Out in the open Vernet's nerve was as good as Montbron's; he understood this part of the charade and took it all in his stride. It was good to be out on the loose, even with big brother hovering around. But he wasn't worried about him, not any more. He was Paul Vernet, and he was equal to any of them. He had status, he was legal, and the hard lump of metal grinding into the soft flesh above his belt confirmed all this. It gave him confidence every time he glanced out of the corner of his eye and saw the shadow dogging his footsteps.

He didn't try to hide his tension when Montbron took him firmly by the arm and steered him, just as the automatic doors hissed their warning and began to close, on to the destination Robinson train.

They stood apart for most of the journey until they drew into Bourg-la-Reine and the carriage emptied as people changed for the St-Rémy-les-Chevreuses train. At a nod from Montbron, they moved away from the doors and sat down.

'What's going on, Philippe?'

Montbron studied his half-brother surreptitiously. Vernet's new standing was showing. He seemed to have grown in stature, and there was an air of confidence about him. Something had happened to give him that extra two inches in height and this new-found ability to look him directly in the eye. It must be the smell of blood and cordite mix that had worked its way into his nervous system. He turned in his seat to face him.

'It's all finished, Paul. The game's over, closed down. We're getting out. You're going back into the woods, and I'm going under a blanket. Don't worry. Leave it up to me.'

'Leave what up to you? I'm not bloody worried, I like what I'm doing. Fuck you, Philippe! I don't want to go into the bloody woods and live like a fuckin' mushroom.' Vernet looked as if he was about to jump out of the seat and throw himself through the open door of the train. Montbron reached out and placed his hand gently on his arm. Not to restrain, just to calm down. One or two people glanced out of the corners of their eyes. Vernet shrugged off Montbron's hand, but relaxed into the wooden-slatted backrest and lowered his voice to a harsh whisper. 'But what about this job, the one you wanted me to research? I thought we were going to make another Gautier kill?'

'Forget it. It wasn't what it seemed. It was never on.' Montbron was in two minds. Tell him everything – the put-up, the infiltration, the double-cover – or tell him nothing until he was tucked up, out of the way where no harm could come to him. But was that the problem? Montbron gave a quick sideways glance. No. The bloody problem was not what harm would come to him; it was what he, with his crazy lust for the scream of pain and the bullet in the head, would do to others.

Another station came and went. Vernet was sitting quietly, expressionless, staring out of the window, seeing nothing but buildings flashing by. Thinking?

Montbron made up his mind. 'The Gautier business went wrong. You turned it into a blood bath. There was never going to be another killing. It was all a put-up affair, Paul. What we did was against the OAS, not for them.'

'I don't follow.' Vernet didn't. This was over his head, but it only got more confusing. Montbron told him at length the depth of the infiltration – the origination, the scope. His brain refused to accept what it was hearing. When Montbron had finished he sat dumbfounded.

'Jesus!'

'We get out at the next stop.' Montbron rose to his feet and moved towards the door.

Vernet hadn't moved. He was still in shock. But his mind was coming out of it; there was advantage to be taken here. Filli . . . *Oh, sweet Jesus!* How was he going to let Filli know about all this? And if Philippe was on the same side as Filli, how was it going to affect the new status of Paul Vernet?

'Come on.' The doors hissed open and Montbron stepped out on to the platform. Vernet had to move himself.

'So what happens now?' asked Vernet as they moved out of Robinson Station and into the café on the corner.

'We're going somewhere safe while we sort this thing out. There might be a way to clean you up. I'm fairly sure your name's not on the list. We'll play it as we go along.'

Jeanette kept well out of the way. She saw Montbron on his approach to the house through the surrounding trees and she saw that he'd another figure with him. Prudently, she decided this was none of her business.

Montbron took Vernet through the concealed back door and up the servants' stairs to the attic. Vernet was not at ease. Montbron put it down to pressure; he didn't feel all that relaxed himself. He poured a large whisky for himself and added a little water, then a shorter one for Vernet. Vernet drank the unfamiliar spirit neat, in one swallow, then moved away from the window to the other side of the room.

'What about this Rostand-Bercy,' asked Vernet, 'who was he reporting to?'

Montbron thought for a second. *It can't do any harm now . . .* 'An Élysée Palace department; a special Presidential security and intelligence organization. It's called Maurice.' Montbron gave it another searching examination. 'And it's a method that will put you in the clear . . .' Montbron almost grinned, but didn't quite make it. 'It might even receive a thank you!' He went on to tell

Vernet of the scope of Rostand-Bercy's assignment and his final moments on the banks of the Canal St-Martin. 'How's your memory these days?'

Vernet shook his head. 'I can remember my name and date of birth.'

'Add this to them then.' Montbron leaned on the dressing-table, drew a sheet of paper towards him and began writing. As he wrote them down, he read out the names of the people he'd identified at the Cambronne meeting; then he added to them the additional names, the political affiliates, that Rostand-Bercy had listed, and the disturbing intelligence of the Metz Brigade factor. He kept the paper on the dressing-table and looked round at Vernet. 'Can you memorize all those?'

Vernet didn't reply immediately. Montbron had done it again, the bastard! He'd slithered and twisted like a bloody snake from Filli's boot and now he was about to climb out of the pit for the last time, smelling sweetly of roses. He and Filli were blood-brothers. They were both on the same bloody side – the winning one – and he, Vernet, was the loser, the poor little bastard trotting behind them clearing up the horse shit! But you never knew, Filli could always trip up and fall flat on his face, and Montbron wasn't immortal! And then who would be left to bounce the rubber ball into the court of those who mattered?

Vernet's eyes glazed over. His mind was on a merry-go-round with thoughts and ideas whirling about like the tiny fragments in a kaleidoscope, each twist jiggling them into different patterns. He tried to concentrate on one, the one that ensured Paul Vernet's survival, or, better still, that he was the one who walked in from the battlefield with the stuff Montbron had just mentioned . . . It even had the proper ring about it: 'Paul Vernet, special DST agent of the Filli Group, who brought about the end of a three-year-old revolt by a bunch of very unpleasant little generals and political dog-ends . . .' Somebody would have to be very pleased about that. So what about Georges Filli? Vernet shrugged mentally. A Corsican tiddler whose future went only as far as the end of the war. Montbron? An OAS master assassin until he cleared his face with the people who mattered in Paris. And if he didn't, and went down the hole with the black ring round his name? Everything was possible. But nothing would stay still long enough to make a picture with a hard edge. He blinked at Montbron and brought his brain back into the room.

'Why? What d'you want me to do with them?'

Montbron shrugged off Vernet's strange manner. It was understandable. Things were moving too quickly for him. He spoke slowly and clearly.

'According to Rostand-Bercy, the Maurice people are waiting for these names. With them they finish the game. Once they've put this lot into the Santé, the whole of the OAS structure in France will disintegrate.' He wrote on the paper again. 'This is the important factor: a special number, issued to Rostand-Bercy, that will reach the top man. He's known as Maurice. This information handed to him will allow me to demand that my credentials as an undercover officer of the Inter-Army Coordination Group be examined and cleared with the civil intelligence agencies in Paris. If anything happens to me, if we get separated, you complete the job. Ring the number, use Rostand-Bercy's name as an entry, and tell them what you've got. Make sure you speak only to the man at the top, to Maurice. OK?'

Vernet's taut expression belied the ice-cold workings of his mind. This was it; this was the key that unlocked the future. He knew where it was leading to. It was all a question of guts now. 'Why don't you ring this Maurice thing now, from here?' He pointed at the phone on the side-table. 'Get it over and done with?'

'It's not as simple as that, Paul. I'm on the list. I put myself there, I'm one of the OAS Committee – I'm marked. They won't trust me and I can't move until I get some sort of clean note from Elm. And Christ knows how I'm going to do that, unless . . .' He stopped and frowned, then glanced at the phone. *Unless Lemercier, for some reason, is playing a death card. For everyone but me? Why not? It won't be the first time somebody's pulled a coffin lid over his head for a breathing space . . .* 'There's only one way to find out.'

'What's that? And what about cleaning me?' Vernet edged further up the camp-bed and made himself comfortable on the pillows. The H&K pressed into the soft flesh around his ample waist, but it didn't worry him, quite the opposite; it gave him the impetus for the final hurdle. He knew what he was going to do; this was what it had all been about. This was the end-game – or the beginning of the new one. 'And what about the Gautier killing?' He stared hard at Montbron. This was the important one. 'And the bodyguards. Who takes credit for that? Who's going to get his arse kicked all the way to the brick wall at Ivry for it, you or me?'

Montbron stared at him. This was a different Vernet; even the voice was different. It must be the adrenalin . . . 'You're outside of that one, Paul, and you haven't done anything since. You're already clean. You're still unknown; your name's never been mentioned. No one's looking for you. You could walk through. And if something silly does happen, you've got the insurance.'

'What insurance?'

'I've just given it to you. The Department Maurice phone number and those names. Don't carry the list around with you. Memorize and then destroy it. You know the procedure.'

Vernet nodded. It was all done. He was clear and running. One more hurdle to go. 'How are you going to find out whether you can get a "clean note"?'

'Like this.' Montbron turned his back on Vernet, picked up the phone and began dialling.

It didn't ring long enough. It was almost as if a hand had been hovering over the receiver, waiting for his call.

'Hello,' the voice said.

Wrong.

'General?' said Montbron, hesitatingly.

'Yes. Guy-Montbron?'

Wrong again.

Montbron replaced the receiver gently and stood for several seconds staring at the wall.

'Something wrong, Philippe?' Vernet pulled himself upright

against the wall at the head of Montbron's camp-bed. He didn't look very comfortable, but it didn't matter. He took a deep, silent breath and waited for his tingling nerves to quieten. The whisky was helping.

Montbron didn't turn round. Something wrong? Everything was wrong. Lemercier wasn't playing games. Lemercier was dead, and they were all queueing up for a share of the Guy-Montbron prize. They'd even stuck a vocal ringer in General Lemercier's chair. Oh yes, it had sounded like him; it could have been his twin, if he'd had one. But one thing Lemercier didn't do was grab the phone before it had spelt the message, and even if he had done so in a moment of aberration, he wouldn't have said 'Hello?' Whoever had shoved him to one side hadn't done their homework – or hadn't worked the needles deep enough under the nail! Even giving Lemercier the benefit and supposing he'd really gone to sleep on this one, the last thing he'd have done would be to use the name Guy-Montbron, even if he'd been expecting the call. They should have known he'd cover Montbron's face with a code. 'Éliane' – very personal, the perfect code-name for a pseudo-traitor. But they hadn't even tried. He closed his eyes for a second. He'd have to scrub the General and start all over again. But where?

'Yes. A dead end. I'm staying outside, Paul . . .'

The click of the safety-catch was almost inaudible.

But not to Montbron. He stiffened, and without moving his body or his hands slowly turned his head.

Vernet had raised himself on to his knees so that his shoulders were supported by the wall; it provided something solid against his back as he steadied his right hand by gripping his wrist with the left. The H&K automatic was an extension of his arm, pointing, with just a faint nervous tremor, at a spot between Montbron's shoulder-blades. A silly thought crossed his mind. Not 'Why?' There didn't seem to be a logical reason. It was like one of those strange enduring dreams where the inexplicable seems perfectly acceptable. It was the noise that worried him. No suppressor on the H&K. It was going to blow their eardrums in this small room. The thought died, silly as it was, but he didn't say anything. He just looked Vernet coolly in the eye and waited for the explanation.

There wasn't one.

Neurie and Metcalfe heard the first shot as they stood by the car studying the house. Metcalfe's knees were still weak and his thigh muscles refused to stop twitching. It had been a frightening car journey from the centre of Paris. But that was all forgotten as the two men, with a quick glance at each other, rushed for the door.

Then a second shot.

And a third, and a high-pitched scream, a woman's, in anguish, as they thundered up the main stairs.

Jeanette Fabre was on her way to Montbron when the first shot was fired. She dropped the tray of coffee and rushed for the backstairs to the attic room. As she burst in, Vernet hit her across the face with the automatic, then dragged her off her knees and thrust her back through the door. He went right behind her, but stopped briefly in the corridor. It took no longer than a second. He raised his hand and pointed the HK4 at Montbron's body and squeezed the trigger. BANG! Another bullet thudded into Montbron, lifting him with a jerking shudder as it found its target. Aiming for the back of his twitching head, Vernet fired again and then, without breaking his stride, he grabbed the cowering Jeanette by her hair, pulled her upright and, with the automatic jammed into the side of her neck, rushed her along the corridor, down the backstairs and out into the rear courtyard.

'Quick! Where's your bloody car? Come on! Come on! Come on!' Vernet wiped the pistol down the side of her face. 'Quick, quick, you bitch! The car!'

She couldn't speak. Fear. Pain. Horror. She pointed to the end of the house.

'Go on.' He thumped her in the small of the back and she stumbled forward, scrabbling to keep her feet, but he was moving faster than she was and, sticking his hand under her armpit, he half dragged, half pulled her to the corner of the house. He glanced quickly over his shoulder as he turned the corner and brought the automatic to bear. But there was nothing there – nobody. He heard a door slam somewhere inside, a shout and the thumping of feet on the staircase, and then they were across the front courtyard, both he and Jeanette scrabbling on the thick layer of chippings to reach the Mercedes parked outside the garage.

'Get in!' he screamed. 'Drive the bloody thing – quick!'

His arm was straight and the pistol aimed directly at her face as she fell, terrified, into the car and scrambled behind the wheel. She turned the key. The engine roared and the skidding wheels sent up a shower of stones and gravel that rattled against the open garage doors like machine-gun bullets.

'Go for that car! Close to it.' He bellowed over the howling engine and pointed the gun at Neurie's parked Citroën. Then, 'Stop!'

She stood on the brakes and the Mercedes' nose almost touched the gravel alongside the Citroën.

Vernet leaned across her, his arm pressing into her throat. Then, as she gagged and choked, he leaned out of the window and fired at close range into the Citroën's front tyre. He altered his position slightly and did the same to the rear. With a bang and a hiss it too settled on to its rim.

'Right, move!' He eased his arm from her throat and drew himself back into the car. Then he saw Metcalfe and fired through the open window.

Metcalfe had too much impetus to stop. He hurtled out of the front door and was halfway across the courtyard when Vernet's bullet caught him high in the stomach. As he fell he had a blurred vision of a snarling face, lips drawn back over teeth in triumph as it vanished inside the car. He saw Jeanette, her head pressed into the backrest, and tried to focus on the silhouette of Vernet's head. It would have been a marvellous shot under any circumstances, but Metcalfe hadn't a hope. Dragging himself on to his knees, he pointed the Czech automatic, tried to stop it wavering, then squeezed the trigger. Not a hope! The trigger was like lead;

the squeeze turned into a pull and the bullet howled over the roof of the Mercedes and vanished somewhere over Buc village. He tried another shot at the now skidding car as it juddered in a half-circle, screeching across the courtyard and round into the tree-lined drive, but nothing happened, his finger wouldn't answer his brain, and he dropped the weapon and clasped his hands over the terrible numbing pain in his stomach as he toppled on to his side. He gave in to the enveloping red mist that swept into his vision from somewhere deep inside, and as he slipped into the darkness, the last image that engraved itself into his fading mind was the snarling face leaning out from the window of the Mercedes.

47

VERNET MADE JEANETTE drive round the backstreets of Robinson until he found the spot he was looking for. About half a kilometre from the RER station, it was a narrow street lined with trees on one side. Beyond the trees, there was an open park – a recreation area with children's swings, a sandpit and brightly coloured climbing-frames. But there were no children, no mothers. The place was deserted.

The other side of the street was bordered by a high brick wall that stretched from one end of the road to the other. It enclosed the outer reaches of the station and a huge new power plant that had been constructed alongside it. There were one or two other cars parked haphazardly, with no one in them. The whole area was completely deserted.

Jeanette did as she was told. There was no argument in her mind; her brain was paralysed. She'd glanced at the man in the passenger seat. One glance was enough. He was mad. All she wanted now was to get away from this ghastly place and get this man's face out of her mind.

She switched off the engine. As she sat back in the seat, she could see him out of the corner of her eye as he clicked the magazine out of the butt of the pistol, flicked the empty plate with his finger and then, after a moment, returned the magazine to its housing. He eased the slide of the automatic back fractionally until the shiny brass rim of the last cartridge showed in the breech. He let it slide back into place, then looked up and, without warning, brought the muzzle to within three inches of her temple. With his left hand held up as a shield, he squeezed the trigger. The front of her forehead disintegrated. Bits and pieces of bone and blood splashed against the side-window. The rest of her head slammed in amongst it and bounced back, but her shoulder met his left hand and juddered upright. After a slight pause, she slithered to a slouching position, jammed between the back of the seat and the steering-wheel.

Vernet stuck the empty HK4 into his waistband and stepped out of the car. There was still no one in sight. The pistol-shot had gone unnoticed, and there was nobody to see him leave the car. He didn't look round as he crossed the road and walked, without hurrying, to the station entrance.

There was a train waiting when he arrived on the platform.

He boarded and stayed on it until Denfert-Rochereau, then changed to the Métro and moved haphazardly across the system until he finally surfaced at Nation. There he found an empty phone booth and dialled the number Montbron had given him.

Striped waistcoat had all the patience in the world.

'I need a name,' he insisted.

'He wouldn't know my name.' Vernet was surprised by his own coolness; it was as if having killed Montbron he'd acquired some of the confidence and self-assurance he'd always admired in his half-brother. Vernet's new character was taking him over. He'd survived whilst his former idol had fallen, and he was quite pleased with the new Vernet. He let the other man have a few seconds to work that one out.

Maurice's man had already done that. 'Give me the name of the man who gave you this number,' he asked in a calm voice.

'Rostand-Bercy. You can mention the name Filli.' Vernet paused. There was no reaction. 'And the undercover operation against Diderot.'

'Can you wait a moment, please?'

'Not really. I'm in an exposed position. Be quick.'

It wasn't even a moment. It was just long enough for the phone to be placed in another hand.

'What was it you wanted to talk to me about?' asked the new voice. This one had authority; it was a no-nonsense voice. For a moment Vernet felt a surge of the old Vernet, the old uncertainties and hesitation, but it was a very brief glance backwards.

'Rostand-Bercy was killed this afternoon by an OAS assassin named Guy-Montbron,' he said.

'Go on.'

'He'd been left for dead. I arrived too late to help him, but before he died he gave me certain information to pass to someone whom he called Maurice.'

'Where are you?' The voice showed concern.

Vernet gave him the name of a café on the opposite side of the road.

'Stay there. You'll be picked up. Just a minute . . .' The sound was totally deadened by a hand over the mouthpiece. When he lifted his hand Maurice said, 'A DS, colour maroon. Name of driver, Rivières. Half an hour. And, er—'

'Yes, sir?'

'We owe you a great deal. I'm looking forward to meeting you.'

As simple as that.

Vernet sat in a corner of the café where he could see the road and ordered a double Pernod. He diluted it with ice only and coughed over the first mouthful. He tried again and then his hands began to shake uncontrollably. He felt as though he'd just finished a marathon, all forty-two kilometres of it. Everything felt like jelly, even his brain.

He let go of the glass and put his hands in his pockets. Eyes locked on the traffic and the people, he sat and waited, a lonely, hunched-up figure sitting in the weather-protected corner of a café's pavement, seeing no one, hearing nothing until, slowly, his nerves began to settle.

It didn't take long, about ten minutes, and then he began to whisper to himself: 'You've made it, Paul Vernet! You've bloody made it!' He repeated it over and over again until the shivering inside him stopped and the rational thinking took over. *You're free! Montbron's out of the game, and bloody good riddance! Rostand-Bercy, whoever he is, or was, is down the bloody shute too! They've all gone – Filli, Rosso, Pietri – and who's the great survivor? Who's the guy still standing upright when the whistle blows? Jesus, Vernet! You can't lose. You're the only one left. You're the man who brought the good news, the stuff that's going to clear the OAS/Métropole out of Paris. Somebody owes you a favour, he said as much, and he's somebody big, very big. You're in, there's only one way to go and nobody knows enough about you to pull you back. Montbron said – what the bloody hell did he say? Think . . . Ah, he said – now get it bloody right, Vernet! – he said, 'You're already clean. You're still unknown; your name's never been mentioned. No one's looking for you. You could walk through.' So what's holding you up? Let's 'walk through'. And it's goodbye Paul-bloody-Vernet and welcome Paul Alembert to your new life!*

Vernet gave himself another few minutes of self-congratulation, then took his hands out of his pockets, sat up straight and picked up the glass. It was still shaking, and when the maroon-coloured Citroën DS drew up outside the café a couple of minutes later, he still needed both hands to hold it steady.

PART TWO

The Man Who Would be President

48

Paris, April 1993

PIERRE LAINE, PRESIDENT of the Senate, pushed his chair back from the table, crossed his legs and studied the faces of the other men sitting and talking round the long table in the dining-room of his official residence. The movement alone was enough to draw their heads towards him.

'Gentlemen,' he said. 'The President is on the verge of sacking Madame Lemaine and putting Paul Alembert in her place as Prime Minister.'

'Who the hell is Paul Alembert?' The Minister of Defence choked on his ninety-year-old cognac.

'You might well ask.'

'I do.'

'Very well . . .' Laine nipped the end off a cigar and studied it as he spoke. 'Alembert is the shadow behind Jean-Marie Le Pen. He's the mastermind behind the National Front, the man who organized the fat one's political campaign and brought him to the forefront of the less acceptable face of European politics. He's a bloody Nazi, and he's also a damn sight more dangerous than Le Pen.'

'So how does he get himself elected as Prime Minister of France? If I've never heard of him, he hasn't come up through the ranks, so where the bloody hell has he come from and how do we accept a total stranger, a man without political credentials, into one of the top jobs in Europe? It must be unconstitutional.'

'Which question d'you want answered first?'

There was a stony silence as they considered the President of the Senate's announcement. He studied the set faces around the table and settled on the Minister who'd been asking the questions. 'It's not unconstitutional, Jean-Pierre, for a non-elected representative to assume the office of Prime Minister. It becomes the will of the President, and that's nothing new in French politics. The danger, however, is that unelected Prime Ministers have a nasty habit of becoming President.'

'I know only of de Gaulle.'

'Then let me give you a little modern-history lesson. You are right, of course, about de Gaulle. He left politics in 1946, returned to the Matignon as Prime Minister in 1958 and went on to become President. And so did Georges Pompidou, who was not a member of anything but a bank when he became Prime Minister in '62 and succeeded to the presidency in '69 when de Gaulle resigned. There is ample precedent for this fellow Alembert to end up as President.'

'When did you know about this?'

'Why weren't we informed earlier?'

'Where'd he come from?'

'What's his background?'

'People don't just walk off the street and into the Matignon because our President likes the way he knots his tie.'

'And talking about our brand-new President—'

Pierre Laine held up his hand like a traffic policeman. The carefully selected dinner party of senior politicians was turning into a Wild West show; everybody wanted to say something and nobody wanted to listen. He let them have their heads until they started getting in each other's way and ran out of questions, then he shook his head disapprovingly.

'The President informed me of his intentions three weeks ago—' The barrage started up again; indignation this time. He ignored it. 'And I sought the help of Maurice.' The mention of the name Maurice, head of the special intelligence group Department Maurice at the Élysée Palace, silenced the voices as if a plug had been pulled. 'It seems, according to Maurice, that Alembert was at one time a senior Maurice operative. This was before the present Maurice took over as head of the department. Apparently Alembert spent some twenty-five years in Maurice, most of them abroad in an executive capacity, and was destined for the senior position at the Élysée. However, he resigned when the present Maurice took over the department and vanished into the crowd some seven years ago.'

Laine paused and looked round the silent table before continuing: 'In keeping with that department's practice, nothing is known of his origins. He came from nowhere, and he went back into nowhere. We do know, however, that he joined up with Le Pen at the beginning of Le Pen's rise and engineered his attempt on the presidency in '88. It failed, of course, but they learned their lessons. Alembert never showed his face or allowed his name to be mentioned. He remained firmly in the background. It would probably be appropriate to say that the total secrecy surrounding his activities with Maurice continued until three weeks ago, when the President informed me, in strictest confidence, of his intentions to make the man his Prime Minister.'

'This is ridiculous. What was the man doing before he joined Maurice in . . .' The interruptor made a rapid calculation: seven years, or thereabouts, with Le Pen; twenty-five years in the Maurice shadow . . . 'In the early sixties?'

'Nineteen sixty-one, to be precise,' said Laine. 'And that's all.'

'What d'you mean, that's all?'

'That's all. No curriculum vitae. The man joined Maurice in 1961 and left in 1986.'

'I don't follow this. Where was he born? Where did he go to school? What about his national service?'

'Nothing. This is usual in Maurice. Funnily enough – if anything could be termed funny in this bizarre affair – this practice of shielding Maurice operatives started in 1961. Make of that what you will. However, the bare facts are that Maurice agents start as newborn babies and their activities from the day they join to the day they die, including details of the service they carry out for France, is the best-kept secret in the Intelligence Service. To all intents and purposes, Alembert was born in 1961, was covered in a thick blanket of fog, and has suddenly crawled out to be your next Prime Minister.'

The silence thundered around the walls of the dining-room,

shuddering from gilt-framed portrait to gilt-framed landscape, and over the silence was the tension of fear. These men were in shock. Laine didn't allow them to recover.

'And with every chance of becoming the next President.'

'How do we stop it?'

'The appointment of the Prime Minister of France is the prerogative of the President. One can talk to him and suggest disagreement. One could tell him it would be unpopular with the people, but he wouldn't take a blind bit of notice because *he* knows, you know and I know, that far from being unpopular with the people, Le Pen, or in this case, Le Pen's *éminence grise*, is the people's choice. The people, the ragged-arsed, bloody-minded French proletariat, have frightened him into this. They wanted Le Pen himself because the man's tapped a political gusher with his stance and pronouncements on recent immigration issues, but even Le Pen knows that the rest of Europe won't stand for him in the Matignon or anywhere else, at least not yet. Later, perhaps, but not yet, and in the meantime he has his friend and mentor in the Matignon. That's bad enough, but in seven years, or sooner if the President decides to stick his head under the duvet and let someone else try his shoes for size, this Alembert'll go straight into the Élysée Palace.'

Laine didn't give them a chance to throw him off course. 'And you don't need me to tell you who he'll nominate as Prime Minister twenty-four hours after he lowers his bottom for the first time on the Presidential lavatory. Another twenty-four hours after that and the National Front will have walked into total control of the country, with him as President and Le Pen as Prime Minister.'

'This won't bloody do!' barked the Minister of Defence. 'Someone's going to have to force the President to change his mind about this appointment. I think it's up to you, Pierre, as President of the Senate. On behalf of us, a majority of the Constitutional Council, you've got to tell him that he has lost the confidence of the Government and must stand down.'

'Presidents of France "standing down" in the middle of their term has no historical basis.'

'De Gaulle did in '69.'

Another voice, one with authority took over. Robert de Cantenac, Minister of the Interior, had sat in silence as, grim-faced, he'd listened in disbelief to his colleagues.

'De Gaulle was a law unto himself,' he said disdainfully. 'And he didn't resign, he walked out.' He pointed his finger at the last speaker. 'But tread carefully, my friend, this is beginning to sound distinctly Commune-like. Or worse.' Cantenac was a different kettle of fish. He was a rarity, an honest and dedicated politician who'd handicapped himself by being a patriot. He'd already been the topic of an intense dialogue between the President of the Senate and the head of Department Maurice.

'Cantenac? He's a cold bastard, a stickler for the constitution and its rules. He was also a Department Maurice man in its early days and close to the original Maurice. He wouldn't condone shifting Presidents around the board, either!'

'Somebody's going to have to have a very close look at your organization, Maurice. It sounds like a spy boys' polytechnic; a school for funny politicians. What about this Cantenac? Could you carry him with you if the crunch came?' They both knew what 'crunch' he was talking about.

'I don't know. We'll have to wait and see. Let's hope it never comes to that.'

'Perhaps he'd like to be Prime Minister . . .'

As if they were being operated from the same piece of string, the President of the Senate and the head of the country's supreme intelligence organization both allowed a slight movement of the lips when their eyes met. It wasn't mirth, more a satisfied understanding that successful conspiracy hung on the vanity, ambition or sheer greed of the key conspirators. Sadly, Robert de Cantenac, Minister of the Interior, suffered none of these symptoms, but his willing participation was vital.

'You could do worse,' Maurice had counselled.

Now de Cantenac had touched a raw nerve for the putative conspirators. Their fear was overriding their political acumen. They were worried, and they had reason to be. There was a scent of danger in the air.

Laine lowered his eyes and studied each of the men around the table in turn. Some were alert, one or two suspicous, another had an impossible-to-conceal glint of opportunity, and one, de Cantenac, barely concealed cynicism, but they were all definitely wary. Laine gave them a barely perceptible shake of the head. Whichever way he looked at it, it sounded conspiratorial: *We're talking of changing the President. We're thinking about having a new one. But the old one doesn't know it yet!* Definitely conspiratorial! And, as de Cantenac had reminded them, talking of inviting the sitting President to give up his office was getting dangerously close to that dreaded word – the Republicans' nightmare – the Coup. And with it went that other word, the one usually accompanied by the swishing of a heavy blade hurtling down its well-oiled grooves: Treason! A very serious business indeed!

The silence couldn't go on. 'You paint a grim picture, Pierre, and I for one can't dispute your fears over this Alembert and his colleagues of the Front, but . . .' The Minister of Defence paused and stared about the room, not at his fellow guests, but at the walls, as if suspecting tiny microphones waiting to record indiscretion. Slowly he brought his gaze back to Pierre Laine. He needn't have worried. *He* wouldn't have been speaking so freely if he hadn't had the walls and cornices washed. 'But will the President listen to your counsel?'

'I doubt it,' said Laine sombrely. He was not going to commit himself any further than that. 'My advice is to avoid any action that might prejudice the President's decision, as well as any further discussion on the question of the President's tenure of office, before the public announcement of the new appointment.'

He'd made his position clear. If it ever came to court, he, Pierre Laine, President of the Senate, had had nothing whatsoever to do with inciting the Constitutional Council to commit treason.

The serious faces stared at him for some seconds and then one by one the senior politicians around the table slowly nodded their agreement. They didn't want anything to do with treason either.

'When is the announcement to be made?' asked the Minister of the Interior.

'A week tomorrow,' answered the President of the Senate. 'There will be a press release and the normal media hoo-ha.'

'Pictures?'

'Sure to be.'

'Maybe someone will recognize the bugger and pronounce him unclean!'

'Wishful thinking. But it would solve a lot of problems if his purity was only skin deep.'

'I think I'm going to drink to that.'

'You'd be better off going to church and getting down on your knees and asking for divine intervention!'

Nobody laughed.

49

PAUL ALEMBERT'S FACE, as the prospective Prime Minister of France, gazed evenly and unsmilingly from the international pages of most of the world's newspapers. He looked dignified, serious and a fitting incumbent for one of Europe's leading political positions.

Those who made a profession out of studying things like new faces rising in the political arena raised their eyebrows, though not in surprise, only at the fact that it hadn't happened for such a long time. Solidly installed prime ministers being replaced caused no racing of the pulse. In most countries of Europe it used to be a weekly occurrence; it was not something that brought the world to a startled halt, particularly when it was the Prime Minister of France. France was just up to her old tricks again, trying to make herself interesting to a disinterested world. And yet there was one very interesting observation, not from a political commentator, but from someone who opened his newspaper, stared into Alembert's one-dimensional face and flat, unseeing eyes for the best part of a minute, and, without lowering the paper, said:

'So that's how the bastard hid himself!'

He folded the newspaper, propped it against the milk jug and stared at the picture as he dipped his toast into his bowl of coffee. After a moment he pushed the bowl away, lit a cigarette and rocked his chair on to its back legs so that he could reach the telephone. His eyes left the newspaper only briefly while he dialled the international code and then a London number, and he continued studying the picture through the spiral of smoke generated by his cigarette as he listened to the ringing tone in London.

It clicked to a halt. A brief silence, and then, 'Harry Metcalfe.'

Philippe de Guy-Montbron, the bottom half of his face twisted into a rigor-induced grimace, his speech impaired by the permanent distortion of his mouth, sounded like a cleft palate struggling for comprehension. His left hand was shaped into a tight fist and was twisted at an angle pointing inwards with the only flexible digit, the thumb, gnarled and steel-like with more than thirty years of extra strain.

But there was nothing wrong with his thinking processes.

The bullets from Vernet's automatic thumping into his back and head had caused horrendous physical and neurological damage, but had left the brain as sharp as it had ever been. At the age of sixty-four, Montbron was almost a physical wreck, but otherwise he was as hard and as calculating as he'd been at half that age.

His speech at the best of times and under ideal circumstances was difficult to follow; on the telephone it was an ordeal for the listener. But Harry Metcalfe had infinite patience and an enormous regard for the man making the effort.

'Philippe, this is bloody ridiculous! How can you be certain after all this time? Jesus! I wouldn't know my own mother if I hadn't seen her for thirty-odd years.'

'I might look like a fuckin' idiot, Harry, but one of the few things that bastard didn't destroy was my eyesight. There's nothing wrong with my memory, either. I tell you, the man they're eventually going to squeeze into the President's shoes is Paul Vernet.'

PART THREE

Paris by Night

50

GÉRARD NEURIE SIGNALLED to the waiter and asked for another bottle of Chablis, then turned back to Harry Metcalfe.

'Harry, it's a foregone conclusion. As the incumbent Prime Minister and with the backing of all the political mandarins, the man'll walk it. Sure, when the time comes there'll be other candidates – there'll have to be – but mark my words, he will be the next President. Can you imagine the effect on this country as a whole when the bombshell drops that the Prime Minister and future President is a murderer several times over, an unrepentent OAS activist who personally assassinated the then Minister of Special Affairs in 1961, who killed a top Government agent by shooting him in the back of the head in a public square, crippled for life an Army undercover agent by shooting him in the back, and murdered in cold blood, and at point-blank range, two helpless and defenceless women! Christ! You know all this. D'you need any more?'

Metcalfe shook his head absently.

Gérard Neurie reached for his glass of wine and almost knocked it over the crisp white tablecloth. His eyes were cold and hard. The memories of 1961 had never faded. 'The vicious, evil bastard!'

'We're none of us perfect.' Harry Metcalfe knew it was a mistake the minute he opened his mouth. This wasn't the time for an English sense of humour. For Gérard Neurie it wasn't the time for any sense of humour.

'Fuck you, Metcalfe! I'm in no bloody mood for your British bloody condescension, or your bloody sense of humour. Somewhere along the line there's been a slip-up, the system's broken down. This sort of thing's not supposed to happen. Our leading politicians, Presidents in particular, are expected to be pure and sweet and innocent of any past unpleasantness. This—'

Metcalfe stopped him before the steam started puffing out of his ears. 'I was the one who slipped up, Gérard. I had him in range and in my sight . . .' He touched his chest where Vernet's shot had brought him down into the dusty courtyard at Jeanette Fabre's house at Buc and winced at the recollection. 'I should have emptied the magazine into his face when I had the opportunity. If I'd known what I know now I would have said to hell with the woman and taken the chance of stopping him. I was afraid of hitting her.'

Neurie shrugged and pulled a face. He knew what he would have done had it been him and not an Englishman with the opportunity. 'It wouldn't have mattered; she was already dead. But that's beside the point, Harry. You didn't and the bastard's still here to haunt us. What's more, he's going to be President one day.'

'Is the Prime Minister of France immune from prosecution for a civil offence?'

'No. He'd go into the dock like any other criminal, and like any other criminal you'd need to produce evidence against him, and we haven't got any bloody evidence. We can't even prove that he's the fellow we're talking about.' Neurie drank a large mouthful of wine, wiped his lips and nearly smiled. It was only nearly; Gérard Neurie hadn't smiled genuinely since 1961. 'Of course, we could always lay down charges and produce our old English friend and ask him to show the bullet-hole in his chest! But I don't think it would sway the court one way or the other. No, we can only sit and grind our teeth. Prime Minister or future President, the result'd be the same.' Neurie leaned across the table and lowered his voice. It only just carried. 'But I'll tell you something, Harry, it would save us all a lot of trouble if the miserable little bastard tripped and fell under a bus.'

Metcalfe dropped his voice too and joined in the fun. 'Can't that be arranged?' he asked lightly. He offered Neurie a little smile to show he was joking. But he'd misjudged Neurie again. His sense of humour wasn't up to it.

'Jesus Christ!' he hissed and unconsciously glanced around the elegant surroundings. He needn't have worried. In the George V grill discretion was paramount and the tables far enough apart for the Rev Ian Paisley to hold court and not be heard. 'That's bloody treason talk, and in a place like this, you silly bastard! You'll have us both beating our mugs on the bars at the Santé if anyone hears you talking like that!' He nearly smiled again. 'Or rather I'd be the poor bastard screaming for water and you – you'd probably find yourself going back to London in a Camembert box!'

Metcalfe smiled. He'd no inhibitions about smiling, but he hadn't done much of it since his phone conversation with Philippe de Guy-Montbron.

'You didn't seem all that surprised when I told you what Montbron said about Alembert. D'you mind telling me why?'

Neurie took a mouthful of Chablis from the newly refilled long-stemmed crystal glass and touched his lips again with the napkin. 'I never liked the man from the first time I met him. In fact, I took an instant dislike to him.'

'Was he with Maurice before you joined the club?'

Neurie shook his head. 'No. I didn't see, or meet, him until he arrived in Paris from Washington, where he'd been for Christ knows how long. Maurice was getting very old then and the lines were being drawn up for his successor. That would have been the early 1980s. I didn't want the Maurice job. I think he did, but as it was he was pipped at the post. I think that was a surprise to everyone but Maurice. Maybe Maurice knew more than we gave him credit for. But, as I was saying, I thought Maurice had fallen for our future Prime Minister in a big way. You see, he came out of the blue . . .' Neurie narrowed his eyes at Metcalfe. It was equivalent to touching the side of his nose with his finger. Metcalfe understood. 'Overseas jobs, big ones, everywhere. It was almost as though he'd been kept under wraps for the purpose of eventually stepping into the top job. But there you go . . . And as I said, I didn't like him. It doesn't pay to ignore these primeval instincts, does it? Anyway, there was something about him that made me feel uncomfortable, a feeling that you should never let the bugger come up to you from behind. It was the same feeling I got when some mad sod with evil intent stuck a Luger barrel into my neck and told me to say my prayers.'

'Your devotions must have been very powerful ones, Gérard!'

Neurie shrugged – a very French gesture. He didn't find it necessary to tell Metcalfe that prayers had never been part of his working armoury and that anyone who managed to get that close to Gérard Neurie in the past had usually ended up wishing they'd gone somewhere else. 'This Alembert', Neurie continued, 'had covered his tracks far too well for a man with nothing to hide and only security of office on his mind.' He paused to sip the delicate green-tinted wine again and brought his lips together in appreciation.

But he wasn't going fast enough for Metcalfe.

'How deep did you dig? I'm assuming that's what you're trying to tell me, that you began to dig into the bugger's vegetable patch because you didn't like the look of his face and the funny feeling he gave you behind your ears?'

Neurie frowned for a moment, then nodded. 'Something like that. The designation given to Maurice agents ensures total anonymity and his file is sacrosanct – well, almost sacrosanct. I managed to get into his DST/Maurice transfer schedule. It went back to the early 1960s . . .' He stopped.

'And?'

'It cut out there. That's the system. A dead end.' Neurie studied the sceptical expression on Harry Metcalfe's face and nodded with a grim smile. 'Nothing unusual in that. When the old Maurice made the sign of the cross on a supplicant's forehead that's when his life began, in this one's case, in 1961. His name went into limbo and he lived with a number until he died, or became Maurice himself, when he could wipe it off the record altogether.'

Metcalfe waited. No prompting. Neurie knew exactly where he was going.

'Our future Prime Minister came to Maurice as Paul Alembert.'

'So?'

'You're not a scholar of the classics?'

'Gérard, I had no time for those sort of luxuries when I was growing up. Ian Fleming is the nearest I ever get to anything classical! What's this Paul Alembert got to do with my classical education, or lack of it?'

Neurie gave Metcalfe a look of pity. 'Jean le Rond d'Alembert was the close friend and collaborator of Denis Diderot.'

Metcalfe shook his head. 'And who's Denis Diderot?'

'He was an eighteenth-century philosopher who spent most of his life working on the French *Encyclopédie* with his close friend d'Alembert. Somebody played an unkind trick on the future President of France. They didn't want him to lose himself in the system, and like you, the poor ignorant bugger didn't know enough about his country's scholars to spot what had happened. It seems somebody had as much regard for Monsieur Alembert then as I do now.'

'I'm still not with you.'

'Take your mind back to '61,' said Neurie patiently. 'What was the name of the hot-cock OAS mastermind Gaby Violle and I wanted to crack knuckles with and the guy whose tail I set you to put salt on?' He paused. Metcalfe didn't take him up; he continued to stare blankly across the table. '*Merde*! You bloody English. You remember all about the Battle of bloody Agincourt but fuck-all about what happened a few years ago! Think, Metcalfe. For Christ's sake, think.'

'Remind me.'

'Diderot. His bloody code-name was Diderot! Colonel-fucking-Diderot! In other words, our friend with the back of his head for a face, Philippe de Guy-Montbron.'

Metcalfe woke up at last. 'Who had a mad-dog half-brother, Vernet! Jesus!'

Neurie nodded patiently. 'Alembert is Montbron's brother, or if you prefer, his half-brother Paul Vernet, the treacherous, murderous little bastard!'

Metcalfe smiled wryly. 'I can see why you didn't start swinging from the candelabra when I told you of Montbron's phone call. You knew already!'

'Not *knew*. It was a wild hypothesis, the sort of thing that has you waking up in the middle of a freezing night covered in sweat and the brain grinding away at some impossible dream. But this is no dream, it's a bloody nightmare, and, of course, these bloody names make it all real.' Neurie picked up his glass and frowned into it.

Metcalfe studied him for a moment, then said, 'I wonder who gave Vernet his working name? The guy must have had a marvellous sense of humour.'

Neurie looked up slowly. 'I bet he doesn't have it any more.'

'Why'd you say that?'

'Anybody who knew the pre-Maurice Vernet in any capacity at all would have taken the high road as soon as Vernet saw where he was going. He'd have cleared his past as cleanly as if he'd dropped it into a vat of steaming acid. There won't be a bloody soul left standing to scratch his chin and say, "I think I knew him". I'm sure our nasty little friend has made himself bomb-proof. He's untouchable. He's got a clear run.'

But Metcalfe was on a high. 'What about those mechanics of Filli?' His memory was now primed and jumping over the sticks like a Grand National favourite. 'Remember them? The watch crew in that shithouse you took me to after our meeting with the earlier Maurice? North-east Paris, wasn't it?'

Neurie hadn't forgotten. 'The nineteenth. DST records of that period give four names on a watch schedule in a house over at Buttes-Chaumont. They're all dead.'

'Causes?'

'Various. Nothing usual, none in bed.'

Metcalfe wasn't surprised. 'But there's still one man.'

'Yes. Philippe de Guy-Montbron.'

'Have you discussed this with him?'

'Yesterday. Vernet popping up out of the blue like this has rekindled an old desire of his.'

'What's that?'

'He wants to kill the little bastard. So do I, but he's untouchable. I've had a private look at him. As Le Pen's Svengali, Vernet has the best protective ring around him in Europe. If you pull a face at his car as it slithers up the Champs-Élysées somebody'll stick a gun in your ear and ask you what you're staring at. I never met Vernet when he was on the rampage with Montbron in '61, and neither did anybody else, apparently, but it bloody irks me to think that I've been within an arm's distance of him and that it's only now, when I can't get anywhere near him, that I realize he was the target of a life's ambition.'

'Gaby Violle?'

'You remember?'

'I remember you saying you were going to chase the bastard who killed him to the end of the pier and then drop him, no matter how long it took. But aren't you getting a bit long in the tooth still to be cherishing these unkind thoughts?'

'Shut up, Metcalfe! This is bugger-all to do with you. You've helped old Philippe a lot over the years, and me, too, come to that, I suppose. But you pack up your kitbag now and leave this business to me. Vernet's my pigeon. Don't interfere.' Neurie smiled, unusually, to take the sting out of the remark. 'Not again!'

Metcalfe shrugged it aside. 'So all that tearful and patriotic stuff about the state of the nation and how unhappy you're all going to be if this murderous bastard gets a decent job is so much bloody guff? What you actually mean, Neurie, is that it gives you a nice clean conscience. You can convince yourself you're going to kill this fat little bastard for your country, and not to satisfy something that's been gnawing at your vitals since 1961!'

'Get stuffed, Metcalfe!'

Metcalfe grinned. He knew he'd found the spot; so did Neurie. But it put everything on to a nice sound footing. Vernet's political passage had bugger-all to do with Neurie's finer feelings. It was an act of retribution, nothing more than that.

'Besides,' said Metcalfe, 'I came to help Montbron, not you. But you're going to have trouble if you think you'll be able to jog round the track on your own. You said yourself that Vernet's untouchable. So what are you going to do, turn yourself into some bloody fictional hard nut and shoot him with a metal crutch?' Metcalfe grinned again, genuinely, and tapped his empty glass at the same time, stopping Neurie from answering. When his glass was refilled he added, 'Have you discussed this kamikaze mission with the man who really has a debt to be repayed?'

Neurie stared at Metcalfe for several seconds. Metcalfe had always had that unerring ability to dampen highly emotional intentions. It was most annoying, but what could you expect? He was a bloody Englishman. Neurie pulled a face. 'I spoke to him briefly. As you know, it's difficult to understand what the bloody hell he's saying on the phone, which is why I prefer talking to him face to face. I haven't managed to see him since this little titbit popped up, so I don't know where his mind is at the moment. One thing's for sure, though, I'll bet he's thought of some bloody crazy scheme to take Vernet's head off.'

Metcalfe gave a nervous laugh. 'I think you're both bloody mad, and as for buggering off and leaving you two old cripples to your own devices, forget it! Remember, I've been the loser on two occasions trotting around behind you two devious buggers, so I think I'm allowed a walking-on part this time. Against my better judgement, I'm going to stay and see how this thing develops.' He raised his hand as Neurie took a deep breath to begin his objections. 'It's bugger-all to do with you, Neurie, whether I stay or go. You retired ten years ago. The days when you wandered around Paris waving exclusion orders under my nose are finished, so calm down. Let's give this thing some thought. When can we meet?'

'Day after tomorrow. Dinner?'

Metcalfe stared in surprise. He had been expecting a stiffer fight. He even forgot his wine, warming in his hand under his nose. 'You're a funny bugger, Neurie! Where?'

Neurie didn't smile. 'My place. Half-past eight. How about Montbron?'

'I'll ask him. It'll be nice to see Monique again.'

'You won't be seeing her. She won't be there.' Neurie stared blankly at Harry Metcalfe. 'And whatever idiotic thing we decide over this, she won't be involved in any way, is that clear?'

'Are you paying for this lunch, or am I?'

'Did you hear what I said?'

Metcalfe nodded. It was very serious again, just like old times. 'Nineteen sixty-one was a bloody long time ago, Gérard.'

'Not long enough for my memory, Metcalfe. Just bear in mind what I've just said, OK?'

'Whatever you say.'

'Good. Pay for the lunch.'

'Do you know my brother-in-law?' Neurie asked halfway through a dozen oysters. Montbron shook his head. Metcalfe said, 'It sounds like the beginning of a joke.'

'Then let me put you straight, Harry. As from now there are no jokes in this game, it's bloody serious. At the end of it somebody's going to die. It could be you or me.'

'What about me?' asked Montbron.

Neurie studied him for a moment. 'You're not going to die, Philippe, because you're not going to be in the physical game. You listen, you pick holes, and you advise. You're not equipped for violence, not any more. Where are you going?'

Montbron had pushed back his chair and was standing up. 'I didn't come here as a sightseer, Neurie. If you've got plans that don't include me in the final move, or any other part of it, then I'm wasting my time. I'm going to kill Vernet. Don't get in my way.'

'Just a minute, Philippe. Don't be bloody silly.' Metcalfe carried on eating. He stuck a thin slice of brown bread in his mouth and pointed an empty oyster shell at the standing man. 'Neurie,' he frowned across the table, 'tell Philippe he can play in the front row. Tell him that he can have first go at getting killed, tell him—'

'Cut it out, Metcalfe. I just told you, there are no jokes. I don't want to hear any more of your bloody silly humour – it's getting on my nerves.' He swung round in his chair. 'OK, Montbron. You want the starring role? You can have it. Let's see you run a hundred metres in ten seconds and then dispose, silently, of six of the best body-watchers in France.'

'Stop taking the piss, Neurie.'

'I agree,' said Metcalfe. 'Sit down, Philippe. Gérard, go on about your brother-in-law, and what he's got to do with Paul Vernet.'

Neurie went back to his oysters. Montbron sat down again. They were on edge – except for Harry Metcalfe. Neurie swallowed another oyster, touched his lips with his napkin, and said, 'He's the Minister of the Interior.'

'He's the what?'

'Minister of the Interior. Robert de Cantenac.'

Metcalfe stopped eating. 'Your brother-in-law? Monique's brother?'

Neurie nodded.

'You haven't been discussing—' began Montbron, with difficulty.

Neurie cut him off kindly. 'Trust me, Philippe. I had a long chat with him last night. I didn't offer any specifics, I mentioned nothing of the past. I only made suggestions that the man who wants to touch thighs with him at the top table might have some unsociable little habits. Although take my word for it, Robert's as safe as any of us. He's an old Maurice man himself—'

'Which is neither here nor there,' interrupted Metcalfe.

'Quite,' agreed Neurie. 'But next Saturday he's having a private little do – a celebratory dinner for the next Prime Minister, who, incidentally, had been briefed by someone to court de Cantenac for a starring role in his new political roadshow. Vernet – let's call him by his real name – doesn't normally go to other people's houses for his dinner. Going to de Cantenac's is something of an exception, and this—' he paused dramatically, although his voice remained on the same flat, even plain '—if we're going to do anything about it, is the one chance we have of getting anywhere near him.'

'Isn't this a bit coincidental?' asked Metcalfe. 'Vernet coming to dinner at your brother-in-law's just at the time you and Philippe want to kill him?'

Neurie nearly smiled. 'He was invited at my request. Philippe, have you got any interesting thoughts?'

Montbron stared at him flatly, but his eyes gleamed. 'Who are the other guests?'

'A very exclusive little affair. Pierre Laine, the President of the Senate, Fontblanc, the President of the Assembly, me, my wife and daughter, and the de Cantenac family. That's the dinner party, small and select, which suits Vernet down to the ground apparently. I told you I'd had a discreet chat with Robert. If you've got any bright ideas he might be persuaded to gaze out of the window while things are going on around him. There's only one stipulation . . .'

'There always is,' commented Metcalfe. It was ignored by Neurie.

'He wants no blood on his lawn.'

Montbron had been deep in thought. He came out of his reverie. 'What sort of transport does Vernet use?'

'Something special for himself and a Renault 25 – the V6 Turbo – for four hand-picked bodyguards.'

'Can we find out what's special about his?'

Neurie didn't smirk. 'Robert had a guided tour and trip round Paris in it. Apparerntly Vernet designed this thing himself and guards its capabilities like a mother with her first-born. But he was out to impress the Minister of the Interior and got a little touch of the "show-offs".'

'When was this?' asked Montbron sceptically.

Neurie acknowledged the scepticism; it sounded like coincidence again. But it wasn't. 'I know what you mean, Philippe, and you can forget it. There's nothing suspicious in the Minister of the Interior showing an interest in the future Prime Minister's go-cart—' He broke off to finish up the plate of oysters as his housekeeper appeared to prepare the table for the next dish. With her coming in and out the conversation drifted until the meal was finished. Neurie waited until the door finally closed behind her before joining the others with a large glass of chilled Pineau de Charente and resuming where he'd left off.

'I asked Robert about Alembert's form of transport as a matter of curiosity. Whatever Robert may think of my interest is something that doesn't worry me. I told you he's sympathetic. The last thing he'd have on his mind is the thought that I myself would undertake a top-grade assassination. He would quite rightly dismiss such a suggestion as ridiculous. I'm inclined to do the same myself . . .'

'I'm not,' said Montbron curtly. 'You didn't say when your brother-in-law had his guided tour.'

'Yesterday afternoon.'

Metcalfe sipped his Pineau and glanced at Montbron. Their eyes met and Montbron frowned. He wasn't happy. He'd seen many times before the results of too many people stirring the same pudding. He looked away from Metcalfe and shrugged aside his misgivings. 'Did he come up with anything constructive?'

'More than constructive,' said Neurie. 'Don't forget he's played the shadow game himself. He knows that anyone wanting to study a face over a high-powered gun sight needs more than the rate of acceleration of the target's motor. Sitting in the back of Alembert's car, he saw through a special mirror a pair of eyes that would have made Heinrich Himmler's look like a kindly rabbi's – Robert's words. He was referring to André Marchal, Alembert's very personal bodyguard. Where Alembert goes, so does Marchal; they say he sleeps on the carpet at the foot of Alembert's bed. He's devoted to the man, and like his master a total mystery. Nobody knows where he came from or when, but he's got all the skills and he can use any weapon. His favourite's a .45 Colt and he's supposed to be able to shoot the toenail off a moving fly at a hundred metres.'

'What about the car?' prompted Montbron.

Neurie shrugged. 'Specially constructed. It has the chassis of a small lorry with a solid two-inch steel underseal. Only a charge of enormous size could penetrate from that direction. The body is tested to withstand a close shot from a projectile of anything up to 90mm. It would take a tank to destroy it from the outside. Inside? As I've explained, nobody ever gets there without Almebert giving a conducted tour. It has all the right equipment. A specially strengthened glass screen separates passengers from the driver and bodyguard, but speech is two-way. The passenger can close his transmitter for privacy or security. The radio is driver-controlled and on permanent stand-by with the guard car, but can be switched off. There is a radar trace on the car from Le Pen's HQ and also a special radio-frequency stand-by for emergency. On a more mundane point, it has a well-stocked drinks cabinet set into the bodywork.' Neurie stopped talking to sip his Pineau. Montbron did the same.

Still savouring the liqueur, Montbron asked, 'Anything more about Marchal?'

Neurie pursed his lips, then nodded. 'André Marchal doesn't mix with the follow-up body crew and has no known friends. When on duty he never leaves his place in the passenger seat of the car. There is a central-locking device under Marchal's control to prevent the doors and windows being opened in the unlikely event of an ambush. Once activated it cannot be overridden by the passenger in the back of the car. In an emergency, the front-seat bodyguard takes total control.

'The driver remains at Marchal's side at all times and he is also a highly competent and personally selected operative. Like Marchal, he's a crack shot and totally reliable. Robert de Cantenac reckons there is no scope for compromise in either of these two. They make a formidable team. He said if anyone got as far as this pair they'd be very lucky. To get beyond them would be a miracle.'

If Montbron was discouraged, it didn't show. 'What about the rest of the body-watching team?'

'Ah, top people. Former parachute commandos – twelve of them. Four of them on duty at a time, the others resting so that they don't get tired. Trained in every aspect of aggressive protection, they have dispensation, while on duty, to shoot to kill on suspicion alone. Robert de Cantenac, on purely academic grounds and without knowing my thoughts on the subject, offered me some advice.'

Philippe de Guy-Montbron wasn't interested. Harry Metcalfe was.

'What was that?' he asked.
'He said forget it!'

By the following day Montbron had got it all worked out, or he so reckoned.

He rang Harry Metcalfe and they arranged to meet for lunch in one of the restaurants overlooking the Marne. Safe, secure and away from prying eyes. As if there'd be any eyes prying on two elderly gentlemen sampling the speciality, the *grande friture*, and drinking a bottle of Aligoté on the veranda overhanging the river on a mild spring afternoon.

Harry Metcalfe took Montbron's proposals in his stride. He kept his feelings from his face and refused to allow them to affect his appetite. There was a certain romantic idiocy about it all. The man wanted his pound of flesh in return for more than thirty years of pain and anguish, but there was no doubt that Montbron at least was going to lose his life buying it, and probably Harry Metcalfe's as well. And one thing was for certain, Gérard Neurie's reaction was going to be very interesting!

'Well, the first thing', said Montbron, 'is for Neurie to get me into his brother-in-law's house unseen, unreported, unnoticed. Secondly, all the guests except Vernet have got to be thrown out in good time. I want Vernet crawling into his car no earlier than half-past one.' He filled his mouth with the chubby, crispy whitebait and followed it up with a lump of bread and butter. The mouthful kept him quiet for a few moments, but he didn't take his eyes off Metcalfe. He cleared his palate with a large sip of Aligoté and continued. 'When Neurie leaves, he can drop off his family and wait for us here.' He pulled out of his jacket pocket several sheets torn from *Maxi Paris*, fiddled through them until he found the one he wanted, and then turned it round. He stuck his finger on the spot, then raised it so that Metcalfe could read the name. There were no marks on the map. 'You'll tell him all this.' Montbron gave his head several little twists to release the locked muscle over his mouth. 'He hasn't got your infinite patience, Harry, in waiting for the bloody words to come out sensibly. It's not his fault, I don't blame him. Anyway . . .'

Metcalfe stopped spearing fish for a moment and pointed his fork at Montbron. 'You said he'll meet *us*?'

'That's right.' Montbron ignored Harry Metcalfe's expression and unfolded another sheet from the map book. 'You're going to be waiting here.' He smiled, but it wasn't much of a success. 'You *did* say you wanted to be part of the playschool, Harry. This is your part. You're not going to let me down, are you?'

Metcalfe shook his head and went back to his little fishes.

'OK. That's everything, then. You'll talk to Neurie. After we've finished here I'm going out to Noisy-le-Sec to see a friend, and then you, Neurie and I will meet to tie all the little bits of string together before Saturday. Is that all right with you?'

'This friend you're going to see, is he anything to do with this suicide pact we've entered into?'

Montbron managed another smile; it was improving. 'You don't remember Denis, do you?'

Metcalfe shook his head. 'I don't think I want to know any friends of yours that need remembering. I didn't think you'd made any since 1961.'

'I haven't. Denis helped mc out of a little puddle just before I got my brains scrambled and we became quite close. He was part of Lemercier's group at Elm before it folded up. I still see him occasionally. He's the commandant of the DGSE training centre over at Noisy-le-Sec. There are one or two little trinkets I want to borrow from him.'

'Borrow? Is he that good a friend?'

'Yes, he's that good a friend. Treats me like his idiotic father!'

Denis hadn't changed much. A few grey hairs, and that tightening of the mouth which develops with lengthy experience in the close-quarter killing business. His eyes had lost their youthful twinkle of expectation as well, but no, he hadn't changed all that much.

'You don't get any prettier, Philippe!'

'And I'm not likely to. Denis, I want a few simple little toys. Can you oblige?'

'For you? Providing your indent falls short of a nuclear warhead, anything we've got.'

'Two kilos of Semtex?'

'Jesus!'

'And a pair of wireless-activated detonators tuned to a couple of miniature radio transmitters?'

'I suppose it would be silly for me to ask what the bloody hell you're going to do with this stuff?'

'Denis, I thought you were an experienced field officer?'

'I was.'

'Then don't ask bloody silly questions. Just make sure there are no trace marks or origination codes.'

'Anything else?'

'Fifty rounds of .22 long rifle, and a .22 adaptor tube for this . . .' Montbron opened his coat and slipped out of the small leather bracket on his belt a much used 7.65 Mauser HSc. He removed its magazine, ejected the round from its breech and dropped it gently in Denis's lap.

Denis picked it up and studied it. 'You're wasting your time, Philippe. This is a centre-fire piece. The .22 is a rim-fire round. That means you've got to change everything – pin mounting, magazine, the lot. Why bugger around like that? You'll just end up with something of a bastard. You won't know what the bloody thing's going to do.'

'It's unmarked, untraceable – and I trust it.'

'You're out of date, Philippe. Leave it up to me. Whatever it is you're up to, you're going to need something more reliable that a botched-up Mauser. Has it got to be .22?'

Montbron nodded. 'It'll be close range and I'll only have two effective shots. It's got to be silenced sufficiently for me to get the second one in.'

Denis weighed the Mauser up and down in his hand and stared thoughtfully into Montbron's face. After a few moments he shook his head in disbelief and stood up. 'Come with me, Philippe. I think we'd better do this thing together. I shan't sleep a bloody wink wondering what the hell you'll be doing with all this stuff . . . Before we go, though, is there anything else you want from my private stock?'

Montbron stood up beside him. 'Have you got a magnetized "plattermine" with a fifteen-second fuse?'

'Bloody hell!'

Denis sent the armoury workshop staff on a twenty-five-kilometre training run and went to work with the stuff he'd collected from different parts of the establishment. The weapon. He brought this out of the canvas holdall and handed it to Montbron. 'It's a self-loading PPK Manurhin, home-produced for home consumption – that means ours – so it's unmarked. Brand-new, not a thing on it. Easily adapted to take .22. OK?'

Montbron glanced at it. 'Barrel's too long.'

'So what?'

'Denis, the barrel's too bloody long!'

Denis stared down at it. 'Eighteen centimetres. How long d'you want it?'

'As short as possible. There's a silencer got to go on it too that's going to be a minimum of fifteen centimetres. I can't afford all that. What're you doing?'

Denis had blocked the beautiful weapon in a vice and was now picking up a hand-held electric metal-cuter and a measure. 'How close did you say you were going to get to your target?'

'Point-blank.'

'Then we'll reduce the barrel to seven and a half centimetres. It won't make any difference at that range. You'll need at least eighteen centimetres of silencer. How does that suit you?'

'It's going to ruin that gun.'

'Bugger the gun!'

The saw cut through the metal as though it were butter. Denis worked on the cut edge of the barrel in silence, then moved to another part of the workshop where he spent some time with another machine, cutting in the minimum amount of thread to accommodate the suppressor. This was a rough tube, 18cm long, 20mm in diameter, which once threaded tightly onto the muzzle of the PPK turned it into the complete ugly duckling. Montbron shook his head sadly when Denis placed it in his hand. 'Let's try it out.'

He picked up the internal telephone and asked for the cookhouse. Montbron sat in the far corner studying the weapon, aiming and balancing it as he listened to Denis's instructions.

'D'you have any rutabaga in your vegetable store? You have? Good. Send me two of the largest you've got. North workshop. Right away.'

'What d'you want swedes for?' asked Montbron.

Denis lit a cigarette and joined him. He perched his bottom on the edge of the workbench and offered the packet to Montbron. Montbron shook his head. 'I've taken a rough guess, Philippe. You're going to shoot some poor bugger in the head while he's not looking, which is why you get only one shot. There's also going to be someone else hanging around who, if the first one falls in time, will get one as well. Correct? Never mind. You want my opinion?'

'Go on.'

'I think you're taking too much of a chance with only one shot. I'd go for a minimum of three, four even – OK!' He put his hands up as Montbron's deformed mouth began to shape his objection. 'I know, you told me, you've only got the one chance, so let's see if we can make the best of it. First of all, let's make sure the two-two is enough bullet, which we can do by popping it into a swede at close range. If you can put the bullet in just behind your target's ear lobe, it'll meet about the same resistance as it would in a swede. We can cut it open and see whether it's gone in far enough to kill him. Even then it might take a bit of time, and you could find him spitting back at you while you attend to the other guy, so we'll change the straight .22 for a jacketed Hydra-Shok bullet with a delayed expansion rod.'

'What does that do?'

'Switches off the light. When the bullet reaches as far as it's going, the expansion rod swells and explodes. It'll scramble the whole of the inside of his head. If he hangs around after that he won't be in a position to get in your way, so you can attend to your other target with an ordinary .22 long rifle. You'll even have time to use three or four. Come on, let's go and play with it. We'll also see how effective this suppressor is. You happy now?'

'I can't wait. About this Semtex?'

'Everything you asked for is in here.'

'I'm worried about trace marks.'

'Don't. This is all stuff from the *Eksund*. It was scheduled by the IRA for use in Northern Ireland. This is part of my share for familiarization. I said it was unmarked and it is, but if someone finds a few bits and pieces, they won't find an origination point anywhere here. It's all Irish! OK? Is there anything else you want? My help at your end, for example?'

Montbron shrugged. 'Thanks, Denis, but this is private. You don't happen to have a good night-powered telescope?'

'Am I ever going to know how you got on?' Denis stared at Montbron's blank face and shrugged. 'OK, no more questions. You're not going to tell me anything anyway. A night sight? Yes, I have. We'll pick it up on the way out. When we've finished playing with our new toys, I'll drive you home. I've got that nasty feeling I had when I saw you kneeling on the side of St-Martin's lock. I know I'm running, I know I'm moving fast, but I don't seem to be getting anywhere. Philippe, I've a nasty feeling about this one. I don't think I'm going to be seeing you any more, so perhaps we ought to have dinner together tonight – supper, the last one!'

'I bet you behave like this with everyone who comes scrounging a few bits and pieces from you.'

51

00.45 HRS. MONTBRON stood by the window in the unlit room overlooking the side and rear courtyards of the Minister of the Interior's official residence and watched the last of de Cantenac's political guests depart. The heavy damask curtain provided a solid barrier behind which he could observe the activity of the security teams as, in their dark-coloured, high-powered cars, they shuffled off, one by one, with their precious charges. Montbron was further protected from the view of the remaining agents – should any one of them have had 100 per cent night vision and X-ray eyes – by the thinner, blast-proof transparent curtains, and he concentrated Denis's night sight on the one vehicle remaining in the courtyard under the full glare of the security lights.

Montbron had been watching, still and unmoving, for the best part of half an hour. Finally, with a silent sigh of satisfaction, he edged away from the window, took a white linen coat off a hanger in the wardrobe and hung it on the back of a chair. From the bottom of the wardrobe he lifted a plastic Printemps shopping bag and placed it on the marble-topped table in the centre of the room. He held his hands out in front of him and studied them. They had a slight tremor; the good hand and the twisted one were in concert with tension. He shook his head in exasperation, gripped them tightly until the movement stopped, then wiped them down the sides of his trousers and opened the bag. The shaking had stopped; he'd won that little battle. But then a new sound below distracted him for a moment and he backed away from the table and glanced quickly over his shoulder through the window. It was nothing, just a car door slamming. He silently cursed his nerves, went back to the bag and brought out the dull-metalled PPK Manurhin and laid it on the table. He sat on the edge of the chair, carefully eased a Hydra-Shok round into the breech, then removed the magazine, flicked off the top round and polished it before replacing it and testing it for ease of movement. He replaced the magazine, lowered the firing pin on to the round in the breech and applied the safety-catch.

With the PPK still in his hand, he peered into the plastic bag and by the reflected light from the window found, without scrabbling among the other contents, Denis's home-made silencer. It was crude and roughly finished. It looked as if it had been turned in somebody's garden shed, but there was nothing amateurish or crude about its effectiveness as a noise suppressor. He and Denis had tested it on the swede to its extreme. It had reduced the explosion of the modified .22 cartridge to the sound of a polite cough – one that would have gone unnoticed in an auditorium during the middle of a violin adagio. He carefully tightened the tube on the minimum area of thread available on the end of the shortened barrel and weighed it in his hand. It wasn't the weight that interested him – he'd been all over that before – it was the length. With the suppressor, it was still nearly thirty centimetres long. It worried him.

He put the weapon to one side and removed the remaining contents of the bag, placing them carefully on the table. He'd gone over the procedure all through the previous night. Failure of the equipment was not an option.

Montbron handled the bulk of the equipment casually. There was nothing lethal about it – not yet. Two kilos of fresh C4-Semtex were about as dangerous as two kilos of treacle toffee without the contribution of the rest of the stuff in front of him. This he handled with more sensitivity: the double wireless-activated fuses, a finger-blowing job on its own, and the two miniature single-wavelength transmitters, about half the size of the palm of his hand, with simple on/off switches. They made up two complete sets, a hair's breadth difference on each tiny wavelength. He made sure the wavelengths didn't coincide and that the black length of tape over the activating switches hadn't loosened. It was all custom-made; Denis had guaranteed it. There was no chance of malfunction.

He stood up, moved to the side of the window again and with his back to the wall, once more studied the courtyard. Nothing had changed since his last inspection. The car was still there, standing on its own. Some of the lights in the courtyard had been switched off, casting a shadow over the car. He knew there was another – the Turbo V6 Renault – and other guards, but these were round the corner of the house, out of his sight, and out of sight, presumably, of the car below the window.

His face, as much of it as was capable of forming an expression, revealed nothing. He could have been watching rain falling, yet there might have been a tiny gleam of satisfaction in his eyes as he turned back to the room and distributed the explosive with its detonators and initiators among the pockets of the white linen jacket hanging on the back of a chair. With only the Manurhin left on the table, he tried on the jacket. Moving fractionally towards the window so that the shadowy light fell on him, he was able to study the effect in the full-length mirror on the back of the door. The pocket was overloaded, obvious, the Semtex bulky and pulling everything out of shape. He should have checked it before and now he cursed himself for inefficiency. But he didn't get excited. Last minutes were all part of the business; in a moment the exasperation would start pumping the adrenalin, and then would come the thrill. But not yet. He patted the explosive hard to flatten it against his hip. It was still bulky. He took it out of the pocket, laid it on the hard, cold table surface and pressed it flat, then tucked it into the back of his waistband and tightened his belt over it.

He studied the effect again, then turned round and did the same from over his shoulder. He tightened his lips in a contented grimace.

Another trip to the window. Nothing had changed.

One more job.

The wooden butler's tray was standing on its side propped against the wardrobe. He picked it up and turned it face down on the table, then positioned the PPK on it, left side up, and taped it into position with heavy-duty industrial tape. He picked up the tray and shook it vigorously. The weapon didn't budge. He turned the tray right side up and held it at eye-level. Pity about the suppressor. But even so it would need a bright light shining directly on it for it to be noticeable. And who was going to be flashing torches around when there were overhead security lights?

Montbron laid his left hand on the butt of the taped Manurhin and felt for the trigger. The tip of his finger bent round it. He squeezed. It would work. He touched the safety-catch and then ran his fingers round the back of the breech. No obstruction. It would slide cleanly and there'd be a second shot ready. And two were all he needed. He'd get them; if he didn't, he wouldn't be in a position to worry about the rest of the programme. He touched the safety again, debated for a fraction of a second, and left it on. One final thing. He put the tray down and wiped his hands again. They weren't shaking, but they were damp; fear has many ways of expressing itself. He wiped them once more, and held the tray up at eye-level. He closed one eye and lined up on the small bore of the suppressor. With a sliver of white chalk, he made a barely visible mark on the tray's rim.

He glanced at his watch. 01.05. Neurie said they'd start yawning at half-past one. Ten minutes for the message to get home; ten minutes to get to the door and say goodnight. Forty-five minutes. He rested the edge of the tray on the corner of the table and placed on it two unopened bottles of Perrier, a bottle of Evian and two plain tumblers. Without turning on the light, he opened the door a crack, glanced along the corridor, then made his way down the backstairs and through the empty scullery. Bypassing the dimly lit kitchen, he limped without stealth towards the garage and the glass-fronted reception annex.

The four bodyguards studied him through a cloud of Gitane smoke as he came to the door. The remains of a post-dinner snack littered the table and cups of coffee half full and cold and stale-looking, their saucers overflowing with crushed cigarette-ends, indicated their boredom. But boredom didn't affect their vigilance. Boredom was their way of life. There were no alcoholic drinks visible. They were all stone-cold sober.

Montbron went through his ritual. He pressed his chin into his collar-bone and forced his twisted mouth to enunciate.

'The Minister wonders whether you'd like some light refreshment, gentlemen?' That was what he meant to say.

The white coat and black trousers reassured them, but they were still wary. Eight eyes studied him.

One of the men said, 'What was that?' There was no mockery in his voice, he wasn't being unkind. Montbron's speech impediment and deformed features had taken them by surpise; his diction needed concentration.

He repeated what he'd said, slowly.

They all shook their heads.

He turned to go.

'I wouldn't bother asking the guy in the car at the front,' said another of the men. 'Or the driver,' added a third. They all grinned. 'Those two don't even piss on duty!' Everyone laughed except Montbron, who turned and walked towards the front of the house. He'd given them a couple of minutes entertainment – he was OK. They didn't attempt to stop him.

André Marchal picked up the movement in his wing mirror. He did two things. He nudged the shoulder-holster under his left arm slightly forward and steadied it there with his left elbow, then he flicked on the car's reversing lights.

The man in the white coat coming towards him was clearly illuminated. He came openly, without stealth, and slowly began to fill the wing mirror.

Marchal watched him without moving his head, his eyes unblinking, his brain automatically assessing the danger and eliminating its potential with every step the man took. The fact that he'd come from the direction of the corner of the house and would have had to pass the scrutiny of the rest of the team gave him no reassurance. He was a paranoiac. Everybody wanted to harm his master; a footman in the high security of the Minister of the Interior's official residence was not excluded from that paranoia. He sized the man up. Uniform: white coat, black trousers. A member of the staff. Old, over sixty. Trouble didn't come from grandfathers! Hands, occupied and both in full view, and – *Jesus Christ, the man's a bloody cripple! Look at his bloody face . . .* Marchal stared, his tense concentration slipping for a moment. *It's twisted like a bloody Hallowe'en mask! How the hell does an old wreck like that get a job handing out drinks at a Minister's dinner party?* For once in his life Marchal overlooked the unusual; he asked the question and ignored the answer. Suspicious? He nearly laughed at his own fears, but didn't make it. Life in André Marchal's narrow confines was too serious for laughter.

The old man stopped at the car window, put his face close to it and grimaced. Marchal stared back blankly through the reinforced glass. Montbron's crooked hand pointed to the bottles and glasses on the tray while it remained balanced, with some effort, on his good right hand. Without changing his expression, Marchal shook his head.

'Piss off!' he mouthed.

The driver glanced across with interest. 'He can't hear you, you silly bugger, though by the look of him, he wouldn't understand if he could! Why don't you open the window and treat the poor old sod with a bit of dignity – or d'you think he might strangle you with that gammy hand!'

'Mind your own fuckin' business!' Marchal didn't take his eyes off the grimacing face and gesturing hands. 'I said piss off!' he mouthed again, then: 'Oh, Jesus! All right!' He reached for the button and with a muted whine the heavy plate window moved down four inches. 'I don't want anything to drink,' he said through the gap. 'And neither does he.' He jerked his chin sideways at the driver. 'What's that?'

Strange sounds came through Montbron's twisted mouth.

'I can't understand what you're saying!' Marchal turned his head to the driver. 'What the bloody hell's he on abou—'

Ahumm.

The bullet hit him just below the jaw where it joined the neck, then ploughed straight through to the back of his head, severing the main nerve on its way to the brain. Marchal was all but dead, but he still had a short time to go, a little bit longer than he needed to realize what had happened. The driver hadn't time to react before Marchal's head lolled on to his shoulder, although once his brain told him to do something, he moved quickly. But the bodyguard's head hampered him, and when he'd got it all together the wooden tray was already resting on the window-ledge. He just had time to register the bulbous tube underneath it when the second light cough removed his eye, and then his life.

Montbron moved quickly. The sound of the two shots hadn't been noticed. Not surprisingly. They wouldn't have been heard at the back of the car. He ripped the small weapon from its attachment under the tray and placed the tray and its bottles out of sight behind the front wheel. He glanced round again quickly. Nothing had changed. There were no galloping, scuffling feet; the backup crew remained in their room around the corner. He leaned on the bonnet and studied the entrance. The solitary uniformed guard gazed dutifully outwards as if what might happen inside was none of his business.

Montbron went up on his toes and slid his hand and arm through the gap in the window. He gave a short prayer of thanks to Neurie and his brother-in-law's information when his groping fingers reached the arm rest and found the emergency door-lock button. He was sweating profusely. He touched the button and held his breath. A gentle hum, a whine and an inaudible click. The door was open. *Shit!* The interior light!

He glanced around again. Nothing. Then he dived into the car and straightened André into a sitting position, tightening the seat-belt around him. He switched off the reversing lights. At a casual glance the upright André looked his normal on-duty, alert self. When Montbron reached across to click open the driver's door, André looked him in the eye. He knew what was going on. He was still dying, probably drowning in his own blood, but it was slow and there was nothing he could do about it except wait. Montbron ignored him as he straighted up, closed the passenger door and, without hurrying, went round to the other side. He checked his watch. Twenty-past one. Another ten minutes and they'd start yawning at each other. The heavy feeling pressing down on his bladder didn't reflect in his face, and he seemed to have solved the problem of nerves and shaking hands. His expression was the same as when he'd left the room upstairs – except for the sweat. He could feel it running down his back, and soaking his shirt. The bulk of the explosive was becoming uncomfortable, but he shrugged. There was no time for self-pity – there was no time for anything!

He dragged the driver upright, then pushed him in a bundle so that he rested half across Marchal's lap and half on the floor at his feet. The two of them looked crowded, but they weren't going to complain. He jammed the PPK under André's backside and placed the explosive and the detonation equipment at his feet. Then he closed the door.

The front was in darkness again and from the side everything looked normal. Montbron wiped his eyes with his sleeve. *Until some silly bastard comes along and asks if André wants a cup of coffee . . .* He shrugged to himself and glanced at André's silhouette as he made his way to the front of the car and retrieved his tray and bottles. The dying bodyguard looked comfortably vigilant. Montbron caught his eye again, briefly, as he walked past and returned to the house.

'Did he tell you to bugger off?' The talkative bodyguard looked up from stubbing out his cigarette-end and grinned sympathetically at Montbron.

Montbron grinned back. His heart wasn't in it and the effect wasn't pretty. To accompany it he gave them all a casual nod and carried on his way. He was almost past the door.

'Just a minute!'

His knees locked. They refused to function. He stopped dead and waited. He didn't turn round.

'How about leaving one of those bottles of Perrier, mate?'

Montbron's knees unlocked. 'Why don't I leave them all?' He didn't give them a chance to understand or object. He placed the tray gently on the table and retreated from the room without haste. Nobody ran after him.

As soon as he got through the kitchen and scullery he threw caution to the wind and mounted the stairs as quickly as his useless leg would allow him. Safely in the upstairs room, he stripped off the sweat-soaked white linen coat, screwed it up and threw it into the back of the wardrobe. Draped round a coat hanger was another jacket – a chauffeur's dark grey. He slipped it on and without bothering to inspect himself in the mirror moved to the door. After a brief glance up and down the corridor, he slipped out and made his way to the main stairs. He waited at the top for several seconds and listened to the conversation drifting up from the open door of the main drawing-room. He looked at the time again.

01.40.

He went down the stairs and turned for the main entrance. Neurie had left, thank God. He could hear a voice quite clearly. It had to be de Cantenac's, but he didn't stop to listen. Then one of de Cantenac's women had something to say. Alembert wasn't talking. Maybe he was out at the front studying his dead or dying bodyguard surrounded by four hard bastards waving H&Ks into the night sky! He glanced around him. There was no one about, only a light glimmering from an open door along the corridor, probably the butler's pantry, with the butler's ears cocked for the goodbyes. Neurie must have done a good job on de Cantenac and got him to send the rest of the staff to bed. They wouldn't have complained. Nor did Montbron. He waited a few seconds and glanced at his watch again. Something must have gone wrong – thank God! Alembert should have been on the move by now. Somebody was overstaying his welcome, or de Cantenac was brokering an insurance policy while he waited for the sound of gunfire. *Don't yawn too loud, de Cantenac. Not yet.*

Montbron opened the front door without a sound and moved out on to the porch. He slipped across the courtyard and, after studying the apparent vigilance of Marchal, went round to the driver's side of the car on his toes. Sliding into the back seat, he admired the luxury Alembert had designed for himself, then switched off the interior light, leaving only the diffused illumination from the open drinks cabinet. He went down on his knees and inspected its interior. It held two fine antique crystal decanters, both full – a good Scotch whisky and, even better, a champagne cognac from one of the exclusive Cognac estates – and, nestling in their neat holders, two equally fine dual-purpose glasses. A small humidor of good Havanas completed the contents.

Shielding the light with his body, Montbron studied the cabinet's interior before moving everything out on to the thick carpet. He reshaped the Semtex into an oblong brick and worked in both detonators, leaving visible only the tips containing the tiny activators tuned to the wavelengths of the two transmitters. When he removed the cigars, everything fitted neatly in the humidor. From his pocket he took a small tube of extra-strength superglue, spread a thin coating round the lip of the box, closed it and replaced it with the decanters and glasses in the cabinet.

He reset the interior lighting, shut the door and slipped into the driver's seat.

The dead driver's hat wasn't a good fit but he doubted whether at this time of the morning Alembert would seriously consider commenting on it. He decided it didn't much matter either way.

André Marchal was still dying. He was making a very hard job of it. His eyes remained open, not entirely glazed, whilst his mouth had set into a rigor-induced grin. He sat bolt upright, constrained by the tight seat-belt across his chest and round his middle, and waited for the black blind to fall over his eyes. He hadn't long to wait. Montbron gave him a quick glance and assumed the posture of a tired, but vigilant chauffeur. He was just in time.

Paul Alembert slumped into the soft upholstery and stared at the back of his driver's head.

'Neuilly,' he grunted and then closed his eyes.

The car pulled out of the Interior Minister's house and was

followed, locked in by radar and radio, by the dark, anonymous guard car some two hundred metres behind.

Alembert relaxed. A good evening. And if he was half the judge of human nature he gave himself credit for being, he could say with conviction that he'd got that awkward bastard de Cantenac in his pocket. He'd virtually said he'd put his weight behind him in the proposed new administration, and de Cantenac's weight was sufficient when all his friends stood on his shoulders. He was as good as home! The coming years had a nice feel of the momentous about them. From Paul Vernet, the poor little bastard, to Paul Alembert, Prime Minister and future President of the Fifth Republic of France! Alembert sucked his teeth with satisfaction at the picture and returned his agile and active mind to contemplating the evening's entertainment. He groped with his tongue, displacing a sliver of irritating *confit* from his back tooth as he considered the advantages of high office. They'd felt it necessary to do their homework – *confit d'oie* was his favourite dish! It was all very satisfactory. Alembert smiled to himself in the comfortable darkness and allowed his mind to drift under the soporific effects of the magnificent dinner, the well-chosen wines, the cognac – definitely the cognac – and the success of the evening. He was lulled into a sense of total contentment. This early morning, like any other 2 a.m., all was well with the state of Monsieur Alembert's world.

But not so Monsieur Vernet's more primeval instincts. Something jarred.

Not that bloody Cantenac? No. It was something else. What the bloody hell was it? His eyelids flickered, then opened, and rested on the back of Marchal's head. He looked asleep. Vernet frowned away the disquiet; there wasn't much chance of that. He glanced at the driver's back. Then at his head. That hat was far too small for him . . . His eyes swivelled to the window. They were crossing the Place d'Italie. It was deserted. The car turned onto the *périphérique*.

'Where the bloody hell d'you think you're going?'

The people in the Renault were worried too.

Vernet sat up with a jerk. He was wide awake now. He

punched the intercom button on the armrest and stared at the back of the driver's head. 'Jacques!' There was no response. He jabbed the button again. 'Jacques!' He'd had enough. '*What the bloody hell's going on?*' He waited a fraction of a second. '*Answer me, you bastard . . .*' His voice trailed as he stared at the back of Jacques' head.

That bloody hat . . . Jesus! That bloody hat! That's not Jacques . . .

'André!'

Marchal didn't move. His head had dropped on to his chest; his eyes were still open. He was dead.

Vernet's stomach lurched. There was hardly any traffic on the *périphérique*. He sat bolt upright, tense, and glanced quickly through the smoked-glass rear window at the sign of sanity behind. The car, full of bodyguards, calm and alert as they assessed the danger ahead, was holding well back but keeping pace, its headlights dipped. Vernet frowned through narrowed eyes. That was all he could do.

The agent in the passenger seat, his eyes glued to the car ahead, murmured continuously through the mouthpiece of the handset he was gripping tightly. Something was wrong. But what?

'Keep station on leader . . .' The other three all heard it. 'Leader's car is not on air. Take no remedial action until situation clarifies. Stand by.'

'Do as he says.'

Vernet turned to the front again.

'Who are you?' he said to the back of the driver's head. 'What's going on? What d'you want?' His voice, calm and questioning, belied the state of his mind. He had a nasty bubbling feeling in the pit of his stomach. 'Answer me,' he commanded.

Montbron slowed the car and turned off the *périphérique*. As he breasted the slope at the top of the slipway he went down another gear until the car was moving at little more than a walking pace. The car behind followed suit.

'Leader's vehicle almost stopped,' intoned the man in the front seat.

'Get ready . . .'

The two men in the back of the black Renault and the front-seat passenger all had guns in their hands, two carrying squat H&K machine-pistols. With the rear doors unlatched but held closed, they prepared to dismount.

But the car in front didn't stop completely, it continued crawling just above stalling speed, as if the driver was studying the buildings looking for a number.

The men behind watched and waited.

After several minutes the driver seemed to have found what he was looking for. Not a number, not a shop, but a pool of light, and he found it, an overhead white strip that splashed its crisp, shadowless fluorescence across a dangerous crossroads. Montbron stopped in the middle of it and turned fully in his seat, removed his chauffeur's cap and smiled into Vernet's startled face.

Behind them men were pouring out of the Renault and moving with expert casualness into the shadows on either side of the road before closing in on the stationary car in the middle of the junction.

Montbron paid them no attention. He stared, his grin set in place, for a few more seconds, then turned to the front again and jabbed his foot on the accelerator. The armed agents tumbled back into the moving Renault and the man with the handset continued his litany as they once again took up their position a hundred and fifty metres behind.

Vernet was none the wiser. It wasn't a lucky maniac who'd cracked his security, it was a bloody imbecile, someone who'd ducked his keepers and made the wall of one of the St-Sulpice lunatic asylums. 'Who the bloody hell are you, and what the bloody hell d'you want?' Vernet was Alembert again. Whatever Montbron thought about him, there was nothing wrong with the man's nerves.

They were about to be tested to their limit.

'We've already been through all that, Paul.' The voice, and its physical distortion, came through the system crisp and clear. Montbron could have been sitting in Vernet's lap talking into his ear. But the voice meant nothing to Vernet. Nor did the words, or the hideously contorted face with the lunatic grin.

Vernet was still in control of himself. 'You'll have to speak a lot clearer than that if you want any conversation with me – whoever you are. Start again, and if you want my ad—'

Montbron cut him off with a wave of his hand. He concentrated on loosening the muscles of his face the way they'd taught him, hour after hour, day after day. And it worked. He centred his mind on his mouth and tongue and let his brain take care of the words. Vernet shot upright again when the voice, the words carefully enunciated, came over the intercom:

'I thought you might have recognized your brother, Paul.'

There was no reply from the back of the car.

'Shall I say that again, Paul?'

Vernet's face had changed colour. He'd heard what the twisted mouth had said, and he'd understood the words. But it didn't make sense. 'I haven't . . .' His voice dried up. He tried again. 'You're mad. Why don't you stop the car and I'll see that you're properly taken care of. No harm will come to you . . .' *Not much, you crazy bastard – whoever you are! Some bloody heads are going to roll for this . . .* He tried the door handle. He should have known! Procedure – his own – meant that the door could only be opened by Marchal's hand, using the button on the right-hand-door armrest. Not the best idea, not in these circumstances, but it hadn't been envisaged that some bloody nutcase would have control of the bloody button! Vernet brought his mounting agitation under control with logic. *The man's a bloody lunatic. Look at his bloody face! And what the hell's he talking about, my brother? But he can't be all that crazy to pull off a stunt like this . . . How'd he do it? And who's put him up to it? Ahhh! Who indeed?*

Montbron turned his head again but this time didn't grimace. He slowed the car down and switched on the driver's interior light. From the back seat the vision was even more frightening.

But Vernet didn't close his eyes, he stared at the face – and then it made sense.

'Jesus Christ! Philippe?'

Montbron made no reply. He'd seen enough; the pot was simmering near boiling-point. As he turned his eyes back to the road, he stretched out his arm and touched the switch on the radio console; the tiny transmission warning light faded. They were on their own.

'It can't be . . .' Vernet had second thoughts. It was beginning to sound like the old nightmare again, the one that used to trouble his sleeping hours on his way up. 'Philippe de Guy-Montbron is dead. There's a grave in the St Cyr hospital burial-ground with his name on the headstone. I checked it,' he said slowly.

Montbron allowed him another glance. He really ought to have been enjoying Vernet's nightmare, perhaps with a celebratory laugh, but somehow laughter wasn't readily available. He hadn't laughed for more than thirty years. He wasn't going to start now. 'There's a headstone, Paul. Nothing else. My friends didn't think I was ready to go underneath it.'

'How did you manage it?'

Montbron didn't answer. He was studying the road ahead. And there it was, where he'd indicated with his finger on the *Maxi Paris* map for Harry Metcalfe, the narrow street on the right-hand side with the 'No Entry' sign. He flicked the headlights twice and turned abruptly. It didn't matter; the Renault was far enough in the rear to take it all in. It slowed almost to a standstill, suspecting a trap as the car in front jolted into the turning.

Two hundred metres along it, a Citroën *camionnette* blocked half the street. Montbron went past it without reducing speed, then braked violently and watched through the rear mirror as the van swerved on to the pavement and swung across to block it completely. Harry Metcalfe leapt out of the van's driving seat and trotted up the road.

Montbron was already out of the car. He had punched the

button for the passenger door and was reaching in, his arms around Marchal's body.

Metcalfe peered into the front compartment and stared at the dead men. 'Jesus! No prisoners?'

Montbron didn't stop. 'No bloody jokes, Harry! Just shut up and grab this bugger's feet. OK, drag him out – quickly!'

Marchals' body flopped untidily into the road.

'Now this one.'

'Been having fun, Philippe?'

'Quick! Get in. You drive. Watch it!'

Bang! Brrrr! Bang!

Sparks shot off the road as three of the men in the Renault dismounted and hurtled round the Citroën van, firing as they came. One leapt into the *camionnette*, dragged the wires from under the dashboard and its engine roared in agony as he thrashed it to one side. But Montbron and Metcalfe were now inside Vernet's car and with a shriek of tortured tyres Metcalfe gunned the car down the narrow street.

The whole operation had taken less than two minutes. It took even less for the Renault to make up the lost ground.

'I don't believe this.'

Vernet's voice came clearly between Metcalfe and Montbron. Montbron motioned Metcalfe to silence and turned round comfortably in the seat vacated by Marchal. 'Believe it, Paul,' he said. His breathing was almost back to normal. 'It's all happening. Let's have a proper conversation, shall we?' He reached down and selected another button. With an almost soundless hiss half the glass security screen opened and Vernet found himself within touching distance of Montbron's twisted features.

Vernet stared, mesmerized, and then found his voice again; it didn't seem so grotesque without the glass separating them. 'How did, er, that happen?'

'My face? What's the matter, Paul, can't you say it?'

Vernet didn't react. 'How did it happen?' he repeated.

'A treacherous little bastard shot me in the back, and then tried to finish me off with one in the head. But as well as being a treacherous little bastard he was an inefficient little bastard . . .'

It was the first sign of vehemence Montbron had shown. But he didn't allow it to develop. It was the cool, controlled, matter-of-fact manner that inspired fear. He'd worked it all out. He removed the edge from his voice. 'You were half an inch too low. The bullet severed the facial nerve and slipped round the brain and bounced out of the side of my skull.' He held up his twisted hand. 'This and my leg were minor problems. It was quite a butcher's performance you carried out. Why, Paul?' It was a simple question, simply put. Vernet's brain raced.

'They ordered me to do it. I had no choice. If I hadn't, they would have done it. They'd marked you, they'd got a hook waiting for you. It was better my way. They were evil bastards—'

'You mean I've got to thank you for this?'

'No. But you've got to believe me. You don't think I did what I did out of personal choice?' Vernet managed to inject a note of indignation into his voice. He didn't feel it. He was frightened; any tone was better than the whine that was fighting to take over.

'Who were these "evil bastards" who gave you your instructions?'

This was better. 'DST. The Corsicans. A man named Filli. Like I said, I had no choice.'

'And he told you to come and shoot me in the back?'

'It wasn't like that . . .'

'What was it like, Paul?'

Vernet told him what had happened to him from the time he'd been picked up by Rosso and Pietri and taken to the tiled room in the Boulevard Montmorency HQ, to the final chapter at Buc and then his progress – progress beyond his wildest fantasies – to the office he was about to occupy. As he spoke he lost some of his fear. It all sounded so logical and inevitable, and he seemed to recover some of his confidence by recounting his own achievements. He finished on a note of banality, as if his explanation had given him absolution so that the record was now straight and everything could go back to where it had been an hour before.

'Philippe, you realize of course I'm now in an extraordinary position. I can do an enormous amount for you. I can help you – anything you want. I know you understand . . .' He didn't look Montbron in the eye but focused on a point just above his eyebrows. As long as he was looking in his direction, it seemed as if things would be all right. If only the bastard would show some expression!

He hadn't noticed that the car had turned off the main road and was now on the old 'A' road heading in the direction of Versailles. A short while later it turned again. Nor did he notice the signpost: BUC 18KM.

The black Renault had recovered its position. After a brief, interested but cynical glance at the bodies of André Marchal and his partner as they manoeuvred past, the man with the handset had reported their new direction and been instructed to continue openly shadowing the target vehice but to take no action until its destination became obvious. Teams were marking them and would close in when assistance was called for, they were told. They looked at each other and shrugged as their control HQ told them what they already knew: 'There is still no radio contact.' The driver looked round at the grim faces behind him. So what! Their problem couldn't get any worse.

In his own car Vernet's voice broke the brief silence that had descended.

'OK, Philippe, what is it you want then?'

'I've got it,' said Montbron, evenly.

'I don't understand.'

'Paul, you're going to die in about half an hour.' Montbron gazed coolly into Vernet's eyes while he digested this. The searching scrutiny was too much for him. He closed his eyes and pressed himself into the corner of the seat. His dignity was still intact and his brain was working overtime; there was fear, bladder-crushing fear, but on the credit side there was still an overpowering curiosity. It was this that kept him from screaming, but only just. The moment his brain told him to believe what the man with the twisted face was telling him, and the self-assured master of the intelligence business, the cool calculating Alembert, the brain, the future Prime Minister and probable

President of the Fifth Republic, would revert to Paul Vernet, the frightened fugitive of the savage little war of the 1960s. But his cunning hadn't deserted him yet. He was ready for the opportunity. He opened his eyes. The face was still there, studying him.

'I suppose it would be silly of me to say sorry, Philippe?' He tried an apologetic smile – it had always worked with Montbron in the past – but his facial muscles had set solid and refused to cooperate. It was a ridiculous suggestion, even from a man who'd just been sentenced to death.

Montbron didn't attempt a smile either. 'It took a year', he enunciated carefully, 'before I could raise or lower my eyelids. It took three years before I could make a sensible word out of what you'd left of the workings of my mouth and tongue, and another year on top of that before I could walk five metres unaided . . .' He paused for a moment. 'No, Paul, "Sorry" doesn't quite compensate.' It was almost as if the overpowering sense of satisfaction with the situation was the therapy that had been missing from Montbron's process of recovery. His speech was almost normal. 'But I'm not the only one who owes you pain, Paul. There are others waiting their turn. They're not going to get one, but I'm sure they'll read your obituary without tears.'

'Success always produces casualties.' Vernet surprised himself. It was a remark more fitting to the grandeur of his penthouse study than to the back of a car being driven by a madman bent on revenge.

Montbron tried to smile. He saw the irony of Vernet's situation. 'This Englishman sitting beside me will, I've no doubt, be comforted by those words.' Without taking his eyes off Vernet, Montbron turned his head slightly and said, 'Are you all right, Harry? You know where you're going?'

'Sure,' said Metcalfe. 'I hope our friend got there in—'

Vernet wouldn't let him finish. 'Englishman?' he stammered. 'What bloody Englishman? What've Englishmen got to do with it?'

'You tried to kill him as well, don't you remember? Harry, say hello to Paul Vernet.'

Metcalfe turned his head briefly and locked eyes with the small fat man in the back of the car. There was no sign of recognition from either of them. But for Vernet there was recollection.

He sat transfixed. Perhaps in a moment he'd wake up and get over this with a glass of warm whisky while he gazed across the pre-dawn tranquillity of the Bois. But the nightmare ran on and on; there was no let-up for him. It all came flooding back – too much of it. The man running at him from the Fabre house, the automatic in his hand . . . He could see it all clearly, as if it were yesterday. The shot across the woman's body, and briefly – there it was – the face that had just studied him as if he were a dirty shirt, but then, all that time ago, grimacing at him as he crashed into the gravel in front of the house. *The woman! Oh, Jesus Christ! The bloody woman! Slow down, Vernet. Montbron hasn't mentioned her – maybe it doesn't matter . . .*

It did.

'Why'd you kill Jeanette Fabre, Paul?'

The big nerve in Vernet's face started to jump. He probed it with his fingers to coax it back to sleep but it was uncontrollable. The twitching was an old impulse he'd been unable to control, but funny, it was years since he'd experienced it. He took a deep breath, then exhaled slowly and thought about the decanters standing solidly in their recesses behind the panel in front of him. But he didn't go beyond the thought; a large cognac wasn't going to get him out of this situation. He moved his head fractionally and glanced out of the corner of his eye through the rear window. It was a reassuring sight, the slow-moving headlights of the Renault holding its station, the hand-picked agents ready to take Montbron and blow his head into the gutter. And when they'd done that, the whole bloody lot would be looking for another job. But first there was Montbron, obviously totally mad. He'd have to be put down like a bloody madman, without a bloody chance, not even a whispered Hail Mary . . .

'Why'd you kill her, Paul?' repeated the madman.

Vernet looked to the front. 'I'd have thought that was obvious. With you dead and Filli put away in the Camargue there was no one left who could put anything together to spoil my version.

When you told me about the Air Force chap – what was his name?'

'Rostand-Bercy.'

Vernet's confidence was returning. This had gone on too long. If Montbron had wanted to kill him he'd have done it by now. He wanted something. Everybody wanted something; they all had a price. Montbron was trying a bit of blackmail; death wasn't coming into this. Not his, not Paul Vernet's . . .

'That's the fellow. When you told me about the real game you had both been playing, plus his Department Maurice connections, I realized I had a bolt-hole with a future. I didn't fancy going back to that bloody village and serving croissants and hard-boiled eggs in the local café, which was what you seemed to have mapped out for me. Suddenly I saw the light. It all fitted. The young DST operator who had a background that started yesterday and who was certified by Georges Filli, the head of a DST Special Group, coming to Maurice, the man who counted, with the information that was going to put an end to the OAS Paris organization. Not only that, but he did it all on his own! Just the sort of man Maurice wanted. And that's how it happened. He offered me the key to the door—'

'And for that you stuck a gun against a defenceless woman's head and pulled the trigger?'

'I've just told you – it was necessary.'

'Some of Filli's people could have identified you.'

'I worked it all out while I was waiting for Maurice to collect me. Went through it from beginning to end. There was nobody left except two goons who shared the watch with me in that room over at Buttes-Chaumont. You remember—'

'You killed them?'

'They were worth nothing.'

'Was anybody by your reckoning? The Minister in the car park at St-Germain – you didn't give him a chance either.'

'He was a pig.'

'And that made it OK? What about the young girl, Lucienne, who thought she was helping a cause?'

'All sorts of people die in war.'

'Gabriel Violle?'

'Who's he?'

'A man who was killed by you in the Place de la Contrescarpe. You might meet his friend shortly.'

'I can't remember everybody. If anyone got it that day it was done either by Filli or one of his people. Come to think of it, Filli did put one in the back of an SDECE agent's head that day . . . It should have been your head, Philippe. You had a lot of luck at Contrescarpe!'

'I think his friend'll find you guilty of Violle's murder by implication. You had quite a bloody career until you crawled into Maurice and pulled the flap over your head. Was it Maurice who gave you the name Alembert?'

'No, Filli. I cut out everything before—'

'He played a joke on you, Paul. That name and a bit of flattery cost you your life.'

Vernet's stomach froze again. 'How d'you mean?'

Montbron ignored the question. 'Why did Maurice find a hole for you?'

'Like I said, I brought the war to an end, I was blue-eyes. He wasn't interested in minor details. He'd got a result, and he'd got the boy who'd handed it to him. He marked me as a goer and sent me to Tokyo as special services to get me out of the way. He thought you'd have friends from the sandpit who might want to see me about your death, but of course he was mistaken on both counts, wasn't he? You didn't have any bloody friends – and you weren't even bloody dead!' Vernet sounded quite bitter about Montbron cheating over his death. 'When nothing was reported about the business at Buc, I presumed one of the agencies had moved in and cleared up the mess. You were dead – I'd killed you, hadn't I? – and I was home and had a clear run. I stayed in Japan, covering the Far East for Maurice for twelve years – a beautiful life – and then Washington. But never head of station. Maurice knew what he was doing. No publicity. He'd got me marked, same size shoes and hat. In '81 I came back to Paris to take over the job itself, but instead went in with Le Pen. Much more rewarding than chasing spies!' Vernet was in a different world, he was picking out only the best bits. He'd have gone on for ever if Montbron hadn't brought him back to his present problems.

'You did well for yourself,' he said caustically, then turned his head briefly and jerked his chin. 'D'you recognize this place we're coming up to?'

'No – should I?'

'I think you should, even after all your good years. Have a look around!'

Vernet stared out of the side-window. The view meant nothing to him. But the dark car cruising behind, ominous and threatening as it came ever closer, did. His stomach settled again; his curiosity had risen. He turned his head and stared back into Montbron's face. 'I'm not interested in Paris by night – but I am interested in you. Tell me, Philippe, how, erm . . .?'

Montbron did it for him. 'How did I keep out of the hole and out of the way for all these years? I don't think we've got time for my story, Paul, we're nearly there.'

'Nearly where?'

'Nearly at the end of the road.'

It didn't make sense. Vernet sat forward with a scowl on his face. 'What the hell are you talking about, you bloody lunatic! The end of what bloody road?'

'Yours, Paul. You can stop worrying. It's nearly over.'

'I'm not interested any more.'

Montbron took no notice. 'That fellow you were dining with this evening—'

'De Cantenac?'

'No, the other one, Gérard Neurie.'

'What about him?'

'He was the man who wanted our heads. He was the leader of the Special Group formed to run down the Diderot team after the Boulevard St-Germain massacre. It was his best friend who was gunned down in the Place de la Contrescarpe. He wasn't going to let it lie until the people responsible were under the ground. Filli told him it was you. I agree. Shooting a man in the back of the head sounds the sort of murder that's right up your street.'

'It was Filli.'

'You were bound to say that. Filli's dead.'

'I don't give a fuck either way! It was all a long time ago, it's forgotten—'

'Not by Neurie. He eventually confirmed my role in Diderot. You didn't see him at Buc; he didn't see you either. You were lucky there, but he knew he'd meet you one day. He reckoned it was written!'

Vernet didn't like this bit. He flopped back in his seat and stared, mesmerized, at the silhouetted head in front of him. 'D'you mean Neurie knew about me all along?'

'No. As you said, you and Maurice played a wonderful game. Neurie didn't know who you were until I saw your picture in the papers and told my friend Metcalfe here. He was the one who brought Neurie into the play. And even then you nearly got away with it. He didn't take to Metcalfe's story – too over the top, too bizarre – until he coupled the names Alembert and Diderot and then it all suddenly began to make sense. It was Neurie who saved my life. He put the stone in the graveyard. He hid me in a private hospital until the Diderot dust had subsided and the OAS had beome just a bitter memory, and then he arranged the rest of my life. It's costing you your life, because if he hadn't saved mine you'd have lived. You've got just a few minutes to work that one out, Paul.'

Vernet said nothing. There was nothing more he could say; it was all there, 'written', like the bloody man said. He sat back in his seat and let the jelly-like tentacles of fear wrap themselves around him. He stared out of the window again. Something jogged his memory.

It was the brick wall on the right. It seemed to stretch high and forbidding into the distance. Time had painted it with the corrosive filth of thirty years' pollution and the grubby overhead street lamps did nothing to diminish the sense of desolation. His eyes flickered back and forth, up and down, with a feeling of the inevitability of it all. He ought to have known all those years ago that he'd be coming back. He leaned forward and turned his head away from the wall. His mouth dried. He knew what he was going to see. It was still there, the children's playground, but there was no more playing to be done; this playground had long been abandoned. He stared, unseeing, at the overgrown site with its large signboard depicting an unlikely impression of a towering and expansive hypermarket. But by the illumination of the developers' security lights and the orange-coloured street lamps he could see the rusty remains of a bank of children's swings and, on its side, grotesquely pointing to the dark sky like a dead monster, the barely recognizable remnants of an infants' slide. Everything was derelict and changed, but not out of recognition. Paul Vernet knew exactly where he was; the place hadn't changed all that much in thirty-two years. Desolation remains desolation regardless of the passage of time.

'Recognize it, Paul?'

Metcalfe saved him the necessity of replying. He grunted an obscenity as, just before he turned the corner, he studied the distance between him and the Renault. He shook his head slowly and drew breath through pursed lips.

Montbron swung round. 'What's the matter?'

Metcalfe shook his head again. 'It's going to be close.'

'Have you seen Neurie?'

Metcalfe took one hand off the wheel and made a little jabbing motion with his finger. 'That second buttress.'

'Did he signal?'

'Yeh. He's ready. But he'd better be quick.'

The man in the back seat of the car was for a moment forgotten. But there was nothing he could do. He knew that. He glanced out of the back window again. The Renault hadn't turned the corner. Wise. They'd creep along, probably with one man on foot skirting the wall. All that was left for him was to take an interest in what these two lunatics were up to.

As he turned to the front again he just missed spotting the man who darted out from the shadows of the wall, moved in behind them and then carefully laid the object he was carrying in the gutter where, in the darkness, even if anyone had had eyes for it, it was completely invisible. With a quick wave of his hand, Neurie darted across the road and threw himself into the undergrowth of the abandoned park. Montbron watched him crawl until he was out of sight, then turned his eyes back to the corner of the road.

The Renault, its headlights dimmed, did exactly what Vernet had prophesied. It poked its nose round the corner and waited. One man on foot, an MP5 in his left hand going before him, eased round the corner in time with the slow-moving Renault and peered along the gloomy, derelict road.

'Wait,' he cautioned, and studied the brake lights of Vernet's car some two hundred metres away, then whispered hoarsely, 'It's stopped!'

'What the bloody hell's going on?'

The man in the passenger seat stared along the road for a moment, then touched the driver's arm. 'Slowly. Stay on this side. Be ready to stop when I give the word.' But it never came. With the man on foot, his back pressed against the wall, moving parallel with them, the Renault crawled into and then along the road. Twenty-five metres. The front wheel went over a solid object and a second later there was a muted thump and a gentle clang.

They all knew what it was.

'Fuckin' hell!'

The driver fiercely jammed on his brakes, instinctively pulled the heavy MAB automatic from the holster under his arm and grabbed the door handle. The two men on the back seat did the same. But they knew they were going to be too late. They were.

The fifteen-second fuse left them behind; they had no chance. Half in and half out of the Renault, they went up when the magnetic plattermine, stuck immovably to the underside of the Renault, exploded with a brilliant, lightning flash. For a moment the street was as bright as a film setting, and everything was frozen. A deathly hush, a fraction of a second, and then, with an almighty clap of thunder that stretched the eardrums to their limit, the Renault was picked up and thrown against the wall, where it disappeared in a ball of flame with pieces of shapeless metalwork thudding and bouncing into the night.

Montbron and Metcalfe kept their heads buried in their arms for several seconds after the explosion. Vernet, unprepared, was thrown on to the floor of the car by the tremendous whoosh of the blast that lifted the heavy vehicle off its four wheels, waggled it like a toy, and crashed it down again on to its chassis.

Montbron was the first to recover.

'Move, Harry!'

'Jesus Christ!'

'I said bloody move, Harry! Drive! That way, quick. Get off the road – go on! Don't worry about the bloody ditch, this thing'll jump it!'

It did. Metcalfe swung the wheel violently, cut into the derelict playground and, avoiding the broken swings and roundabouts, roared across the pitted tarmac and skidded to a halt before the surrounding trees. The night sky was lit up by the burning carcass of the Renault, casting an eerie, nightmarish glow as jagged flame-streaked shadows flickered across the startled faces of the two men in the front seat of the car. Vernet, strangely quiet, began to drag himself off the floor. When he felt the car stop and the engine die, he remained where he was, on his knees, his face and arms pressed into the luxurious upholstery of the back seat.

'You two going to sit there until daylight?'

They hadn't spotted his approach from the cover of the undergrowth. Neurie's calm, matter-of-fact voice through the shattered driver's-side window broke the sudden silence inside the car. He leaned in and glanced into the back at the kneeling Vernet. 'Christ! Is that what it was all about? Good morning, Vernet. Saying your prayers?'

Vernet struggled into a sitting position and stared at the three men. He didn't say anything. He didn't like the look of the Englishman; Montbron with his distorted face frightened the life out of him; and Neurie . . . If he got out of this one alive he'd make it his life's work to see that these three bastards went all the way for what they'd just done. And it was always possible.

He held out a faint chance that their object was to frighten him, but it was very faint. Montbron took over again.

'Thanks, Gérard. Any of those chaps get out?'

'Buggered if I know. I didn't stay to watch. But that's part of the job, it's why they're well paid. They could have got jobs in the supermarket if they didn't want to take a chance. You going to finish off here?'

Montbron wiped his forehead with the sleeve of his coat. His hand wasn't shaking, but he didn't stop to marvel at it. 'You and Metcalfe go to the car. You left it where I suggested?'

'It's far enough away.'

'Good. I'll join you in a minute.'

'What about me?' Vernet found his voice. All three men looked at him, but none of them said anything. Neurie and Metcalfe glanced at each other from the corner of their eyes and Neurie inclined his head slightly.

'I'll catch you up,' said Montbron.

'Are you OK, Philippe?'

'Yes, thanks, Gérard. I'll be with you in a moment. See you at the car.'

Neurie met Vernet's eyes, briefly. There was no message, no satisfaction, no goodbye – nothing. 'Don't be long, Philippe. There'll be people here any minute now.' And he was gone.

When they were alone, Montbron switched on the interior light and studied Vernet's face. There was a certain dignity about the man, but it was too late now.

'Just over there, where your crew went down, was where you murdered Jeanette Fabre. Does it do anything to you?'

Vernet said nothing.

'That's what you're dying for, Paul, Jeanette's murder. I'm not concerned with all the others. Just as long as you know.'

'It doesn't make you any better than me, Philippe.'

'That's a matter of opinion. I think you'd better pour yourself a drink, Paul.' He reached down to press one of the buttons on the door rest and with a gentle hum the window between them slid to a close. He turned his head and fiddled among the buttons. The front door clicked open. He got out, closed the door and walked round to the side-window and studied Vernet. You had to admire the man. He was on his knees and was reaching forward to open the drinks cabinet. He looked up and their eyes met again. Vernet, with a look of resignation, shrugged, then lowered his eyes and stared into the recess as if trying to make up his mind whether it should be whisky or cognac. He didn't reply to Montbron's 'Goodbye, Paul,' or acknowledge his 'You've got about four minutes. Make the most of them.'

As he climbed into the passenger seat of Neurie's borrowed car, Montbron took one of the transmitters from his pocket and placed it on the ledge in front of him. Neurie stared at it for a moment and said, 'You inviting me to push that tit?'

Montbron looked tired. He left the car door open as if the smoky night air would do something to jolt some life into his flagging system. He didn't look up. 'Give it four minutes,' he said and continued to study the progress of the minute hand on his watch.

'Why?' asked Metcalfe from the back seat.

'Because I told him he could have four minutes. It's two and a half now . . .'

'For Christ's sake why?' repeated Metcalfe.

Montbron didn't reply. He didn't look up from his watch.

Vernet kept his face averted from Montbron in case he saw the look of triumph in his eyes. As soon as Montbron turned his back on the car, Vernet straighted up, threw himself across the carpet and stuck his fingers in the gap between the glass partition and its housing. He'd noticed it, but Montbron hadn't; he'd been too busy fiddling with the door catch. He'd taken his finger off the button too soon and hadn't bothered checking that the partition was completely closed. *The inefficient bastard! If I can reach the armrest I can open the door. Open the bloody door and I'm free and running. You can do it, Paul! You've got to bloody do it, Paul!*

He gripped the glass and tried to slide it open. It was immovable. He pulled, he jerked. Four minutes, Montbron had said.

What had he done? A bomb? It had to be. Timer or fuse? *Oh, Christ!* He tugged again. Nothing moved. He stuck his fingers in it and gauged the gap – ten centimetres! *Jesus!* He ripped off his jacket. His shirt was soaked and the sweat poured out of the ridges over his eyes, almost blinding him as he tore his shirtsleeve and rolled it up as far as it would go. His watch thudded on to the carpet. He glanced down at it quickly. *Oh, my God! I don't know how long, how much longer . . .* He wanted to be sick, to urinate; he wanted to cry. He thrust his hand through the gap, then his arm as far as it would go and felt the skin peel off with the force of it. It was no bloody good! He was too bloody fat! It jammed at his elbow. He stood up and pushed downwards, groping with his fingers for the armrest and the door buttons. *Oh God, how many minutes is that?* The sweat was building up on his arm, between his elbow and the glass. It helped. The elbow moved. *God! I'm going to do it!* He waggled his fingers about again. He could almost feel something. His bladder burst as he pushed. The agony was unbelievable, but his finger touched something solid – though only just. A button. *A button!* He stretched everything as far as it would go. His finger rested on it and the button moved . . .

'It's coming up for five minutes, Philippe. Press that bloody button and let's get out of—'

He didn't finish. For the second time in fifteen minutes the air was rent with the force of an explosion. Louder than the earlier one, this split the clouds and flattened everything within two hundred metres. The air was full of flying, screaming metal, bits of trees, lumps of tarmac melted by the heat. The air shook, and underneath the car the ground heaved as if trying to throw them off. And then the vacuum, the whoosh of displaced air, and the silence. Neurie ducked automatically, and when he straightened up he gripped his nose and swallowed, then rubbed his ear and glanced sideways at Montbron.

'You did that, Philippe, without moving your lips!' He pointed to the transmitter. Its button protector was still in place. 'What's the secret?'

Montbron didn't smile. If anything he looked sadder than usual, but his new-found diction was still intact.

'I thought I'd let him do it himself. Seemed poetic. I stuck the other transmitter on the armrest and left a gap in the glass partition. I can't make up my mind whether an enormous debt has just been repaid. I'll tell you something though, Harry.' He glanced over his shoulder. 'I wouldn't like to think too hard on how his last few minutes were passed.'

Neurie agreed, but he didn't say. Metcalfe said, 'I didn't think you had such a nasty streak in you, Philippe.' But it was said lightly. It was understood. It was what was known in the Business as debt repayment.

Neurie started the car, but before he moved off he said, 'Has anyone got a cigarette?'

'I thought you'd given up?'

'I've just started again.'

'How about a cigar?' said Montbron and produced three large Havanas from his inside pocket. 'Compliments of the late Paul Vernet's motor car!'

Neurie stuck the cigar between his teeth and turned in his seat to look out of the rear window. The flames were bouncing off the clouds and all round them the world had woken up with the sound of the two explosions and the distant cacophony of noise from fire engines, police and – a wasted journey – ambulances pouring into the area from every corner of the region. He studied the reflection of the carnage for a few seconds, then turned back and said, 'I know it sounds silly, but has anyone got a light?'

He didn't laugh. Neither did Montbron or Metcalfe.